THE MAMMOTH BOOK OF

Sea Battles

Also available

The Mammoth Book of Arthurian Legends
The Mammoth Book of Astounding Puzzles
The Mammoth Book of Battles
The Mammoth Book of Best New Horror 11
The Mammoth Book of Best New Science Fiction 13
The Mammoth Book of Brainstorming Puzzles
The Mammoth Book of Bridge
The Mammoth Book of British Kings & Queens
The Mammoth Book of Cats
The Mammoth Book of Chess
The Mammoth Book of Comic Fantasy
The Mammoth Book of Comic Fantasy II
The Mammoth Book of Dracula
The Mammoth Book of Erotica
The Mammoth Book of Eyewitness History
The Mammoth Book of Fairy Tales
The Mammoth Book of Fantastic Science Fiction
The Mammoth Book of Gay Erotica
The Mammoth Book of Gay Short Stories
The Mammoth Book of Heroic and Outrageous Women
The Mammoth Book of Historical Detectives
The Mammoth Book of Historical Whodunnits
The Mammoth Book of History of Murder
The Mammoth Book of Humor
The Mammoth Book of International Erotica
The Mammoth Book of Jack the Ripper
The Mammoth Book of Killer Women
The Mammoth Book of Lesbian Erotica
The Mammoth Book of Lesbian Short Stories
The Mammoth Book of Life Before the Mast
The Mammoth Book of Love & Sensuality
The Mammoth Book of Men O'War
The Mammoth Book of Modern Science Fiction
The Mammoth Book of New Erotica
The Mammoth Book of New Sherlock Holmes Adventures
The Mammoth Book of Nostradamus and Other Prophets
The Mammoth Book of Private Lives
The Mammoth Book of Pulp Fiction
The Mammoth Book of Puzzle Carnival
The Mammoth Book of Sex, Drugs & Rock 'n' Roll
The Mammoth Book of Short Erotic Novels
The Mammoth Book of Sword & Honor
The Mammoth Book of Symbols
The Mammoth Book of Tasteless Lists
The Mammoth Book of Terror
The Mammoth Book of the Third Reich at War
The Mammoth Book of True War Stories
The Mammoth Book of West
The Mammoth Book of True Crime (revised edition)
The Mammoth Book of Unsolved Crimes
The Mammoth Book of Vampires
The Mammoth Book of Victorian & Edwardian Ghost Stories

THE MAMMOTH BOOK OF

Sea Battles

Great Stories and Classic Tales from
the Golden Age of Naval Warfare

EDITED BY MIKE ASHLEY

CARROLL & GRAF PUBLISHERS, INC.
New York

Carroll & Graf Publishers, Inc.
161 William Street
New York
NY 10038–2607

First published in the UK by Robinson,
an imprint of Constable & Robinson Ltd 2001

First Carroll & Graf edition 2001

ISBN 0–7867–0914–6

Printed and bound in the EU

CONTENTS

COPYRIGHT AND ACKNOWLEDGMENTS

PREFACE

Mike Ashley

The Mammoth Book of Sea Battles follows in the wake of *The Mammoth Book of Men O'War* which so many of you have enjoyed. I've followed much the same tack. These stories all hail from the Golden Age of British maritime history when Britain ruled the waves. The stories run in chronological order, the earliest set in 1760 and the last in 1821 – in fact from the time when Horatio Nelson was just a toddler to the last days of Napoleon Bonaparte.

Although several of the major naval conflicts figure strongly – especially the Battle of the Nile and the Battle of Trafalgar – what I find exciting about the stories and the real thrill of compiling an anthology such as this is the sheer variety of naval life and adventure. The first story, for example, has two scientists setting off to observe the transit of Venus only to be attacked by the French – based on a true event. In fact most of the stories here draw upon real historical events or circumstances around which to weave a story. We have an American captain whose ship is stolen by Napoleon and he determines to get it back. We have Cornish smugglers who help fight off French opposition. We have a young boy, press-ganged into the navy, whose desire to get home again leads to a major confrontation between the French and English in the Channel.

Over half of the stories were written especially for this anthology. This includes a new Nathaniel Drinkwater story by Richard Woodman and new material by Derek Wilson,

Keith Taylor, Peter Garratt, Guy N. Smith, Peter Tremayne and others. There are also rare stories by William Hope Hodgson, Jacland Marmur, Frederick Marryat and others, some being reprinted for the first time in many years. I am also delighted to be able to include an extract from David Donachie's new novel about Horatio Nelson, *On a Making Tide*. What's more, David Donachie has also provided a long and fascinating introduction about his work and interest in historical naval fiction.

At which point I think it only fair to hand over to Mr Donachie to declare this anthology well and truly open.

INTRODUCTION

David Donachie

I don't think you can be a writer of naval fiction and not love the genre. I certainly do, though the thought that I might produce stories of my own surprised me when I first started and still does. It is also impossible to avoid examination of the subject and wonder at its enduring popularity. And popular it is, as this volume and its companion *Men O'War* testify.

The sea exerts a powerful pull on our imaginations, the greatest of the elements, more potent in its rages than earthquakes, volcanic eruptions and killer winds. We mortals know we cannot tame or control the sea, but we do feel we can use and understand it. For all the terrors it can produce the sea is perceived as a friend, a giver of life and opportunity, albeit one that sometimes turns to anger and destruction. Thanks to modern technology it is safer now than at any time in history, yet we still know that ships will sink and men will die, sometimes in circumstances that leave us to wonder at the events that brought such tragedy about.

For the people of the United Kingdom it has always been an avenue to adventure. You cannot leave our homelands without encountering water, or walk very far without sight of the sea, which is inclined to stir something in the breast. Even a trip on a ferry across the narrows of the English Channel can bring about a surge of feeling, an atavistic connection to the generations of sailors that made our islands, for a hundred years, the masters of the known world. I doubt any lover of naval fiction, on any ship, can stay indoors, even when the wind is blowing hard. They will, like me, need to go on deck and feel that wind on their face; need to allow their imagination a free run, to try and see in the heaving mass of water that surrounds them something magical.

Look into the water running down the side and you can easily suppose it passing wood instead of metal. You can hear the cry of the lookout from high in the crosstrees, see with his eyes the topsails on the horizon that will bring all the officers, including the captain, on deck. As the commander of the ship that captain will run through his mind a mass of calculations. Foremost will be the wind, its speed and direction, the single most important factor next to the sea-state: force of the waves, leeway and, if close to a shore, the need for sea room. He would look to his sail plan, to ensure that should he choose to close or run he can get aloft the spars and sails he requires. He would wonder, as his warrant officers report, at the state of his hull, a victim of weed, so important to the speed his vessel can make through the water.

Imagine the tension that will remain until that sail is identified. Half a hope that it is a friend, the other half a deep desire that the vessel, as it comes hull up, will be recognized as a foe, and one that to fight and beat will bring glory to every man aboard. Close your eyes and you'll hear the sound of the marine drummer beating to quarters, the crash of wedges being knocked from bulkheads, the squawk of animals as they are loaded into the ship's boats, which will still be loud as those boats are heaved over the side, lowered through squeaking blocks into the heaving sea, to be towed astern.

Every man aboard who can write will find time to pen another section to that long letter-cum-diary that awaits only a landfall or a passing friendly ship to be sent winging back to loved ones and friends at home. They will also write a last will and testament, commending their souls to God and the worldly goods to whomsoever they cherish. Will they, in their mind's eye, see the surgeon setting out the tools of his bloody trade, imagine themselves as screaming wrecks beneath the saws and blades, or worse, sewn in a hammock and committed to the deep with only a cannonball for company? Some will, some won't but all will resolve to do their duty.

Back on deck, to the uninitiated eye, all would be confusion. But men who have been in the King's service most of their lives will see order where the inexperienced eye observes chaos. Powder monkeys running with charge and shot; the master-at-arms preparing his boarding weapons for issue; the rigging of the fire engine, so important in battle where the fear of fire comes second only to the fear of being cut in two by a ball. Nettings and extra stays are being rigged at the same time as sails are trimmed or changed, the deck a mass of shouted orders that will continue till the guns are run out, and all is ready for the forthcoming battle aboard HMS *Opportunity*. And then calm will descend, that hiatus of near silence that will proceed the maelstrom of close-quarters battle.

Opportunity! A siren word to the men of the eighteenth century, none more than the sailors. Where else could a fellow go from penny-pinching obscurity to fame and wealth in an afternoon? All he required was an enemy to fight, a deck under his feet, men who would ply his guns with gusto and a rate of fire that would always outdo his opponent, men who would then board if necessary with an irresistible brio. That he faced death from roundshot, langridge and musket ball was part of the pact he made with God and the devil.

One day, I moved from the avid reading of this to writing it, and, in retrospect, what looks like an accident now appears to be fate. As someone who had always evinced a desire to write, I set out to acquire none of the skills that would seem to be necessary. My handwriting starts legibly then descends into a scrawl, and I somehow never really learned to type. I can't spell and still don't know a noun from a verb. (This is nothing to do with dyslexia – more to do with persistent truancy at school.) I sat down to write a land-based radio play and ended up thirty days later with a 400-page novel set in the eighteer th-century navy.

What happened was simple: I discovered the freedom that comes from writing what you like without the constraints of broadcast media. I discovered the joy of making up a story that I myself would want to read, existing for a whole month in a world where imagination was king and I was free to plunder every experience I'd ever had, while making up many more. This first novel was not in praise of naval heroics! It was intended as a humorous look at the reverse of the medal: at those officers who plagued our fictional heroes, the cowards, poltroons and greedy prize-grubbing sods who would shy from battle to line their pockets, flog men unmercifully and lie to see themselves advanced while another career was checked.

Two weeks after being submitted a major publisher made an offer for it, the kind of dream response to which all budding authors aspire. You won't have read it because I turned them down, on the grounds that the money wasn't good enough. It never occurred to me that no one else would want it, but that's what happened. It went the rounds and all I got was polite rejection. There it sits, a reminder of my folly, but also the proof that I could tell a story that a publisher would want to buy. All I had to do was to find another tale to tell. And so Harry Ludlow was born.

To be perfectly truthful Harry Ludlow had a previous incarnation, as the hero of a television script that I occasionally read with deep embarrassment. Why is it so bad? Because the genesis was based on cost and practicality rather than a love of the subject. You may wonder why you are offered so few sea stories on television and on film. The truth is they are horrendously difficult to make, as well as expensive. Without going into too many technicalities, ships have an annoying habit of moving about from one minute to the next, the tide goes in and out and the state of the sea changes as rapidly as the wind. And ships are expensive to hire, that is if you can find them at all. One day soon, using computer-generated graphics, someone is going to make a maritime blockbuster with whole fleets engaged. Personally, I can't wait.

It was to that script that I turned when looking for a book. And it took very little time to realize that I had given myself a whole raft of advantages. Harry wasn't a King's officer but a privateer, which allowed me a greater degree of fictional freedom. And he had a past, a temper and some very questionable habits in the veracity line. But then he had a brother, James Ludlow, a know-nothing guest aboard his ship who nevertheless felt he had the right to question every action Harry proposed to take. In the course of the book he came across Pender, an ex-thief with a deep pool of common sense as well as an innate understanding of the foibles of his fellow men.

While I wanted to write about all the usual things – battles, storms, floggings, the relationship between captain and crew, life aboard a man-o'-war – I also wanted to do something different. So the first story was a murder mystery set in the confines of a seventy-four-gun ship, and that set the tone for the series. Maritime adventure mixed with criminality. People asked me, after about four books, if I ever got bored. I used to say no quietly, without actually going on to say just how much I enjoyed sitting down to write. It was like letting a child loose in a toyshop.

It was only when I started work on my latest project, a novel about Horatio Nelson, that I really began to examine the genre and its evergreen attraction. I also realized that as readers we are not just some amorphous mass who will devour anything with a sailing ship on the cover. There are those of us who prefer action to depth, others who will happily immerse themselves in philosophy at the expense of activity; we are, in short, as diverse a bunch and as critical a group of readers as any other.

Nelson, his death and apotheosis to national saint, spawned a whole raft of memoirs. Anyone who'd passed him on the Portsmouth hard or tipped their hat at the sallyport felt the need to write about the experience; quite a few to explain how their presence at sea had contributed to the downfall of Napoleon. Whatever their purpose, the books found a ready audience, who knew that Wellington could not have triumphed in Spain if the navy had not controlled the seas.

It was once put to me that I should write a biography of C.S. Forester. In researching that, I found myself trying to imagine him at the point at which he decided to write the first Hornblower. He was, and had been, a successful novelist for nearly twenty years. What turned him to naval fiction, to the world of sailing ships, a genre that had been moribund for a long time? It seemed to me that he was affected by the same motives that propel us, both writers and readers.

As a novelist he would have been attracted by the diversity of characters aboard ship; it took so many people to sail and fight even the smallest warship that no writer will ever lack for a personality, be he a seasick lubber, a flogging bosun, a sanctimonious parson, a right sod of a hard horse captain or an eccentric surgeon with disreputable habits. The whole of human life was within those wooden walls, packed so tight that they could scarce get away from one another. Those sailors saw exotic landscapes, survived horrendous storms, engaged in hard toil, enjoyed humour and suffered pain, experienced friendship and enmity, and faced the prospect of wealth and death. I can think of no situation with so much dramatic potential as an eighteenth-century warship.

Nelson stands at the apex of our naval history. Yet look at him in the context of his time and it was the heroics and abilities of others that inspired him. The Seven Years War was the conflict that made Britain a major naval power and it was against the heroes of that contest that Horatio Nelson measured himself. Yet his greatest hero was not a sailor: it was James Wolfe, the general who died to secure Canada for his country.

He also had, like his contemporaries, the memory of Admiral Byng, whose father Lord Torrington had been a hero of the Seven Years War, the son shot on the quarterdeck of *Queen Charlotte* for his perceived failure off Minorca. Every officer in the navy knew that the trial and execution were political. They also knew that they too could suffer the same fate; politics had not changed very much in twenty years. The price of failure could be very high indeed.

All the more remarkable then the risks they took, particularly Nelson at the Battle of Cape St Vincent, when he totally disobeyed the Fighting Instructions that forbade any form of fight but line ahead, by pulling out of the line to head off the escaping Spanish fleet. Had he failed to bring the Dons to battle we would certainly never have heard of him again. He would have been at best beached, at worst executed as an example.

But the real genesis of the naval fiction hero is Cochrane. Tall, red-haired, he was an aristocratic Scot who mixed imagination and insubordination in equal measure. As a young officer, newly appointed master and commander he fought and defeated a Spanish frigate in a brig. As a very senior officer he bluffed a whole Portuguese fleet into surrendering to his single warship off Brazil. In between he innovated, fought single ship actions, engaged in politics, fell out with his seniors, was dismissed the service for fraudulent speculation and reinstated by the King, died as Admiral of the Fleet, the Earl of Dundonald. But, more important than that to his posterity, was the fact that he had aboard one of his frigates a young midshipman called Fredrick Marryat.

Here is the true father of all these books and stories we so admire, a young man who ran away to sea and served with the most quixotic commander alive in an age of strong personalities, who experienced first hand life aboard a man-o'war. They have the edge of first-hand experience on their side and no youngster, even today, could have a better introduction to that world. I remember them well, cloth-covered in orange and red beside my bed as a youngster. If the passage from reader to writer started anywhere it was there, and the real joy is that it's not over.

As I write this introduction, I have only a very limited idea of the stories that Mike Ashley will include in this *Sea Battles* volume. I devoured *Men O'War*, and I look forward with keen anticipation to putting my feet up with what follows, and losing myself in a time and a place where I feel so at home.

DEADLY TRANSIT

F. Gwynplaine MacIntyre

Although most of the stories in this anthology are set during the French Revolutionary and Napoleonic Wars, we start our journey through naval history several years earlier, in fact in the midst of the Seven Years War. This lasted between 1756 and 1763. Things don't seem a lot different. Britain is still at war with France, this time over colonial supremacy. In fact Britain wasn't originally involved in this war, which was a conflict between France, Austria and Russia on the one side and Prussia on the other. Britain supported Prussia. So it was another opportunity for the British and French to be at loggerheads. Life did try to go on as usual but such rivalry had a tendency to get in the way, as the following story shows. It is based on a real incident when the British astronomer Charles Mason set off in 1760 with his colleague Jeremiah Dixon to observe the transit of Venus. These are the same scientists to be immortalized by the Mason–Dixon line which they surveyed a few years later in America to decide the boundary between Pennsylvania and Maryland. Here is an earlier exploit in their eventful lives which also shows their ingenuity.

F. Gwynplaine MacIntyre (b. 1948) is a Scottish-born, Australian-raised, American-resident author, primarily of science fiction and fantasy, including the novel The Woman Between the Worlds *(1994).*

She was not, by strict measure, a ship-of-the-line, for her guns were too light and too few. HMS *Seahorse* was a barquentine rig, classed as a twenty-four-gunner. The *Seahorse* arrived in the Royal Dockyard at Portsmouth on 27 October 1760, just in time to receive word of King George's death, in a sudden fit of syncope, two days before. On hearing this, the master gunner at once asked the date of the new King's birthday. In the Royal Navy it is an old lurk – going back to Queen Anne's time – for the master gunner of each ship to conspire with his storekeeper of ordnance every year, straight after the monarch's birthday. They vouch a warrant to the Ordnance Board for a new supply of gunpowder, claiming falsely to have fired off all the guns in a birthday salute to "his most excellent majesty". The stores obtained by this stratagem are then pilfered and sold, and the gun-money is translated into booze.

Yet the *Seahorse*'s guns were now strangely subtracted. No sooner had she berthed at Portsmouth, than four of her study nine-pounders were unshipped from the gun deck and trundled ashore by a guard of marines, without ever so much as a thank-ye. The *Seahorse*'s lieutenant-at-arms told his quarter-gunners that these cannon had been removed by agents of the Lord High Admiral's office, under warrant from Trinity House, so as to make room aboard ship for "the gentlemen's bundles, y'see".

Why had the *Seahorse* been ordered to Portsmouth of a sudden? Captain James Smith told his senior officers that their destination was a secret, to be kept mumchance until the ship was under sail in the English Channel. Meanwhiles, the ship must be refitted, armoured, provisioned and victualled for the voyage ahead.

The sea holds its secrets, yet sailors have means to discover them. In November all the hull of the *Seahorse* received a fresh application of brimstone, tallow and tar. This was a clue that the *Seahorse* was bound for tropical waters. The sulphurous coating would protect the *Seahorse*'s oaken hull from the gnawing of shipworms that dwelt in warm-watered latitudes.

Then "the gentlemen's bundles" arrived. Hogsheads and puncheons with unknown contents were taken below decks, to be stowed in the traditional chine-and-bulge arrangement which enabled the stacking of the most barrels into the least space.

Still more mysterious were the packing-cases that were shipped aboard under armed guard in late December while the crew were busy with a winging-out: this was the long ritual in which the heaviest objects in the ship's holds were moved from amidships to the wales, to make the ship steadier in the water, while the lighter pieces of cargo were rummaged further inboard. The able men and ordinaries were kept so busied with this task, none had chance to examine the packing-cases before these were whisked below decks and stowed inside the padlocked hold that was usually reserved for spirituous liquors. The master-at-arms stationed two sentinels to guard the locked hold. When several curious jackies wondered aloud about the contents of this locker, the captain's clerk sent them away with a never-ye-mind.

And who were "the gentlemen", pray? There were two of them, but their names and business were known only to Captain Smith. Both men had been piped aboard in late December, during the break-bulk and the ship's lading.

Both of the strangers were young: the leader of the two looked not older than thirty. He wore the plaincloth and breeches of a tradesman, and he spoke in the broad Cotswold accent of Gloucester. He was stocky of frame and middling of height. His assistant, some three years younger, was tall and gentle of manner. He wore a long scarlet coat, its pockets bulging with quills and penknives and what-ye-call-ums. His lanky frame was surmounted by his ill-fitting cocked hat. He had a Geordie accent, yet he evidently took his chapel among the Society of Friends; whenever he spoke to any crewman or officer, he tempered his speech with "thee" and "thou" and such Quaker locutions: "I tell thee sure, thou must make safe those casks!"

At last, December stood her watch and was relieved by January, and so the year changed in its fashion. In its *new* fashion, aye: for scantly nine years had passed since the honest English calendar was cozened into Popish ways. Now the almanack vouched that this was 1761, yet few men of the *Seahorse* were accustomed to starting a New Year in January.

And now the final readiness. Coils of new-turned hemp from the Navy Board's stores were cut into shorter lengths of rope; these were wormed, parcelled, served, whipped and seized in the long process that would transform them into fresh rigging and lines. Dead-eyes were turned in, blocks were strapped. Then at last came the glorious day when the sheets went aloft, and the *Seahorse*'s barquentine masts billowed white as the ship carried sail.

And on Saturday morning, 10 January 1761 – a day with clear weather, and no clouds to obscure the bright sun – the *Seahorse* put forth from Portsmouth harbour.

The ocean was an unknown universe to him. At age thirty-one, this was Mason's first sea voyage. Solid land had always been his favoured realm, for he was a surveyor by profession. He was accustomed to measuring hills and quantifying valleys. A mountain, at least, had the good grace to stand still and permit a man to calibrate its size and its dimensions, and, once surveyed, nothing less than an avalanche could alter those aspects. But the ocean's province showed no constancy. The sea had its peaks and valleys, but they shifted shape and traded places each-the-other every moment. How could any man chart the oceans? The task seemed impossible, unless the map were made of liquid that kept shift with the tides.

Mason had striven to master the sea's ways. Desiring to learn how the helmsman controlled this vast ship, he had gone to the *Seahorse*'s weather deck. At once, he was cautioned by the yeoman of the sails: no man was permitted near the helm until he had divested himself of his knife and every other metal object that might beguile the ship's compasses. Obeying this stricture, Mason approached.

He had observed that the helmsman stood sometimes to the right of his wheel, sometimes its left. Now the yeoman explained that the helmsman always stood at the helm's weather side, which, of necessity, was inconstant.

As Mason stood abaft the helm, he had some sense of the natural order of men under sail. The *Seahorse* mustered 200 able seamen and ordinaries, besides her officers. The rawest recruits and the oldest veterans were deckmen – afterguards and waisters – whose tasks involved drudgery rather than skill. The largest and brawniest hands were the forecastlemen, charged with the headsails and studdingsails of the topmast. Men of medium size were stationed in the lowest and aftmost sections of the rigging, where they had charge of the crossjack and jeers, and the spinnaker. The smaller and more agile hands – many of them mere boys – were topmen, working aloft. And the lightest and smallest of *these* were charged with the topmost sails on each mast, which (the yeoman explained) were styled the royal yards. Just now the weather was fair, so the yeoman of the sails ordered the deckmen to raise the windsails: in this wise, they diverted a cool breeze to the gunports below decks, and gave some welcome ventilation to that most stifling and stenchsome portion of the ship.

Now the ship's trumpeter sounded three notes, mustering the ship's company: "All hands, a-hoa!" called the mate of the watch, as Captain Smith came on deck.

The quarterdeck is the most spacious section of a ship-of-war: it gives service as the captain's sermon bench on the rare occasions when he sees fit to address his crew directly rather than sending word to them through his petty officers. As there was no place aboard the *Seahorse* large enough for all hands to assemble, the topmen stayed aloft in the rigging, with one eye on their clews and luffs as they listened, while the deckhands paid heed from their stations. Only the sentries on watch, and the man at the helm, showed no attention to Captain Smith as he gave sign for Mason and his younger partner to step forth.

"We are now," said Captain Smith, "34 leagues south-west of Portsmouth, 2 leagues west: far enough at sea, I think, for our guests to reveal their intentions." The captain nodded to the two men flanking him, and then stood at his ease as the older and stockier of this pair stepped nervously forward and spoke.

"I am Charles Mason, of the Greenwich Observatory,"

Mason began, hoping that the acoustics of the open seas would lend a tone of authority to his voice. "This man beside me is my assistant, Jeremiah Dixon. By the captain's consent, I permit you all to speak freely and ask questions, for I have need of your chief reliance and confidence."

"Where are we bound, then?" a maintopman called from above.

"For the East Indies," Mason answered. "We've set course for Bencoolen, on the western coast of Sumatra." This news provoked a general murmur of approval from the crew, for Sumatra was a Dutch colony. The current hostilities between Britain and France had dragged half the nations of Europe into the conflict, either as allies or enemies, yet Holland had maintained her neutrality.

"We are going to Bencoolen," Mason continued, "on a mission of surveyance."

"What, surveying Sumatra?" someone muttered from amidships.

Jeremiah Dixon doffed his cocked hat, and peered into the assemblage of deckhands to see who had spoken. "No, friend. We are charged with surveying the celestial spheres."

This news put all the crew a-huzzbuzz. Mason gestured for silence, then spoke: "Less than six months from today – on the 6th of June – there will occur a transit of Venus. The Royal Society has engaged Mr Dixon and myself to equip an observatory at Bencoolen, where we are to witness the Venereal transit."

"And what's *that* when it's at home, then?" a foretopman quizzed.

"The planet Venus will pass directly across the face of the sun, as viewed from Earth," Mason explained. "Such an event has not transpired in this past century and more; the most recently previous transit was in 1639. If we fail to witness the forthcoming event, we may never have another chance."

"But what's it to do with the King's navy?" called out a deckhand, whose location in the ship's narrow midsection beneath the foremast indicated that he was a waister.

"By timing the progress of our sister planet across the sun's countenance," said Mason, "we shall reckon the diameter of Venus's orbit, which the German astronomer Kepler has estimated to be seven-tenths as large as the path of our own sphere. By ascertaining this, we may more truly affix the Earth within its rightful ambit in the heavens."

"Do you intend to gaze directly into the sun's face?" asked a midshipman. As an officer in training, he naturally had some knowledge of astronomy.

"Of a certainty, not," said Mason. "Staring into the sun is a fool's hazard. And to gaze at the sun through the powerful magnifying lenses of our telescopes would be sure blindness. The mirrors of our telescopes will throw a bright reflection of the sun's disc upon a nearby plate of white enamel, and we shall observe the phenomenon against that surface."

"Couldn't you do it just as plain from Greenwich?" asked an afterguard.

Mason smiled. "The weather in Britain is too unreliable to grant us certainty of clear skies. As well, the Venereal transit must be witnessed from as many latitudes as possible, so that we may more easily deduce the solar parallax. The Reverend Maskelyne is leading an expedition to St Helena for that purpose. Other expeditions are bound for Madagascar and Siberia to witness this selfsame event; and to Canada, despite our current war against the French in that province. Of all those vantage posts, Sumatra has the clearest weather and the latitude most nearly equatorial, so Mr Dixon and I expect to perceive the transit's most favourable aspect."

"And into the bargain," said Dixon, "we hope to observe the movements of the Nodes of Venus." As soon as he said this, a gale of mocking laughter erupted from the crew, and several midshipmen and officers hastened to conceal their grins. Dixon's face reddened in anger, then blushed anew as he realized that his words held a meaning more bawdy than he had intended.

Captain Smith raised one arm, and the laughter stopped: "The Royal Society and the Astronomer Royal have seen fit to despatch these two men on their celestial endeavour, and we of the *Seahorse* are ordered to conveyance them at all speed. Even with favourable winds, it will take us many weeks under full sail to reach Sumatra. So, if nothing more need be said . . ."

"One thing more, I think," said Mason. "Good men, know this: the movements of the heavens will not wait for us. We *must* make landfall at Bencoolen in sufficient time to erect a base camp for our makeshift observatory. We must set up our telescopes, our zenith-sector, our quadrant and our longitude clock – and we must have time to verify their trueness. All our instruments must be in readiness *before* the moment of our tryst with Venus. Delay would be most fatal to our enterprise. If any hazard detains our voyage, Venus will not favour our dalliance, and she will proceed in her orbit without us."

"Let us beseech the Lord, then, for swift currents," said Dixon. "And, if such is divine will, we may have a safe transit of the oceans as well as a transit of—"

"What's that shape coming towards us?" said Captain Smith suddenly.

"French colours, off the larboard quarter!" came a shout from the crow's nest, and the decks rattled as the deckmen rushed to battle stations, while the masts shuddered and creaked as the topmen adjusted their sails for a quartering wind away from the pursuer.

Mason shaded his eyes as he turned directly into the sun's glare, and saw a ship bearing down from the eastern horizon. At the vane of her topmast was the French naval flag: three golden *fleurs-de-lys* on a white standard. Beneath this, a scarlet banderole with the *auriflambe* of St Denis rippled in the breeze. The newcomer was a full-rigged frigate: three-masted like the *Seahorse*, but much larger and faster.

The lieutenant-at-arms raised his spyglass. "Gammon her for a pox-trap! I know that ship: she's the *LeGrand*. A thirty-four-gunner: eighteen-pounders, if I dispart her cannon rightly. And for all her weight in the water, she's faster than us with all sails drawing. We can't outgun her and we can't outrun her."

"What ought we do, then?" Mason asked, as the *LeGrand* bore steadily closer. In the vast expanse of the English Channel, there was no place to hide.

The lieutenant-at-arms was already bellowing commands: "Larboard gunners, bring your guns to bear! Up top, a-hoa! Lace on your bonnet!" This last was apparently an order to add sail to the foremast, and so gain some speed.

As all hands secured their stations, Mason and Dixon stood alone while deckmen rushed past them. "Thou and I must lend our assistances where best they are useful," said Dixon to his senior partner. "But how can we help?"

Before Mason could answer, there was a flash of fire from the *LeGrand*'s starboard gunports: then a roar. Mason's intellect had only an instant to observe that the light of the cannon's eruption crossed the water more swiftly than the sound of its report. Then the *Seahorse* shuddered violently as a cannonball splintered her foremast. The tarred lines of the fore-rigging burst into flame, and Mason looked on helplessly as the inferno spread across the foresails.

"Foretopsail afire!" bellowed a master's mate. "Clew her up, and strike the yard!"

A moment ago, the wind had been the *Seahorse*'s ally: now it was her enemy, fanning the blaze as it spread through the billowing canvas. Swiftly, the helmsman put the ship before the wind, slackening her sails. At the same time, foretopmen with knives in their jaws scaled the rigging, slicing the burning forecourse from the yard. There was a shout of "*Hoy below!*" as the flaming mass came tumbling to the deck, where quarter-deckmen manned the fire-pumps. Hammocks soaked in sea-water were passed up top, hand over hand, so the riggers could use these to beat out the flames.

Now the French guns roared again, and the *Seahorse* shook beneath another assault. Mason looked towards the enemy ship – much closer now – and straight away he saw the fatal truth.

"We must steer *towards* the enemy!" he said aloud, to none in particular. The cannon of the *LeGrand* had a much larger bore and calibre than the *Seahorse*'s guns – and they fired a heavier round. The *LeGrand*'s guns had much the longer range: by keeping her distance, it was possible for the French ship to bombard the *Seahorse* while staying beyond reach of the British chaser guns. In order for the *Seahorse* to get within striking distance of her enemy, the barquentine would have to sail directly into the French line of fire.

With some vague plan of aiding the gunners, Mason rushed below to the gun deck.

The larboard gun crews were all at their stations. Two gunports on either side of the ship were idle, showing the empty stations of the four cannon that had been unshipped at Portsmouth. As Mason came below, he saw two starboard gun crews straining to wheel their massive gun carriages athwartships to the larboard line of fire. With a will, Mason tore off his coat and lent his own weight to the effort. Alongside four men and two boys, he manhandled the nine-pounder into position, then stood gasping while two jackies reeved the cannon's tackles through large ringbolts either side of the gunport. Tools were seized from the starboard gunport: hand-spikes, crow irons, sponge-staves and a wooden tub which the smallest boy hastily filled from a butt of seawater.

"How can I help?" Mason asked, but the gun crew ignored him. He stood aside, if it were possible to stand *aside* in such a cramped place as a gun deck. Then the ship lurched again, as another French gun found its target. Glancing across the larboard row of gunports, Mason saw that each artillery-piece was serviced by six men and boys who worked together as a squad, with the leader among them as gun captain.

"At your stations, lads, and make sure of your flints!" roared the captain of the nearest gun. His second gunner used a handspike and crow-lever, thrusting these under the carriage to elevate the cannon's breech, while a third man levered the wedge-shaped quoins at the rear of the gun carriage to steady the gun and a fourth man lifted a flannel bag filled with gunpowder and dropped this into the bore, followed by a wad of cotton wool to keep the powder compressed. The fifth man, brandishing a rammer, thrust the wad home while the third man lifted a 9-pound cannonball and held it ready, then dropped it into the barrel as soon as the rammer was clear. The fourth man put another wad inside; this was rammed home too, keeping the cannonball steady. The sixth member of the gun crew, Mason observed, was the smallest boy, whose job it was to run back and forth under fire, fetching gunpowder sacks from the magazine and ammunition from the shot locker. Each cannon had its own boy charged with this task – some of them as young as ten – and the constant traffic of these lads atwixt the lockers and their several guns was most industrious. Seeing their helter-skelter scamperings, Mason suddenly understood why these boys were known as powder monkeys.

Now the gun was levered down into firing position, and her gun captain jammed a pricker into her breech-hole, ripping the thin flannel sack and exposing the powder within. The second gunner poured a thin trickle of black powder – more than a scruple's worth, less than a dram – down the cannon's firing hole and into the flintlock pan.

"Run her out!" howled the gun captain, and the wheels of the gun carriage grumbled as the five men of the gun crew – all except her powder monkey – strained against the tackles to thrust their cannon's heavy muzzle through the gunport. The gun captain jumped free, and tugged a lanyard on the flintlock. Mason felt his eardrums shudder in the sudden change of air pressure as the cannon fired. At the same instant – truly in an instant – the cannon recoiled on its carriage some 10 feet inboard, straining against the stout breech-lines which were secured to the ringbolts and tied fast at their bights to the large pommel of the cascabel at the cannon's rear.

The gun crew continued amain. Again the breech was elevated by the second gunner, while the fifth man seized a wooden staff surmounted by a sea-sponge tied round with sheepskin. This was dipped into the water tub, then rammed home into the cannon. Mason sensed its purpose: the sodden sponge-staff must purge every last remnant of the spent powder-charge before a new charge was inserted: if this were not done, the cannon would explode while its gun crew were setting the new charge. And the seawater in the sponge helped to quench the thirsty cannon, betwixt its frequent bellowings of fire. Now the sponge-staff was removed, and the fourth man was inserting the next charge.

Again the cannon roared, and then again. Mason stood well aside while his right hand took the blood-pulse in his left wrist. By this impromptu timepiece, Mason was astonished to discover that the well-trained gun crews of the *Seahorse* fulfilled their tasks so rapidly that each English cannon fired at intervals of ninety seconds. The French frigate, for all her grand artillery, could not match this rapid rate of fire. Mason wondered if perhaps his timekeeping was false: in the fever of battle, his pulse-rate was naturally quickened. No, he was certain of it: in spite of all the requisite manoeuvres, each cannon on the *Seahorse* fired twice in every three minutes.

A sudden hand touched his shoulder, and Mason turned to see a sharp-faced crewman. "You! Stand clear, mind! I want no landers getting killed on *my* watch, thank ye kindly," said this newcomer. "I'm Jem Hodgett, quarter-gunner in command o'these four guns. Captain Smith has ordered me to keep you clear of trouble, and he's told me to answer your questions. The captain hopes your scientific knowledge can ambition a strategy against those Frenchy gunners."

Mason had noticed certain able seamen – not members of any six-man gun crew – who moved between four gun crews apiece, and seemed to have some authority over them. Evidently these men were the quarter-gunners. Hoping to discover some clue that might suggest a means of turning this battle in England's favour, Mason said to Hodgett, "Our own ship and the *LeGrand* take it in turns to shoot their guns each-the-other, never firing both at once. Is this some courtesy of war?"

"Courtesy? La, sir!" The quarter-gunner spat into the nearest water tub. "Not in it! The French navy always fire their guns high, when their ship's on the crest of a wave, in hopes to set our masts and rigging afire. The froggies think that's the best course of attack: leastways, so I'm told by Frenchies we've took prisoner in other battles. But we jacks know better, o'course. On His Majesty's ships we train our gun captains to pull the lanyard on the down roll of each wave. Our guns fire *low*, so's we can smash the hull of Jawn Franswah – and kill his gunners besides. You, there! Look lively wi'that rammer!" This last was directed to one of the gun crews.

Someone moaned. Mason turned, and saw the gaunt figure of Jeremiah Dixon, hatless, unsteady in his boots. There was blood on his face and his hands. "Lord, man!" Mason shouted above the cannon-fire. "Are you wounded?"

"Not yet, praise the Maker. But there are many injured on the quarterdeck." Dixon's face was ashen, beneath a layer of his own perspiration and other men's blood. "I've been conveyancing wounded men to the scavenger's cockpit."

"To the *where*?"

"The ship's surgeon: the crew call him the scavenger, and his medical bay is the cockpit, for its walls are bloody enough for any cockfight." Dixon's face had been pale; now it turned suddenly bilious. "I was commanded to hold down a screaming man on the orlop deck while the surgeon's mate sawed off the shattered bones of his . . . *hwulp!*" Dixon turned away suddenly, and vomited into the nearest water tub.

The gun deck's demeanour had changed. Most of the guns on both ships had gone silent, and the battle now stood at an ominous lull. The crew of the *Seahorse* were making ready for combat at close hand against the oncoming French. The powder boys were distributing Brown Bess muskets and grenadoes. The gun captains were armed with rifles, and now these men were sharing round several parchment tubes which Mason recognized as cartridges.

Dixon wiped his mouth on the remnant of a flannel powder sack as Mason trembled in rage. "Our safe transit has become a deadly transit. Very likely we'll die here, or be taken prisoners of war. You and I at least may well be recognized as civilians and set free, yet 'tis obvious we'll never reach Sumatra in time for the transit of Venus. Think on it, Dixon! The Royal Society have been planning this expedition since last July; yet here we are, not four hours out from Portsmouth, and already our enterprise lies in tatters!"

Dixon nodded grimly. "And think on the equipment loaned to us: the quadrant belonging to the Earl of Macclesfield, Mr Sisson's zenith-sectors, and Mr Short's telescopes; to say nothing of Mr Ellicott's longitude clock. They have charged us with these instruments' safe-keeping. But I tell thee true, I would sooner cast the lot of them into the sea, before surrendering them into French hands."

Mason knew that his partner was right. Of all their cargo, the two large telescopes most especially were precious: these were brand-new instruments, made by James Short of Surrey Street in the Strand. One of these was supplied with a micrometer, and both telescopes were equipped with newly ground convex lenses of 24-inch focal length and 120 powers of magnification.

Now the ship shook again, in another onslaught of the French guns. In this dreadful moment, Mason's intellect sought haven from warfare in the scientific knowledge and equations that were his favoured domain. The gun captain beside him tugged his lanyard again, and the massive gun carriage lurched backwards as it thundered its charge. Observing the recoil of the artillery-piece, Mason took desperate comfort in this demonstration of Isaac Newton's third law: action and reaction. War had no rules, yet the universe's laws were inviolable. If only the rules of physics might offer some weapon which . . .

"Hold a moment," said Mason to Dixon. "Our telescopes: are they not of the Newtonian design?"

"They are," said Dixon. Even in this modern age of King George III, most telescopes were merely spyglasses grown large: crude embellishments on Galileo's prototype. But Mr Short's firm of telescopes had engineered their wares in the new-fashioned catoptric design, with reflectors of the sort devised by Sir Isaac Newton and improved upon by the Scottish astronomer James Gregory.

"Do you recall a certain legend?" said Mason to his younger associate. "Perhaps apocryphal, yet still within the bounds of scientific laws: the tale of Archimedes at the siege of Syracuse."

Dixon began to shake his head, then of a sudden his eyes widened. "Surely, thou cannot intend to . . ."

"I do."

Both men turned round, and ran to the companionway.

As Mason came up from below decks, escaping the hell-stench of gunpowder and brimstone in the cramped gun deck, he was struck by the odours of blood and burning pitch in the salt breeze of the foredeck. He saw fragments of men. Seamen and boys sprawled dead or dying on the quarterdeck. Corpses dangled from the burning rigging. Their shipmates ignored them: all the crewmen still alive and able-bodied were busy snuffing out the many fires, or attending to the chaser guns fore and aft.

The long-shanked legs of Jeremiah Dixon brought him first to Captain Smith. "Hasten, sir!" cried the Quaker cartographer. "Thou must put about, and away!"

"Retreat, you mean?" said James Smith.

"We want distance between us and the *LeGrand*," said Mason, panting for breath. "My partner and I have a stratagem: pray, give us twelve men with strong arms and steady hands. And have the carpenter stand by."

The captain's jaw clenched. "I need every man at their guns!"

"We cannot outgun that frigate," Mason said in plain truth. "You must put about, and gain some distance from the French, while Mr Dixon and I make sure our gambit."

"And do thee give us access to the safe-hold," said Dixon.

Captain Smith looked doubtful, but his training had enabled him to make quick decisions. As circumstance now stood, a French victory was assured. If Mason's stratagem failed, the *Seahorse* and her crew were doomed anyway. But if his plan – whatever it might be – should succeed . . .

The captain ordered his lieutenant: "Muster twelve forecastlemen – or the strongest men still standing – to the safe-hold. Give Mason and Dixon anything they require."

"But, sir!" the second-in-command protested. "The French are—"

"The French can ride the devil to Peg Crankum's bawd-shop," said Captain Smith. "Order the helm to put about." The captain fished within his coat, and brought forth his ring of keys for the padlocked storage compartments: the safe-hold.

With keys in hand, Mason ran to the companionway. Just before he rushed below, he took a desperate glance beyond the larboard rail. The crew of the *LeGrand*, sure of victory, had been making ready to board the conquered *Seahorse*, and in consequence had left their own guns and sails undercrewed while they took up boat-hooks and weapons. Now there were shouts of dismay from the frigate's decks as the barquentine suddenly raised sail and put about. This ruse was unexpected, and the French crew were unready to give chase. As Mason rushed below decks, he was pleased to see the English ship achieving some distance from the pursuer.

The armed sentinels had kept their post outside the safe-hold: their orders required them to guard the cargo in these lockers even when the ship was under fire. Now Mason jangled the captain's keys, and – at a nod from the lieutenant – the two sentries stepped aside. While Mason unlocked the hasps, he heard heavy footfalls on the gangway behind him as the fore-castlemen arrived.

"Six of you men, take yon packing-case and fetch it to the afterdeck," said Mason, pointing to one of the largest articles of cargo. "You six, that other one. *Have care!* The contents are heavy and fragile."

The twelve men seized the two long wooden cases and made towards the companionway. Dixon hurried ahead, clearing a path amid an obstacle-course of dead men and splintered wreckage.

As carefully as possible aboard the lurching ship, the cases were carried topside. As Mason returned to the ship's waist, he saw in anger that all three of the *Seahorse*'s masts had been flindered by French cannon-fire, which had also shattered his hopes of reaching Sumatra in time for his rendezvous with Venus. Just as he thought of this, Mason felt a sudden burst of shame: the *Seahorse* and the lives of her men should be his prime concern. Damn the heavens, but Venus must wait!

The two large crates were borne to the afterdeck, and the aft chaser guns were trundled aside to make room for them. The ship's carpenter and the carpenter's mate came aft, with their tools. In a minute or less, both crates were prized open and their contents stood revealed.

"Dam' me!" said a quarterdeckman. In front of him on the deck lay a long tapered cylinder of steel, fashioned in graduating sections of diminishing size, with brass fittings between them and bands round their diameters. Athwart the afterdeck lay the twin of this object. Just then the deck lurched, and both cylinders would have rolled away had not several deckmen held them fast.

"Fetch ropes, someone!" said Mason. "We'll use the gun carriages of the chasers to hold the mountings at stablehead." Under his guidance, the two telescopes were lifted on to the wheeled platforms of sturdy white oak. "No, not that way!" Mason shouted. "Turn it round, sir! The polar axis of the telescope's equatorial mounting must support the declination axis!" These words were Greek to the deckmen, but they made shift to obey Mason's directions while several mizzentopmen hurried aft with lines. Quickly, they made fast the two telescopes to their carriages.

From the many pockets of his coat, Dixon produced several small tools. Using these, he unscrewed the casings of the starboard telescope and then he inserted his long right arm into the barrel of the instrument. Mason nervously glanced over the stern rail: the French ship was in rapid pursuit, and closing fast. The sun was almost directly overhead now, as the noon hour approached.

"We must counterpoise the telescopes, to position both the azimuth and altitude," said Mason, holding out both arms and accepting what Dixon gave him as the younger man went to the other telescope and repeated his movements. With both hands full, Mason nodded at a nearby gunner. "Bear a hand to those quoins, man, and bring them to the gun carriage."

Several deckmen stiffened. "Captain on the deck!" said one of them, as Captain Smith came aft. One look at the captain's face told Mason the tidings.

"Eleven men dead so far, and half again a score of wounded," said the captain, ignoring a trickle of blood from his own forehead. "And the Mounseers are closing in. This plan of yours is our last hope, and there's the truth on't."

"Nearly ready," Mason answered, without looking up from his labours. Hunched over the gun carriage behind the telescope, he was holding what Dixon had given him: a large circular mirror, nearly 2 feet in diameter. With some tarred oakum, Mason fastened the backside of this to the quoins at the rear of the gun carriage. Dixon did likewise with an identical mirror at the opposite gun.

"Before we die here, might I ask of your intentions?" said the captain.

Mason stood with his back towards Captain Smith, and he faced the oncoming warship. Quickly adjusting the quoins of the chaser, so as to manipulate the silvered mirror behind the telescope, Mason gave answer, never slackening his labours as he spoke: "This telescope, sir, has a Newtonian reflector. Between its convex lenses, a plane mirror is set at a 45-degree angle inside the prime focus, thereby directing the focus to one side of the telescope's tube." Mason's forefinger tapped an eyepiece projecting from the telescope's flank. He had blinded the eyepiece with a cud of tarred oakum, preventing the escape of any light from within. "A concave secondary mirror, outside the prime focus, reflects the ambient light towards the primary – instead of refracting the light, in the manner of your spyglass."

Dixon wiped perspiration from his brow. "We have removed the primary mirrors from within these telescopes, and positioned them *behind*." As Dixon spoke, Mason was directing the gun crews of both chasers to aim the telescopes towards the oncoming French ship.

"*Now!*" cried Mason to four afterguards: two men on either side of each telescope. At once, the deckhands raised the telescopes to a nearly vertical position on the chaser carriages, directly towards the noonday sun.

A blinding glare dazzled the captain's eyes, then shifted aside as Mason adjusted the distance of the nearer mirror underneath its telescope: precisely 24 inches from the lens, in correspondence with its focal length. A glowing diadem of concentrated sunlight appeared within the mirror's centre.

Now the *Seahorse*'s captain understood: each telescope caught the sun's rays and focused them on the mirror below. By adjustments of the mirror's angle, the reflection of this sunlight could be directed afar. Was Mason hoping to *blind* the French gunners? "God's truth, man!" Smith shouted at Mason. "My men are being killed while you dandle this gimcrack!"

"This is no toy, sir." Charles Mason spoke grimly while he shifted the mirror below his telescope. At the other gun carriage, Dixon in the same wise moved its counterpart. "This is an instrument of science, transformed into an engine of war. The telescope's lenses have caught the sun's rays, and concentrated them. Have you never remarked that a convex lens, designed for magnification, can as well give service as a burning glass?"

Captain Smith wiped his bleeding forehead. "It'll burn, right enough! And set fire to my ship!"

"Never a one, sir." As Mason spoke, a thin beam of white light came forth a-dazzle from his mirror. Turning the reflector, he directed this beam across the waves towards the topsheets of the approaching frigate. "James Short's firm of telescopers have crafted their most excellent mirrors of silvered glass which has a low co-efficient of expansion. Even with a vast increase in temperature, the glass will not warp greatly."

"But, across such a distance . . ."

The sun's rays have travelled a goodly distance to get here, and can travel a deal further," said Dixon. "Mr Short's mirrors are of the most admirable contrivance, with no chromatic aberration: they reflect the sunlight without dispersing it into its diverse spectral colours."

On the gun deck of the *LeGrand*, a cannon boomed, and its 18-pound cannonball came whistling past the *Seahorse*'s gunwales.

"Confound the oceans!" said Mason, as a swelling wave lurched the ship. "How can I keep this focus steady, if the ship keeps heaving up and down?"

By this time, the gap between the *Seahorse* and the oncoming *LeGrand* was so narrow that Captain Smith could hear the taunts of the French frigateers. Now he saw, out of nowhere, a bright red circular apparition forming in the centre of the *LeGrand*'s forecourse sail. Suddenly, the sail burst into flame. The taunts of the Frenchmen became shouts of alarm, as the flame spread up the forecourse and ignited the lower topsail of the frigate's foremast. Meanwhile, Dixon was adjusting the mirror of the other telescope, and now the lower topsail of the French ship's mainmast likewise burst aflame. 'Twas done with mirrors, as Archimedes was rumoured to have set afire the Roman galleys of Marcellus.

The *LeGrand*'s canvas sails were highly flammable. In a moment, the flames on both masts had risen to the upper topsails, and thence to the topgallants. With shouts and curses, the French abandoned their guns, and manned their sea-pumps. Mason and Dixon had redirected their mirrors to the frigate's mizzenmast, and now this too was afire. The red flames spread like a scarlet pox across the leeches and throats of the French sails, and the tarred lines and rigging burned merrily. The square-sailed rig of the *LeGrand* carried a denser concentration of canvas and lines than the simpler fore-and-aft rig of the English barquentine: this had given the French ship more power under sail than the *Seahorse*. But now, with the frigate a-burning, the flames leaped easily from one sail to the next, and the *LeGrand*'s inferno spread more rapidly than her crew could extinguish the flames.

With all her sails afire, the French ship quartered to retreat. The vanquished *LeGrand* evidently had no intention of engaging an English ship that could project rays of hellfire.

"She's putting about!" yelled a mizzentopman, and fivescore Englishmen huzzahed.

"The devil she is!" shouted Captain Smith, racing to the helm.

Now the *Seahorse* gave chase. Dixon gave aid to the wounded, while Mason bent to the task of reassembling his telescopes. "The Royal Society will expect me to return these intact," he said to no one in particular, as he unplugged the eyepieces and reshipped the mirrors.

"Well done, sir!" said the yeoman of the sails, coming aft to Mason's station. "Would you like to know our strategy of pursuit? We will keep the tide upon our lee quarter, for the French ship is running directly into the wind's eye, and the tide runs to leeward."

"Is that good?" Mason asked.

"Good? Quotha! It is superlative! The enemy can have no advantage if we pursue her in this wise. If the *LeGrand* bears down afore the wind, she will have the tide further forward than ourselves, and so we will receive the greater benefit."

Indeed, the *Seahorse* seemed to be gaining on the French ship, which formerly had been much the faster. But the *Seahorse*'s masts were groaning in protest now as the wind caught her sheets. Just as Mason detected this, there was an ominous creaking sound from the ship's waist, and a cry of "*Down mast! Look below!*" With a sickening crunch, the shattered mainmast collapsed beneath its own weight, in a knot-maze of rigging and lines. Deckhands jumped aside to escape being crushed, then ran amidships to plunge marlin-spikes into the broken mast and hold it safe before it could roll overboard.

"Blast the luck!" said Captain Smith, as the French ship made good her escape. The captain came aft to where Mason was standing. "Well, there's nothing for it now. We can coak together that mast with some spars, and it will answer well enough for us to limp home. But your journey to Sumatra must end where it began: in the Royal Dockyard at Portsmouth. We shall require at least two months for this ship to be refitted and provisioned for a new voyage. And we must have replacements for the brave men we have lost."

Dixon placed a consoling arm across the shoulder of his senior partner. "Have courage, friend Mason! The governors of the Royal Society cannot fairly blame thee for this misfortune."

Charles Mason shook his head. "I doubt that the Royal Society – or the Lords of the Treasury, who have financed us – will display much generosity. Captain, your original mission still stands. Immediately we reach Portsmouth, you and I shall plot a course to the southernmost port which the *Seahorse* can attain in time for the transit of Venus. If Bencoolen is beyond our reach, there is still Scanderoon. I have not given up."

"Nor have I," said Jeremiah Dixon, as the *Seahorse* put about and set course for home. "I do not know why Providence has thrown this obstacle in our path, but if we two are not fated to reach Sumatra, then I believe 'tis because the Maker has chosen some other destiny for us. We may know it in time, perhaps. Who can say, friend Mason? At some future time . . . oh, let us say five years, then: five years after the transit of Venus has elapsed, wherever we two find ourselves – either apart or in company – perhaps thou and I shall understand that what has transpired here this morning was all a chapter of some divine scheme."

"Five years, you say?" asked Mason bitterly. "If these French have caused us to miss the transit of Venus, then – wherever I may be five years after – I feel certain that I shall not be inspired to merriment."

Indeed, Mason and Dixon never reached Sumatra; not in time for the transit of Venus, nor afterwards. Yet the paths of their lives remained parallel.

Five years after the transit occurred, on the evening of Friday, 6 June 1766, Mason and Dixon were in America. To be precise: on this night, they were encamped slightly west of Warrior Mountain and slightly east of Savage Mountain, in the second ridge of the vast Allegheny Range, at a position 165 miles 54 chains 88 links from the western benchmark between the colonies of Maryland and Pennsylvania. The two partners were able to set their position precisely, because they were charged with the task of surveying the borderline between these frontiers. As their assistants made camp for the night, Dixon reminded Mason of where they had been five years before.

"I had nearly forgotten this date's significance," said Mason. The night sky was clear, and as he looked upward he easily found Vega, Algol and Capella: three stars of low zenith distance, which were invaluable to him in his surveyances. "But is it not strange how diverging points may yet converge? My destiny and yours were fashioned by two simultaneous events, on opposite sides of the planet: in July 1760 the Royal Society commissioned us to witness the transit of Venus, while here in America that selfsame date, Lord Baltimore and the Penn brothers signed the document that would bring you and I to the New World: an indenture of agreement to chart the border of their lands."

Dixon nodded. "And we have learned, meantime, what happened in Sumatra: on the morning of Venus's transit, the skies above Bencoolen were so gravid with rain that no observations were possible. If the French had not accosted us on our first day out from Portsmouth, we would have made straight for Sumatra, and on the crucial day of the Venus event, all our energies would have availed us for naught."

Mason looked to the stars. Yes, it was true: after the battle against the *LeGrand* had forced them to return to Portsmouth, he had petitioned the Royal Society's consent to an alternate voyage to some other port nearer to England, whence the transit might still be observed. Thus, in April 1761, Mason and Dixon had reached the Dutch colony at the Cape of Good Hope, with sufficient time to erect an observatory.

"When the transit of Venus arrived," Mason recalled now, "the skies above Cape Town were hazed with clouds for the first twenty minutes, and I feared that we had striven in vain. But then the heavens cleared, and Venus revealed all her secrets to us. Immediately the transit had ended, the skies became cloudy again. It is almost as if Providence gave especial favour to our enterprise."

Dixon nodded once more. "The charts of the Great Surveyor

are concealed to us, but if we follow their lines, we are certain of wondrous discoveries."

And the two friends stood beneath the stars, and made plans for the rest of their journey.

NELSON: FIRST BLOOD

David Donachie

To this day Horatio Nelson remains one of our most enduring national heroes. He will appear several times in this anthology, but the following story, which is an extract from David Donachie's new novel about Nelson, On a Making Tide *(2001), shows us a youthful and less experienced sailor. By the standards of his day, Horatio Nelson was a lucky young man. His uncle, Maurice Suckling, was a naval hero and an influential senior captain. So instead of the young Horatio being stuck aboard Suckling's command, a guard ship moored in the Thames Estuary, the nephew was sent off on a series of voyages which gave him many advantages over his peers. First he sailed as a merchant seaman "before the mast" to the West Indies, a voyage that shaped his entire future career. That, after a six-month normal service, was followed by his trip to the Polar ice cap, rated as a captain's servant. Then, a month after his fifteenth birthday (in October 1773) came Nelson's appointment to* HMS Seahorse, *bound for the fabulous East! And yes, by a wonderful coincidence (the first of several in this anthology) this is the same* Seahorse *we met in the previous story.*

David Donachie (b. 1944) is the author of a dozen naval books. These include the Harry Ludlow series which began with The Devil's Own Luck *(1992) and the George Markham series under the alias Tom Connery which began with* A Shred of Honour *(1996). He has recently completed a two-volume novel on the life of Horatio Nelson.*

Prevarication could last only so long, and even the various boards had to succumb to the pressure of the Admiralty. They wanted Sir Edward Hughes and his squadron at sea, on his way to relieve the ships that had now been on station in eastern waters for two and a half years. Nelson was on deck, ready to go aloft on the great day, impressed by the band playing on the hard, as well as the presence of several senior officers come aboard to see them off.

He was first to the shrouds when the order came to weigh, and from aloft he looked down on the quarterdeck to see Captain Farmer stagger till he clasped the binnacle. Having been entertaining or indulged by others for a full twelve hours, he was in no fit state to command a ship's longboat. Not that he tried. He stood on the quarterdeck trying to make his swaying look as if it was caused by the ship's motion rather than half a dozen bottles of claret.

Red-faced admirals were heading back to the Portsmouth sallyport. As they landed the signal gun spoke from the Round Tower, a plume of white smoke preceding the boom. This was only a second ahead of that on the flagship HMS *Ramilles*. Signals broke out instantly at the masthead, and on each deck the first lieutenants raised their hats to their commanding officers and set in train the actions that would not only get every vessel to sea but also allow their captains to return to their cabins and sit down.

Nelson, still waiting for his orders, watched the crowds that lined the ramparts, waving their scarves and handkerchiefs in time to the music of the band. Below decks the men began to move to that same rhythm, the off-duty watch and the marines at the capstan, straining to haul HMS *Seahorse* over her anchor, 1,000 tons of inert timber, guns, stores and a 300-man crew, heaving till the call came that she was "thick and dry".

Durrand, head held back and speaking trumpet to his lips, called aloft to let fall the maintopsail, which followed as the bunts were released by the singular sound of falling canvas, like the slow wing-beat of a gigantic bird. The canvas beneath Nelson's feet changed quickly from a creased shapeless mass to a thing of white beauty, as the wind took the sail, billowing it out until it was as taut as a drum. A turn of the head saw the frigate fetch her anchor, sailing slowly over it so that it could be plucked from the bed of the sea.

"Anchors aweigh, sir," came the cry.

"See it catted and fished," called the first lieutenant, as the free anchor was hauled up on the cathead, well clear of the side of the ship, prior to being securely lashed. On the deck below, men were struggling with a wet, slimy hawser, while on slippery planking boys threw fast loops to attach it to the messenger cable so that it could be brought inboard and laid, head to tail, in front of the stout wooden bitts that held the fast to the end. Every other ship in the squadron had carried out the same manoeuvre, creating, to a young, impressionable eye, a wondrous vision of a fleet going to sea. Sure it was a small one, but it was impressive nevertheless.

"Mr Nelson," called Lieutenant Durrand, his voice a loud growl, "I will thank you to attend to the fore topgallantsail, and to cease your damned daydreaming."

He did as he was ordered, but it was hard. He had never seen so many ships put to sea at once: majestic two-deckers, several frigates, down to a couple of scampering sloops, all encouraged by the music of a band. That and a thousand relations, a great many of them wives who would be weeping with the fear that they might never see their loved ones again. He thought of his own family, his sisters and brothers, even his father, which brought a tear to his own eye and a rasping comment from his neighbour on the yard. "Belay them tears, Nellie lad, for if they hit the premier's fresh-swabbed deck, he'll have your guts."

Seahorse heeled over as the wind took enough of her sails to bring a tilt to her deck. Looking down, he saw the water running down the lee side of the ship, deep, green and cold.

Blue and warm and startlingly phosphorescent, the water was now even deeper, as the frigate ploughed through the great swell of the Indian Ocean. The crew of the *Seahorse* were now so practised in their sail drill that they could bend on a sail, take it in or reef it in their sleep. Durrand, his pockmarked face bereft of the ability to smile, might be a bad-tempered martinet but the ship ran well enough to be termed a crack frigate by the admiral, one that could be detached for special duty when the need arose.

They had crossed the line so long ago that it seemed like a distant memory, all the numerous candidates for the ceremony daubed and ridiculed as they made their first foray into the southern hemisphere. The Cape of Good Hope, where they had taken on wood and water, had come and gone, as had Mauritius and La Réunion. Ceylon was behind them and the flagship had set her bowsprit well to the east so that the squadron would master the currents and winds that would carry them on to the Bay of Bengal and the mouth of the Hooghly. He learned this from the man responsible for teaching him seamanship, the master of the *Seahorse*, Emmanuel Surridge.

"For failure to do so, Nelson," Surridge said, as they carried out their fifth consecutive night of lunar observations, "would see us hauled up westerly and foul of the Maldives."

"Yes, Mr Surridge."

"Tell me what that would mean, young man."

There was no attempt to trap him in the question, just a desire to ensure that his pupil had absorbed all that he had been taught. Nelson had come to admire his teacher for the depth of his knowledge, the extent of his curiosity and to esteem him for his kindness and patience.

"Coral reefs and sandbars, sir, many of them uncharted and deadly danger to a ship's hull on a night without a moon, especially with any kind of wind blowing."

"Now, sir, lay me a course to avoid that by taking a fix on Venus and the Orion's belt."

John Judd had taught him to hand and reef aboard the *Swanborough*. Emmanuel Surridge had added more spherical trigonometry, lunar and astrological observation, mathematical considerations about the consumption of stores related to the state of the frigate's trim, plus a thousand other points of learning required by a sailor. The process of assimilation was almost unnoticeable, and only the thickness of the boy's journals betrayed how much knowledge he had acquired.

Captain Farmer entertained them in rotation, an occasion for the ever-hungry midshipmen to fill themselves at a more well-endowed table, and to drink more than was good for their young heads. Nelson was no exception, happy to let the conversation pass him by as long as he could keep his mouth full. On this occasion he had been invited along to hear in which position he was now going to serve, it having been decided that he had spent enough time aloft to be fully competent.

If he had thought the captain didn't notice his greed then he was wrong, since Farmer posed a question just as he stuffed three slices of tough roast beef into his mouth. His attempt to reply was inaudible, and sent flying several pieces of meat.

"We must do something about your manners before we raise Calcutta, Nelson. And not just yours!"

"Slur," Nelson replied, a wad of beef stuck in his gullet.

"Every midshipman I have aboard is the same," he said to Durrand.

The premier, Durrand, responded with his habitual scowl, which looked even worse than it had previously on his peeling face. Nelson knew that the sun had not been kind to him on the voyage: it had left his visage, pockmarked under the shards of skin, looking like a piece of upholstery scratched by a cat.

Farmer had turned his attention back to his still chewing young guest. "Once we anchor, Nelson, there will be a great deal of social activity, some of which might be of benefit to you – not that I want to deny you the common whorehouse, if that is your wish. I'm told the Bengal bawds are a cut above their English counterparts, perfumed, gentle creatures unlike the brutes you'd find in a home seaport."

Surridge, also a guest, coughed slightly, to remind his commander, whose voice had grown wistful, that he had strayed off his point.

"Quite!" said Farmer, recovering himself. "I dare say it would be futile to hope that any of my midshipmen's manners should improve, since none of the young men I have aboard seem to possess an ounce of that commodity, do they, Surridge?"

Surridge replied with a heavy nod. "I've often had occasion myself to bemoan the lack of polish in the mids berth."

"Shockin," Surridge! God help the Calcutta whores when they get that lot between their thighs, eh! I doubt the perfume will suffice to kill off the smell. And as for gentility they'll not last two grains of sand. And what am I to do with them in polite society, I don't know? Weren't like that in my day. We were born to be gentlemen and knew how to behave like one."

He gave Nelson a hard look, just as the youngster managed to shift the last lump of his meat to one side of his mouth. "That's what I'd like to see from you."

"I'll do my best, sir."

Farmer had leaned forward and was peering at Nelson's bulging cheek. "For God's sake, boy, get rid of that lump."

The knock was so slight it was almost inaudible, and the door opened swiftly to reveal the round, red face of Thomas Troubridge. "Flag signalling, sir. Squadron to make more sail, dipped three times."

Surridge had already made to leave, since that meant the admiral apprehended danger, and Farmer had lost his vagueness. The eyes that had seemed sleepy were lively now. "Anything from the masthead?"

"Nothing, sir," Troubridge replied.

"If the best eyes are not aloft already, get them there."

"Sir!"

"And my compliments to Mr Durrand, he is to comply with the signal." The eyes were on Nelson next. "What are you still doing here? Get about your duties!"

In the background Nelson could hear the cry of "All hands". Before that would have meant him going aloft, but he'd been removed from that station. "With respect, sir, I'm not sure what my duties are."

"You may act today as my aide. Tell Mr Durrand I would like things put in hand to clear for action."

*　　*　　*

By the time Farmer appeared on deck they had heard the dull boom of distant gunfire. Every eye was straining to see the source of that sound, with the officers occasionally glancing aloft at the two men who occupied the masthead. Surridge was yelling orders through his speaking trumpet to the men aloft, while on deck canvas was coming up from below, sails to be laid out ready for bending on to the yards.

Seahorse was racing along, her deck canting to the angle of a steep-pitched roof, her bowsprit digging into the heavy swell of the Indian Ocean, throwing up a great mass of water. *Ramilles* and the other 74s were striving likewise, but their bulk slowed them down compared to the frigate, and Farmer had to shorten sail to remain on station.

Nelson felt as if his entire skin were itching, so quickly was the blood racing through his veins. All the ships in the squadron had a full suit aloft now. The sloop *Vixen* – on point duty – which had raised the alarm, had gained on everyone, increasing the gap between herself and the fleet, seemingly determined to get to the centre of the action first.

"Flagship signalling, sir," said Durrand.

"What does he say?" Farmer asked Troubridge, who was now the signalling midshipman.

"Difficult to make out, sir. The wind is angling the flags away from us."

"*Vixen* shortening sail, sir," added Durrand, a telescope fixed to his eye.

"Flagship's orders being repeated by *Euraylus*, sir," said Troubridge, pointing to another frigate, then consulting his book to make sense of the message. He nearly screamed the order as Sir Edward's signal became clear. "Flag is making our number, sir. The message reads, 'Make all sail.'" Everyone on board the vessel was watching as that set of coloured pennants disappeared and fresh lot was sent aloft. "General chase due east."

"Mr Surridge," said Farmer calmly, "I want the very best you can give us."

"Aye aye, sir."

The next hour was a whirlwind of activity, as yards and sails were set up in an endless stream. Nelson was sent dashing in all directions with messages to the various divisional officers, all the time aware of what the master was about, trying to second-guess each alteration to the sail plan before it was made, happy that he managed to anticipate about half of what occurred.

Studding sail booms were lashed on, to be pushed out from the main yards, the canvas they carried spreading well beyond the side of the ship. Royals and kites were hauled up to take what wind there was at the very top of the masts. *Vixen*, too lightly armed to go on alone, spilled the wind from her sails then joined company as the two ships opened up the gap between themselves and the rest of the squadron. The log was cast continuously, as Surridge trimmed sails, added to one side and subtracted from another, until, on the even Indian Ocean breeze, and taking account of the leeway, he had achieved the maximum speed.

"By damn, 12 knots, sir," he called, as the log was heaved again.

"Thank you, Mr Surridge," Farmer replied.

Nelson now stood beside Farmer on the quarterdeck, balancing himself against the motion of the ship, left leg extended to hold his position on the canted deck, right dipping to absorb the motion of the swell. Spray washed his face continuously, blown over the bows to hang in the air as *Seahorse* ploughed on through it. Cool as it was, it did nothing to dampen the excitement he felt, or the feeling that this was where he belonged.

It was what he had dreamed of in that cold coach that first took him to Chatham, the image of himself in command of a warship going into battle. It was the stuff of endless speculation among the youngsters he messed with; would they one day rise to a captain's rank? On this deck now it was easy to forget the presence of Farmer and imagine himself in the role of which he dreamed, to transpose their respective stations and conjure up the notion that he was issuing the orders. He would, God willing, rise to command, and when he did, he would be a better captain than the man he was standing by, at this moment, to serve.

Farmer's eyes were fixed on the scene ahead, an East India merchant vessel that had fought off a pirate assault long enough for the attacker to realize that warships were coming to the rescue. Still partly obscured by smoke, the attackers had been close to success. The Indiaman's bulwarks showed several jagged areas where they were stove in, and what sails she had aloft were shot full of holes. Obviously the enemy had lain off her stern, out of the arc of her guns, firing through the casements of the main cabin, which were so shattered as to be non-existent.

The enemy must have been close to the point of boarding through that very cabin, but had disengaged as soon as they spotted *Vixen*'s skysails, running before the wind to make an escape. The East Indiaman cheered first *Vixen* then *Seahorse* as they went by, with all the officers raising their hats to each other in salute. But Nelson observed that blood was running out through the scuppers, and through the shattered sides he could see bodies strewn on the deck, proving that it had been a close-run thing.

"Signal the flag, Mr Durrand," said Farmer. "Enemy in sight, am engaging."

Those last words proved to be at best premature. The ships they were pursuing turned out to be a couple of *chasse-marées*, small, compact vessels with narrow lines and a low freeboard designed for speed. They were fore and aft rigged, so on their present course the square rigger lost a great deal of the advantage of being able to put aloft more sail. A wind dead aft meant that the maincourse took pressure off the forecourse, which in turn deprived the inner and outer jib, while to come off the wind slightly so that they could draw meant that *Seahorse* had to tack and wear in pursuit. Farmer decided to split with the sloop, himself taking a more southerly course, while *Vixen* trended north. That would create a triangle with the British ships at the base and the chase at the apex.

"Mr Surridge, we require subterfuge. I want plenty aloft, but

I would wish them not to draw too efficiently. They have seen us struggle in their wake, let them see us wallow a trifle on a more favourable course."

"If I could be appraised of your intentions, Captain?"

"We could stay on this course for days, if the wind stays true, and we'll lose them for sure. Their home port has to be north towards the Kerala peninsula. I want them to turn that way, assuming that only *Vixen* stands between them and safety. Let them also believe that even with the most favourable wind we could never catch them."

"Would they not have seen our true ability as we bore down on the action?"

There was a touch of impatience in Farmer's reply. Nelson surmised that the master had asked one question too many, exceeding his duty in that respect and annoying a man who disliked having to explain himself.

"That I cannot tell, Surridge. I'm hoping they were too busy to note it. Now you will oblige me by complying with my request so that I may discover if I have the right of things."

Surridge took the rebuke well, having achieved his purpose, this being that all the men on the ship should know what was required. And Captain Farmer could not have had a better ship's crew for such a task. Nelson watched carefully as Surridge, employing skills honed over many years, did as he was asked. Now the idea of one sail interfering with the efficiency of another was deliberate, the canvas behind spilling just enough of the breeze to keep the one ahead taut, so that it looked as though it was drawing well, when it fact it was working at only three-quarters of its capacity.

"Who do you think they are, sir?" asked Durrand.

"French dogs, for certain," Farmer snapped, "with local Indian crews, either out of Madras or Pondicherry."

"Since we are at peace, they have engaged in piracy." Durrand's peeling face showed real pleasure as he added, "We can hang them."

"There's no peace out here, Durrand, regardless of what

happens in Europe. The best you can hope for is an armed truce, and those ahead of us have just broken it."

Farmer threw back his head and shouted to the men in the crosstrees. "Keep an eye on the enemy decks. As soon as you see them prepare to alter course, I want to know."

Nelson, who had considered George Farmer a bit of a duffer, was now looking at him with open admiration. The captain's eyes were alight, and his whole frame seemed infused with a new spirit of animation. Horatio Nelson would be a kinder captain than Farmer, less inclined to employ the cat, but he would settle for the same competence as a sailor.

"Mr Surridge, I will require an increase in speed on this course, since I intend to deny them the opportunity, if they make an error, to correct it."

"The chase is manning the braces, Captain," the lookout called.

Nelson strained to see, but from his position on the deck, with a running sea creating waves 15 feet high, he only glimpsed the two enemy ships when all three vessels crested at the same time. But he could imagine the men on the ropes, half an eye on the pursing frigate, the other on their own captain, waiting for the orders that would change their course.

"Mr Surridge," said Farmer.

"Aye aye, sir," the master replied. Having discussed what would happen next, more words were superfluous. The main course was goose-winged into a triangle, the raised corner allowing the wind full play forward. Braces were tightened and yards trimmed so that every one drew, with the driver boom, holding the fore and aft gaff sail, hauled to leeward to take full advantage of the wind.

"Enemy going about, sir," said Durrand. There was then a moment while he waited for them to sheet home again on their new course. "Heading north-north-east."

"Mr Troubridge, a signal to *Vixen*, if you please, to read, 'Disengage, course north-north-east.' Mr Surridge, stand by to go about. Mr Nelson, a message to the gunner. I intend a mixture of bar and case shot to be ready and loaded as soon as we clear. Tell him I require double charges to make them fly."

"Sir," Nelson replied crisply, running for the companion-way. Desperate not to miss anything on deck, he raced to the lower depths, hauling back the wetted screen on the hanging magazine to relay Farmer's order.

"Belay there, you daft swab," the gunner growled. He was bent over, sorting charges by the glimmer of candlelight that filtered through the glass window. "Don't you know better, boy, than to rush in here when there's powder laying about?"

"Sorry," Nelson replied, before delivering the captain's message. He got back to the deck just in time to hear Farmer order the new course. The chase was now off the starboard beam, with *Seahorse* at the end of a near straight line drawn from *Vixen*, through the two *chasse-marées*.

The months at sea paid off now as the *Seahorse* came about almost in her own length. The deck was a mass of men hauling and running, first easing the ropes that held the yards in place, then, as the rudder bit and the ship began to turn, pulling even harder to tighten them at an angle to the wind, which was now coming in right over the frigate's quarter. Surridge was yelling and waving his arms, calling for a mass of adjustments, some tiny, others major, so that he could get the best out of the top hamper.

Farmer, immobile through all this, waited until *Seahorse* was settled on the new course, until the master himself, taking the wheel, nodded to say he was satisfied, before turning to Durrand. "I think we may now clear for action."

They pursued the *chasse-marées* for hour after hour, the distance closing imperceptibly, while ahead of the enemy *Vixen* barred their escape. Having overheard the discussion, Nelson knew that Captain Farmer had no intention of exposing *Vixen* to a fight with two of the enemy. In such a small fleet and far from home the number of ships had to be maintained. Capture of these two pirate vessels would avail little if the sloop was rendered useless in the process.

Both the enemy helmsmen were good, as were the crews,

quick to see an extra puff of wind or a path through the run of the seas that would keep them clear. The hands were fast workers when it came to slight alterations to the set of a sail, the combined skills keeping them out of danger for longer than Captain Farmer had thought possible.

As the sun began to sink, they saw the enemy trying to lighten their ships, throwing overboard anything deemed unnecessary to survival: water, food and personal possessions that bobbed on the water until the frigate ploughed through them. Having eased away from the captain, Nelson had questioned Surridge as to what was likely to happen.

"He won't request *Vixen* to haul her wind unless the pirates throw overboard their guns. She will stay ahead of them, avoiding battle until we can overhaul."

"But it will be night soon."

"Aye, lad, and if you look at the sky you'll see nary a cloud. There's a moon due, and that will be bright enough for us to work by."

"Why don't they change course?"

"Because, no matter which way they turn, the wind and leeway favour one of our ships. And that wind can hold steady for a week in these parts. They should have held to the west and run for two days, if need be, to get clear, waited for a dark night to go about and get home safe."

"How long, sir?"

"See that one that's a touch laggardly?" he answered, pointing to the rearward enemy ship. 'We'll have him within long gunshot by dawn."

"Mr Nelson," called Farmer, "gun crews to worm every second cannon. Please go round the officers and tell them to split their men into watches. Two hours' sleep each."

"What about food, sir?" asked Durrand. "They have not been fed."

That remark surprised Nelson, who had always thought Durrand a hard-case premier who would see the men suffer rather than appear soft.

"Neither have we!" Farmer snapped, proving where the

indifference lay, also killing any hope that the cook might be able to relight his coppers. "Give them cold water and biscuit."

Night turned slowly to day, the sky full of moon and stars fading to a cold grey before the orange ball of the sun lit the western horizon. The first bow chaser fired, at extreme range, just after four bells in the morning watch, by which time any enthusiasm for what was to come had evaporated among the crew. They were hungry, and so was Nelson. And he was tired, not having been allowed to leave the deck all night. The ball skipped across the waves, dropping short on the second vessel's stern. Immediately the two ships changed course, heading in opposite directions.

Surridge was yelling again, bringing them round in the lead ship's wake, while a signal went out to *Vixen* to engage the other. The frigate was closing fast on her quarry. And since they knew their fate the pirates were determined to fight, lining the side in the low, brilliant sunlight and casting off their guns.

"Six-pounders, Durrand," said Farmer. "I doubt we have much to fear from those."

"Shall I reload the wormed cannon, sir?"

"No. Put the men into a boarding party, to gather on the forepeak. You, Mr Durrand, may lead it."

The premier's cratered face positively glowed. If the ship was taken by his boarding, the honour would belong as much to him as to Captain Farmer. And if the admiral at Calcutta bought it into the service, he might even get it as his first command.

"Message to Mr Foster, Nelson," Farmer said. "I want his main-deck cannon aimed well forward. He's to clear those swine away from their guns so that when we touch Mr Durrand can board."

Going forward to relay this allowed Nelson to look over the hammock nettings. He could see several Europeans clustered around the enemy wheel, in breeches and shirts, but the rest of the crew were dark-skinned, wearing nothing but white cloths around their loins.

By the time he was back on the quarterdeck, the range had shortened and Durrand had his party ready. Slowmatch smoke drifted up from below, the smell of saltpetre lingering on the nostrils. But that disappeared as Farmer gave the order to fire.

Nelson felt the vibrations through his feet as the whole ship shuddered, the result of half a dozen guns going off at two-second intervals, sending a frisson of fear though him, not helped as, simultaneously, the balls from the *chasse-marée* thudded into the frigate's side planking. The boom was deafening, the great cloud of greasy black smoke rising to obscure the target. Surridge, on the command, put the helm hard down, so that *Seahorse* ran alongside the chase. A second salvo was exchanged, the pirates aiming high at the elevated bulwarks of the frigate. Durrand, standing on the hammock right by the forward shrouds yelling to his men, took a ball that went right through him. Even over the din of battle, Nelson could hear him scream in agony, before he dropped back on to the deck, twitching like a freshly stuck pig.

Farmer's voice seemed devoid of emotion, even though he had just seen his first lieutenant killed. "Ask Mr Stemp to take over the boarding party, Nelson. You take his place on the guns, which are only to fire if the chase looks like getting clear."

Going below to the main deck was to enter a different world, darker, full of smoke and sweating men, the only radiance coming in through the open gunports, streaks of sunlight on the red-painted deck. The crews were kneeling by their pieces and only the gun captains stood, crouched, peering through at the target, which was now a few feet away.

"What do I do, sir?" he asked Stemp, as the lieutenant hurried away.

"Fire them one at a time, and let the gun captains do the aiming."

"What else, sir?" he shouted to the retreating back.

"Stay clear of the recoil, or you'll forfeit a leg."

Every time the frigate's bows rose he could see the enemy's side, splintered and broken where the guns had struck home. Above his head, he heard the yells of the men getting ready to jump for the side. He was in command, with only the sketchiest idea what to do. True he had orders, but they were so vague as to be useless. Suddenly there was a voice in his ear. "It's all over bar the shouting, young Nellie."

He turned to look into Mallory's smiling face. Clearly he was the gun captain on the number one piece.

"Durrand's gone, cut in two by a ball."

"That's no loss." Mallory spat on the deck.

"Belay that, Mallory," he shouted, offended. "I'm in charge of this division now."

"Nellie," Mallory replied, unfazed, his face splitting into a grin, "you've gone and joined the enemy."

Nelson looked set to protest, but Mallory slapped him on the back. "Had to come 'cause of the coat you wear. Never mind, when you'se high and mighty, lad, don't you forget your old shipmates."

The ships, crunching into each other, killed any chance of a reply. Mallory ordered his gun pulled inboard, grabbed the wormer and poked himself half out of the gunport, jabbing at something unseen, the muscles in his scarred back flexing with each stroke. He blocked any view that his newest young gentleman had had of what was going on. All Nelson could hear were the muffled sounds, metal on metal particularly, accompanied by banshee-like screaming. Suddenly it went quiet for a split second, then a great cheer rent the air, some of it coming through the ports but the majority from the upper deck.

"Come on, Nellie," called Mallory, tugging at his coat sleeve and heading for the companionway.

"Have we won?"

"How could we fail? It weren't no more'n a smack. Mind, old Farmer will carry on as if it were a ship-of-the-line when he dines with the admiral."

Everyone was pouring up on to the deck. Hesitating for only a second, Nelson followed, to be greeted by the sight of a British ensign being raised on the *chasse-marée*'s mainmast. The boom of distant gunfire reminded them of *Vixen* and the task she had to perform, which was more difficult given her size.

"Belay that damned cheering," yelled Farmer, before shouting across to the enemy deck. "Mr Stemp, you will take possession of the prize. Mr Surridge, shape me a course to join *Vixen*."

"Three huzzahs for Captain Farmer."

Nelson didn't recognize the voice, but the cry was instantly taken up. He was standing close to Mallory's back, so close that each stroke of the cat seemed like a separate etching or ridge in the re-formed skin. But the tough gunner was cheering like everyone else, and for the man who had bestowed his scars, which made Nelson wonder where sense started and excitement ended. Mallory should surely hate the captain more than any man alive. When he turned, the sailor provided the answer to why he was cheering. "There's money, Nellie," he whooped. "Good coin to make our Calcutta visit one to recall in old age. I'll pay you back for that brandy you fetched me."

"Nelson," shouted Farmer, "what the devil are you doing away from your station?"

"Sir," he cried, before turning to Mallory, his face flushed: "Get the men back on the guns."

The two fingers that went to the cloth wrapped round Mallory's ears were a salute of sorts. "Aye aye, Mr Nelson."

They buried Durrand on the way back to join the squadron. No plain shroud for him, rather the wooden cot he had slept in. It had been made to fit his body and was slung from the deck beams in his cabin. All it required was a lid and some roundshot to weight it. Had he ever pondered as he lay in it at night that his bed might also be his coffin? Somehow, Nelson doubted it; Durrand had been a man who seemed bereft of imagination.

But there was still emotion in this funeral, with the captured French officers in attendance and Captain Farmer reading the words of the service in a sonorous tone. On the voyage he had lost the usual number of men to sickness and accident, but this was the first time Nelson had witnessed a burial caused by action, and it was different.

He hadn't liked Durrand, but his death had made him think differently of the man and see beyond the scabby face and bellicose manner, perhaps to glimpse the fellow who wanted the men fed. The work of a first lieutenant was thankless: they got no praise when things went well – that was expected – but were roundly damned when anything went wrong. Perhaps his manner had been the result of his office and not his true personality. Nelson would never know the truth now that the man was dead.

As Farmer spoke the final words, and the burial party tipped the body over the side, Nelson prayed for the soul of a departed shipmate with all the vigour of his faith. At the same time he shuddered at the thought of where Durrand's remains were going.

SPECIAL DUTIES

Derek Wilson

We now enter the period of the French Revolutionary Wars, at a time when the traditional English navy was trying to come to terms with the development of a military intelligence service which had been set up by the young British Prime Minister William Pitt. In the early stages of the conflict he hoped to bring the war to a swift and successful conclusion with a combination of gold (paying allies to employ soldiers and encouraging insurrection within France) and spies. The following story poses the question of how this new style of warfare would impact upon men brought up in the tradition of the navy.

Derek Wilson is the author of over forty books, and is a leading writer of popular history, biography and fiction. Among his books of naval history are The World Encompassed *(1977) and* The Circumnavigators *(1989). He is also the author of a series of mystery novels featuring art specialist Tim Lacy, which began with* The Triarchs *(1994). Derek Wilson's new series, which began with* Keene's Quest *(2001), is all about Revolutionary and Napoleonic War espionage.*

"5 April 1793. This day I was given my first command. I am now Acting Captain Charles Hawkestone of His Britannic Majesty's brig *Gallant*. I suppose I ought to feel proud."

The young man with the dark, close-cropped hair and still-boyish features chewed the end of his pen and reread the sentence he had just written in his personal log. He sat back in the cushioned armchair installed by his predecessor and looked around the main cabin, appreciating not for the first time that these Frenchies did very well for themselves. The space was small and a sizeable part of it was taken up by the six-pounder standing ready at the larboard port but by comparison with the lieutenant's berth he had occupied until yesterday on the frigate *Promise* the accommodation was palatial. He dropped the pen in the well of the portable desk, stood up and took two paces to the wide rear window. It was no use: he could not settle to the dull routine of writing. There would be time later to complete the logs – his own and the ship's – before he turned into the screened cot against the starboard wall. Perhaps by then he would know what to write.

Hawkestone leaned against the leaded panes, too tall by an inch to stand erect in the cabin, and watched the *Gallant*'s crisp wake uncurling like a white ribbon on the green-black of the English Channel. The prize-ship – if that was what she was – went sweetly under full trim. A fresh wind had pulled round to the north in the dying day and the brig was riding the cream-braided waves joyfully, like a boy out of school. As a first command she was nothing to be ashamed of. If he handled her well and if the war lasted more than the few months most people at home were prophesying he might soon have his own frigate. Three weeks ago there had been nothing he yearned for more. But now?

Three weeks ago.

The frigate *Promise*, Captain Athanasius Tranter commanding, was making indifferent progress after two days of alternating calms and squalls. She had cleared home waters on a sou-westerly course and was standing well away from the enemy coast. When Hawkestone ended his watch at 6.30 a.m. on the morning of 16 March she was 47 sea miles due west of St Matthew's Point, the nearest French mainland.

Old Tutter, as everyone on board called the captain because

of his stammer – though not in his hearing – came on to the quarterdeck just as Hawkestone, the first lieutenant, was handing over to a junior officer. "W . . . w . . . well, Mr Hawkestone?" Tranter, constantly embarrassed by his disability, was a man of few words.

Briskly Hawkestone reported on overnight wind, weather and the *Promise*'s current position.

"Hmm!" Tranter strutted to the starboard rail and peered into the morning murk through his spyglass. He was small, and immaculately turned out, down to the last polished button, a precisionist who tolerated not the slightest suggestion of sloppiness, and a worrier. "C . . . confound this mist. What v . . . v . . . visibility have you had overnight?"

"Clear with a good moon till 2.30, sir. Then showers on and off, giving us no more than a mile's view at best. The mist came down at first light."

"What s . . . s . . . sails s . . . sighted?"

"*Saturn* at 3.15, sir and *Rameses* at 3.40, both inward bound. No French sail, sir!"

"C . . . confound the French, Hawkestone! It's the S . . . *Spry* we're l . . . l . . . looking for." Tranter spun round, glaring.

"Yes, sir." Hawkestone and Second Lieutenant Bradford stood stiffly to attention.

"Yes, sir? Y . . . yes, sir? Is that the b . . . b . . . best you say? B . . . By God, Hawkestone, if we've p . . . p . . . passed *Spry* in the n . . . n . . . night . . ." The captain bit his lip in an effort to control the flow of words. "You k . . . kept a double lookout all n . . . night?"

"Yes, sir."

"Hmm! Mr Bradford, I want m . . . more m . . . men aloft and extra watch all round the d . . . deck."

"Aye, Captain!" The officer hurried away to give the necessary orders, glad to escape Tranter's sharp if hesitant tongue.

"May I suggest extra rum ration for the first man to spot her, sir?"

Tranter snapped the telescope shut and thrust it inside the

top of his waistcoat. "What? Extra r . . . r . . . rum for doing his d . . . duty?"

Old Tutter was notoriously mean about offering rewards and inducements to his men. He had the reputation of being one of the most ardent prize-hunters in the British navy, ever on the lookout for opportunities to enrich himself and, like most avaricious men, he was little disposed to be generous. It was a weakness Hawkestone took a mischievous delight in exposing. Now, as the captain glared at his young subordinate, he was met with an open, innocent look of seemly deference. "Well p . . . perhaps, on this occasion," he muttered. "P . . . pass the word, Hawkestone."

The lieutenant hesitated before descending the companion-way. If the captain was in a mood to grant concessions it might be worth risking a question. "Why are we chasing a prison ship, sir?"

Tranter's face darkened and Hawkestone knew he had gone too far. "Because, I obey orders without asking d . . . d . . . damn-fool questions, Mr Hawkestone, and I'll t . . . t . . . thank you to do the same!"

Back in his cramped quarters, a "cupboard" some 5 feet by 6, the young officer removed his uniform tailcoat and dropped thankfully on to the hard bed running the length of one wall. Like all the junior officers on board and some of the men, he felt frustrated. Since he had joined the navy six and a half years ago Britain had been at peace. Hawkestone had made three tours in those years: two to the Mediterranean and one to the West Indies. In all that time, while he was serving his apprenticeship as midshipman and subsequently as junior lieutenant (a promotion gained with the aid of family influence and a forged birth certificate), he had only on two occasions seen anything that might remotely be called "action". Now, with France's declaration of war in February he had hoped – expected – to be engaged on a real fighting ship, part of a fleet sent to drive the enemy from the seas.

The reality was very different. He had been immediately assigned to the *Promise* and sailed with a squadron on a goodwill mission to Denmark. That had ended ignominiously when the frigate had hit bad weather off Jutland and been obliged to limp home for repairs. The work had been carried out at Chatham and the *Promise* had then sailed for Plymouth to test a new mast and spars and complete her refit. Hawkestone had planned a short visit to his Wiltshire home while the ship was in dock but on arrival Tranter found fresh orders waiting for him. They had sailed again within twenty-four hours, short on naval supplies and scarcely half victualled.

Old Tutter had chosen to share almost nothing with his officers about their new assignment. He only hinted darkly at "special d . . . duties" which involved pursuit of a transportation ship called the *Spry*, which had set out for Australia three days earlier. Hawkestone and his wardroom companions had speculated about the purpose of chasing after an old tub carrying traitors and subversives to their just punishment in the distant penal colonies on the world's wrong side. No one had been able to come up with a convincing answer to the conundrum but all agreed that it was a waste of time. They realized, also, how desperate the captain was to rendezvous with the *Spry*. At every change of watch the duty officer was reminded of the importance of keeping lookouts up to the mark and every few hours he had called Hawkestone into the great cabin to discuss the possible speed of the old transportation vessel and plot her possible course on his charts.

The lieutenant had some sympathy with his captain. Tranter was facing two major problems in attempting to carry out Admiralty orders. The further the *Promise* got into the Atlantic, the easier it was to miss her quarry completely. And with no possibility of a landfall she would be forced, by shortage of provisions, to turn back within days.

The next thing Hawkestone knew was that he was being shaken into consciousness by a one-eyed sailor with a savage scar which distorted the left side of his face and made him look like a messenger from hell.

"What is it, Bairstow?" the sleepy officer muttered.

"Captain's compliments, sir, and will you be so good as to

join him in the Great Cabin?" The ugly face twisted into what was presumably supposed to be a grin. "What he actually said was, 'F . . . F . . . F . . . F . . . F . . . Find M . . . M . . . M . . . M . . . Mr Hawkestone and t . . . t . . . t . . . t . . . tell him . . .' "

"Yes, all right, Bairstow, I understand." Hawkestone got to his feet and reached out a hand for his coat. "You may go, and I'll thank you to show more respect to your superiors." But he grinned to himself as the sailor closed the door behind him.

When he arrived in Tranter's commodious cabin, Hawkestone saw that the captain had assembled all his officers, including the captain of marines and the bosun, who formed a circle round the table. He realized he was the last arrival and glanced apologetically at the captain but Tranter restricted his displeasure to a quick scowl and continued with what he had been saying.

"We s . . . spotted the *S . . . Spry* and confirmed her identity a h . . . half-hour ago. She's a lumbering t . . . tub and we'll be up with her w . . . within the hour. We shall hail her and order her to h . . . heave to. The captain of the transport will be b . . . brought aboard the *P . . . Promise* to receive his orders. When we have c . . . c . . . conferred, the *S . . . Spry* will be under my c . . . command. Captain Carter will return and s . . . s . . . supervise the operation from his end. Then, Mr Bosun, I want all the boats ready, manned and away in d . . . d . . . double-quick time. Mr Bradford, you'll take the first. Report to Captain Car . . . Car . . . Car . . ." He paused and swallowed hard. "Report to the captain and place yourself at his disposal. It will be your r . . . responsibility to convey all the *S . . . Spry*'s officers back to the *P . . . Promise*."

The listeners exchanged puzzled glances and the second lieutenant asked, "*All* the officers, Captain?"

Tranter glared at him. "S . . . S . . . Something wrong with your hearing, Mr Bradford?"

"No, Captain."

"I should th . . . think not. Here are your instructions, Captain Strange." He handed an envelope to the marine officer.

It bore a heavy Admiralty seal. "You'll t . . . take as few m . . . men as possible to d . . . do the job and you'll make sure they discuss their orders with no one. Understood?"

"Aye, Captain." The tall soldier nodded.

"Good. Mr Bosun!"

"Aye, Captain."

"All the other boats, except one to bring off the *Spry*'s crew – as m . . . many to a b . . . boat as possible. I want the whole manoeuvre d . . . done quickly." He looked around the circle. "Any questions?"

The listeners' minds were humming with queries but no one put them into words.

"Dismissed, then! M . . . Mr Hawkestone, you'll remain."

When the others had filed out, Tranter produced another letter and placed it on the table in front of the lieutenant. "B . . . Be good enough to read it n . . . now," he ordered.

Hawkestone picked up the envelope which was of thick, good-quality paper and bore his own name in Tranter's hand. He broke the seal and extracted a single sheet written in the neat characters of an Admiralty secretary. It read:

The designated officer shall proceed aboard HMS *Spry* and locate among the prisoners Mr George Keene. He will convey Mr Keene to HMS *Promise* with the maximum despatch and will attend personally to Mr Keene's needs throughout the remainder of the voyage. Mr Keene is to have no communication with any person aboard other than the designated officer. When HMS *Promise* reaches her destination the designated officer shall deliver Mr Keene into the hands of those appointed to receive him. The designated officer shall not discuss these instructions with any other person either during or after the voyage.

The letter was unsigned.

Hawkestone looked up. "Who is this George Keene, sir?"

"The m . . . man we have to rescue." Tranter's shrug suggested that he shared the lieutenant's bewilderment. "All

I know is that I am ordered to s . . . stop him being taken to T
. . . Terra Australis."

"So, the Admiralty is now in the business of helping traitors
and seditionists to escape justice?"

"These orders came from higher than the Admiralty." Tranter collapsed moodily into an armchair and waved his dismissal.

It was late morning before the *Promise* caught up with the
lumbering transport ship and there was a protracted exchange
of flag signals and shouted instructions before the *Spry* took in
sail and her commander consented to be rowed across to the
frigate. Then, for several tedious hours, nothing happened. The
two captains were shut up in Tranter's cabin. Food was taken in
to them. Hawkestone and his fellow officers took every opportunity to be busy in the adjacent area. Occasionally they heard
raised voices and when they quizzed the midshipman who
served the meal he reported black looks and a brittle atmosphere
but no one could discover what was being discussed behind the
firmly closed door.

Speculation and rumour were, therefore, rife as the occupants
of main deck and quarterdeck went about their routine duties.
Ignorance bred both excitement and apprehension. Men told
each other that the *Promise*'s complement was being doubled for
a surprise raid somewhere on the French coast. The convicts
were going to be used for a suicide mission. The *Spry* would be
turned into a fireship and sailed into the crowded harbour at Le
Havre or Brest.

The wilder guesses seemed to be confirmed when, in mid-
afternoon, Carter emerged, silent and grim-faced, to return to
his ship, and immediately a ferry system was set in motion.
Boatload after boatload of supplies were transferred from the
transport to the frigate; casks, kegs, canvas, timber, cordage. It
was like manna from heaven; all the *Promise*'s shortage problems were being solved at a stroke and the purser, as he stood
by the forward hatch checking every item being stowed below,
looked like a man who had just married a rich brewer's widow.
Was this what it was all about? Hawkestone wondered. Had

their masters in London hit upon a cheap way of reprovisioning the *Promise*? Was the convict-carrier to be stripped of everything of value and its human cargo turned loose at some point on the enemy coast? That still did not explain the traitor who had been wished on Hawkestone as an unwanted cabin mate.

The day was drawing to a close before the lieutenant played his role in this weird manoeuvre. At last he climbed the scrambling net and stood on the deck of the wide-bellied *Spry*. The scene before him was depressing to anyone inured to the essential disciplined tidiness of a well-run naval vessel. Ropes snaked uncoiled about the deck. Tools and items of equipment lay where they had been abandoned. Aloft the half-furled sails drooped in irregular folds from their spars. The only semblance of order to be discerned was the lines of sailors and marines who shuffled towards the starboard and larboard rails in order to transfer to the waiting boats. Hawkestone was overwhelmed with a sense of desolation made worse by his total incomprehension about what was happening.

"Lieutenant Hawkestone?" A stocky marine sergeant with smears of grease across the facings of his red jacket offered the young officer a perfunctory salute. "Captain's ordered me to take you to the prisoner Keene." Without waiting for acknowledgment the man turned and scurried towards a companionway. Holding a lantern aloft he descended three decks with Hawkestone following. He stopped before a low door and unlocked it with one of the keys from a large ring chained to his belt. The first sensation that assailed Hawkestone as he stooped to enter the black space was the choking stench. The smell of every kind of human excretion mingled with the odours of pitch, hemp, mouldy canvas and seeping seawater attacked his nostrils. The lieutenant clapped a hand over his nose and mouth as he stared around him. The low-ceilinged chamber about 20 feet square was carpeted with manacled bodies scarcely recognizable as men. They lay or sat but mainly huddled together for warmth on a slatted platform below which bilge water slopped and splashed with the movement of the ship.

"Right you, on your feet!" the sergeant ordered.

He had stopped beside a youngish man who was blinking in the sudden light from the lamp thrust into his face.

"What's going on?" the man asked, sitting up with an effort, as the soldier unshackled him.

"That's for us to know and you to find out," the marine responded gruffly, grabbing the prisoner's arm and hauling him to his feet. "You lot, hold your tongues or there'll be no grub for you tomorrow!" He directed the last words at several prisoners who were rattling their fetters and calling out "Me too!", "Take these off!", "Let me out, too!"

Thankfully Hawkestone retreated up the companionway to the fresh air of the main deck, prisoner and escort following. The evacuation of the *Spry*'s crew was almost complete as the lieutenant hurried to the rail, saw the man Keene and his guardian stowed in the boat reserved for them, then dropped down to take his seat in the stern.

On the short journey across the water he surveyed the wretch he had been ordered to rescue. He saw a haggard creature of, perhaps, twenty-eight or thirty, though it was hard to read the age of a face covered in grime, sweat and several days' growth of beard. Keene stared back defiantly, eyes bright in their deep sockets, hollowed cheeks giving him a cadaverous appearance. Here's a villain if ever there was one, Hawkestone thought.

Minutes later he stood with his unwanted companion on the *Promise*'s overcrowded main deck. "Wait there!" he ordered the sergeant as he made his way between the groups of seamen towards the quarterdeck. He reported Keene's safe arrival to Tranter whose response was to glower at him and bellow, "Well d . . . don't stand there c . . . c . . . congratulating yourself, Lieutenant! Get him out of s . . . s . . . sight! Now!"

Hawkestone returned to his charge. "Come with me!" he ordered and turned to lead the way aft.

That was the moment at which a sudden bright light illuminated the frigate, followed instantly by the first of a series of explosive cracks and roars. Hawkestone spun round to look across the water and saw the *Spry* fly apart with a burst of lurid flame. The display lasted only a few seconds. Then all that was left of the transport ship was a drift of smoke and a scattering of specks on the ocean that might have been wooden fragments or human bodies.

Hawkestone was still shaking minutes later when he escorted George Keene to one of the tiny cabins opening off the wardroom and prodded him in the small of the back. "This is where you'll be staying and you ain't to leave it, day or night." He pointed to the narrow bunk along the outer wall. "That's my bed, so don't get any ideas. You'll find a blanket in the locker under it. You can sleep down there, by the cupboard. It'll be luxury after what you've been used to."

For the first time he got a good look at the criminal who had been thrust upon him. George Keene was thin and slightly taller than Hawkestone. He was filthy and unkempt, yet there was about him an air of defiance, even arrogance. Hawkestone decided that the next few days were going to be very unpleasant. He shuddered as he surveyed the other man's soiled breeches, torn brown coat and sweat-stained shirt.

"God, what a sight!" He pinched his nose. "And you stink like a farmyard." The officer's lips curled downwards in disgust. "You're not staying here like that. We must get some clean slops for you and have you out of these greasy, threadbare . . ." He stretched out a forefinger to tweak the collar of Keene's jacket.

What happened next took the lieutenant totally off guard. Keene's face twisted in sudden rage. With the speed of a mule's kick his right hand lashed out. His grip fastened on the other man's wrist like an eagle's claw.

Hawkestone struggled to free himself, his left hand fumbling for his sword hilt. "What do you think . . .? Take your hand . . ."

With a quick twist Keene pinned the lieutenant's arm behind his back and forced him against the cabin's only empty wall. He whispered, his lips close to the officer's ear. "You'd best listen to me, without making a noise, for I'm a desperate man. I'm already sentenced to a living death, so I really don't care what I do to you."

Hawkestone squirmed but knew himself to be beaten. "Is this the way to treat your rescuer?" he demanded, with as much dignity as he could muster.

"Rescuer?" The word came out as a growl. "Or executioner. What's supposed to happen to me aboard His Majesty's ship *Promise*? Pistolled and dropped overboard in a sack with some roundshot?"

"No! Why should you think that?" Hawkestone tried to calm his assailant. "Look, my orders are to take care of you. You're to be kept in here and have no contact with the crew until we get to wherever we're going. Sleep here, eat here – everything."

He felt the criminal's breath on his neck as he seemed to weigh up the words.

"Very well, I'll own that I'm here alive unlike all those other poor wretches you've just sent to perdition. So, let's say I believe you; that I am being rescued. That means that someone has gone to a great deal of trouble. So I must be important to that someone, in which case a little civility would be in order, don't you think?"

Hawkestone nodded. He realized for the first time that Keene spoke with the tones of a cultured man and not those of the back-street ruffian he seemed to be imitating.

"Very well," Keene continued. "Now all I'm asking you for is a few answers to some very simple questions. But first, since we've not been properly introduced, my name is George Keene, formerly confidential aide to the Honourable George Granville Leveson-Gower, MP. And you are, sir?"

"The Honourable Charles Hawkestone of Collingbourne Hall, Wiltshire. For God's sake, you're breaking my arm!"

Keene smiled. "Your servant, Mr Hawkestone. Delighted to make your acquaintance and my thanks to you for your hospitality. Now, to whom am I indebted for my deliverance and why wasn't I blown to bits like all the others?"

"I don't know. I assumed you would have the answers to these sorts of questions. I'm just an officer carrying out my orders."

"Well, then, where am I being taken? Surely you must know where your ship's bound."

"Back to England, I suppose. I shan't know for sure till I go on watch and see the helmsman's course."

"Hmm! No one bothers to explain anything to mere underlings, do they? Well, I'm obliged to you, Mr Hawkestone. I'm now about to release you and I trust you'll not take your rough handling too much amiss. I'd be very much obliged for a change of clothes, as you suggest, but I own I'm quite attached to these humble rags. Perhaps they could be washed?" He loosed his hold on the lieutenant's arm.

Hawkestone turned and, after briefly rubbing his shoulder muscles, he smiled and held out his hand. "Mr Keene, I wronged you. I took you for—"

"An uncouth Jacobin rabble-rouser you'd hang from a yard-arm if you'd half a chance?"

The lieutenant laughed. "Something like that. Now I see that you're a man of spirit. Anyone who can endure that stinking hell-hole on the *Spry* and keep his dignity deserves better than I gave you."

Charles Hawkestone was a man given to forming quick impressions and, when necessary, reassessing them with the same rapidity. These qualities had been noted by more than one of his superiors, who had commended him as an excellent officer in a crisis. He had the talent to rise assuredly through the ranks though, as he readily admitted, family contacts had set his feet securely on the ladder and given him a start denied to other young men of equal merit. With a grandfather and an uncle who had both been rear admirals and a father who had died at the siege of Charleston in 1780, young Charles's career had never been in any doubt. Nor had he taken the trouble to doubt it. At least until his grandfather, Viscount Hawkestone, died and he assumed the title, he would serve his King on the high seas.

It was typical of the young lieutenant that he readily adjusted his impression of George Keene. Even before the convict had bathed, shaved and climbed into clean clothes Hawkestone knew that he liked the man and found in him a kindred spirit. Not that he was able to learn much about him, for Keene was reticent about his past. It seemed that, though of humble origins, he had early entered the service of George Leveson-Gower, eldest son of Earl Gower and until recently the British ambassador in Paris. From being that gentleman's confidential aide Keene had graduated to government service, which involved keeping an eye on the English revolutionary clubs which took their inspiration from what was happening in France and which threatened to overthrow the social and political order. Somehow Keene had become involved with the very men he had been employed to keep under surveillance. At that point his employers had disowned him, hence his arrest and condemnation to the new penal colonies of Terra Australis.

As to the destruction of the *Spry* and the death of thirty-two fellow transportees, Keene seemed as stunned and appalled as Hawkestone was. He either did not know or would not say who had ordered his costly deliverance nor what lay in store for him in the future. What neither man could foresee was that that future would bring them together again in unexpected ways.

Three days later George Keene was landed under cover of darkness on a quiet stretch of Dorset coast and Hawkestone assumed he had seen the last of him. The *Promise* sailed to Portland harbour where she disembarked the men from the *Spry*. The frigate's own complement fully expected a spell of shore leave and Hawkestone was, again, hoping for a few days at home at Collingbourne. But scarcely had the *Promise* come to anchor when a harbour boat pulled alongside bearing fresh orders. Within hours Captain Tranter's ship was at sea again with a disgruntled crew. Old Tutter himself seemed even less enamoured of his new instructions. He stalked the quarterdeck, muttering about s . . . special d . . . duties. He was even less communicative than usual and swore roundly at anyone who broke in on his brooding.

The *Promise* anchored after dark close inshore near Lulworth Cove and at midnight exchanged lamp signals with someone on the headland. Hawkestone was in charge of the boat that put away to pick up passengers. There were two of them this time, George Keene and a short, bespectacled, older man with swept-back grey hair whose name Hawkestone later learned was Sir Thomas Challoner. This dignitary was treated with grudging deference by Tranter and with distinct reserve by Keene. Like a sombre, grey bird he flitted everywhere around the ship, constantly checking the helmsman's course and the ship's speed, bombarding the watch officer with questions, quarrelling with the captain about the spread of canvas. Always he seemed dissatisfied with the frigate's progress towards her destination – but he told no one what that destination was. Hawkestone found his presence unnerving. Nor was he alone. The conviction rapidly settled on the crew that Sir Thomas was "unlucky"; that he had taken command of the *Promise* and was sailing her to perdition.

On the second day out the lieutenant tried to prize some information out of Keene as they stood together at the starboard rail.

He nodded in the direction of the quarterdeck where Challoner stood, bracing himself against the rail and surveying the horizon through his spyglass. "Your friend's obviously an important fellow. Old Tutter don't let anybody else come and go as they please on the quarterdeck."

"I wouldn't call him a friend," Keene muttered.

"What then? Who is he? Is it true he's close to the King?"

Keene shrugged. "I've heard it said." He changed the subject. "We seem to be making good time. The *Promise* runs well with this wind."

"What's the hurry?" Hawkestone demanded. "Just where is it you want to get to and why is it so urgent?"

Keene gazed aloft at the full sails and muttered, half to himself.

" 'If it were done when 'tis done, then 'twere well it were done quickly.' "

Hawkestone pulled a long face. "Confound you, George! When you're not biting your tongue like a shy girl you're speaking in riddles. You've no idea how tedious it is not knowing where we're going and why and whether it really matters anyway. Running up and down the Channel on these cloak-and-sword errands upsets the crew."

Keene clapped his companion on the shoulder. "Sorry, Charles. If there was anything I could tell you I would. All I can say is that it's important to get me to . . . where I'm going as soon as possible. Every hour we lose because of a slack wind makes my job more difficult."

"Your job! You weren't so enthusiastic about it a couple of days ago when we sent those poor devils on the *Spry* to kingdom come. I suppose that was Challoner's doing?"

Keene sighed and looked Hawkestone square in the face. "I haven't changed my opinion about that. Challoner and his . . . associates . . . decided that George Keene should 'disappear' and they chose a devilish way to achieve it. But it's done. Life goes on. This damnable war goes on and thousands more wretches – sailors, soldiers, civilians – will get killed unless we can put a stop to it quickly. And *that* is what my job is all about." He turned and stared out to sea. "Now, I've already told you too much, so no more questions, if you please."

Two days later, in the hour before dawn, George Keene was rowed ashore near the little Belgian port of Zeebrugge.

Any suggestion that the *Promise*'s "special duties" were now at an end was soon dispelled. Challoner "required" Captain Tranter to return to the same location in exactly seven days to pick up his agent again. In the meantime he was to take the frigate well away from any possibility of encountering enemy vessels. The *Promise* cruised to and fro in the North Sea while Hawkestone and his fellow officers devised gun drills, boat drills and watch competitions to keep a bored and disgruntled crew occupied. Their task was not made easier by Tranter, whose temper deteriorated by the day. He took to inviting the senior officers to share meals in the Great Cabin to ease the strain of dining alone with Challoner and being civil to him. On one such occasion he demanded why the *Promise* should be debarred from seeking out the enemy.

"Damn it, sir," he exploded, "her j . . . job's ridding the seas of His M . . . M . . . Majesty's enemies, not running a cross-Channel p . . . packet service."

Challoner was quite unruffled. "I'll allow, sir, this is a different kind of war and one you ain't used to but war it is none the less, though it don't hold out much prospect of personal profit." He gazed appraisingly round the appointments of the cabin. "You took some fine prizes in our little contretemps with the Americans, I'm told."

Tranter drew himself up, his narrow chin jutting defiantly. "I had the honour to command the *S . . . Samothrace* for t . . . two years and we brought in a couple of F . . . Frenchies and a Yankee p . . . p . . . privateer. If you're suggesting m . . . m . . . m . . . my . . ." He clenched his fists on the table with the effort of getting his words out. "My only interest—"

"'Deed I ain't, sir, 'deed I ain't.' Challoner smiled his infuriating smile. "Your devotion to duty is well known. That's why their lordships of the Admiralty selected you for this crucial work."

Tranter bellowed for his servant, who appeared on the instant to clear the tureen of vegetable broth and bring hot dishes of chicken and ragout. When the man had withdrawn the captain took up the argument again. "And just what is this 'work'? Damme, how can I be in command of the ship when I don't know from one day to the next what we're about?"

"What we're about," Challoner replied calmly, "is getting this war over as quickly as possible. It's my intention to bring these king murderers to their knees within months."

"Well, the only way to do that is to blockade their ports and cut off their trade with the Caribbean plantations. Starve 'em out."

"I know that's the navy's way. What do you say to it?" Challoner turned his spectacled gaze on Hawkestone.

"I'm no strategist," he replied with a shrug.

"All the better," Challoner insisted. "You can give us an intelligent officer's unbiased opinion."

"Well, then, I agree a blockade is a very slow and uncertain weapon. It wasn't a resounding success against the colonists."

Challoner nodded. "We could have the oceans crawling with English ships and Europe full of English armies but I tell you this, one man in the right place is worth ten battalions in the wrong one."

"And Mr Keene is that one man?" Hawkestone asked.

The little civilian removed his glasses and rubbed a weary hand over his eyes. "I pray to God he may be," he muttered.

But Challoner's appeal to the Almighty went unanswered. At the appointed time the *Promise* arrived at the rendezvous point and waited but no signal came from the shore. For three successive nights the frigate returned and remained on station until perilously close to dawn but there was no sign of George Keene.

With every day that passed Tranter became more restless. "Your man is either t . . . taken or d . . . dead," he insisted more than once. "We c . . . cannot wait here for ever."

Challoner always dismissed the objection. "Keene has a difficult task. There are many things that may have delayed him."

After the fourth fruitless vigil Tranter became more insistent. "My orders are to assist you with this m . . . m . . . mission. Well, S . . . Sir Thomas, the m . . . mission is now over." He added with some satisfaction, "It has f . . . f . . . failed. I'm returning to England f . . . for f . . . fresh instructions."

Challoner's reply was characteristically brusque. "Make course for The Hague, if you please, Captain. I have contacts there who should have news."

By the time the *Promise* had visited the Dutch port and the spymaster had spent time ashore another four days had passed and the mood of the crew was volatile. Hawkestone received several representations from men anxious either to see action or go home. Three sailors slipped ashore at The Hague and the master-at-arms wasted another half-day in a fruitless search for the fugitives.

At last Challoner returned aboard despondently and gave Tranter permission to set course down Channel. Now it was the weather that turned against him. Hour after hour the *Promise* made heavy going against a vigorous nor-wester. In the early light of 5 April she was some miles off Ostend when the lookout reported a sail off the starboard beam. Hawkestone, as watch officer, brought his telescope to bear on the distant craft. "A brig," he muttered to the bosun standing beside him. He handed the glass over. "What do you make of her, Johnson?"

The stocky seaman with a face of rubbed leather braced himself against a mizzen stay and pointed the brass tube at the black speck on the universal grey of sea and sky. "Frenchie by her trim. Out of Ostend, I shouldn't wonder, sir," he observed. He swung the glass to and fro along the southern horizon. "And alone." He returned the telescope and his quizzical expression left no doubt as to what was in his mind.

Hawkestone nodded. "Best send to rouse the captain."

By the time Tranter appeared on deck ten minutes later word had gone round the ship that there was a prize in the offing. Several pairs of eyes were trained on the quarterdeck for signs of the captain's response.

"With a following wind she's at our mercy, sir," Hawkestone suggested. "She'll never make port before we catch her."

Tranter nodded. "Ninety degrees to starboard and full sail, if you p . . . please, Mr Hawkestone."

As the orders were given a cheer went up from the main deck.

The chase was a short one because there was no chase. The British had expected their quarry to turn in a vain attempt to outstrip the faster vessel but she held her slow and steady westerly course. The frigate's decks were cleared for action, cannon run out and the gunners' team trundled shot to the various ports. As soon as the *Promise* was within range she fired a warning shot from her bow chaser.

The brig made no response.

Tranter ordered a couple more rounds to, as he said gleefully, "t . . . t . . . tickle her b . . . backside."

At that moment the agitated figure of Sir Thomas Challoner came up the quarterdeck companionway, two at a time, still pulling on his coat. He strode angrily up to the captain. "In God's name, what are you doing, man?"

Tranter lowered his glass but did not look round. "In the navy we call it 'engaging the enemy', sir."

"You'll break off pursuit this instant, d'ye hear!" Challoner ordered.

"No, sir. Admiralty orders are to engage whenever there's a fair prospect of success."

Challoner grabbed him by the epaulete and pulled him round. "And my orders – which I'll remind you come from a higher authority – are to convey His Majesty's officers to their destination. At this moment that means conveying me, without delay, to Dover. Take in sail, sir, and change course."

Tranter's eyes stood out like marbles from his scarlet cheeks. "You'll not m . . . m . . . make a c . . . c . . . coward of me, damn you! That's His M . . . M . . . Majesty's enemy and I'll not l . . . l . . . let him escape."

"And I'll not have His Majesty's affairs ruined by a prize-hungry buffoon! Change course or, by God, I'll have you before a court martial the instant we go ashore!"

Tranter's hand flew to his sword hilt and he half drew the blade. "Get b . . . b . . . below or I'll slap you in the b . . . b . . . brig—"

The argument was interrupted by a double explosion. All eyes turned to the French ship which had brought her broad-side to bear and loosed off two cannon.

"By God, she wants to m . . . make a f . . . fight of it," Tranter shouted. He ordered the *Promise* to be brought side on to the enemy. Within minutes the two ships were exchanging fire in what could only be an unequal battle.

Through the smoke Hawkestone scanned the decks of the French vessel with his telescope. He saw the brig's captain gesticulating vigorously as he gave orders to his crew. "She don't intend to be captured," he muttered to Challoner who had come to stand alongside. "What on earth . . ." The circular lens had picked up another figure, standing at the brig's starboard rail and gesticulating wildly. Hawkestone gave the glass a quick wipe over and trained it again on the waving man. There was no doubt. It was George Keene. Silently he handed the telescope to Challoner and pointed.

"Keene, by all that's wonderful!" The spymaster unchar-

acteristically shouted his exultant relief. Then he turned back to
Tranter. "Break off or I'll break you!" he ordered. "I want a
flag of truce hoisted immediately!"

Old Tutter drew a deep breath in preparation for discharging
a broken stream of invective but Hawkestone forestalled him.
"With respect, sir, the Frenchie's carrying an English prisoner
– Mr Keene. Perhaps, we shouldn't send him to the bottom,
sir."

For a moment the captain was bereft of speech. Then the
words poured out in a furious, unimpeded flood. "By God,
that's precisely what I'd like to do – Keene and his damned
puppet master with him!" He paused before adding sullenly,
"Very well, offer a t . . . truce."

As soon as the guns fell silent Challoner strode about the deck
issuing his own imperious orders. He had a boat lowered to
convey him to the French ship, now identified as the revolutionary navy's brig *Gallant*, commandeered two marines to
accompany him and, before leaving the quarterdeck, turned
to Hawkestone with a curt, "Come with me if you please,
Lieutenant."

On the short crossing between the vessels, the little civilian
was deep in thought. Only once did he speak to his companion.
"Not a word to anyone, if you please, Lieutenant, especially to
Mr Keene."

When they stood on the *Gallant*'s deck in the centre of a ring
of leering French sailors Challoner presented a picture of
nonchalance. He laboriously dried his spray-spotted spectacles
with a handkerchief and appeared in no hurry to open negotiations. The French captain, not to be put at a disadvantage, also
took his time descending to the main deck. Hawkestone noted
that he was accompanied by a stout, high-coloured gentleman in
the braid-covered uniform of a French general.

Stiffly the captain bowed. "Citizen Captain Philippe Legros
of the people's navy."

"Really?" Challoner replied in French that was careful rather
than accurate. "This is Lieutenant Hawkestone of His Britannic Majesty's navy. He will be taking temporary command of

your ship with the aid of a crew which will be here in a few moments. Your men will go below decks and remain there until I have decided to release them. If any of your wounded require medical attention our ship's doctor will be available. You will accompany us aboard HMS *Promise*, as will these gentlemen." He waved arrogantly at the general and Keene, who had now also come forward.

It would be difficult to say which of the hearers was more astounded by this brief speech. Hawkestone watched the performance with amazement. The audacity, the arrogance of this little man! He stood surrounded by his country's enemies, with only the protection of two armed men who could easily have been overwhelmed, and he quietly took command. Legros blustered his protests but seemed powerless to resist. It was as though Challoner had mastered the strange powers of Franz Mesmer, who had been amazing audiences in London over recent months with his displays of "animal magnetism".

The young officer was still in something of a daze twenty minutes later when he found himself, in very fact, in command of the *Gallant*. A posse of marines had herded the French crew below decks and grinning sailors from the *Promise* now stood to their stations around the ship. They looked to him for instructions and Hawkestone was at a loss to tell them what he required. Only when the bosun came up, saluted and asked, "Orders, sir?" did he come out of his trance. Then he had the guns run back and the ports closed. He sent men to check for damage and others to tidy up the debris left by the brief battle.

He took Johnson with him on a tour of the ship and was very pleased with what he found. The *Gallant* was obviously a fairly new vessel, well appointed and of trim build. Furthermore, it was clear that Legros exercised good discipline. All surfaces were clean – stoned, polished or painted – and would have passed inspection by the most fastidious admiral. Hawkestone felt jealous of the French captain and wondered how long he would enjoy command of the other man's ship. What did Challoner mean by "temporary"? Capture, of course, was out of the question; one could not take over an enemy vessel under cover of a flag of truce.

He had to wait until mid-afternoon for his answer. That was when Challoner and Keene returned from the *Promise*. As they came aboard Hawkestone welcomed the older man with a respectful bow and then grabbed Keene's hand and shook it warmly. "George, what a relief to see you safe and sound. When you failed to make the rendezvous—"

"No time for all that, Lieutenant. We have work to do." Challoner marched to the main cabin, leaving the others to follow in his wake.

"We shall need charts of the north French coast, Lieutenant. Have the Frenchies any that are halfway decent?"

Hawkestone produced a roll of sea maps from the cupboard beneath the table and when Challoner had selected the ones he wanted the three men bent their heads over them.

"Lieutenant, be so kind as to point out our present position," Challoner ordered.

With a slim forefinger Hawkestone indicated a location some 30 miles west of Dunkirk.

Challoner nodded. "And how long would it take to sail this vessel down here to Caen?"

The young officer hesitated. "Hard to be precise, Sir Thomas. The *Gallant* is a trim craft but everything depends on wind . . ."

Challoner scowled his impatience. "I'm well aware of the principles of locomotion as applied to sailing ships, Lieutenant." Observing the flicker of annoyance that passed over the officer's face he immediately changed his tone. With an encouraging smile he said, "I'm relying on your expert judgment in matters nautical. Roughly, how long?"

Hawkestone bit his lip and replied cautiously, "If this weather holds I could probably get you there in a couple of days, Sir Thomas."

"Oh, I ain't going," Challoner said with a light laugh. "Keene is. I have to get back to London. That's why I'm requisitioning the *Gallant*, under your command, for special

duties. Your first task, Lieutenant, will be to set Keene down at
Caen – or Le Havre or some other point on the Normandy coast.
Now" – he turned to Keene – "I can spare you two weeks, no
more, to make your way down through Normandy and eastern
Brittany, Rennes, the Loire valley, Nantes or Angers – you'll
have to arrange your own route – and end up here." He pulled
out another chart from the pile and, smoothing it out on top,
indicated a point on the western seaboard. "La Rochelle.
Meanwhile, you, Lieutenant, will have reached the same point
by sea. There's a strong royalist element in the port and it
should be a safe rendezvous but obviously you'll approach with
caution. The whole operation will be ruined if you're surprised
by ships of the revolutionary navy and you will not initiate any
unnecessary engagement. In God's name, remember I've no use
for headstrong heroics or prize-seeking. Now, if you'll excuse
us, Lieutenant, Keene and I have matters to discuss."

Hawkestone left them to their business while he returned to
the quarterdeck to pace up and down and try to sort out his
conflicting thoughts and emotions.

An hour later Keene and Hawkestone stood side by side at the
starboard rail and watched as the spymaster was rowed back to
the frigate.

"Remarkable man," the naval officer observed. Then, when
his companion remained silently gazing after the retreating
figure, he added, "Now can you tell me what's going on?
Who was that French general and what were you both doing
on this ship?"

"The general? One of their top men, defecting to our side. As
to our being on the *Gallant*, well that's quite a long story. We
had a hard time of it making our escape and when we missed the
rendezvous with the *Promise* we had to find another ship to take
us to England. I'm afraid we tricked poor Legros into giving us
passage. We promised him a safe-conduct to land us at Dover.
You gave us a nasty shock when you tried to blow us out of the
water."

The two men watched the activity on the other ship. Challoner had reached the *Promise* and a couple of marines and half a

dozen sailors were now taking his place in the boat, which immediately began a return journey.

George said, "We'd better get the Frenchies ready for transfer, Charles."

It had been decided to take Legros and his crew captive.

Hawkestone pulled a face. "Can't say I like this business, George. Sir Thomas promised Legros we were commandeering the *Gallant* temporarily. Now, here we are taking his ship and sending him and his crew back to England as prisoners. There have to be some rules. I mean, abusing a flag of truce!"

"There's no honour in war, Charles; leastways not in Challoner's kind of war."

"And what is Challoner's kind of war?"

Keene turned to face him. "Challoner's war – Pitt's war? Something new, Charles. Something fought with gold and intelligence agents instead of soldiers and sailors. Something in which you buy victories and overthrow the enemy by intrigue. There ain't no etiquette in it. No chivalry. That's because it's a politician's war. They'll use people like you and me and Legros and not think twice about it."

Hawkestone stared back. "And you're happy to be a part of that?"

Keene shook his head. "Happy? No. But then I ain't happy about Tranter's kind of war either. At least this way thousands of men don't get needlessly butchered for king and country. Mark my words, Charles, there'll be no big battles by land or sea in this war."

Acting captain Charles Hawkestone turned away from the window and went back to his chair, still troubled by the words the strange man, George Keene, had spoken scarcely an hour since.

A war without rules? Without engaging the enemy in honourable conflict? A war in which tricks and treachery counted for more than courage and skilled seamanship? A war of spies and secret missions and the slaughter of one's own countrymen (what matter that they were convicted criminals)? A war without prize money as some reward for crews who endured the misery and danger of life aboard a man-o'-war? In such a war there would be no place for the likes of Captain Athanasius Tranter. No room for any loyal officers and men brought up in the proud traditions of the British navy. No room for those who prided themselves on following in the footsteps of brave forebears. Would there be room for Charles Hawkestone?

With a sigh he pulled his personal log book towards him and stared at the two sentences he had already written. There was so much to record. And yet, perhaps there was nothing worthy of recording.

FOUNTAINS OF RESOLVE

Keith Taylor

You don't have to invent plots in historical fiction because just about everything you could ever imagine happened for real. Take the following story, based on a real series of episodes. Roger Lowell North was an American sea captain, son of one of the American privateers of the revolution/War of Independence, and a chip off the old block. North has a frigate and is also something of a hothead given to outrageous heroics. He also detests Napoleon: mostly for the Corsican's total indifference to the lives of the men who serve him (Napoleon didn't like the French), but also for a personal reason. When Napoleon was getting ready for his Italian campaign, he resorted to taking a privateer and selling it in order to equip his army. This is the story of that episode and what North did about it.

Keith Taylor (b. 1946) is an Australian writer with an interest in history and myth. He is perhaps best known for his series of historical fantasy novels set at the time of the downfall of the Roman Empire in Britain which began with Bard *(1981).*

In human affairs the sources of success are ever to be found in the fountains of quick resolve and swift stroke: and it seems to be a law inflexible and inexorable that he who will not risk cannot win.

John Paul Jones

I
Dawn, Tuesday, 26 April 1796

"Gentlemen, your seconds have done what they can to make peace between you. Are you determined to proceed?"

Roger Lowell North knew that he had to affirm. He wondered why he had come to the duel in uniform, then asked himself even more bleakly why it seemed important. North had chosen that uniform for identity and distinction when he took French letters-of-marque. His own country had no official naval dress – yet – and he hoped it might serve as a pattern. Not wishing to copy the British navy, he had made it dark green instead of blue, with buff facings and silver buttons. Some had roared with laughter, but then, over the past two years, they had stopped laughing.

Probably, now, they were having a chuckle again.

Chattan was not wearing it. Languid and fashionable in slim-fitting breeches, a tailored jacket and high-crowned felt that, he looked assured to his fingertips. It must be a pose. Nobody could really be so easy at a meeting with pistols. North's own hands were sweating, despite his reasonable confidence of the outcome. After all, he knew himself to be a good shot, and he'd been out before.

Noel Chattan had too, of course – and rather more often. Destyre, his second, though also a lieutenant of North's, chose to act for Chattan, not the captain. Like Chattan, he had shed their uniform. The third lieutenant, young Abel Runsevoort, was not even present: he'd taken himself off to Sardinia.

Strong indications, thought a watching police spy, that North's officers no longer reposed confidence in him. He hadn't been able to find any second but a prison officer. Lately confined for a month, he had been forced to appeal to one of his own jailers to attend him at this meeting. The man had obliged, but it was irony, and humbling.

Supposing a headstrong fellow like North *could* be humbled.

"Are you determined to proceed?"

"Yes," Chattan said.

North nodded resolutely. "Unless Lieutenant Chattan cares to apologize for his insults."

Chattan smiled, very slightly.

They had settled on a damned melodramatic place for the meeting. Certainly it was level ground, but the ancient Roman amphitheatre with its worn, ruined tiers of seats had a solemn atmosphere that seemed to mock this tawdry charade. Affair of honour? Living Lord God! North remembered the hot words of their quarrel, and the impact of his own clenched-fist blow to Chattan's face. A schoolboy stroke. Harder than he'd intended.

A number of gawking fools had turned out to watch, even at this hour, though they kept a decent distance. Well, the quarrel had been public enough, in a wine shop off the main square of Nice (another tawdry aspect) and North knew it must have a certain interest for many. A privateer captain and his first lieutenant, meeting at dawn . . .

The police spy could not have cared less. Bare-headed and balding, he leaned against a crumbling wall above the duelling ground. Let them get on with it, so that he could go! With fortune these two troublesome rascals would exterminate each other.

Privateers, in the spy's view, were almost always more trouble than value. This one commanded – *had* commanded – a frigate of thirty-two long guns taken from the British off Guadeloupe. Then charges of some dire sort had been brought against him. The ship had been confiscated and sold with a most irregular haste. For that matter, why was North at large instead of being arraigned for his crime? It all smelled, the spy thought. Like a month-dead fish. Captain North had protested fiercely. By all accounts he had bribed, cajoled and plain rammed his way as high as General Dumas before being refused any further leeway. Gossip said the captain had made such a scene that Dumas ordered him jailed for a month, despite his famous good nature. A different man would very likely have ordered that North be shaved – to the neck – with a heavy triangular blade.

Well, the American clearly did not appreciate his luck. Nor had he learned a thing. Hardly free for a day, he had quarrelled with his own first officer, who was said to be a lethal shot. The spy had been present, in fact, under orders to follow North on his release from prison.

It had been an entertaining scene. Chattan had angrily blamed North for the loss of their frigate. The captain had rated him sharply for impertinence and vowed – with loud-mouthed folly – that he intended to get the vessel back. He had asked if Chattan was with him.

Chattan had declined. All haughty, bored aristo (lucky for him the Terror was over!), he had asked how North proposed to do that, with no notion of where their ship had been taken, no vessel in which to pursue it, and no crew. He had concluded by calling North a blighted fool.

The two angry men had glared at each other over the table. Then North had sprung to his feet. His hand had flickered in a hard backhand blow across Chattan's mouth.

"Damn your eyes, Chattan!" North had raged. "I would not listen tamely to words like that from God Almighty!"

"Take the consequences, then." Chattan's mouth had bled, and his eyes looked wicked. "Unlike you, sir, I might be humble before the Almighty, but I don't accept a blow from any mortal man. Mr Destyre? Will you act for me?"

The principals faced each other now, their armed seconds tense in the background, the surgeon standing to one side, case of instruments under his arm, bag on the ground by his buckled shoes. The captain's red curls and Chattan's black queue made a conspicuous contrast.

Their arms came up. Both pistols cracked. For a long moment it seemed as though both men had missed. Then the captain, as though bemused, pressed a hand to his side and brought it away with the palm scarlet. He remained standing, though. The wound was evidently not grave.

"Gentlemen, you have stood each other's fire and exchanged shots. Is honour satisfied?"

The question came distinctly to the spy's ears, as did Chattan's curt answer.

"Yes."

"I've received satisfaction," North agreed.

He developed a slight fever from the wound and remained abed in his lodgings for two days. The lieutenants, Chattan and Destyre, vanished on a coaster to some place unknown. North appeared to have been deserted by his whole crew, except the surgeon.

"It causes me to wonder," the spy declared, on making his report. "This American is a popular captain. Besides, he has taken various prizes and enriched his men. Why should they desert him because of a reverse?"

The spy's superior, a former Girondin deputy disappointed in the revolution and all to do with it, proved less than fascinated.

"A serious reverse. No more ship. Besides, directly the frigate was seized, this American sent his crew to ground himself. He hadn't been at such pains to gather and train them only to see them taken by French press-gangs. That was among the numerous ill-advised things he said to General Dumas. I believe they are skulking in Sardinia now."

"North said to his first officer that he meant to get his frigate back. I heard him."

"His first officer had only contempt for the idea. You heard that too, *n'est-ce pas*? And if he did?" The former deputy shrugged. "She's a Spanish ship now, and the Spanish government's concern. It's not long since they were at war with us. They have taken the frigate and paid for her. If they cannot keep her, it is their business."

That appeared to end the matter, then, the spy told himself. Appeared. His experience, his nose for the smell of a situation, warned him otherwise. Perhaps he ought to look into it further.

Ah, no. Why? What could North do? Bumptious young naval officers were twenty to the livre. He had stranded himself on the beach, done some ill-advised shouting, and fought a duel. Banal, all of it. Most likely he would try to recoup his fortunes in the slave trade, and die of fever in some jungle.

Venez au diable, m'sieu', the spy thought.

II
Friday Evening, 29 April 1796

"You are a madman, my Roger, and you may give thanks for the big mulatto's forbearance."

"General Dumas? Oh, indeed." Roger North smiled, more than a bit ruefully. "I confess I acted the madman with him, but I vow I was half crazed with frustration. The charges against me are false as Canadian diamonds, madame; and more than one official seemed to know it, smirking behind his hand! By the time I reached Dumas I knew why. He all but confirmed it. Wasn't unsympathetic. 'Your frigate I dare say was taken on . . . ill-founded charges.' Those were his words."

Wearing the clothes of a merchant ship's mate, he sat in the lesser salon of Genevieve Sospel's house in Toulon and drank wine he scarcely tasted. As Roger Lowell North, privateer captain, he had been a guest in the grand salon several times. She had supplied him with everything from spars and sailcloth to gunpowder, besides being his agent in the matter of captured prizes.

Although handsome yet, she had reached fifty, and preferred to appear by dusk or candlelight. At present it was candlelight, gleaming on white-stranded black hair and a maroon gown adorned with ruchings of gold tissue. She considered North with a certain pity and wondered if he realized the extent of his trouble.

A woman of her age could feel fondly protective towards Roger Lowell North. His appearance made it hard to credit him with even the twenty-seven years he possessed. While he spoke French fluently enough, a strong sense of outrage was making him stammer a little – and that American accent gave a further rustic touch. Freckles did not make a man juvenile, of course, but he had them (inevitably, with red hair, blue eyes and an outdoor life) and they added to the impression. Tall, active and assured, he still made Genevieve think of an honest bumpkin boy who had come to the great city and was about to be swindled of his last sou.

Well, and so he had been. *Tant pis.*

The question was whether she should help him, and how much sense his plans would make from a merchant's point of view. A mother's, too. Genevieve had four daughters, two of them married, one a widow whose husband had gone to the guillotine during the Terror; not an aristo, either, but a passionate, honest revolutionary, too moderate for Robespierre and his madmen, who had been condemned on the undefined catchall charge of *incivisme.* And poor Danielle, to her mother's concern, seemed to have a growing *tendre* for the privateer captain.

"I suppose so," she agreed, responding to North's words anent the general. "I have enquired, while you were fretting in a cell. It wasn't Dumas. His chief, the Corsican, did it. One sees why. He receives the command of the Army of Italy he has so strongly desired. There's a campaign to be fought, with soldiers who turn out to be vilely equipped and starving. His masters are bankrupt, and for the most part cowards. No help there. What should he do? Concede abject failure? My dear, would you?"

"No," North admitted.

"Nor Bonaparte! First he inspires his army with visions of glory and plunder, then he raises money to equip it. My bankers tell me he gained the Directors' sanction to raise a loan from Genoa. But apparently it was not enough."

"It couldn't have been," North said explosively, "since he stole my ship and sold her to plump out the shortfall. When I've been sailing under French letters-of-marque these two years and given good service, the crimson thief!"

Genevieve shook her dark head in reproof – and a certain dawning consternation. "You did not describe Bonaparte in those words to Dumas!"

"I'm afraid I did."

"*Juste ciel*! No wonder he hurled you in prison for a month, incommunicado by strict orders! He handled you mildly! And once you're enlarged, what do you promptly do? Quarrel with your own first officer, who can shoot the pips out of a playing card! Roger, you lunatic, I wash my hands of you and forbid you to speak to my Danielle again!"

North laughed aloud. The candle flames quivered. "I beg that you won't go that far. Believe me, we were neither of us likely to die in the duel, since the pistols weren't loaded. Except with powder."

"What's that you say?" Genevieve's eyes narrowed. "Ah, then! Your quarrel with the gallant Chattan was all a charade?"

"All a charade," North echoed, "and it went better than my audience with Dumas, for which I'm thankful! We reckoned it best to give the authorities a false picture. After all, I'd sworn in Dumas's teeth that I'd never take the loss of my ship tamely. They might remember. Now they believe my officers have deserted me, and I've neither ship nor money – just a pistol-shot wound around the seventh rib."

"No pistol-shot wound, eh?"

"Nothing but a great play-acting fraud with the help of surgeon Devereaux," North said cheerfully. Then his face changed. "We all knew, except the man who acted for me. Duping him like that was a shoddy business; he thought he was my second in a genuine affair of honour. I'm sorry for it."

Madame Sospel's mouth moved into a very wry shape at that phrase, affair of honour. Against her own wish, two duels had been fought over her before she married. In the last one, a man had died. Duels to her were affairs of folly. She much preferred a spurious one to the genuine thing.

"He's none the worse," she said pragmatically. "What he does not know will not offend him. So, your officers in fact are still with you, and I know you do possess money. In various banks. But it's a fact that you have no ship."

"I will have. Madame, I mean to get *Liberty* back again. I said it to Dumas's face – rashly, I confess – but it was no idle talk. Chattan and Destyre are in Sardinia now to gather the crew. They are to bring them here, or close to here."

She said cautiously, "To Toulon? Isn't that perilous? And how?"

"Not Toulon itself. Ile de Porquerolles. I'll join them there and we'll go. You know nothing about us, haven't seen us."

"But then what do you wish from me?"

"Knowledge. Intelligence. Madame, you know everything to do with the sea that occurs on the Côte d'Azur. You must know who bought *Liberty* and where they took her."

She certainly would know. And did. Her husband had been one of the richest shipowners on the Côte d'Azur, and now, twenty-two years after his death, Genevieve ranked as *the* richest. Handing control of her fortune and business to someone else through a second marriage had never appealed to her. Clever, charming men had tried; so had some utterly ruthless ones, during the greatest upheavals her country had known since Joan of Arc's time, and still Madame Sospel retained control.

"So must your own officers," she said, "if they are worth their salt, my dear."

"Noel Chattan told me. Although he's no dolt, and Destyre even less, I reckon you shrewder than the pair of them combined. Besides, they haven't your resources. I must know if he was right."

Genevieve felt her heart beating ridiculously fast for a decision that should be so easy, and so wholly a matter of business. Roger had captured rich prizes – yes – and she had benefited, but now his days of sailing under a French letter-of-marque were over, whether he regained his ship or not. It would be difficult for them to associate. Still, she could scarcely deny him information that would cost her nothing, and once he had it he would, of course, go away hurriedly. Perhaps there was even something in his liaison with Danielle that she could turn to account . . .

"The Spanish government bought her," she said abruptly. "I know because one of my coasters followed her to the new harbour. If it may be called one! She's at Barcelona, or was a week since, and she's there yet so far as I know."

"Barcelona," North repeated. "I've never entered there. Why's it dubitable that one may call it a harbour?"

"It's very bad. Shallow, incommodious, unsafe. My Roger, even though you have never been there, you must have heard about it! Without experienced pilots you cannot cross the sandbar."

"I've heard it's poor. I didn't think it could be quite so bad as that. Not with Barcelona's name for trade by sea."

"It is worse, believe me. My mother's father was Catalan, and cousins of mine are merchants there today. I know."

"Help me, then! I'll be needing one of those experienced pilots, a fast weatherly merchant brig, and small arms: pistols, muskets, cutlasses, boarding axes, all in secret, and quickly. I'll leave you a note on my bank in case the brig should be lost. And pledge you an admiral's eighth from my next prize."

Genevieve thought, Damn you to perdition, Roger North! This changes the matter! I shouldn't be greedy and risk this involvement . . .

But a flag share did change the matter. Genevieve knew the term, a naval one meaning the fraction of prize money taken by the superior officer (of flag rank) of the commander who actually made the capture. Some admirals made fortunes that way.

Roger, of course, could make his next prize a rotten fishing-boat if he wished, and give her 12½ per centum of that. Many privateer captains would not even think of doing anything else. Not, however, Roger. A hothead, perhaps. But transparently honest.

"Roger, I cannot have it said that I gave you a vessel. It must appear to have been stolen. I cannot be connected in any way with the affair!"

"Done. I'll not compromise you."

He did not add, "Of course", or "It goes without saying." Genevieve appreciated that. She had learned to distrust all avowals that came with those words appended.

"This is to be what navy men call a cutting-out affair?"

"Just that."

"Then you must have boats, good swift boats. Cannon for defence, too, not like a ship-of-the-line, but nine-pounders, I expect."

"For extreme need only," North said, all innocence. He added wryly, "If I require to fire 'em till they're hot it will mean there has been a serious blunder, and I want no more of those, by God."

III
Tuesday Morning, 3 May 1796

A strong, wailing mistral had blown for days without stopping. Funnelled into power down the narrow Rhône valley, it spread out over the sea and roughened the waves to an ugly chop. Two merchantmen, a brig and a threemaster raced over the Golfe du Lion with the wind on the starboard quarter, under a ragged grey heaven. The brig led. The three-master, a Neapolitan vessel named the *San Gennaro*, on her way back from Smyrna bound for Marseilles, had got no further than Cagliari with her lawful captain. North's lieutenants had lifted her neatly out of the harbour with no killing. Now, unknown to captain or owners, she was for Barcelona. Chattan commanded.

"No trouble, sir," he had said crisply. "We've handled more difficult cutting-out affairs than that."

"Yes, Mr Chattan. And we're about to handle another. Barcelona looks a trace challenging."

Standing with feet braced a little abaft the helm, bare-headed, North relished the wild wind and the prospect of action. Still, he did not particularly desire any until they reached Spain. He was single-minded when he had an objective before him. While the British held Gibraltar and Leghorn, there was the chance of meeting a roast-beef privateer. Even a Royal Navy ship. Muslim corsairs were less likely, this far north, but they did not always work from their famous galleys. Sometimes they tricked their victims using captured Christian ships. Neither was North eager to be challenged by a French vessel, which might occur even though they flew France's colours. Nobody took flags at face value.

Spain, then, with all speed.

"Roger?"

North supposed he had imagined the voice. Some trick of the wind. Who would address him by his first name at sea? Not the master at the helm, certainly. A young sailor was making his way along the heeling deck, and none too adroitly, either. What was he about, anyhow? He didn't appear to be attending to any sort of duties. His clumsiness was puzzling. North didn't accept lubbers aboard *Liberty*.

The youngster looked straight into North's eyes. The captain thought fleetingly that a youth so pretty might have a hard time among men who had been too long at sea. By the look of that firm jaw and stubborn forehead he'd fight, though North doubted he was big enough to win.

He realized that he had not seen the youth before. Now that was odd. North noticed his crew, knew their names and their capacities. Why didn't he know this one?

The sailor continued to hold North's gaze as though it were urgent. His lips moved, shaping the name Roger. Now, what the devil did he think he was doing? North decided to ask him, and he had better give a quick, satisfactory answer . . .

Him? More like her!

It couldn't be.

But upon the instant he knew that it was, and knew the face once he thought of it as a woman's, even with the hair tucked away under a sailor's cap. *Danielle!* Devil's thunder, why was she here, and who had helped her sneak aboard in that crazy disguise? Whoever it was, her mother would blame one Roger Lowell North. She'd have his family jewels to bait fish.

He almost blurted her name, but clamped his jaw on the impulse. That sort of hothead directness had lately landed him in jail for thirty days. Like a whipcrack he said, "You there! Get below, you clumsy lubber, before you fall overboard! Are you ill, man? See the surgeon, that's an order."

Achille Devereaux was quick-witted, and close with a secret. That spurious duel would never have fooled anybody without him. North gave Danielle a quick wink out of the eye furthest from the helmsman, and she answered gruffly, "Aye, sir," before fleeing down the main hatchway.

Danielle! North couldn't imagine her reason for being aboard. She wasn't romantically running away to be with him, that was certain. Even though they were lovers. Widows with children didn't do that, unless they had never outgrown being harebrained girls. Granted, Danielle had spirit and was a practical joker besides, but surely she could not have stowed away for any sort of trifling reason? Well, whatever her reason might be, it wasn't good enough.

She was lucky not to have been washed over the side.

North felt a chill of fear at the thought. He'd asked for a fast, weatherly brig, and Genevieve had supplied one in *Callirhoe*, no question, but she was a damned wet sailer, taking water over her bows and sluicing the men at the wheel. The decks were slippery as be-damned in a choppy sea. Danielle could have been injured. Or . . .

North quelled that thought. He waited ten minutes and then went swiftly below. The surgeon had hurried Danielle into his own minute cabin once he understood the situation, which had not taken him stellar ages. He appeared amused. Middle-aged, twice married, and a veteran of sea actions, he had passed the time when much could startle him.

"Dr Devereaux," North said, "I believe you may have a new surgeon's mate. It's perhaps the only thing that will answer unless we can set the lady ashore with an escort back to Toulon. It's to remain a secret that she is aboard."

"What, because of scandal?" Danielle exclaimed. "Roger, I am twenty-three, a widow with a child, not a schoolgirl! And you will need me. I have kinsmen in Barcelona, rich merchants who will trust you if I am present. Otherwise—."

North interrupted with what he trusted was firm courtesy. "Only saying Barcelona, *ma chére*, means that you know what you have no business knowing. We mustn't under any circumstances go near your kinsmen, for the same reason you have to be set ashore. Maybe you didn't know – I can see you didn't – but the house of Sospel is never to be connected with this affair. It's imperative. Never."

"Then you will have to explain how you come to be sailing this brig! She belongs to my mother. It's well known."

"And I pirated it. Or that's the tale we will all swear to. Just

as Chattan and Destyre lifted the *San Gennaro* in Cagliari
harbour. The *San Gennaro*, by the way, goes back to her lawful
owners when this is over, if at all possible."

"That is to say," Danielle interpreted, "if you do not get her
sunk."

"You have it."

These open confessions of piracy did not seem to disturb
Danielle much. She had possessed herself of a towel, and went
on drying her drenched hair with complete aplomb. To North it
made a charming sight. When she sneezed several times and
impatiently asked for a handkerchief, it did not lessen her
attractions in the least.

"But why the secrecy?" she asked. "Roger, I know what
you're about. I know *you*! Once I heard you had been robbed of
Liberty, none of it was hard to guess! Will the French authorities care if you lift a frigate out of Spain?"

"They may, before long. Dr Devereaux and Mr Chattan both
think there's a French-Spanish alliance brewing. But whatever
happens, my days of privateering on a French warrant are over,
Danielle. Those authorities of yours won't have me back now.
Nor should I trust them again."

"It's true, madame," Devereaux put in. "A Franco-Spanish
alliance by the year's end, if this Italian campaign is a success.
I'd wager on it."

"If it happens," North said, "I'd not dare hang about in a
ship Spain thinks is her property."

"No, indeed! Roger, you might find yourself too literally
hanging about." Danielle made a noose-adjusting gesture at her
neck. "As to setting me ashore – *can* you turn back to a French
coast in this weather?"

"Perpignan might do," North said, but dubiously. "Doctor,
may we have your cabin to ourselves for half an hour? Say
nothing of this, and be ready to pretend the lady is a surgeon's
mate named André. I must speak with her privately."

Devereaux had been aware for some time that he was *de trop*,
but curiosity had engaged in Laocoon-like conflict with manners. With a murmured, "But of course," he bowed and left.

Sailing with the American, he thought, there was at any rate always something new.

The cabin door had scarcely closed before North had taken Danielle in his arms and kissed her soundly. Laughing, she kissed him in return until she was breathless.

"Half an hour, my dear?" she said demurely.

"Not nearly long enough. I'll be needed on deck. This weather isn't to be trusted. Danielle, what fool of an accomplice smuggled you aboard? I'll flog him! It's nothing to what your mother will do – pistol me, I dare say."

"Oh, nonsense. I'll see that she does not blame you!"

"Sweeting, I've learned by now that no one speaks for Genevieve. Not even her favourite daughter."

Danielle didn't deny being the favourite. She said swiftly, "Listen, Roger, please, you must take me to Barcelona! My Uncle Enelio – he's a distant cousin, really, but I am like a niece to him – can assist. You will need his help. Do you know what Barcelona is like?"

"The harbour's an abomination, I know that much. Most trading ships lie at anchor outside the mole and have their cargoes ferried out. I'm hoping that's how *Liberty* lies. It'll make things simpler."

"But if not?" Danielle widened her brown eyes, a part of her persuasive method that had doubtless melted her father when she was five, North told himself. It was not going to melt him. "Perhaps they have taken her inside, to the shipyards, say. What then? How will you get her out? Do you really know what the Bourbon grip on that city is like?"

Warmth, tousled damp blonde hair, and brown eyes. North admitted it, he was wild about her, but he could well do without her distraction this voyage. No, she must go ashore at Perpignan, like it or not.

What had she just asked him? Oh, Barcelona, yes.

"It's under close control, I hear."

"It's a prison!" Danielle said forthrightly. "The rulers built a monstrous citadel to dominate the harbour, and then a great wall around the city, a jacket of bastioned stone! It's hated as the

Bastille was hated here. Riots happen often. It might be useful to start one if you need a diversion. But you'd require the help of men who know the city, and then you'd need me to vouch for you, be your go-between."

North stared into the fresh-skinned, pretty face. He'd thought he knew her. Danielle was a child of the revolution, of course. She'd seen blood and death. Her husband had gone to the guillotine. Still, this cool plotting to start city-wide riots for a "diversion", if need be, either showed a ruthless side to her nature, or meant that she didn't really know what she was talking about.

"No, sweeting," he said flatly. "I've spoken with your mother's harbour pilot! He's told me all that you said, and more. The city's a garrison and jail in one. Bourbon soldiers swarming like weevils in ship's biscuit."

Danielle pulled a comical face. "Thanks for the charming simile, Roger! On this ship I will eat no biscuits."

"*Sail off the port quarter! League or less!*"

It was Runsevoort on the quarterdeck, repeating a lookout's words.

"I'm needed on deck," North said. "Danielle? Trust to Dr Devereaux's care and stay in men's attire. You came aboard as a man. It's best that you stay in that role."

He mounted the companionway quickly. Waves were running white-capped across a silver-grey ocean. The sun looked like a bright silver coin among ragged clouds, while patches of blue showed intermittently. The wind still came from the north. *Callirhoe*, sailing on a broad reach, had her fore- and topsails close-reefed, while the three-master following had more canvas set. Except for a single stern-chaser and a triptych of swivel guns forrard, she was unarmed.

Abel Runsevoort saluted smartly as North approached. The captain shook his red head. "We'll dispense with that till we're aboard *Liberty*, Mr Runsevoort. We're merchantmen now, and you're a mate. Not a lieutenant."

"Aye, sir." Runsevoort, a young Dutch-descended New Yorker with butter-yellow hair and the muscles of a bull, althought not quick-witted, had proved himself rock steady. And he was bred to the sea. "I shall like it when we're walking her deck again."

"We shall. Now, Mr Runsevoort, this ship in sight – what are her colours?"

The lookout bawled down, "French, sir! Tricolor! Reckon he's sighted *us*, too. He's making sail."

North glanced at his third officer. "Eager fellow, isn't he? Well, if he's standing after us, he must be a navy ship or privateer. Unless he's an out-and-out pirate."

Runsevoort said slowly, "If he wishes for trouble, sir . . ."

"In the ordinary way he could have it. Not now. We've business in Barcelona! Let two reefs out of the tops'ls, Mr Runsevoort, and set t'gallants."

"Tops'ls, two reefs out," Runsevoort roared. "Set t'ga'ns'ls, lively now!" To North he added, "Jib, sir?"

"Presently. If we see that she truly means to make a chase of it." North glanced at the sea and witch-tattered sky. "Squally weather attending. What d'you think, Mr O'Driscoll?"

The sailing master, former mate of a whaler and as old as North and Runsevoort spliced together, gave a pensive sideways nod. "Devil a doubt, sorr. Squally weather. We'll need to make and shorten sail between the blows, and look sharp about it, if it's a chase that's coming."

"More men at the rigging, then. Best hands aloft."

"Aye aye, sorr."

North considered his second ship, the three-master *San Gennaro*. With Chattan in command, Destyre in charge of the foremast, and the bosun, Flowers, to assist them, the ship was well officered. As for crew, Chattan had 170 of the *Liberty*'s hands, while North had the rest aboard the brig – about a hundred. None had deserted while idle ashore in Sardinia. All had returned to join North in this venture. It argued strongly that they hadn't lost faith in him yet, but they would if he didn't lead them to success.

And what sort of distraction was this ship they had sighted? Kitts let him know in the next breath.

"She's a sloop of war, sir! Sloop of war!" He paused, and then yelled down, "I think she's the *Youth o' the Heart!*"

North seldom blasphemed, and almost never aboard ship, holding it bad for discipline and morale. But that news brought him near it. *Jeunesse du Coeur*, or *Youth of the Heart* in English, meant Etienne Robard, the bastard. Of all men North did not wish to encounter without his own frigate's spread of responsive sail and thirty-two long guns at his command, Robard came close to the head of the list.

IV
Afternoon and Evening, Tuesday, 3 May 1796

"I'm going aloft," North said curtly. "Mr Runsevoort, I wish every knot we can make without leaving Chattan in the lurch, and I have no doubt *he's* aware by now that we're possibly dealing with Robard."

"Aye, sir."

North discarded his cloak and hung a spyglass around his neck. Swiftly climbing the mainmast shrouds by the ratlines, he reached the crossing point and went on to the cap, through raw gusts and spatters of rain. It was nothing to the climbs he'd been forced to make as a midshipman. The next set of shrouds led to the topmast cap. North abandoned a captain's remote dignity so far as to grin at the lookout, a lean wiry fellow as nimble as a mountain goat.

"So, Kitts! It may be our friend Robard, eh?"

"Aye, sir."

"Well, we can't be inconvenienced by him just now."

North extended the spyglass.

Yes, indeed, there she was. One couldn't miss her, with that dazzling canvas so clearly new, and recklessly set even to the royals. Her master even had the topmast studdingsail boom run out, ready for setting those as well, if he required them. She remained tenaciously hanging on North and Chattan's lee quarters.

"A corvette, all right," North muttered aloud. "What's more, you were right, Kitts. It's Robard. The sail she carries in this weather is like his signature. Who else would risk it?"

Being Robard, though, he might carry it off. Unlike most privateer captains, he paid his crew wages as well as prize shares (high wages, at that) and in return he demanded first-class seamanship. His men were trained to a hair, and prime hands in the first place, most of them. They could raise, trim and replace sail as fast, and as deftly as – as North's own. He himself used pretty much the same system as Robard, and made the same demands. Only he extended it to gunnery. It was a passion of his. Robard did not have outstandingly good gun crews.

Today they might not have to be, North thought with concern. His brig carried a pair of stern-chasers and four other guns, while *San Gennaro* was naked except for a single long brass nine and those swivel pop-guns. Robard sailed a corvette, fast and light, but not too light for the score of long guns she mounted, all twelve-pounders. If he outsailed them and came close enough, he could make sliced tripe of their sails and rigging, bring down a yard or two – perhaps even a mast. Then they would lie at Robard's mercy, a scarce quality at best, which would not exist at all once he knew he was dealing with Roger North.

All right, then. They must outsail him. And show him some real gunnery if he did come close.

North left the topgallant yard and set a record for reaching the deck.

"Mr Runsevoort, it's Robard for certain," he snapped. "He's never to brag in his smelly haunts that he bested *us*! It's neck or nothing all the way to Barcelona now, and a squall coming. Two reefs back in those tops'ls! Take in t'gans'ls again!"

So the chase started, with North giving thanks that the sea was nearly abeam. Having the swell at their bow would have made matters considerably worse. The white squall struck in another few seconds, howling like Cerberus, and the hands taking in topgallants had a task fit for the chastisement of sinners in hell. North was glad he had trained them navy fashion, and trained them hard. They managed the job in time.

None fell. The shrieking squall lashed them, bludgeoned them, and passed.

"Let tops'ls and t'gans'ls out again," North ordered. "The way this weather looks, we'll have them up and down as often as . . ."

North was about to say, "as often as a light woman's skirts", and then remembered that Runsevoort was an almost excessively earnest, decent lad. *Lad? he's not more than seven years my junior. When did I grow old?* Looking for a purer simile, he finished, ". . . a jack-in-the-box on my nephew's birthday."

He wondered about Robard. Maybe this particular squall had missed him, but in O'Driscoll's seasoned judgment there would be others. Did Robard have new rigging to match those pristine sails? North hoped so. Brand-new running rigging was a bitch until it had worked in. It swelled when wet and could get stuck in the blocks. Stays and shrouds were worse. They stretched. It was a labour of Hercules to keep them taut, and if you did not, at best the masts lost their most advantageous rake; at worst they came out like carrots.

Kitts at the topgallant yard let them know the privateer was gaining. Then, with pleasure, he sang out that strong winds had struck him and that Robard's main topsail was flying loose. The sheets had split. He added gleefully that the jib had split as well. It was gratifying, but not such grand news as all that. Robard's hands had the sail set again in ten minutes, the jib replaced in less than twenty. He continued to gain fast.

The moment Robard appeared, North had thrown aside his plan of setting Danielle ashore in Perpignan. It couldn't be done. If they stayed ahead until nightfall, they might elude the *Jeunesse* (and her twenty guns) in the dark.

Robard surely knew he was dealing with North by now. He'd have heard about his enemy's misfortune during the month that North had fretted in jail. The year before, North had found Robard chasing down an American vessel in the Atlantic, hoisted the stars and stripes, mauled Robard severely and driven him off. Robard had been eager to fry North's liver ever since. He'd be delighted to sink him when such a chance as this offered.

Not today, Etienne. Absolutely not today. Not with Danielle aboard, burn you!

The chase continued through a long morning, under the silvery pale sun and silver-edged clouds, across a silver-grey sea. White squalls were frequent. The wind now blew from the north-east. Roger had directed the sailing master to turn due south some time ago; he had no wish to be trapped on a lee shore somewhere along the Costa Brava, with Robard to his weather side. Chattan crowded on canvas, and all in all *San Gennaro* took it well; Chattan had redistributed her cargo and added more ballast when he found she had crank tendencies. Nevertheless, the next squall split her main topsail, and Chattan set another with a celerity that bettered Robard's, to North's great satisfaction.

He signalled Chattan to come abeam. With barely a chain of creamy water between the ships, he shouted across, "Mr Chattan! If *Jeunesse* comes up with us, bear up, steal her wind; I'll cross her stern, and either smash her rudder or bring down the mizzen!"

"Aye aye, sir!" Chattan answered.

Shortly after two they were struck by a fresh thundering squall, the worst one yet, and the most sudden. North's main topsail yard went, the foremast sprung, and two topmen fell hurtling into the sea with no chance of saving them.

Chattan glanced back at the brig, where North's crew worked like Trojans to woold the foremast, clear the fallen yard away and raise another. Robard's corvette continued to gain like a hunting leopard, and Chattan smiled bleakly to see it.

"Carry on, you bastard, make yourself a complete coffin," he said. "He's a seaman, Mr Destyre, but he's too eager, too greedy."

"Aye, sir." Both lieutenants were strictly formal at sea, the urbane Destyre in particular. "His crew's damned sharp. But he trusts to that more than he should. If these things happen to us, worse has to befall him sooner or later. I'm amazed it hasn't already."

They were sailing south, almost straight down the fourth degree of longitude east, with the wind on their port quarter. The corvette gained steadily, in spite of all her quarry's good sailing. By five o'clock he was nearly within gunshot.

North said, smiling, "Let's tempt the dog, Mr Runsevoort. See how badly he wants us. Let out tops'ls two reefs and set t'gans'ls. And the jib."

Even the steady Runsevoort paused a second before answering, "Aye aye, sir."

Chattan, watching his captain's brig closely, raised his eyes to heaven and then took much the same measures. North ordered the log heaved, and found *Callirhoe* was racing through the yeasty water at 11 knots. He watched the sky and the canvas aloft like a hawk. It couldn't remain set for long, especially on that weakened foremast.

Come on, Etienne my wolf! Act in character!

Robard, with twenty cannon ready to fire broadsides and his prey so close, could not resist. He let another reef out of his topsails, hoisted topgallants, and set his royals. North exulted inside. He briefly dared to hope Robard would raise studding-sails too, on the booms he had actually run out to receive them. No such luck. He refrained. Well, even if rash and free with his canvas, he *was* sane.

But he'd gone too far just the same. North said softly, "We have him!" Looking at the sky again, he added, "Lower that fore t'gans'l and topgallant yard, Mr Runsevoort. Take in the jib. We'd lose the whole foremast, as it is now, to one hard gust."

"Aye aye, sir," the New Yorker responded, with a good deal of relief.

"All gun crews, stand to your guns! Stern-chasers, load! Single roundshot."

Time to give Robard a powder-smoke welcome. He'd come well within range of the long brass nines by now. Owling and Grey, two of North's best gun captains, had the stern-chasers.

Briskly, the loaders rammed their powder charges, rolled the 4-inch roundshot after it and rammed in the wads to keep them from slipping out again. Almost as one, the assistant captains drove their spikes down the touch-hole, to break the powder bag and expose the charge. Next they poured finer-quality powder down the hole from horns hung around their necks. Locks and lanyards had been attached to the guns some time before. The gun captains went down on their right knees behind the cannon, holding the lanyards and sighting along the barrels.

North ceased watching them. His gun crews could manage the details of elevation and traverse to the last hair. A greater concern, and a far less reliable one, remained the weather.

"Take a reef in the forecourse," he commanded. "Lower the main t'gans'l."

The next squall of the day was about to strike. North almost felt it on his skin, smelled its imminence.

"Fire!"

The cannon bellowed. Black powder-smoke covered the stern and the guns recoiled inboard. The half-dozen men on each gun's breeching-ropes braced hard, checked the furious recoil of a ton and a half of cannon. One ball fell a little short of its target, raising a splash, while the other flew high, ripping a hole in *Jeunesse*'s forecourse.

The spongers jumped to swab out the bores. The guns would be ready to fire again in a minute and a half. By then, North suspected, it might not matter, and the greatest value of firing on Robard would be to distract him. Still, it would be fine, it would be very fine, to hole him or bring down a mast . . .

If North was mistaken about the timing of the next sudden squall, he knew Robard would be upon them with a great advantage of canvas, as well as guns. He wasn't taking in a stitch himself. *Jeunesse du Coeur* raced on, heeling far over with the wind in her royals, the lee cathead buried in foaming water.

Callirhoe's stern-chasers roared again. Both roundshot struck Robard's bow, well above the waterline. *That* would send some splinters flying inside the hull; nothing like the devil's mess a full broadside made, but no comfort, either. And rather good shooting, not to mention a swift reload.

Then the squall, a howling wild dog of a squall, hit from nowhere. Lightning, lashing rain and hail all were part of it, but best was the wind, great brutish gusts hitting like clubs. Before North's eyes, the fore yard of *Jeunesse* went flying. With a bursting of stays and shrouds, a splitting of canvas, the fore topmast followed, to crash across the bowsprit and carry it away. The main topgallant mast went by the board, ripped sail and lashing ropes a-whirl around it. Expert topmen fell helplessly with the masts and rigging, to die on the deck or vanish in the creamy sea.

The wind shifted then, and struck from a new quarter. *Jeunesse*'s sails blew aback, those that remained. So did the brig's and the merchantman's, but they were in better case than Robard to set the situation right. Still, it was trouble; North ordered the men at the wheel to starboard their helm, and glancing aloft he bawled, "Brace about, cheerly, there! I want those sails to *draw*!"

Men aloft swarmed to obey, heaving on the braces, angling the yards. Wind hammered into the sails. North expected to see the main course split from head to foot, but it stayed whole, though the yard bent like a bow and made vile cracking noises. The foremast held too. Then *Callirhoe* was gliding across the corvette's weather quarter, with a clear view of her eight open gunports in passing, a reminder that she was still a floating arsenal to North's vessels.

They were clear, then, lurching away through wind gusts and rain into the deepening twilight and the safety of night. North made a quick estimate of how long the chase had lasted. Twelve hours, he thought. They had probably sailed 40 leagues in the time. Barcelona would be very nearly due west of their present position. Distance? That was harder to judge, but 20 leagues seemed fair; at the most, 25.

Etienne, you passed a long arduous day for nothing at all, he thought smugly. You'd have taken us if you only had the patience. Crowding on sail in weather like this – but I knew you'd do it if you were properly tempted. Now you'll be unwise to let me sight you when I come out of Barcelona, for I'll be sailing a frigate of thirty-two long guns!

V
Wednesday Morning, 4 May 1796

"She's here," North said with relief and delight. "Genevieve Sospel never gave me wrong intelligence yet! She's *here*, and all we have to do is take her."

"All?" Danielle repeated with superb Gallic irony. Superb Gallic female provocation, too, North thought, from a woman who knew how perversely fetching she looked in the snug weskit and breeches of a surgeon's mate. Her derrière did mighty interesting things to the fit of those same breeches. North reckoned himself a fortunate man to be her lover – and a strong-willed one to keep his mind on the frigate yonder.

They were eyeing her through the stern window of the captain's cabin. Oh, *Liberty* was splendid, long and lithe even for a frigate. (Some naval officers said too much so, but North loved fast, agile vessels that sailed close to the wind, and he'd yet to find a sweeter blend of stability and speed than *Liberty*. Saliche had built her in 90, and among frigate designers the noisy Marseillais ranked equal to Hackett.) She carried courses only, now, and those neatly furled; there was an officer on her quarterdeck, and in the waist, soldiers.

They were preparing her for sea, too, the dogs. Two deeply laden boats were coming alongside her now. The atmosphere of tension and care in the crews could be felt at this distance. There was a look about the barrels and boxes, and the way they were stowed, that all but shouted magazine stores. They were stocking her with powder, cartridges and shot! Mighty obliging of them, so long as no one made a mistake. North felt hellishly disturbed. Although he'd heard little but praise for Spanish hardihood and courage, less was said about their careful efficiency, and it would be bad to find *Liberty* again just to see her destroyed in an accidental clap of man-made thunder . . .

"All," North repeated. "That's right. I told Mr Chattan that it looked a trace challenging, but that was far away, when I thought our ship might lie within the harbour. Snatching her from under the artillery of that fortress would be no trifle, and then getting across the harbour-mouth sandbars . . ."

"It couldn't be done!" Danielle protested.

"It wouldn't be easy."

North felt that Providence had been good to him. *Liberty* lay at anchor offshore, like most of the other shipping. Even the haughty authorities of Bourbon Spain would find nothing suspicious in North and Chattan's doing likewise. It called for a swift strike. Boarding parties, small arms, cut and run, never mind the anchors. North did not foresee much difficulty, now that he was here; his men had cut their teeth on such actions.

Danielle said gently, "Well, then, I am glad you think it will not be too difficult, for I must tell you there is one thing more. Roger, do you remember I spoke of my uncle? Enelio i Llobre?"

"The courtesy uncle who is really a distant cousin? I remember, but this is no time for family visits, Danielle. I regret you cannot even go ashore. We won't be here so long – I hope. He wouldn't help us anyhow; rich merchants don't stir up trouble with their rulers."

"Sometimes they have nephews who do," Danielle said, as though treading on eggshells. "I'm sorry, Roger. The time wasn't right to tell you until now, even though I'd have said all rather than have you set me ashore. It was needful, imperative, that I come to Barcelona."

North began to feel like a fox that hears horns and dogs. "Danielle, I'm a happy man at present. This business is shaping to be gloriously simple. A quick neat cutting-out by night, and goodbye. I've a notion you are about to make it a crabbed, Byzantine tangle."

"Nothing so bad!" she protested. He didn't believe her. "Roger, listen. The nephew's name is Gaspar i Llobre. He's passionate for freedom. His family desires him to be a merchant like the rest, and stay out of trouble, only – it is a little late. He's in hiding, they wish to arrest him."

"What has he done, then?"

"Print sedition in a cellar. Then distribute it in city and country. The soldiers arrest men for much less, but they want him chiefly because he's a Llobre. The rulers would like to squeeze money from his relatives. If you take him to Toulon, Mother will send him to sea and the trouble will finish. But the family will not trust you unless I vouch for you."

"Not trust *me*?" North said incredulously. "Devil's lightning, who asks 'em to? Or says that I trust them?" With late comprehension, he turned on Danielle. "Your mother will send him to sea to oblige them? Are you saying this scheme is hers? *She* smuggled you aboard in that silly disguise?"

"I knew you would be angry. I'm sorry, Roger. I'm not the easiest person to compel, but she is my mother. You know what she is like."

"I thought I did," North growled. "She's devious, sharp at a bargain, but I never knew her foolish before. Why the busking, Danielle? Why the nonsense? She might have asked me."

"That is what I told her! Mother said you'd refuse. That you had one thought in mind, to take back your ship."

He still did. Running a hand through his copper-red hair, North took a turn around the cabin, thinking hard. Madame Sospel had been devious. And how did he know he had yet heard it all?

"No wonder she was so obliging with the brig and arms," he muttered. "And I pledged my own money against its loss! She's taken me for a gull."

"No, Roger! She does wish to help. It's only that she—"

"Didn't see fit to ask me honestly. She thought to leave me no choice." North shook his head. "And she sent you. Danielle, she used her daughter! No, that's too much, and I will have words with her for it. If I rescue this rebel nephew of a rich merchant house, it'll be much obliged to the house of Sospel, I suppose. Genevieve won't suffer thereby."

"Neither will you! Roger, Maman has always—"

"Done well out of me," North said in ire. "Why's Genevieve so concerned for this man's welfare? It isn't to win his family's gratitude only. I'll never believe that. And why did she go so far as to send *you*?"

"Roger, don't be angry. This won't interfere with your own mission. All you need do is take him with you when you go! I know Gaspar i Llobre. He's like your father, and like you. He hates tyrant rule. That is why he's in trouble now."

"Not interfere? It could wreck everything, as well your mother knows!" Fiercely, North gripped Danielle by the shoulders. "So this is more important in her view. But why?"

His eyes burned like sulphur flames as he stared into hers. "It's a match, isn't it? She wishes you to marry this Gaspar. Joining two rich merchant houses. A stronger link than gratitude."

Danielle tried, with a strong twist and wrench, to pull away from North. When she failed, her own gaze caught fire.

"That is my mother's wish. I didn't come here to marry Gaspar, but to rescue him! He's my kinsman, Roger. I'm fond of him. Nothing in that gives you cause to manhandle me."

North said angrily, "You came to induce *me* to rescue him. And it looks as though you haven't left me much choice. Where is Señor Gaspar i Llobre?"

"His family has him in hiding. I don't know where. Uncle Enelio will tell us, once I vouch for you, and you must see his agents anyhow, on the pretext of buying a cargo. That will mean some going back and forth in boats. It's not hard for a man too many to join the crew of a boat if they have leave to visit a wine shop while they wait. Is it?"

"Not hard at all," North said. "It's more usual for men to slip away and vanish. And you and your mother," he added, "are two of a kind."

Danielle said with asperity, "That flatters me."

"I don't think so. Perdition! I'll talk with your uncle, and even with his nephew – maybe. A drunken, trouble-making lecher who fancies himself a hero, I suppose."

"Not at all!" Danielle smiled at him winningly. "You are magnanimous, Roger. And you will like Gaspar."

North wasn't prepared to lay dollars on that. Danielle appeared to like Señor Gaspar too well. Apart from jealousy, and of far greater significance, this whole venture might be ruined because of the fellow. *Like* him? Danielle was dreaming!

North glowered through the brig's stern window. In the morning sunlight he could look past gold-flecked green water and the imposing harbour mole to the Ciutadella, the massive symbol of Bourbon conquest. A five-sided fortress with a huge bastion at each of its five angles, it covered 150 acres, with barracks, stores and arsenals within its frowning walls, a township in itself. Its commandant could bombard the city to rubble if he chose, with its heavy mortars.

From its western face a high moat-fronted wall, studded with more bastions, stretched up the city's north side and angled back down again to the harbour. A man who aroused the suspicion of that city's masters would be lucky to come out of it, and they were watching the Llobres closely, he gathered. No. North wasn't prepared to like Gaspar.

And Genevieve Sospel needed a lesson.

VI
Wednesday Afternoon, 4 May 1796

Gaspar i Llobre turned out to be a darkly handsome devil a few years younger than North, and to have a sense of humour. At least, he laughed to see Danielle with cropped hair in the guise of a clerk. In a Spaniard, though, it showed small concern for what was proper. Danielle was a relative, after all, and supposed to be this Gaspar's friend. North, neither Spanish nor especially proper, didn't think he would laugh on learning that a kinswoman and friend had made a voyage, unchaperoned, on a lawless errand with a privateer crew, in a man's disguise.

It seemed to him that Danielle looked hurt. For certain, Gaspar's Uncle Enelio looked like thunder.

"Danielle is here to help you, and you show little enough grace or gratitude! I could not risk trusting Captain North, unless she were here to assure me that Genevieve sent him. They were hunted most of the way here by a rogue of a French pirate. It's God's mercy that she is here and not lying on the floor of the ocean. Because of you!"

"Santiago!" Gaspar swore. He wasn't laughing now. "I am sorry, little Danielle. You should not have come."

"Oh, should I not? They are seeking to garotte you, cousin, you colossal fool! And you needn't be afraid for me, when I was in Captain North's care. He can outsail three like that pirate—"

"Privateer," North amended.

"And on my word, you can trust him. Most of all against a king."

"North," Gaspar repeated. "Captain, are you a kinsman of Thaddeus North?"

"I've the honour to be his son, Señor i Llobre."

"And honour it is," Gaspar agreed. "You can certainly be trusted, unless you are the precise and complete opposite of your sire, in which case you would not be approved by my little cousin."

"Gaspar, I had rather you called me *little* less often. It is not I who am silly and young, but you, or you would not be hiding here."

"That's very true," Enelio growled.

"And where is *here*?" Gaspar asked ironically. Yellow lamp-light painted the scene in soft light and deep shadows. "A secret cellar under your large, imposing warehouse, uncle – a cellar for contraband. We are not rich enough, eh? I'm grateful to you for helping me, though not for taking a high moral tone over my breaches of the law, when half your merchant goods are smuggled!"

"Señores, that'll do," North intervened. "I didn't come here to take sides in a family quarrel. Our business here is to take you, Señor Gaspar, safely to France, and I cannot see that it will be difficult. If you don't make it so."

Gaspar said cheerfully, "I have no wish at all to do that. Bourbon prisons are not salubrious, Captain. Bourbon garottes less so. Instruct me, and I shall be all compliance."

"All you need do is dress as a sailor, join a group of my men, and return to my ship with them. It'll be by daylight. Men are less suspicious of things done in daylight. Walk along as though you belong with my crew by right, señor, and if someone looks at you, look back boldly. The surest way to draw attention is to flinch."

Gaspar grinned again. "Flinching is not my custom, Captain."

North grinned back. Damnation, it *was* hard to help liking him. Just where did he stand with Danielle, though?

"Then I look forward to seeing you safely aboard my ship. One thing, though. When a place and time is named, you must be there. We can't wait."

He refrained from saying which ship. The Llobres did not know he had really come here for the *Liberty*, and they were not going to know until it was achieved. Gaspar might be delighted; North felt pretty sure the news would perturb his uncle. Greatly.

That evening North dined aboard *San Gennaro* with Chattan and Destyre. Having been pursued by Robard together, as escaped him together, made enough of a pretext. North took Runsevoort along, as well as Major Archie Gamble, his chief of marines, a laconic crack shot from the North Carolina frontier. (Gamble had promoted himself from lieutenant during his time with North.) He required their presence, for the dinner served as a council of war.

Tomorrow he would instruct the men. It mattered quite as much that each of them should know what he must do, when, and in what fashion. Normally he addressed them from his quarterdeck. It wouldn't do this time, of course, but the next address he gave them *would* be from his own quarterdeck – or a Bourbon prison.

VII
Thursday Morning, 5 May 1796

North surveyed the eighty-odd men gathered in *Callirhoe*'s hold. Pride filled him. There could scarcely be a more oddly mixed lot, and he had made them a fighting ship's company.

Clearly American himself, he had taken all the most obvious Americans and Carribee natives aboard *Callirhoe* with him. About thirty were Jamaican Maroons, descendants of rebel slaves who had built their own communities in the mountains and fought the English army to a draw. Major Gamble's marines – or half of them – watched North shrewdly, men from the Blue Ridge Mountains and westward, the best riflemen breathing. The rest included thirty-odd deserters from the Royal Navy, survivors of a mutiny against a flogging madman of a captain. They had much in common with escaped slaves, in North's view.

"Men," he said, "you know why we are here. Each jack of you has eyes. That's our ship yonder, the *Liberty*, stolen from us and sold like casked beef. We're here to take her back, and that we shall do this very night! I'll lead you. Are you with me?"

A deep throbbing murmur rose from the Maroons, laughter and whoops from the frontier men, an English cheer – low, but enthusiastic – from the tars.

"Good for you. I expected nothing less. You had better know all. There are a hundred Spanish soldiers on the *Liberty*, and, as best I know, 150 seamen."

"Then it don' need more than we, Captain. Two hundred fifty they, eighty we – that's fair."

Makero had spoken, the fiercest fighter even among the Jamaicans. Marines and Englishmen voiced their approval. North felt more than pleased. Spirit like theirs was halfway to winning.

"Beggin' your pardon, sir." It was Evans, the man who had led a mutiny in the Royal Navy. "I'm agreed with Makero. We can deal with the odds. I just wonder why there's that many aboard. Spanish navy ships are mostly undermanned; and why's she being fitted out in such a hurry?"

"Not important to taking her, Evans. We needn't let it occupy our minds, but I did find it out, ashore, and there's no reason why you shouldn't know. She's being sent to bring home the Viceroy of Peru. His tenure of office is ending. I gather he's stolen a fortune and wishes a fast, well-armed ship to protect it."

"His Excellency's goin' to be disappointed," drawled a marine.

"We attack three hours before midnight. Each man is to wear dark clothing, not a thread of white or pale colour about him. Muffled oars and wrapped thole-pins for each boat, except perhaps mine. I'll explain why later.

"*Liberty* is anchored fore and aft, bow towards the land. We'll approach her in six boats. You men will be in three of them. They'll be roped together in line, stern to bow, on setting out. You lads who formerly knew the rare delights of serving King George on the sea" – bleak chuckles answered him – "will go in the first, under Mr Runsevoort. Marines in the second, Jamaicans in the last. All three boats will round *Liberty*'s stern and strike from the larboard side. Mr Runsevoort's party will board at the bow, after casting off the rope to the second boat. The marines will board amidships, at the gangway, after casting off their rope to the last longboat. The Jamaicans, under the master-at-arms, are to board and clear the quarterdeck. You must cut the stern cable, douse all lights aft, then set the spanker and mizzen tops'l. Within five minutes of boarding there must be no light showing on that frigate anywhere."

He then described what the boats approaching the starboard side of *Liberty* would do. One would contain the rest of the marines, and they too would board amidships, at the gangway above the waist. Another would take the starboard quarter, while North himself with two dozen picked men would attack at the starboard bow, cutting the cable there and setting the foretops'l.

"Afterwards, to be sure, we'll need to leave smartly. Tide doesn't matter hereabouts. Wind does. If there's no breeze from the land, the boats can draw *Liberty*'s head about and pull her clear. We'll abandon the brig if we must."

North reviewed the plan twice more, asking questions of men at random, until he was satisfied that even the slowest wits present had a firm idea of what he required.

"I said my boat may be the exception to our rule," he continued. "So she may. If they are still loading *Liberty* tonight, with tenders from the harbour, then I'll pretend to be one, a special one, and hail them openly. That ought to distract them while you lads approach."

Later, crossing to *San Gennaro* in the pinnace, he addressed his boarding parties there, in the after cargo hold. As aboard the brig, he outlined everything the men needed to know and made each boat's role clear: time, position, weapons, tactics, priorities. He emphasized that all lights aboard the frigate must be doused without delay.

While issuing the orders, he heard noises alongside of a shore-leave boat coming back. Mounting the companionway, he met Chattan on deck. The first lieutenant murmured, "The passenger has arrived, sir. Disguised as a sailor among our hands, and a bit disguised in drink, too, but all went smoothly."

North should have been pleased by the news. Instead, it irked him like a hangnail to have his attention drawn to young i Llobre. Bringing him aboard was a risk to them all, to the ships, to the success of their purpose.

No use in worrying now. He visited Gaspar in the tiny cabin assigned to him, before he left *San Gennaro*. Calling him drunk was going too far, perhaps, but he must have shared the shore party's wine without stint before accompanying them to the boats, and was certainly merry. He greeted North like a long-lost brother.

North remained more formal. "I'm glad to see you, señor." It wasn't wholly a lie. "By tomorrow night you should be far out of Bourbon reach."

By next morning, in fact, but North did not wish to confide much in a man he knew only slightly.

"Captain, I am most grateful for that. But some day I will have to come back. There is necessary work to do here."

North sympathized. His own nation's continued freedom had immense importance for him. Still, Gaspar's "some day" would have to remain just that. He might change his mind with time and the realization that he was free and safe. Even passionate Spanish ideals could chill before the image of the garotte.

VIII
Thursday Evening, 5 May 1796

The mudhook went down into 20 feet of water, lowered without a splash. Men shipped their dripping oars. Twelve had been rowing since the onset of darkness, taking a round-about course to reach their present position. The boat must appear to be coming from the harbour when it moved out to attack *Liberty*. The second dozen men would take the oars when that time came. And first there would be forty minutes' rest.

"If you're troubled by rheum or coughing, go back to your quarters now," he had said. "That's an order. If you step into that longboat, you are silent until we attack, no matter what happens. If you should feel yourself irresistibly about to cough or sneeze, put your hands around your throat and choke yourself to death. As for talking – the man who speaks had best have something mighty important to say."

He stared across the water towards *Liberty*. So close, so close. She shone with lanterns like a busy coaching inn. Laden boats were still going out to her from the harbour, though not with powder and shot any longer. Other sorts of supplies: food and wine, mainly.

North wore a coat, unbuttoned and loose. Under it, he felt the weight of four long pistols slung across his chest, lying in echelon one above the next. The opened coat allowed swift access to his firearms, while hiding them from a distant or casual inspection. Beneath his seat, the hilt handy, he'd stowed his naval cutlass.

He allowed the men to employ their preferred weapons, within reason. A couple of freed slaves, brothers from Guade-loupe (that seemed for ever ago) had chosen to try their fortunes at sea. They were still with him. For a boarding action they favoured their big cane-cutting knives.

North's own coxwain, a burly Delaware Bay man named Yorrick Miller, sat patiently in the stern chewing a plug. Miller carried a yard-long horned cudgel and a pistol. Most had cutlasses tucked under the thwarts and dirks at their belts. Some preferred boarding axes.

The most bizarre personal arm in the boat, though, had to be the Chinese billhook sword under Vicente's seat. Vicente, a Portuguese, had sailed the eastern seas out of Macao for years before he settled in New York. He'd fought more Chinese pirates hand to hand, he said, than he had attended masses.

North felt somewhat sorry for the men holding his frigate.

Now and then he glanced, with satisfaction, at the sky. The weather had been his one real dread. He remembered well the series of wild white squalls that had attended him across the Golfe du Lion, pursued by Robard. Little use to recapture *Liberty* if a howling gale trapped him on a lee shore afterwards, but the stars shone brilliantly on as balmy a spring evening as he could desire.

North looked at his watch.

"It's time," he said.

North glanced at the Catalan harbour pilot beside him. Since his accent would arouse no suspicion, and he had shown himself quick-witted, he was to do the hailing and explaining. North knew enough Italian and Spanish to tell if he was playing them false. Besides, Madame Sospel had employed the man for years, he was trusted . . .

Liberty drew closer.

"Who comes?" someone challenged from the foc's'le.

"More cargo, what else?" the pilot answered, manifestly bored.

"Thy mother! What cargo? There's no more to come but extra sail and spars."

"Thine also! This isn't on your lading. Luxuries for His Excellency and His Excellency's lady, on their voyage home. It's been carried from Madrid. I was roused from a good warm bed to bring them out in this undistinguished boat! It might with ease have been left till the morning, and now I am here, you think to obstruct me?"

Good, North thought. The aggrieved tone was just right. Louder, my friend, draw all the attention you can.

North's coxswain looked over his shoulder at that moment. Clamping his big square teeth on a curse, he said urgently, "Captain! Boats under way from the harbour mouth, rowing hard! Gunboats, I reckon. Two."

North stared aft. Yes, by God! He could hear the oars dip and drive, see white at the cut-water. Two. They'd sent gunboats out where ships-of-the-line – even a brig, riding light – would have run aground, and that meant they suspected. Because of the stupid, ten-times-damned digression with Gaspar i Llobre?

He strained his sight further back into the darkness. Not two. *Three!*

"Longboat approaching the frigate! Hold, there! Lay alongside us. In the name of His Catholic Majesty Carlos of Spain!"

No, señor! To hell with you and your king! I'll not be interrupted tonight!

North's men could take the frigate without him, if the gunboats didn't meddle. He was nearest to stop them. This might even be better; it should certainly rivet the attention of the Spaniards in *Liberty*.

"Hard, hard about, boys!" he said fiercely. He pointed at the gunboat that had challenged him, the leader. "We're taking that one, and then the other!"

The longboat shuddered and bucked from her suddenness in putting about. Oars bent in the rowers' hands. North's crew were not inclined to be stopped this night either, and they knew better than to respond slowly when he commanded.

"Two points a-port." That would take them clear of the gunboat's single cannon, aimed straight forward in the bow. "Then turn sharp and we'll strike 'em on their beam." To the pilot he muttered, "Ask them what passes."

"What passes, señor?" the pilot called over the dark water.

"You have no business near the frigate! You were commanded to lay alongside us in the King's name. Comply, or we fire!"

"Yes, señor! We are doing it. See, we hasten! Our errand to the frigate is lawful, we take personal effects for the Viceroy of Peru! I've written authority here . . ."

He continued babbling. Just so the gunboats were bamboozled for a few more precious seconds. Just so they did not fire until it was too late . . .

Drawing and cocking a pistol, North reached down for his cutlass. With amazed yells, the Spaniards saw that the longboat meant to ram them. One of the other gunboats fired, but the ball went wide in the darkness. (It sounded like a roundshot, none of grape's shrieking whistle.) Then came the impact, a cracking of oar-looms, a heel and lurch of the boat, and North sprang over the bows into the Spanish craft.

Clenching his teeth, he fired at a horrified face, stumbled into a peak halyard and slashed it through in his irritation. They ought to unstep the damned mast if they were not using sail. A lean figure lunged at him with a knife. North cut downward, feeling resistance and the jar of blade on bone; the man fell back, dropping his knife, a wedge of muscle flapping loose from his upper arm, blood spraying darkly in the starlight. An officer with a sword met him next, a good fencer, too, growling curses. North parried and cut. He didn't look back to see if anybody had followed him.

Surest way to make one's men falter, anyhow.

His foeman stumbled in the crowded, rocking boat. North opened the front of his head with a drawing slash. The man fell, screaming, and North rammed forward, afire with the need to clear this boat, conquer it, then the next one, and *quickly*.

Vicente was beside him, bearded, left-handed, swinging that grotesque Chinese sword. Miller, the coxswain, only came more slowly because of his bulk. He broke one Spaniard's collar-bone with his cudgel, then trod him down while heaving a second into the water.

North met two more men with swords. Taking their measure, he quickly identified the more dangerous one, not large, but nimble, fierce, the one who led while the other supported him. This, of course, was the one to disable first. He hacked short-armed at North's head in the furious press. Drawing his guard, he laid a long cut across the American's ribs. Except that North shifted his balance and turned sideways just as the Spaniard struck, it might have opened his belly.

North chopped down at the other's hip. His edge bit through lean muscle and hit bone. The man staggered. North clubbed him down with the empty pistol he still held, then drove the barrel hard into the second man's midriff. He sank to his knees, gagging, and Alphonse, one of the former Guadeloupe slaves, finished him with a blow.

The fight raged from end to end of the gunboat, and North's men had cleared it in less than two minutes. Some Spaniards lay dead, a few too badly wounded to move, and the rest were splashing in the water.

Cutlass glued to his hand with blood, North looked around for the second gunboat. If he'd been in command it would have been alongside by now, making a hand-to-hand affair of it, but it was holding back, weaving around like a drunk in a country dance, looking for a chance to fire its pop-gun effectively. Where the third had gone, North was damned if he knew.

"Get to the thwarts, every jack who can row! Oars out! Let's take that nearer gunboat, us to port, you, Miller, on her starboard side! And 'ware her shot."

Half North's men scrambled to the longboat, half to the captured Spanish craft. North wondered what ailed the bungler in the boat they were about to attack, and why he hadn't fired on them while the two craft were so close together. Maybe he hadn't realized as yet that the first gunboat was taken.

North moved to the prow. He wanted their cannon ready. Owling the gun captain was there before him. "Four-pounder, sir, loaded an' primed," he reported. "Not much use in this dark. Except at pistol range."

"Then let's come within pistol range," North snapped.

He left the cannon to Owling, who was more than able to handle it. Straining his eyes into the night, he gave orders with the fixed purpose of keeping his craft out of the enemy's line of fire, until they could come to grips and overwhelm him.

One Spaniard discharged his gun anyway. North heard grape shriek overhead, and his whole body tensed against red-hot, smashing blows that never came. Too high, by heaven, and off to the side as well. As Owling said, with no moon, you were gunning almost blind at more than 20 yards. It served one purpose, though: everybody ashore would know something was far wrong with those cannon roaring.

Lighter fire rattled and cracked from the frigate's anchorage. Muskets. North knew his men must be boarding her, and his heart sang. Glancing that way, he saw one of his own boats driving through the sea to reinforce him. Well enough, so long as only one of them left the main objective. Keeping these inopportune craft from meddling with *Liberty*'s capture was vital.

Now! They had the second gunboat now! North and Miller strove to pincer it between their two vessels. Not quite, and it squeezed from between them with a grating of oar blades. North and Miller almost collided. Beyond them, the gunboat began to turn, bringing its cannon to bear. North sprang to his own gun, and ordered four hands to the check-ropes. Owling sank down behind the four-pounder, one leg out to the side, squinting along the barrel.

Briefly, the Spanish boat lay beam-on, 15 yards away. Owling yanked the firing lanyard. The cannon blasted its shot, recoiled, and knocked Owling back to the mast with a shirtful of broken ribs. Either the lanyard was too short or the check-rope men had not braced firmly enough. But the Spanish gunboat's sheerplank, amidships, flew in splinters that whizzed about like arrows. Men yelled in pain.

North's men swarmed over the wales. They dealt with the second craft even more hotly than the first. The remaining one turned about and fled for the harbour again, thanks be for their poltroonery. The longboat that had come to North's assistance raced in pursuit. North wondered for an instant if he should go too, but no; his place was aboard *Liberty*, now that the gunboats were routed.

"All into the longboat," he ordered. "Spanish wounded too. Smartly, now. Then make for *Liberty*. Let the gunboats drift."

North went aboard at the frigate's starboard bow, as planned, driving the backspike of a boarding axe into her planks to give him a foothold up. He came over the foc's'le railing straight into a group of white-uniformed Bourbon soldiery gamely trying to take and hold the foremast area. Four of them turned on him at once. They carried pikes.

Having three of his pistols yet unfired kept North alive. He yanked out two and shot point-blank. Lunging forward, he grabbed a third man's pike and wrestled him for it. The fourth soldier by then was fighting a tall Jamaican, bare-chested, bloody, and also wielding a pike.

North slipped on gory planks. He fell flat on his back. His adversary yelled in triumph, and levelled the pike to impale him. North swung both legs around in a violent scything sweep to kick the man's feet from under him, bringing him down. He flung himself atop his foeman and caught him by the throat with one hand, fumbling out his last pistol. He levelled it straight at the man's nose from an inch's distance.

"Surrender!"

The soldier dropped his pike.

Resistance was ending on the foc's'le. North handed his captive impatiently to someone else and glared about him. Ship's timbers were bloody and men lay dead or groaning wherever he looked. Runsevoort was down, his thigh run through by a pike, clutching his leg and swearing like a pirate. North hadn't thought that earnest young fellow could command such a flow of profane speech.

In the frigate's waist the battle was essentially over, too. Gamble's marines had control there. On the quarterdeck, some thirty sailors still resisted, but they could not win and their spirit was failing. Suddenly they called for quarter and threw down their weapons.

Liberty was North's again. Now he had to keep it.

"Well done, boys!" he thundered. "Clap pris'ners under hatches! Mr Clough, take twenty men and lay the wounded on the main deck, under the gangways. Mr Flowers, let's have four boats bringing this ship about! I want her head turned to the sea within five minutes, not next year."

As though to emphasize the need, the Ciutadella's great artillery began booming. North's sailors set records for filling four boats with straining rowers, spread out in a fan before the bow and linked by ropes to *Liberty*'s stem. Foot by foot they turned her bowsprit to the sea. *Callirhoe* and *San Gennaro* took similar measures, with two boats each, while resounding splashes (sometimes alarmingly close) showed that the gunners in the Ciutadella were still trying. They must have been watching both ships all day.

North knew why. Gaspar i Llobre. The commandant's spies must have had notions of where Gaspar was hiding, and who was concealing him. His kinsmen: hardly a difficult guess. Very likely North's own movements ashore, and later between the brig and merchantman, had made some shrewd fellow wonder. Well, they might wonder, but with Gaspar out of Spain they could *prove* nothing against his uncle.

Lord above, some wind, some wind! Was that too much to ask? If warships couldn't come out from Barcelona, more gunboats could, or longboats with boarding parties. North envisioned, with his belly knotting, what might happen if the Spaniards chanced to have a captured corsair galley in the harbour, and thought to launch it in pursuit. With soldiers crowded aboard.

Booming thunder and flame on the Ciutadella's ramparts.

Reports of casualty numbers came to the quarterdeck. Seventeen men dead and about forty wounded, fifteen too sorely for working ship. Eighty rowing, yard by yard hauling *Liberty* out to sea, left fewer than forty in the frigate, some of those manning the stern-chasers. He certainly couldn't spare any for the gun deck. Until they caught some wind, his frigate might as well be no better armed than *Callirhoe*.

Archie Gamble, free and easy as ever, climbed to the quarterdeck and broke naval custom – nearly sacred custom – by addressing North without being addressed first.

"We've done it! Mightn't have, sir, without you keeping they gunboats off'n our necks. You wounded at all?"

North shook his head. It was breath wasted to rebuke Gamble for informality. He ran *Liberty* navy fashion, but just now he felt too weary to insist.

"No, Major. Not a scratch."

"You think? What's that on your coat, and your right leg? Tar? Some day some rogue's going to offer you a pinch of snuff," Gamble predicted, "and you'll take it."

"I hadn't noticed, Major. Well, I couldn't be standing if it were serious. You did extremely well, all of you, to capture this ship."

Gamble spat tobacco juice to leeward. "We surprised 'em, sir. You drawing their attention, and then the gunboats, had 'em all watching you until we was almost over the gunnels. My boys caught them Spanish soldiers in a crossfire, but I'll say they kept their heads handsomely. Made for the quarter-deck, got there, and nearly threw our men back into the sea as we was boarding aft. They never fired any steady volleys, though; used their pikes more'n muskets. We charged along the gangways to the quarterdeck an' took it with our bayonets before some officer got 'em to shooting right. Some fought their way past us to the foc's'le, though, sir. I b'lieve you met 'em."

"They welcomed me aboard," North acknowledged. "Now we must just pray for a wind from the land. I fancy the Ciutadella's gunnery is growing worse as we move out, not better."

Nevertheless, a sweating hour ensued before North felt the first breath of a light wind coming down from the Pyrenees to swell the frigate's sails. He ordered the boats raised aboard. By morning they were leagues east of Barcelona, making for the Strait of Bonifacio.

Morning, too, showed the faces of the dead, seventeen of North's, more than sixty Spanish, to be shrouded in canvas and buried at sea. It showed blood on the decks, and the faces of the wounded whose groans North had heard all night. He wondered how right he was to be sceptical of the Last Judgment.

Come. He wasn't immortal either. He'd run the same risk as they. Neither were any of his crew pressed, serving against their will. That surely made a difference.

But *Liberty*'s crew, making sail, scrubbing down the decks

and examining the guns, noted a sombre mood in their captain that day.

IX
Wednesday, 8 June 1796

His humour was more buoyant, far more so, the next time he paid a visit to Genevieve. He swaggered into her lesser salon like a carefree tiger and spun his hat on to the nearest table. Aware but heedless of her irritation, he bent over her hand with a flourish.

"*Bonjour*, madame. You seem in good health."

"*Pardieu*! Good health, you say? Captain North, it has been a month, more, since you regained your ship, and I have not even received a letter! You sent Danielle and Gaspar home from St Raphael in a hired carriage. Not so much as a note with them! Not a word of the brig I loaned you!"

"I sold the brig," North said casually. "She's too incriminating for you to take back. No matter, madame. I'll keep her price, you cash the bank draft I left as surety, and thus we're quits."

"Quits?" Genevieve echoed. "Not quite, I think. Was there not an agreement we made? An admiral's share for me from your next prize after you regained your frigate?"

North had known she would raise that point. Even so, he found her gall amazing. After sending Danielle on such a mission without even telling North she would be aboard, and forcing him – at the risk of disaster – to snatch Gaspar away from the garotte, she could mention that!

"True," he said, deliberately looking awkward. He even shifted his feet. "I did pledge that. As it happens, we took a prize just after sending Danielle home. A rich one. Mighty rich. Still, madame, after the trick you played on me and the danger to which you exposed your daughter, I think holding me to that agreement would be unfair."

"Roger, you pledged your word and made no conditions." Genevieve's eyes gleamed with pleasure. "You said, *uncommonly* rich?"

"Oh, yes," North admitted with a pretence of regret. "She's all of that."

"Ah. Tell me."

Genevieve was going to be sorry she had asked in just a few short moments. North could scarcely wait. But he decided to rack her with impatience a little longer.

"Perhaps some wine, Genevieve? I desire to talk about something else, anyhow. Danielle. It's of huge importance to me."

"Better perhaps not to mention Danielle."

"I can't avoid it." North waited for the wine, tasted it with enjoyment, and set down the goblet. "I came here to ask you for her hand."

Madame Sospel shook her head firmly. "No, Roger. I regret. You are a brave, resourceful and personable young man. It honours Danielle that you wish to marry her, but you see she is to espouse Gaspar."

"Is that her wish?"

"Ah, Roger. You are disappointed, I see. And rather angry with me that I sent her aboard your ship."

"Rather more than rather."

"Gaspar would have been taken and killed otherwise," Madame Sospel said coolly. "It was a family affair."

"Gaspar is such a distant relative he hardly counts as family."

"Perhaps not in America. In any case he is to be my son-in-law."

"Danielle is of age, and widowed, with a daughter. She's free to choose. I love her, madame, and I can provide for her better than Gaspar can. Besides, it's my impression that he's in love with the cause of Catalan freedom more than any woman."

"A couple of voyages as supercargo will make him more mature. Besides, I have never lacked authority over my children yet. I truly regret disappointing you, Roger. I like you. Let us not pursue this, eh? Come, tell me about this fine prize you took."

"And that's your last word?"

"I fear so."

"Madame, I must tell you that I don't accept it. I'm going to do my utmost to persuade Danielle to have me and not Gaspar."

"I shouldn't, Roger. It would please me much more to have you still welcome in my house. Now. Let's talk of something else."

"The prize, I suppose?" North said.

"I'm sure it was a bold stroke that took her! Come, what is she? An English merchantman?"

"No, Spanish. Spain isn't quite allied with France yet. I don't believe my French letters-of-marque have been revoked, either. Not yet. By specious legal hair-splitting it should be allowed."

"Yes, yes. Where did you find her?"

"Majorca. We had trouble with our Spanish prisoners the night we escaped; had to fire down a hatchway to keep them quiet. I set them ashore in batches on a quiet cove in the Balearics. Noticed a tempting prize while we were there, so I returned after bringing Danielle and Gaspar back to France."

"You always did have a quick eye for a chance, Roger. And then? Tell me all!"

"A fine large ship, not long built. She was lying in the Bay of Palma. The main protection there came from shore batteries.

"We distracted those by running in and firing on 'em, I in *Liberty*, Mr Destyre in the brig. In the meantime, a force under Mr Chattan's command rowed up in longboats to cut out the vessel we wanted. Very nearly a facsimile of what we'd done in Barcelona, and in one respect more easy. There were far fewer men aboard the ship!"

Genevieve was all admiration. "Don't belittle the feat, Roger! The batteries made it different. Besides, the ship was moored at the dockside, and soldiers from the garrison could have come out to interfere in a moment, couldn't they?"

"Running the batteries was no joke, I confess! And soldiers did come charging down to the quay. Chattan had hard fighting to shake them off while getting under way, but he managed. The ship's ours."

"And her cargo? Or was she empty? If she's as fine as you say she can still be sold for a great sum."

North waited a little, relishing the moment before he gave his answer.

"No cargo. Did I not mention it? We captured a warship. The *Juana*, Genevieve, a fine new two-decker of fifty-eight guns."

Madame Sospel screamed in outrage. A warship, and Spanish! Name of a name of a name! Was Captain North so dense that he didn't see the trouble it would cause her? France and Spain were sure to be allies soon, and if it should be exposed that she had sold a Spanish warship lifted by Roger North, of all men, it would mean the guillotine! Even granting perfect safety, to handle the sale of a *warship*! Where and how did he think she could do that? At what sort of price? She wasn't a sovereign nation! She wasn't the Admiralty!

North had thought of all these things. He had spent much of his leisure time since Majorca thinking of them. Happily. Genevieve needed a lesson, and this seemed like the perfect one. The effect had not disappointed him.

"The first prize you took – and I dare not touch it! Despite its value," she added yearningly.

"Madame, I've kept my promise. All you have to do is sell the ship for me."

"You know it can't be done."

"I made the offer fair," North said virtuously. "If it's not acceptable to you, I suppose you forego your admiral's share, madame. May I hope you will continue to broker my prizes for me?"

"Take your accursed prizes and—" Genevieve halted. At last she laughed. "Yes! It'll be secret from now on. But yes, you devil. And I shall rob you of your eye-teeth."

North grinned at her. "No doubt you'll try."

"Tell me one thing," she said. "What, under heaven, do you want with such a ship? Fifty-eight cannon! It would take 300 men, trained men, to serve half of them! You can sail her, I suppose, but not fight her."

"I won't need to fight her. Think, Genevieve, what a fine scarecrow she'll make! Not against navy ships, but against merchantmen. Picture her coming down on them with gunports open. They'll lie to at the first warning shot. I'll take prizes galore, and when the game ends – when I have to leave the Mediterranean at last – I'll sail *Juana* and *Liberty* home. I'll present them to the United States navy, which consists, just now, of paper authority for building six frigates. None launched yet."

"Pirate," Genevieve said. She pronounced the word with grudging respect.

North took his leave.

Behind her Toulon house, Genevieve kept a walled garden of white and crimson roses. North's objective had only been the back gate, until he saw Gaspar and Danielle. Then he halted and moved behind a pillar.

Genevieve, no doubt, would have said they made a handsome couple. North didn't deny it, but he had formed his own assessment of Gaspar i Llobre. A passionate dreamer, the sort who shed rivers of blood for the noblest ideals and made fearful, needless trouble. Always around the next corner, or behind the last, he looked for perfection. North also suspected that for Gaspar, as in politics, so with women.

Genevieve did not see it, but then she was willingly blinded by his family's riches. The question was whether Danielle saw it. The handsome bastard was talking into her ear with what looked like earnest, persuasive passion. Telling her, as her mother hoped, that he'd make a steady husband? Or something more rakish?

Danielle listened, and smiled, but wryly, and in the end a slow, firm shake of the head was her response.

It's now a perfect day.

North, his soul singing carols, reckoned it exactly the right time to saunter down and join them.

DAVY JONES'S LOCKER

Harriet Hudson

You may notice the following story is set on exactly the same day that the previous story finished! And it's all true. The HMS Unicorn *was a fifth-rate thirty-two-gun frigate launched from Chatham Royal Dockyard on 12 July 1794. The* Tribune *was indeed a British ship which had been captured only recently by the French. And on 8 June 1796 the* Unicorn *and the* Santa Margaritta *encountered the* Tamise *and the* Tribune *just west of the Scilly Isles.*

Harriet Hudson is the pen name of author Amy Myers, best known under her real name for her series of historical mystery novels featuring chef-detective August Didier. These began with Murder in Pug's Parlour *(1987) and the most recent (and possibly the last!) is* Murder in the Queen's Boudoir *(2000). As Harriet Hudson she has written a number of romantic historical novels including* The Wooing of Katie May *(1992),* The Girl from Gadsby's *(1993) and most recently* To My Own Desire *(2000) which, with its main character's fascination for the unicorn, has something in common with this story.*

"Do you know, sir, when I might go home?"

The roar of laughter that greeted the boy's polite request to the burly seaman who seemed to be in charge of this table bewildered him even more. He stared at the unappetizing salt meat before him, unable to eat, although for once his stomach was not heaving as it had ever since this ship had weighed anchor.

Three days ago he had been delivering meat to a public house near Portsmouth Royal Dockyard when he realized with terror that the gang of a dozen or so rough-looking men was not passing him by but surrounding him.

"Here's a likely one. Know anything about the sea?" the one nearest to him demanded, sticking his cudgel under the boy's chin and forcing it upwards.

"No, sir," Davy replied truthfully. In this year of 1796 he was only just twelve and spent all his time helping his father in his butcher's shop.

"You will soon, boy," thundered another, seizing him by the arm. "What's your name?"

"Davy Jones, sir."

There'd been a roar of bewildering laughter then too.

"You'd best look after your locker, lad," and despite his protests he was pushed and pulled into the hold of a tender which was already packed with men and a few other boys like himself. They were battened down until morning with nothing to eat or drink, and nowhere to relieve themselves, and the long hours passed terrifyingly slowly in the stinking, airless dark. At last a cry came from outside: "Take 'em to the guard-o," and Davy had gratefully breathed fresh air once more. Although to his dismay, the "guard-o" proved to be another ship, there at least some notice was taken of him. There was even talk of sending him home because of his age and inexperience, until someone asked, "Do you know your duty, son?"

"Yes, sir, to deliver meat," he had faltered uncertainly.

A smirk. "And powder too now. We're in need of monkeys like you with old Boney roaming the seas."

Instead of being sent home, he had been sent aboard this ship, and now he was far out to sea in one of His Majesty's thirty-two-gun frigates. He was told it was a fifth rate of 776 tons, and that in addition to the thirty-two-guns she carried six carronades on the quarterdeck, but it meant nothing to him. After he had helped carry endless boxes of supplies aboard, stumbling his way around the unfamiliar companionways and decks, he had felt the waves rocking the ship with sudden violence as the wind caught the sails. Orders were barked, bells and pipes sounded, and as the sails billowed out, he could see they were outside the harbour and at sea. He was being taken further from home. Incomprehensible orders were barked at him, and though he obeyed every command as best he could, whether it be to scrub that, or fetch this, his mind was occupied with only one thought: how to get home.

He knew his father picked carefully from which farmers he bought meat, for mean faces meant mean meat, but there seemed nothing but mean faces in the crowded space between the two enormous eighteen-pounders that he was told was his mess shared with eight others, all grown men. There was a rough wood dresser, but nothing like the one at home, and he was given a chest in which he could keep his belongings, but he had nothing to keep there, except his treasured conker from last autumn. It was June now, and the conker was shrivelled, but he placed it inside carefully.

Davy mulled over his predicament. He needed a friend if ever he was to return home. He decided therefore that he would be polite to one and all, even to the burly Taffy Thomas, a bull of a man with huge hands and a face to match, who was in charge of the daily beer and grog ration, as well as the huge buckets of food. Apart from that, Davy knew nothing and understood nothing, and no one explained. The constant bells and pipes, the smell of tar, wood and hemp and the endless motion of the ship were of another world, and one to which he did not belong. He was pushed and pummelled to wherever Taffy decided he should be, and fear and seasickness predominated over all else. There were a few things he liked, such as looking up at the sails billowing before the wind, and watching the bows churn up the water, but mostly he hated everything and everyone.

"Don't you take to life at sea, butcher's boy?" Taffy jeered tonight, ignoring Davy's question as to when he might go home.

Davy said nothing and another, kinder, said, "Eat your supper, lad. You need your strength."

"What kind of meat is this?" Davy asked timidly.

A sneer from Taffy, and a wink to his messmates. "What else would you be eating aboard the good ship *Unicorn*? Unicorn meat, of course. Don't your pa sell that?" More laughter.

"No, sir," Davy replied humbly, then daringly repeated his question: "When might I go home, do you think?"

Taffy looked round at his mates for approval. "Don't you even know you can only go home when the old unicorn himself comes to fetch you?"

The roar that followed made Davy belligerent. It wasn't his fault he didn't know, and it wasn't his fault he was here. "What is a unicorn, if you please?"

Taffy dug his elbow into his neighbour's ribs. "Ah well, some say the unicorn has magic powers; he stops you being poisoned by the navy victuals, and its horn makes the old prick bigger, don't it, lads? The ladies like that, so we take the nice unicorn with us on our ship. If you catch sight of him, you'll be homeward bound within the hour, butcher's boy, so you'd better be on the lookout. Tell you what," he roared as fresh inspiration came to him, "you clean the heads tomorrow morning, slop-boy, and most likely you'll see him."

There was a murmur of unease at this, since it was easily the worst job in the ship, but no one dared protest.

"But I don't know what a unicorn looks like," Davy said, alarmed at this, even more than the prospect of cleaning the terrible area in the beak of the ship where all the seamen and boys relieved themselves.

"It's like a large white pony, white as milk it is, with one large horn stretching out from its forehead. You can only catch him, they say, by dodging behind a tree when he's chasing you so that the daft old thing gets his horn stuck in the trunk."

"But are there any trees aboard this ship?" Davy asked, very puzzled now.

"You don't know nothing," chortled Taffy. "Ain't you ever heard of trestle trees, crosstrees and tree nails?"

Davy had never heard of them, nor had his father, who was a great authority on English woodlands, ever mentioned them. He was not going to show his ignorance amid all this mocking laughter, though. Instead he asked, "Where does the unicorn sleep at night?"

Taffy was nonplussed, but then he had a brainwave and guffawed, "Well, mates, I reckon he sleeps in Davy Jones's locker, don't you?"

"What locker, sir? Where is my locker?" Davy asked eagerly.

"Your sea chest, boy," someone sneered.

"But I have never seen him in it," Davy said doubtfully.

"That's because you don't look at the right time. They say if you see him in it, though" – Taffy paused impressively – "it means you'll be made an admiral straight away, it's that lucky. You just take him along to the captain, and tell him you're in command now."

The unicorn must be a very small animal, David thought dubiously, but no one contradicted Taffy, so he assumed he must be right. Helped by the nightly grog ration, his messmates were passing on to the usual talk, of which he did not understand a word. Unable to join in, he battled with the salt meat, which made him feel ill again.

It wasn't only the men who jeered at Davy next morning. It was other boys like himself up early to scrub the decks with their buckets and deck bumper brushes. Except for one other unfortunate lad, they were not assigned to the heads, but were scrubbing the decks. The heads stank as usual, and the filth Davy had to clear away made him sicker than ever.

He knew he had to find that unicorn *now*. He'd already peered into his chest, and seen it wasn't asleep in there, so it must be here somewhere. Dropping his bucket, he ran for the waist, away from this stench. Regardless of the shouts from below, he rushed up the companionway, only to find himself on the half deck face to face with a lady clad in a blue gown and blue bonnet, which framed her round pleasant face. She reminded him a little of his mother, though Mother was plumper, and her face softer. Just thinking of her made Davy want to weep, for this woman wasn't smiling at him as Mother did. She looked very annoyed.

"What are you doing here, boy?" She gestured to the red-coated marine sentry to leave him alone for the moment.

"If you please, ma'am." Davy blurted out the truth. "I'm searching for the unicorn to take me home."

She did smile at that. "This is the captain's poop deck. What stories have they been telling you? And what is your name?"

"Davy Jones, ma'am. They said the unicorn would come to fetch me, but he hasn't. He isn't in my locker where they said he slept, so he must be here. Where will I find him, ma'am? I must go home. My mother will fear me dead."

Betsy Williams, the captain's wife, looked at him, not knowing what to say. How could she tell him that it might be years before he saw his home again? In the end she said, "He'll come for those that do their duty patiently, Davy, for frigates are the eyes of the fleet. Don't you want to serve your country?"

"Yes, ma'am, but it is better to serve it at what I know. I am going to be a butcher."

What might have been insolence in another boy, impressed Betsy in Davy. This was a lad who used his brain, and her husband would be amused when she told him of her encounter. She racked her brains as to how to encourage him, without giving him false hope. "How old are you, Davy?"

"Twelve, ma'am."

"There was another boy not much older than you who went to sea in his uncle's ship, but he began by loading stores, just like all you young boys. And now young Horatio Nelson is a commodore, and many say will soon be an admiral."

"But, ma'am, I have no uncle aboard this ship."

"You do not need one, Davy. In the Royal Navy a man makes his own path to the top. If you work hard, my husband might even make you a midshipman in a few years' time."

Appalled, she stopped, realizing what she had admitted tacitly: that there was no hope of his seeing his home for a very long time.

"Thank you, ma'am," Davy said firmly. "I'm much obliged, but I'd prefer to go home."

That night Davy's sleep was fitful. Suppose the unicorn too could not sleep? Perhaps it would come searching for him this very night. He got down from his hammock, careful not to disturb the scores of snoring seamen around him, and went to his sea chest to see whether the unicorn were there. He might not want to be an admiral, but at least he'd have some say over his future.

To his dismay the chest was still empty of all but his conker. The unicorn must be out searching for him, and would never find him in his hammock. The hammocks were so close that there was scarcely room for the men, let alone a unicorn. He must get up to the deck again. Davy staggered sleepily aloft to see if the unicorn were coming. It was so dark he could not find his way to the poop deck, but stayed in the waist. If only the moon would come out from behind the clouds, he might see more clearly, but there was only one dim light on the ship and that was at the steering position and far away. The ship was rocking less violently now, as she made her way through the waves, and all was quiet save for the swish of the water, and the occasional flap of the sails.

Suddenly the moon did shine out, and there on the horizon, before Davy's amazed eyes, were three shapes. Two were indistinct, but the biggest was the unicorn. There was absolutely no doubt. His horn reached out on the horizon as though he were ready to charge the tree and in the moonlight it was as white as milk. The unicorn must surely be looking for him, but he was so far away.

"Here!" Davy shouted at the top of his voice. "I'm here."

Immediately he was seized by several pairs of arms as the marine sentries pulled him away from the bulwarks, stifling his screams. "Get back below, boy, or you'll be clapped in irons," a voice hissed in his ear.

"I can't, I can't." Didn't they understand? "I must stay until the unicorn comes," Davy yelled, wriggling out of their grasp and running frantically to the bulwarks again to see the magic sight. There was nothing to be seen. All was dark, and once again he was dragged away.

"Quiet, you'll have the captain here."

"But it's the unicorn," Davy cried. "I want to go home."

"What's all this hullabaloo?" A gentleman clad half in night-shirt, half in blue frock coat, appeared, and at his roar the sentries, several sailors and one uniformed officer who had also come to investigate the noise sprang to attention.

"Now you're for it," the latter said with relish. "It's the lash for you, lad, at the very least, and well deserved too."

Captain Williams's furious face peered down at the boy, but before he could speak the lady Davy had met earlier appeared at his side, also hastily dressed, and with her hair hanging down under a night bonnet.

"Oh, ma'am, my unicorn. He's there . . ." Davy, oblivious of all else, pointed out to the horizon, sobbing in relief that a friend had appeared who would believe him.

"The boy's mad. Put him under restraint," the captain barked.

"Wait, Tom," his wife pleaded. "This is the boy I told you of. It is not his fault he has been misled."

"I'm not misled, ma'am," Davy put in eagerly. "I've *seen* the unicorn. He's really there. Look."

He pointed again, and at that moment the moon reappeared and there it was. *His* unicorn, and what's more, he could now see it was a whole family of them, two big ones and a baby.

Half curious, the captain turned to look, and immediately stiffened.

"God-a-mighty, lad, that's no unicorn. That's the bowsprit of a ship-of-war and two others with her. Mr Palmer," he bawled at the first lieutenant. "Make signal to the *Santa Margaritta* that we intend to close. Enemy on our lee beam. There's not one of His Majesty's ships hereabouts, so they're Frenchies, I'll be bound. Turn the hands up, Mr Palmer. Middle watch to report to me at eight bells. This lad has sharper eyes than they, and I'll know the reason why."

"Aye aye, sir."

Within moments men were already appearing out of the gangways, each hurrying to his own position. Davy stood back, trying to work out what had happened to his unicorn, and it was some time before he was noticed again by the captain.

"I don't approve of impressment, Davy," he grunted, "especially when it takes boys against the rules, but our country's at war, and we need lads like you. You want to fight for your country, don't you, Davy?"

Here it came again. Everyone was so eager for him to fight for England, but how could he? He wasn't a sailor. "Yes, sir," Davy agreed doubtfully, "but I'd like to go home first. I'm sure the unicorn—"

"Down to your hammock, Davy," Betsy Williams intervened diplomatically.

Amazingly the captain smiled. "Report to me at two bells, Davy. That's in seven hours' time, nine o'clock. You'll hear the bell strike twice an hour or so after the 'Up all hammocks' pipe. We'll see whether you still want to go home then. We'll make a seaman of you yet, or I'm the Flying Dutchman."

The ship was full of noise and movement now, and Davy could sense the difference now that a quarry was in sight. Men were still appearing from every side, each to his action station, but Davy went below, deeply disillusioned. He had found the unicorn, and though the captain seemed pleased, he still could not go home, unless of course he was to be sent home in the morning. Even Davy realized there was scant chance of this, however, since they were in mid-ocean. Hopefully he peered into his sea chest again before he went to sleep, but it still remained empty of all save the conker, and eventually he fell asleep through sheer weariness.

"What the devil are you doing here, young 'un?" Taffy snarled, when he saw him at the mess-table in the morning. "Up to the heads with your slop-bucket."

"But the captain wants to see me at two bells, because I saw a unicorn." Davy was full of renewed hope. After all, they were chasing it, the captain had said so.

His remark was greeted by jeers of laughter. "You've been

dreaming again, boy," Taffy pronounced, and a clip round the ear despatched Davy to the heads again.

There was a sense of purpose in the ship now as the sails billowed out under the wind. HMS *Unicorn* was cleaving her way through the sea cleanly and quickly, and despite the awfulness of the job he was doing, Davy looked admiringly at the way she was moving so determinedly after what the captain thought was the enemy, but which he knew was the unicorn itself.

He heard two bells strike, but Davy had now convinced himself that either Taffy was right or the captain had been joking, as there had been general mirth at the idea of a ship's boy having to report to the captain. He was surprised, therefore, when he heard a boy in uniform, not much older than himself, calling for him.

"Captain sent for you," he said sharply. "Don't bring your bucket, you idiot."

Davy promptly dropped it, and fell in behind the boy, following him up aloft to the poop deck, oblivious of Taffy on the fo'c'sle staring in disbelief.

The captain glared at him. "It's past two bells. You'll have to make better time than this. There's your unicorn, young Davy," he snapped. "We and the *Santa Margaritta* have been chasing it all night."

Davy looked, not at their sister frigate, but at the spread of sail still far off but which he could now see clearly. "They are ships, sir. You were right." He battled with his disappointment.

"And worth more than unicorns, I'll be bound, for all they've no colours hoisted. Two frigates and a buss a prize indeed if we take them. If you hadn't seen your unicorn, young Master Jones, they might well have taken *us* in the darkness."

Taken them where? Davy wondered curiously, but had the sense not to ask. In the daylight he could see that the captain's frock coat was threadbare in places and had patches at the elbows. Perhaps His Majesty's navy did not pay well, and his officers needed such prizes?

"They're running from us now in close bow and quarter

line," Captain Williams grunted. "They hope to tempt us away from the Scillies and too far towards their shore."

"Which shore is that, sir?" Davy was interested, for the only shore he had ever seen from Portsmouth was the Isle of Wight.

"The French shore, Davy." The captain had his eye to his telescope, and Davy suddenly longed to peer through it too. Perhaps when he returned home, his father might buy him such an instrument.

"They're keeping close, sir," the first lieutenant reported. "The front one's under short sail so they don't get separated. That means they want us to chase," he explained to Davy, seeing that the boy had won the captain's favour. Then all was shouting of orders, and men and boys rushing up and down from the poop deck, and once again everything was incomprehensible. Davy didn't mind that so much, however, as at least it was exciting and he was in the fresh air, not on the smoky, stuffy gun deck.

Since he didn't seem to be required, he found a place to sit down out of sight, unsure whether he should go or stay, but wanting to remain. He found himself getting increasingly caught up in the excitement, as the *Unicorn* and *Santa Margaritta* drew nearer to the mystery ships. After all, there was still a chance that the unicorn was trotting around them somewhere.

"Still no colours hoisted, sir," the first lieutenant reported an hour or so later, then: "Buss hauling windward, sir." Davy could clearly see the smallest of the three ships passing across the *Unicorn*'s bow some distance away.

"Run out the guns, Mr Palmer," the captain roared.

Guns? There was going to be a battle? Davy sat so still, he dared hardly breathe. He sat there for another two hours, but it seemed like minutes there was so much to watch, to smell and to experience. Then two bells sounded again, although the second bell was almost drowned by the captain's roar.

"There she goes. They've hoisted their colours at last. Frenchies, as I thought. Guns to bear, Mr Palmer. We're almost within range."

Almost immediately came the sound of gunfire from the

French ships, followed by a deafening broadside from the *Unicorn*. The whole ship shuddered and the air was suddenly full of smoke. To his amazement, Davy realized he was not scared, even though he saw that one of the immaculate white sails above him had been torn clean away by the gunfire.

"Avast there, boy!" shouted the captain, "tell the sail-maker to report to me. Make yourself useful."

"Yes, sir." To his relief, Davy knew where he would find him, because while he was carrying supplies on board he had seen where the sail-makers and carpenters worked in the orlop.

"And, boy," the captain barked after him, "off with your shoes and stockings. You'll find it easier. These decks are slippery."

"Thank you, sir." Davy obeyed, and did find it easier barefoot. Running down the companionways past the lower gun deck, however, he bumped straight into Taffy who, grasping him by the arm, snarled, "Not so fast, powder monkey. Where the devil have you been? I'll have you lashed for this."

"I've a message from the captain for the sail-maker." Davy wasn't scared of Taffy any more.

Taffy paused, unable to be sure the boy was lying, then reluctantly let him go on his way with a "Tell the bloody captain we need powder monkeys here, not a snitch like you." Then he pulled Davy from the companionway so violently he fell headlong, but he hauled himself to his feet, ignored Taffy, and continued down to the sail-maker to deliver the message. That was more important than bullies. When he returned to the open deck the air was even denser with acrid, pungent smoke, and he could see more sails were shredded, and the rigging too. A terrible fear came to him that they were losing the fight, and, if so, he might never get home.

The captain caught sight of him. "Stay here, boy. I need you."

"Yes, sir," Davy replied thankfully. He wouldn't have to face Taffy till messtime again, and besides, he didn't want to be down there with the hot smoking guns, he wanted to be up here seeing what was going on.

He could feel each judder as the huge guns thundered out beneath him, replying to the Frenchmen's fire, and saw the reason for the colours. Without them, in the heat of battle it would be hard to tell which was their sister ship the *Santa Margaritta* and which the ships of the feared Napoleon Bonaparte. Davy felt a certain pride. His mother still frightened his younger brothers and sisters into submission with the threat that old Boney would get them, and here was he, Davy, about to help in the battle to make sure he didn't. Mingled with the pride, however, was a determination to get the fight over and go home. And *that* meant finding the unicorn.

He was kept busy with messages, returning breathlessly each time to the poop deck. Ships loomed out of the smoke at intervals, but they were not at close quarters, although the gunfire continued.

"Master gunner to report to me, Davy," Captain Williams commanded.

Davy shot down to his own mess deck. "Master gunner to report to captain," he piped, not knowing who this gentleman was.

To his horror it was Taffy who lurched up to him, face, vest and arms all black with smoke and grime. "Still the captain's little molly, then?" he growled.

Davy had no idea what he meant, so he ignored it and simply repeated the captain's message in a firm voice.

"Found that unicorn, yet?" Taffy sneered, as he made his way aloft. "Making you an admiral, is he?"

"No," replied Davy simply.

"You want to be an admiral though, don't you, little molly?"

Davy thought he should reply this time. "I would like to go home," he assured Taffy. "I never asked to come here."

"Poor little molly," sneered Taffy, following Davy on to the poop deck, then he transformed his expression into respectful obedience to meet the captain.

"Enemy wearing round, sir," cried the first lieutenant.

"I see that, Mr Palmer," Williams replied with satisfaction.

"Our fire too hot for the lad, eh? Await my orders, master gunner."

The guns of the smaller frigate thundered out a broadside across the bow of the oncoming *Santa Margaritta* and a roar of appreciation went up from the watchers on the *Unicorn*.

"What's happening, if you please?" Davy asked Mr Palmer breathlessly.

"The old *Margaritta*'s putting herself alongside her quarry. Can't you see that, boy?"

Davy peered through the smoke and did indeed make out their sister ship was steering herself parallel to her attacker. Then Davy lost sight of her too. Their own firing ceased, though they could hear the roar of the guns of the two frigates locked together in combat. At last a roar went up.

"By George, she's struck," shouted Mr Palmer.

"Struck what?" Davy cried. "Are we hit?"

"The colours," he snarled, not too unkindly. "The Frenchie has struck her colours, she's surrendered."

"By heaven, that's a prize indeed for the *Margaritta*," Captain Williams said admiringly. "That's the *Tamise*, Davy. She's taken twenty of our best ships in the last two years, and before that she was British, so we'll be heartily glad to welcome her back into the Royal Navy."

"Signal from the *Santa Margaritta*, sir," the yeoman of signals reported. "Taking in the prize, with but two dead. Leaving the lion to the *Unicorn*."

The captain laughed. "This will be one time when the *Unicorn* won't let the lion win. Are you with me, gentlemen?" he roared.

The cheer that followed from the quarterdeck from his officers left no doubt of their answer.

"They're crowding sail, Mr Palmer. *Tamise*'s brave companions think to run from us," Captain Williams continued, his telescope to his eye. "Master gunner" – he turned to Taffy – "tell the lieutenant every gun to bear. This prey won't escape us, by heaven."

"Aye aye, sir. And I'll take this boy as powder monkey," Taffy said oh-so-politely.

Davy's heart plummeted, more because he would miss what was going on rather than through fear.

"The boy stays here," the captain told Taffy curtly.

Taffy seized hold of Davy's arm and gave it a quick twist as he passed on his way down, making sure it was unseen by the captain. "I'll have you yet, boy," he hissed. "Lash you into shape, I will."

"Not if I see my unicorn, and we *are* still chasing him," Davy pointed out sturdily, kicking Taffy sharply on the ankle.

Stifling an oath, Taffy snarled, "Oh, you will, boy, I'll see to that."

The *Unicorn*'s guns were still firing as she chased the remaining two French ships, and the cries of the seamen and the general noise of battle told Davy that the chase was still on, and that the *Unicorn* had suffered damage.

"Fore yard and maintopsail gone, sir," reported Mr Palmer. "Damage to the mizzen stay."

The captain turned to Davy. "Sail-maker and bosun to report to me. Carpenter to report to me."

"Aye aye, sir," Davy answered automatically, before disappearing on his mission.

He was kept continuously busy running messages for several hours as the afternoon wore on. Gradually he began to feel a part of it all; he had a role to play that would all help towards his speedy return home.

As the hours passed, sometimes their prey was in sight, sometimes it wasn't, especially as it grew dark. There seemed to be only the one French ship now, the one which Davy recognized as *his* unicorn. He refused to leave his post for food, for he wanted to make sure it was captured, as he had a personal stake in it. A lingering hope remained that somewhere aboard it might be a unicorn. It was time, he realized, for "lights out" to be piped, but there could be no sleep for the hands with such a prize in sight, and Davy had never felt less like going to sleep in his life.

"Well now," Captain Williams said jovially at last, "it's dark now. What to do, Master Jones, what to do?"

Davy realized the captain did not really want an answer, or not from him, but he was determined to help if he could. "The wind has dropped, sir. Perhaps we will come nearer to the" – he nearly said unicorn, but remembered in time – "the French ship now, sir. She will not sail so fast."

The captain swung round. "You hear that, Mr Palmer? We'll make a sailor of this lad yet. Carry topgallantsails," he ordered crisply. "We'll draw near on our Frenchie's weather quarter to take the wind from her sails."

As soon as they at last caught up with the Frenchie, battle broke out once more, although it was very dark by now.

"Alongside, Mr Palmer," Captain Williams ordered. "Guns to bear in close action."

Shortly afterwards, Davy was thrilled to hear the sound of cheering, not just from the quarterdeck of the *Unicorn*, but from below, from the whole ship it seemed, as the *Unicorn* ranged herself alongside her enemy. From what had happened earlier between the *Santa Margaritta* and the *Tamise*, Davy understood that the battle was not yet won, but that the cheering was a sign that the *Unicorn* was *going* to win. He joined in enthusiastically.

As the guns roared out again, Davy not only lost his fear in the heat of action, but his dislike of the gun deck itself. "Should I go to help the master gunner, sir?" he asked, anxious to be of best use.

"No." Captain Williams eyed him sharply. "Is that where you'd prefer to be?"

"No, sir, I would rather stay here, sir, until we have won." This time Davy did not even think of adding, "to capture the unicorn".

"I like your spirit, young man," the captain grunted.

Once again, it was hard to work out what was happening, as the guns thundered repeatedly, and the huge French frigate lurched so close it seemed they must surely hit her. The noise of falling wood and the cries of men could be heard in the brief intervals that the guns were not firing, but when at last the smoke cleared, Davy saw that the French ship was no longer alongside them, but falling behind.

"She's close-hauled, Davy Jones; that means she hopes to cross our stern and gain the wind," Mr Palmer volunteered in his own excitement. "We can do better than that, eh?"

"Mr Palmer," the captain called. "Haul in your weather braces."

To Davy's breathless pleasure, as he watched the men at the braces altering the position of the sails, he could understand what the captain was planning to do. By holding the *Unicorn* back, he could manoeuvre her once again alongside the enemy, and begin the battle again. And so it happened. Here was the Frenchie looming by them once more, and so close that he could see before his eyes the mainmast of the French ship beginning to fall, crashing down amid the gunfire, and the proud sails with it. He was torn between the thrill of imminent conquest, and pity that such a ship should be destroyed.

"Enemy fore- and mainmasts down, sir," Mr Palmer reported, followed by: "Enemy mizzen topmast down, sir."

The captain didn't need to be told, for he could see just as clearly as Davy that the splendid ship was crumpling before their onslaught; the lion was dying, but the *Unicorn*, though damaged, was still intact. Davy looked up at their own three masts, still standing proud, and felt this were some achievement of his own. He heard shouting from the other ship amid the gunfire, and he could see men crowded at the ship's side. There were no colours for them to strike, for they must lie upon their deck torn to shreds.

"They're surrendering, Mr Palmer," Captain Williams said quietly. "Take the deck, if you please. I shall go to the surgeon immediately. He will be tending our own wounded."

But before he could leave the poop deck, however, the surgeon himself reported to him.

"Injuries, Mr Saltwood?" the captain barked anxiously.

"None, sir."

"*None?*"

"No, sir. None killed, none wounded."

"Thanks be to God," Captain Williams whispered in relief. "The same cannot be said of our gallant enemy. Methinks they will have suffered heavy losses."

Then he spoke to Mr Palmer again, and Davy caught the words "prize boat". Of course, he realized, a crew would have to be put on board to take the enemy ship into an English port, or else she might just run away. Perhaps the capture of this prize meant the captain might be able to buy a new uniform. Davy hoped so, for he seemed to work even harder than his father in the butcher's shop.

"Mr Palmer, who will you take with you? It will not be a pretty sight," the captain asked.

"Could I go, sir?" Davy asked eagerly. Both men turned in surprise, for the boy was long since forgotten. He blushed, wondering if he had said the wrong thing, but he still had a lingering hope that there might be a unicorn on board. After all, there might also be pressed boys, like him, with mothers of their own, and the unicorn might be busy with them.

"It's no place for lads like you," the first lieutenant replied gruffly.

"One moment, Mr Palmer. Kindly recall that it was this boy who noticed the frigates first. He deserves his chance provided he realizes what it would mean." Captain Williams turned to Davy. "What think you of our navy now, lad?"

"I liked the fighting, sir, though I am sorry if there were people hurt. The enemy sailors must be much like us, even though they sail for Bonaparte. And also," Davy added, "I liked seeing how you plan a battle, sir."

"The prize crew is a job for experienced seamen, not boys. There will be many dead and wounded, and you are of tender years," Captain Williams observed. "Yet you are right to say the hands are just like us. One must learn the hard way how much blood, pain and suffering gunfire produces, before one says 'I wish to be in the navy.' That is part of one's duty, and part of the adventure, but it has to be faced."

"Then I should like to face it now, sir, if you please." Davy was in no doubt that he should seize this opportunity.

"Mr Palmer?"

The first lieutenant nodded reluctantly. "Fetch your sea chest, lad. We shall be gone a few days. We'll be taking the French frigate in to Portsmouth, where she'll be repaired to join His Majesty's navy."

"Portsmouth?" Davy cried. "Might I go home after that, please?" he asked the captain politely. Only then did it occur to him that perhaps this was the unicorn's way of getting him home. He forgot the unicorn, however, in the realization that he would be going home on a prize ship that had been taken in a battle in which he had shared. He would see Mother again.

In his excitement he hardly heard the captain's final words, when he replied, "If you still wish, Davy. I'll have a word with their lordships. You're too young to be aboard. But I'll be sorry to lose you, and so will the navy."

Davy ran quickly below to the mess deck where the men, released from gun duty, were eating. He had forgotten food and how hungry he was, and crammed a few hard biscuits in his pocket.

"Where do you think you're going?" Taffy snarled. There was a sort of grin on his face, though not a pleasant one.

"In the prize boat," Davy announced proudly.

Taffy sniggered. "Found your unicorn, have you?"

"No, but—"

"I'd look in your sea chest if I were you. Might be there. You can go to the skipper, tell him you're Admiral Jones now, and order him to take you back to Mama."

Davy picked up his sea chest, peering inside to see his precious conker was safely there.

It was, but there was something else too. There was a crude white-painted wooden animal with a twist of hemp for a long horn sticking out from its forehead. And roughly scrawled on a piece of paper was: "Davy Jones is hereby promoted admiral. Captain Williams."

The whole table broke into laughter, and Taffy most of all. "You can go and shout at the captain now, lad. He'll be at his victuals but don't let that trouble yer. After all, you're a bloody admiral."

Davy looked at them, and then at the crude unicorn in his hand. He realized now they'd been mocking him all along, that they wanted him to look a fool in front of the captain. But he didn't care any more. He was going to Portsmouth, then he would go home for ever. The captain had said so.

Or would he rather be an admiral? Davy stared at the unicorn. He knew now how hard a life it would be at sea. There would be more battles, but sooner or later he would be fighting them in a ship of his own. His mother would understand, and he'd go home on leave sooner or later. He'd only to learn the ways of a ship, but already he knew how to get the better of the Taffy Thomases of the mess deck.

He grinned at them all cheerfully. "I'll take my conker and my locker," he said. "And I'll take my unicorn, for which I thank you, sirs. It *will* make me an admiral, and it will take me home, you'll see. It will be when it decides to do so, though, not you. I'll manage it somehow, because I'm in the navy now."

THE FRIENDSHIP OF MONSIEUR JEYNOIS

William Hope Hodgson

William Hope Hodgson (1877–1918) ran away to sea when he was thirteen. Although he was caught and brought back to school, he eventually got his way and was apprenticed as a cabin boy in August 1891. He remained at sea (except for his years of study) for the next eight years and would later use his experiences as the basis of a series of remarkable novels and short stories, many of them with supernatural elements. Perhaps his best extended ghost story is The Ghost Pirates *(1909) but you will also find an excellent selection of his best stories in* Men of Deep Waters *(1914),* The Luck of the Strong *(1916) and* Captain Gault *(1917). It was a great loss to supernatural fiction and naval fiction when Hodgson was killed in the First World War. Many of his later stories were not supernatural. The following, one of his few genuine historical naval stories, is set at the time of the French Revolutionary Wars and explores the tensions and problems that arise on board a British privateer.*

Captain Drool and the two mates sat in the cabin and argued, gross and uncouth; but Monsieur Jeynois said nothing. Only smoked his long pipe and listened, while the bosun held the poop deck!

I had grown to like Monsieur Jeynois, for the brave, quiet way of him, and the calm speech that seemed so strong and wise against the rude blusterings and oathings of the captain and the mates.

The *Saucy Lady* was a private venture ship – in other words, an English privateer – at the time of the French war. She had been a French brig, named *La Gavotte*, and had been sold at Portsmouth for prize-money.

Monsieur Jeynois and Captain Drool had bought her, and fitted her out against the French, with six twenty-four-pounder cannonades a side, and two long eighteen-pounders – the one mounted aft and the other for'ard, for chasers.

The brig was a matter of 350 tons burthen, and sailed very fast, and made good weather of it.

We had ninety-six able-bodied sailors for'ard in a fine, great, new fo'cas'le, that was fitted up when Monsieur Jeynois and Captain Drool had the vessel altered. There were also six gunners, that we had helped to run free of the Royal Navy, and good men they were, but mighty opinionated, and nothing would serve them but to sneer and jeer at all and aught because we were not so fine as a King's ship. And, indeed, why they troubled to sail in us was a thing to make a man wonder!

There were, also, twelve boys in the ship. Six of these were named midshipmen, and were from rich tradesmen's families of Portsmouth Town, and paid some sort of premium to walk the lee side of the after-deck and play lob-lolly to the captain and the two mates.

I was one of the other six – just common lads off the water front at Portsmouth, though I was no Portsmouth lad, but Lancashire bred and born, but part reared on the Welsh coast and afterwards in the south, for my father had been a shipwright in Liverpool, and then went to Cardiff, and came in the end to Portsmouth, where he worked in the Royal Dockyards till the day he died, which was two years before this story. And a poor and ignorant lad I was, as I do mind me, and talked a strange mixture of dialects and rough words. But this by the way.

We wanted to fight the French, and make good prize-money

at brave work. And there you have the crew of us, with added thereto the bosun and the two carpenters.

Now, if you have never heard tell of Monsieur Jeynois, you might wonder to hear that he helped fit out a ship against the French. But, indeed, in Portsmouth Town, we had no trouble on this score, for a better hater of Frenchmen, and a greater fighter, never put a pegged boot to good deck-planks.

There were some that said he had been a great man the other side; and this I can well believe, for he was a great man, as all in that ship knew in their inwards. He had a steady, brown eye, that looked down into a man; and you knew that he feared nothing, save it might be God, which I do believe.

As for his hatred of the French, there were many tales to account for it; but none of them to the mark, as I must suppose. Yet, because he was a Frenchman, despite the many times that he had proved himself upon them, there were a thousand to hate him for no more than his name or his blood, both or either, as suited their poor brute minds. Also, while many had a deep respect for him, few loved him, because he was too quiet and aloof. And, indeed, I doubt not that, because there was something great of heart within him, there were many of the poorer souled that hated him for no other cause than that he waked in them – though scarce they knew it – a knowledge of their own inward weeviliness.

And this was the man that sat in the cabin with Captain Drool and the two mates – Hankson and Abbott – and would listen to their rude arguing, that even I, the cabin lad, could oft see the gross folly of. And then, maybe, by a dozen quiet words, he would show them their own poor selves, in a mirror of brief speech that made them and their thoughts and child's plans of no more account than they were; so that I have seen the three of them stare at him out of eyes of dumb hatred.

And then he would show them the way that the thing should be done, and they would be forced to admit the rightness of his reasoning; yet hating him the more for his constant rightness, and the way that he seemed to know all and to fear naught.

Only one thing he did not know, and that was the science to

navigate; else I venture he had never sailed with any captain other than himself.

And there, in this little that I have told, you have the causes that led to the greatest fight that ever a single man put up against a multitude.

It came about in this wise. After dinner the captain and the mate that was not in charge of the deck would sit awhile and drink a sort of spiced rum-toddy. But Monsieur Jeynois drank only plain water, flavoured with molasses, and often left the table with a quiet excuse that he would see the weather.

Then, when he was gone, the captain and whichever of the two mates that was with him, would fall to cursing him, from his keel upwards, and taking no more heed of me – whom I do venture to think they thought no more of than a wood deck-bucket! – than if I were not there; save, in truth, one of them needed the molasses or the hot water or the ground nutmeg; whereupon I was as like to get a clout as a word, to make known their wants.

And clout me they would do at any moment and were at first as handy to it if monsieur were with them as if he were on deck. Not that monsieur said ever a word, one way or the other, for he had no foolish softness about him; yet he never struck me. And once, when Captain Drool had opened my head with his pewter mug, I looked quick over at monsieur, and there was a look in his eyes that made me think he disliked to see me treated so, though he forbore to say aught, but yet I could think had come near to that point at which he might speak.

And, indeed, this is but poorly said; yet, in part, expresses the thought that came to me, before I was knocked down again, for not hastening to fetch another dipper of rum.

But late that same night, when I was lying very sick and hot-headed under the cabin table – for I was allowed no hammock – monsieur stooped and looked under the table, and asked me how I was; and he fetched me, presently, a draught with his own hand, and afterwards put a wet cloth on my head, so that in a while I went over asleep, and woke pretty fresh in the morning.

And I found the cloth on my head to be a strip off one of

monsieur's neck-clothes; and I put the thing inside my shirt, along with a big memory, as a boy will do that is badly treated, and has a great kindness where no kindness was ever expected; for I was but a common ship's boy, and monsieur a great soldier and a shipowner, as I have told.

And after that time I noticed that neither Captain Drool nor the mates touched me when monsieur was in the cabin; so that I supposed he had spoken quietly with them, when I was not there, against striking me.

Yet, when he was up on the deck, they would clout me as ever, and talk very loose and rash before me, as I have said, against monsieur. But threats are easy blows, so that I took little heed for a good while.

Then, one night after dinner, when we were heading up for the channel, they got talking in a way that set me taking sudden note of their words; for there was a real meaning and intention in what they were saying.

Presently, Captain Drool sent me to fetch aft the bosun to drink with them, which was a thing they had done several times of late after monsieur had gone up on to the deck.

They drank more that night than ever before, and the bosun so much as any. And every now and again Abbott, the second mate, would come down into the cabin and have a tot with them, and join in their talk; and me kept mighty busy, in the small pantry-place, scraping nutmeg for their spice-rum-toddy – that was the captain's own invention – and keeping water a-boil over a slush-lamp, all of which I did, despite the rolling of the ship, by holding the kettle with one hand and rubbing the nutmeg on to an iron grater with the other. And all the time I listened, so well as I could, for I had begun to see that they were planning to kill monsieur quietly in the cabin, and afterwards to dump him secretly over the side, and so let it be supposed he had been washed overboard at night; for we were shipping a deal of heavy water with the strong gale that we were running before.

Then Captain Drool should have the ship entire his own, for Monsieur Jeynois was a lone man, and none in England, so it was thought, to be an heir to him and his moneys. And to pay the two mates and the bosun for their help in this dire and brutal murder, the captain proposed to pay them the share of the prize-money that was coming to monsieur, and also a hundred golden guineas between them, each to share equal, but that they should claim no rights in the ship. And this they were well enough pleased with, being but vulgar and brutal men, and each as ignorant as the other; for it was only Captain Drool that knew the science of navigating.

And whether the man for'ard should suspect or not, seemed no great matter to these brutes as they guzzled and planned this foul deed; for there were a deal of men, I doubt not, as I have told, who could not get it out of their stomachs that monsieur was a Frenchman, and should be treated as such. There was not much love that we had those days for Frenchmen. Yet, in the main, the four men desired to keep secret the method of the end of monsieur, lest the crew should demand that monsieur's share of the prize-money be distributed, which the crew might certainly have done, deeming it their right, because monsieur was French, and because they would suppose that if the captain and the mates murdered monsieur, it would be with intent to "nig" his share of the prize-money. And this would most surely offend the crew, who would refuse to have them profit without the whole ship's company should profit. But, were the crew deceived in the matter, to believe that monsieur was truly washed overboard in a natural and wholesome fashion, then they would demand nothing, but expect the usual routine in such matters, which was that a man's prize-money be paid to his widow or to his heir, and this Captain Drool would provide for, by the aid of his brother who was a penman, and could write the name so clever upon the will that monsieur would think it his own were he to return again to life.

There you have it all, with the methods of their poor and brutish reasonings, which truly betray them for what they were. And I, you must picture, holding the kettle above the slush-lamp in the pantry-room off the cabin, and grinding scarce enough nutmeg to supply their needs, for the grinding of the nutmeg upon the iron scraper made a noise that prevented me from hearing them; and so I was fain to keep stopping every moment to listen. And, indeed, once I set all my sleeve alight, with the ship rolling so, for I was taking no heed of the way I held the kettle, but stopping, as I have told, to hark very desperate; and suddenly I smelled the stink of my sleeve burning in the lamp, for I had my sleeve over the flame and the kettle nowhere near.

Yet they never so much as knew, for they had drunk a matter of four dippers of rum between them, and they could think of nothing but the dreadful murder they planned so earnest.

Now, at four bells – by which I mean ten o'clock of the night – monsieur came down from the deck, and for the first time in all that voyage I heard him speak his mind to the captain, nor minded who heard him; only first he had word with the bosun.

"Bosun," he said, "you are in the wrong part of the ship. Go up on to the deck and take charge until you are relieved."

Just that and nothing more, and spoken as quiet as you like, with good English that no man could better; for monsieur was French, to my thinking, only in name.

And the bosun! A great hulk of a man that weighed 15 stone as he lolled there. It was fine to watch, as you will acknowledge! I peeped out of the pantry and saw him make first as if he had heard nothing, and then in a moment, though monsieur said never another word, only looked at him, he tried to catch the eyes of Captain Drool and the two mates, smiling in a silly, ugly way as he did so; but they looked everywhere but at him, like animals that have had guilty intentions, and are full of unease when their master comes near them.

There was not a sound in all the cabin, only the cracking and groaning of the bulkheads as the ship rolled in the storm, and the shuffling of the captain's mug as he pushed it to and fro upon the table top. And still monsieur stood and looked quiet and calm at the bosun.

Then the bosun rose up slowly, looking very awkward and oafish. He made to drain his mug, to show that he was at ease, but I heard the rim of it clitter foolish against his teeth, and he slopped the half of the toddy down the front of his serge shirt.

And still monsieur never spoke, nor said a further word, only looked after him, calm and quiet as he went out on to the deck, through the cuddy doorway, which opened out of the fore-end of the cabin.

Then monsieur turned to the captain and the two mates.

"I should think shame, gentlemen," he said, "to so demean yourselves upon the high seas by this drinking and easy speech with the rough shipmen; and more than this, by the neglecting of your duties as officers, so that the ship has been the great part of this watch without an officer upon the decks."

He said never another word but what I have told, and all spoken quiet and almost gentle. And those three rough men, that had just been planning his murder, answered him nothing; nor did one of them look at him, but sat there and shuffled their mugs and looked at their hands, all like the oafs they were; only, I could tell by the purple of Captain Drool's ears, that he was like a mad beast that is like to burst with the great stress of its anger and its cowardice.

Monsieur stood a matter of a few seconds; then, saying not another word, he went into his own cabin and closed the door.

When he was gone, the three men at the table stopped playing with their mugs and looking at their great hands, and they stared at each other. Captain Drool turned, and put out his tongue at monsieur's shut door, also he put his thumb to his nose and twiddled his great, coarse fingers; then he got up and went towards the companion steps. He tiptoed as he went, as if he were afraid monsieur might hear him. He crooked his finger to the two mates to follow him. And the three of them went up the steps into the night.

Presently, when I had cleared up the odd gear upon the table, and washed all, I put out the slush-lamp in the small pantry-place, for there was a lamp that hung always alight in the cabin. Then I fetched out my blanket from the locker, and hove it under the cabin table. I had no proper pillow, but used my sea-bag always, with my spare shift in it, for this purpose.

Also, it was my habit, each night when I turned in, to rig a length of spun yarn from one leg of the table to another, about a foot from the floor, so that if Captain Drool or the mates should want me in the night, I should escape being kicked in the head or face, for it was their way to wake me at any time by kicking at me under the table; but the spun yarn saved me a deal, for they never bothered to see what it was that their great sea-boots brought up against.

Now, when I had fixed all up for the night, and was rolled comfortable in the blanket, I lay a good while thinking, and half-minded to go to monsieur's door and knock gently to wake him. Yet, if they were watching the cabin from the deck – which they could do very easy without me seeing them – through the glass of the skylight, then I should be discovered, and they would, maybe, kill me when they murdered monsieur.

However, in the end, Monsieur Jeynois saved me the need of this risk, for he came out of his cabin presently, with his pea-jacket on, by which I saw that he meant to go up again on deck.

Then I put my head out a little from under the table, and said, "Monsieur!" But I was so in fear of them seeing me from the deck, that I spoke too low, and he was gone half across the cabin with his great strides – for he was a big man – before I had courage to call him proper.

But now I pushed my head out from under the table, and took my risk as I hoped a man should take it.

"Monsieur! Monsieur!" I said out loud. "Monsieur!"

He stopped, and I came out clean from under the table, dropping my blanket upon the floor, and standing there in my shirt, for I had no drawers.

"What is it, boy?" he asked in his quiet way, yet seeming to smile ever so little as he looked down at me.

"You're in horful danger, sir," I told him, for that was how I spoke those days, before even I was given the good schooling that I had later.

"How, boy?" he asked me.

"Cappen Drool an' Mestur Hankson an' Mestur Abbott an' Mestur Johns the bosun is going to murder you, sir. An' Cappen Drool is to have th' brig, an' he've offered t'others yourn share o' the prize-money an' a hundred guineas, an' they'm not to make no claim to own the ship," I told him, getting my words out all in a heap, because of my earnestness and eagerness to warn him.

And I can vouch that I had not one thought in that one and particular moment concerning my own safety, for which I am pleased to this day to remember.

"Go on, boy," said monsieur, still in his quiet voice. "What reason have you for saying this?"

"Aa heerd 'em, sir, whiles I were boilin' yon kettle an' grindin' the nutmeg for the toddy. Aa'm feared, sir, they'm meanin' to hout you ta-neet. Doan't 'ee go up on deck, sir, but hide yere in the cabing, an' I'll load ye a mint o' pistols, sir, an' we'll blow 'em into hell when they come down to murder ye."

"Boy," he said, "I put my trust in God, clean living, and a straight sword. And by these means, and your honest warning, am I prepared; but first, before we go further, if you must kill a man, why send him down in to hell? I would rather pray, as I slew him, that he might find heaven and a gladder wisdom."

I can remember now the quaint smile, kindly and human, that he gave me as I stood there in my shirt, staring up at him, and puzzled somewhat to know all the meanings of his speech, yet not entirely to misunderstand him.

"Now," he said in a moment, and clapping me twice gently upon the shoulder, "get back into your blanket, boy, and leave me freedom to meet my kind-intentioned visitors when they come."

Then suddenly I saw that he looked at my legs.

"Boy," he said, "where are your drawers?"

"Aa've got none, sir," I told him. "Maybe I'll buy two pair with my prize-money for next trip when we reach port."

He looked at me for a little; then, without a word, he turned and went back into his room. He came again in a moment, with a pair of fine silk drawers in his hand, the like of which I'd never seen.

"Put these on, boy," he said, and tossed them over my shoulder.

But I feared to touch the things, they were so fine and wonderful.

"I daurna wear 'em, sir," I told him. "They'm too fine."

But he laughed quietly.

"You'll have to turn the legs up," he said, and went back into his room.

I saw then that he meant it, and I put the things on, never thinking for the moment of the captain and the mates, or whether they might be watching me through the dark skylight.

When I was into the drawers, I feared to get back into my rough blanket, lest I should dirty them; and it was while I stood there in the fine silk drawers, and looked at my old blanket, that I knew suddenly that danger was upon us, for I heard the ladder that led up to the after companionway creak, like it always did when anyone put their weight on it. And this I heard, despite the constant creakings and groaning of the bulkheads as the ship rolled; for I knew that particular creak, having kept ears for it through many an hour at my work, to let it warn me whether any of my oaf masters were coming below. Yet whoever was on the ladder was creeping down surely in their bared feet, for there was never the sound of any clumsy boot to be heard.

I waited not a moment, but ran to the door of monsieur's room, which he had hooked open to prevent it slamming to and fro with the heavy rolling. I could see his back. He had taken off the heavy pea-coat, and was priming his pistols – four brace, all silver mounted.

"Monsieur!" I said – and, maybe, I looked a little white to think that murder was even then so near. "Monsieur, they'm comin', sir! They'm comin' down th' ladder."

"Under the table, boy, and into your blanket," he said quietly, turning to the door.

"Aa'll feight 'em along with ye," I said, feeling suddenly that a man – that's how I named myself! – could die only once. "They'll get tha' behind, through yon cuddy door through the fore-cabin. Gi'e me one o' them pistols, sir. Quick, sir, I hear 'em!"

I was surprised to find myself speak so usual to monsieur.

And then, to stop him thwarting me, because I feared they would stab him from behind if I did not guard the cuddy door, I stepped up close to him and said, very hasty and speaking scarce above a whisper: "They seen me warnin' ye, sir. It ain't no use me hidin'. They'll just cut my throat after they'm done murderin' you. Quick, sir! They're into th' cabing now! Gi'e me one o' the pistols!"

He said nothing, just pointed his thumb to where three of the pistols lay. He had the fourth in his right hand, and his sword out now in his left. He fought always with his sword in the left hand, as I knew, for I had seen him before at the taking of our prizes. I made no more ado, but took up a pistol in each hand, and as I did this monsieur stepped out of his room into the big cabin.

"Well, gentlemen," I heard him say, "you see, I have done you the honour of staying out of my bunk to welcome you. Perhaps, Captain Drool, you would prefer that I take you first? Or – no, is it to be all together? Ah, Master Abbott!"

Before this I had run out into the big cabin. There had been a loud and violent thudding of bare feet as they rushed monsieur, and as I reached the doorway of his room, I had seen Captain Drool and the two mates running at him with their cutlasses out. I had seen monsieur turn off a stab from Captain Drool with the barrel of his pistol, and then, with a wonderful quick movement of his wrist and forearm, he put his long sword right through Abbott's chest. Monsieur was wonderful with the sword.

Now, I had thought well when I had planned to guard monsieur's back; for at this moment the cuddy door, that led to the main deck through the fore-cabin in the fore part of the poop, was hove open with a great crash, and the noise of the seas and the gale filled the cabin as the bosun and the chief carpenter Maull came tumbling in, each with a drawn cutlass in his hand.

There was a loud shouting from Captain Drool and the mate, and the bosun and Maull the carpenter answered it with other shouts as they ran aft round the big table to get at monsieur's side and back.

I heard monsieur say, in a quiet voice: "Guard my back, boy!"

Just those words he said, and never looked round, but fenced off the mate's cutlass with the long barrel of his loaded pistol, and kept Captain Drool in play with his sword, all as easy and calm as if he were playing some game of skill for a wager rather than for his own life.

And you shall see me in that moment as proud as a young turkeycock with the trust he put in me; and full of good courage, both because of his calmness, that infected me the same way, and because of the fine pistols of two barrels each that I held ready in my hands.

"Mestur Johns and Mestur Maull," I shouted, "bide where ye are, or I shoot ye dead this moment!"

But, maybe, they thought of me as no more than a boy, and of no account, for they came with a great cheer and shouting round the end of the table, to get behind monsieur. And Maull, who was first, made a great stroke at monsieur with his cutlass, but the beams of the deck above his head were a better guard than me. For I had been too late with my pistols to save monsieur, if one of the great deck beams had not caught the top of the carpenter's cutlass and stopped the blow midway.

Yet monsieur was more watchful than I knew, for he spared one brief moment of his sword-fence with Captain Drool, and cut sideway with his left hand, so that his sword shone a moment like a flame in the lamplight. And immediately Maull loosed his cutlass, that was notched hard into the oaken beam, and clapped his hand to his neck, and went backwards into the bosun, singing out in a dreadful voice that he was dead. And dead he was in less than a minute after.

But before this I had loosed off twice into the bosun, and shot him in the arm and again in the thigh. And he also dropped his cutlass – or cutlash, as we called them – and made to reach the cuddy door, which he did in the end by creeping upon his knees and hands.

I have thought that monsieur had some notion to spare the lives of Captain Drool and the mate, for he had the loaded pistol in his right hand, and might have shot the mate at any moment; and equally he had the captain's life upon his sword point all the time, as it might be said.

But sudden the mate jumped back out of the fight, and whipped a pistol very smart out of the skirt of his blue coat that was a fancy of his from the body of a man he killed in the taking of our first prize.

Then monsieur used his own pistol in a wonderful quick way, and still fencing off Captain Drool's cutlass. As he loosed off, he called out in a low, quick voice: "I commend you to the mercy of God, John Abbott."

And with these words he had fired, before the mate had his aim taken. I have thought often upon those words.

At this moment, and as the mate fell upon the deck of the cabin and died, there was a great shouting out upon the main deck of the brig. I caught the meaning of certain of the shoutings:

"Monsieur's killing the cap'n! Monsieur's killing the cap'n!" I heard someone sing out twice, and maybe three times. Then the bosun's voice: "Smart, lads! He've cut Chip's throat, an' I be all shot through an' through!"

You must bear in mind that noises came oddly to me by reason of the great excitement of the moment, and the constant skythe, skythe of Captain Drool's cutlass along the blade of monsieur's lean sword, and the stamping of the captain's bare feet. There was also the noise of the gale and the sea-thunder that beat in through the open cuddy doorway out of the black night, and all the time the creaking and the groaning of the bulkheads, and the bashing and clattering of the cuddy door as it swung and thudded to and for with the brig's rolling.

Then, immediately, I heard the shouts rise clear and strong through the gale, and coming nearer until, in a moment, I heard the thudding of scores of feet racing aft along the decks.

And suddenly Captain Drool leaped back from his vain attacking of monsieur, and turned and ran for the cuddy door, shouting to the men to save him, though monsieur made never a step to follow.

Yet Captain Drool showed his deathly hatred of me in that moment, for he hove the cutlass out of his hand across the table in my face as he passed me.

But I stooped very quick, and the heavy blade struck the bulkhead over me. Then, stooped as I was, I shot Captain Drool in the head over the edge of the table, with no pity in me, for he had made so wantonly to kill me; also, I had been beat and kicked too oft by the brute. Moreover, while he lived to urge the men on, neither monsieur nor I might hope ever to come alive through the night.

Thus died Captain Drool, after monsieur had spared him a hundred times.

Now, in the instant after I shot the captain, I had jumped very speedy into monsieur's cabin, where I caught up his powder-flask and his bag of pistol bullets. Then I was into the big cabin again in a moment.

"Monsieur!" I called out, very breathless. "The cap'n's cabing, sir – the cap'n's cabing!"

And I ran past him into the captain's cabin, which had the door open, and was behind him as he stood there with his sword, staring very earnest and ready towards the cuddy doorway.

"Coom in, sir!" I began to call to him. "Coom in, sir!"

And then, before I could say another word, the big cabin seemed to be full of shouting men all in one moment, for they came leaping over the washboard of the cuddy alleyway, all helter-skelter through the cuddy doorway, which was in the forepart of the cabin, as you know by this.

There were maybe twenty and maybe thirty of them; but I never had time to think how many there were, but only that they filled all the for'ard part of the big cabin.

Those that were into the cabin stopped their shouting, and seemed to hang backward when they saw monsieur standing there with his sword in his hand. But there were more in the cuddy alleyway and out on the main deck that pushed and shouted to get in, so that the men in the cabin were all a-sway, they pushing backward and the men in the alleyway and upon the main deck pushing for'ard to come into the cabin.

I saw Jenkson, Allen, Turpen, and three or four others among the men that had broke into the cabin, and all of them were of the poorer sort, being no more than the rough scum of Portsmouth Town that had come to sea along with better men to make easy money; though, truly, there was not much easy money that ever I found this way!

Now, I knew these men were among the worst in the ship, and they had never a good word for monsieur behind his back, though quiet enough to his face, but had often called him a frog-eater and a French spy, and many another oafish name that had no base in fact; though, I doubt not, they near believed the ugly things they gave breath to.

And so you must see that last great scene, with monsieur standing there, and me behind him in the open doorway of the captain's cabin, and loading the fired-off barrels of the two fine pistols, the while that I stared at the men and monsieur. And I put a double charge of powder into each of the barrels, and upon each charge I dropped three bullets, for I saw that I should have less need of a nicety of shooting than of power to kill oft and plenty with the greatest speed.

As I have said, you must see that last great scene – how the men, though so plentiful, hung off from him, with their knives bare in their hands, ready for brutal slaughter, yet fearing him, while he stood quietly, and had no single thought to fear them, not if they had been a hundred strong. And every few moments there would fight through into the cabin another of the men, and would fall silent with the rest, staring like dumb brutes from monsieur to the dead and back again to monsieur. And all that brief while I loaded the pistols, with my hands trembling a little, though not so much with fear as might be supposed.

Now, there was hung on the bulkhead of the captain's cabin, close to my elbow, a great brass-mouthed blunderbuss, and, having a sudden thought from Providence, I stepped back into the captain's room, and reached this down very quick. I had pushed the two pistols into the front band of my new silk drawers, and now I took monsieur's powder-flask, and near emptied it down into the blunderbuss.

There was a pair of woollen hose that belonged to Captain Drool hanging over a wood peg, and I snatched one, and pushed it down with my hand into the great barrel of the blunderbuss that was so wide I could reach my arm down it. And after that I took the bag of pistol bullets, and emptied them, every one, down into the barrel upon the powder and the woollen hose; and afterwards I thrust down the other hose upon the bullets to hold them steady in the barrel. Then, very hasty yet with a proper care, I primed the great weapon. Afterwards I cast the powder-flask on to the deck, and ran very quick with the blunderbuss to the door of the cabin.

There was scarce any shouting now, for as this man and that crowded himself into the cabin, and saw monsieur standing there with his sword and the pistol, and the dead men lying about the deck of the big cabin, they grew silent.

But suddenly some of those that were at the back began to sing out odd questions and abuse concerning me.

"What's the cub doin' wi' the blunderbuss?" shouted one.

"It aren't never loaded!" sang out another of them.

And so they began to get their courage to attack monsieur by miscalling me that they had no fear of.

"Coom back inta th' cappen's cabing, monsieur!" I kept whispering, so that he might hear me yet the men hear nothing.

In the end he heard me, for I saw him shake his head as if he were bidding me be quiet. Then in a little he spoke to the men, choosing a moment when they were silent.

"For what reason have you come aft?" he said, speaking very ordinary.

"You'm murdered cappen – all vour of 'em!" shouted a man. "We'm coom, maybe, to zee if you'm likin' to be murdered, same as poor cappen an' dree oithers!"

"They'm geet na more'n they axed for!" I shouted out. "They tried to murder monsieur—"

"Quiet, boy!" said monsieur, without looking round.

"Yes, sir" I answered him; and then, in that moment of time, I heard a sound on the companion-ladder, and I shouted out to monsieur: "Thee's sommat coomin' down th' ladder, monsieur!"

As I shouted this, there was a slithering noise and a dull thud, as if someone had fallen, and then a low groaning. I stared hard at the doorway that led to the companion-ladder, and everyone in the cabin stared the same, save monsieur, who watched the men.

"It's the bosun!" shouted one of the men. "Howd'y, bosun!"

I saw the bosun's great head and face come round the edge of the doorway, about two feet from the floor. It was plain to me that he was creeping on his hands and knees, because of the wound in his leg.

Then, in a moment, he had whipped his hand in round the door, and I saw that there was a ship's pistol in his fist. He had fired before ever I could bring out a shout, and he hit monsieur somewhere, for I heard the horrid thud of the bullet, and I saw monsieur jerk his body as he was struck.

Then the bosun roared out in a great voice: "On to him, lads. On to him. He's done for!"

And, at the shout, the men broke forward upon monsieur in a crowd with their knives. Yet I was to see a wonderful thing, for monsieur stood firm and swaying to the roll of the ship, despite that he was hit, as I knew, and as the men rushed upon him his sword made a dozen quick flashes in the lamplight, so that it was like an uncertain glimmer among the men; and suddenly they gave back from him, and there were four of them went thudding to the floor and five more that were wounded.

Yet they had got at monsieur; for, as I ran forward to aid him with the blunderbuss, I saw that there were three knives in his breast, though he still kept upon his feet, with his great strength of body and his greater strength of mind, or will, which are both the same thing, as I do think.

"Monsieur!" I cried out, like a lad will call out when he sees his hero all destroyed. "Monsieur!" And he looked down at me and smiled a little, steadying himself with the point of his sword upon the deck of the cabin.

There was not another sound in the place, for they saw that he was done; but, indeed, I was not yet done.

"Great men ye are!" I called out. "Forty to one, ye swine, an' him wounded dead, an' ye fear him like death—"

I'd got no further, when one of them threw a knife at me, that cut me a bit in the arm; and on that I dropped upon my knee and lunged forward the great blunderbuss.

They gave back from it, like they might from death, which it was. But one of them called out that it was not loaded, and they came forward in a great rush once more with their knives. But I pulled the trigger of the blunderbuss, and loosed into them near half a flask of good powder and maybe two pounds' weight of pistol bullets.

The cabin was filled with the smoke of the great weapon, and out of the smoke there were dreadful screamings and the thuddings of feet; but for my part I lay flat upon my back, all shaken and dazed from the kick of the blunderbuss.

Then I rolled over and got upon my knees; and as I did so I saw that monsieur lay quiet beside me.

I dropped the blunderbuss, and caught monsieur quickly by the shoulders, and dragged him, upon his back, into the captain's cabin. Then I shut the door very hasty, and slid the bolt, and afterwards I drew and pushed one of the captain's sea chests up against it.

When I had done this, I felt round for the box where Captain Drool had kept his flint and steel, for there was no light in the place, now that I had shut the door upon the lamp in the big cabin.

Presently, in no more than a minute, I had the captain's lamp alight, which burned very bright with good whale oil; and I stooped then quickly to care for monsieur.

I found him lying silent where I had drawn him; but his eyes were open, and, when I knelt by him, he looked at me, quiet and natural, yet with a little slowness in the way that he moved his eyes.

"Monsieur!" I said, near sobbing because he was so near gone. "Monsieur!"

There was a minute of silence between us, and I heard the uproar ease outside the main cabin; but the door was thick and heavy for a ship's door, and deadened the sounds maybe more than I knew.

Abruptly, there came almost a stillness out in the big cabin; and then, sudden, a great blow struck upon the door, that set all the bulkheads jarring and the telescopes in the beckets leaping.

But I had them upon the hip, for I shouted out in my lad's voice, very hoarse and desperate: "If ye break the door, I'll blow the ship to hell. Aa've geet the powder-trap oppen, an' Aa've me pistols. Sitha! If ye break in the door, Aa'll loose off me pistol into the powder!"

Just that I sung out to them; and never another blow was struck upon the door, for the powder was stored under the deck of Captain Drool's cabin, as all the ship knew, and I better than any, being the lad that had cleaned his cabin many a score of times. And this is the reason that I chose to retreat there from the men.

"Boy," I heard monsieur saying from the floor, "is the hatch open?"

"No, monsieur," I said, grinning a little at the easy way I had driven the men off.

"Open it, boy," he said gravely. "Nor tell ever a lie with a light tongue. And when you have to deal a man the bitterness of death, be not over eager to consign him to hell, but rather to God, who understandeth all and forgiveth all."

"Yes, sir," I said; and opened the powder-hatch, with a great fear at my heart that I was truly come to the end of life.

"Am I to shoot into th' powder, sir?" I asked him, all strung-up and ready to shut my eyes and fire at his bidding.

But he waved his fingers a little for me to come to him; and when I was come to him, he lay a moment and looked up at me, seeming to smile a little in spite of his pain.

"You are a strange boy," he said at last in a weak voice. "Fetch me a sheet of paper from the captain's desk – nay, fetch me the logbook and a quill and the ink."

When I had fetched these, he bid me put them upon the deck, to the left of him, and to open the logbook at the last entry, also to wet the quill ready.

"Now, boy," he whispered, "make good haste and gentle, and help me over a little upon my left side. Quick now, before I am gone, or it will be too late to do God's own justice."

His voice was very weak, and whistled thin and strange as he spoke; and when I had helped him with all my power of gentleness on to his side, I saw how he had been lying there in his blood.

"Steady me so, boy," he whispered; and I steadied him while he wrote.

And as he wrote, labouring to hold in his groans and to contain all his senses to his purpose, I could see the handles of the knives in his breast. And so he writ, and made no ado of the agony it cost him; but truly a greater victory over mortal pain I could think a man never won.

Now, this is the letter, which I have by me to this day, though I was too ignorant at that time to know what it was that he wrote:

To Master Alfred Sylles,
    The Corner House,
        Portsmouth Town.
Dear Master Sylles, – I write this near death, and with no power to write much. See that justice be done me in this fashion, to wit, that the boy who bears this, John Merlyn, shall be mine heir. See that he go to a good school, well equipt. I will tell him the names of my dead lady, so that you shall know that he is indeed the youth of this my will and last testament, though none here can witness, for I am alone save for this boy, who hath fought by and for me as I could have wished mine own son to fight.

From him will you have all the story.

Farewell, dear Master Sylles.

ARTOIS JEYNOIS.

When this was writ, he laid the quill down between the pages, so that the rolling of the ship should not squander it. But when I would have helped steady him again on to his back, he bid me wait and listen, for that he would certainly die with his words unsaid when he moved to lie down again.

"Remember these three names, my boy," he said; "nor tell them to any on earth save Master Sylles of the Corner House of Portsmouth Town, whom you know by repute, and to whom I have writ this letter. The names are Mercelle Avonynne Elaise. Now, repeat them till you can never let them slip."

He waited while I said them over a dozen times, maybe, then he caught his breath a little, and seemed as if he were gone; but presently he breathed again, but with a louder noise and bleeding very sadly.

"To Master Sylles tell all that you know," he said; "and because you have been a brave and a faithful lad, I bequeath to you my sword, to use only with honour."

He caught his breath again, and I trembled with a strange lad's ague of pity to know how to ease him; but after a little while he began again, but whispering: "How you shall escape, lad, I know not; but hold this cabin, for here they are in fear of you, because of the powder. Presently, when the ship is into the Channel, you may have chance to swim ashore. But wrap the letter up safe first in an oilskin. Tell Master Sylles all. Now, may God be with you, boy. Lay me down."

He sank his great shoulder against me as he spoke, and slid round on to his back with a strange, deep groan, and in that moment the light went clean out of his eyes, and I saw that he was truly dead.

And I knelt there beside him, and cried as only a lad can cry over his dead hero.

Of the manner of my escape, I need to tell but little here, for that night the men, being in fear of the law, ran the brig ashore below the Lizards, thinking to drown the ship and me, and so hide their foul work upon the stark rocks.

But they made a bad business of their landing, and many were drowned because of the heavy seas; but I, who stayed in the ship, was safe, for she held together until the morning, when the weather was grown fine; and I swam ashore, with monsieur's sword made fast to my back.

Yet it was a matter of twelve weary days after this before I came safe into Portsmouth Town, where I learned from good Master Sylles that I was the heir of monsieur. And how good Master Sylles did weep – for he had loved him – when I told him all concerning the vile murdering of monsieur.

But he stayed not at weeping, being a practical man as well as a warm friend, for when the bosun returned to Portsmouth Town a while after, supposing me to be drowned in the brig, Master Sylles had the watch upon him within the hour, and hailed him to high justice, so that a week later the bosun was hanged in chains at the corner of the four roads outside Portsmouth Town, to be for a warning to shipmen and landsmen that the trade of murder shall bring eternal sorrow.

And at last I am come to an end of my telling of that dear friend of my youth, who is with me in my memory all the long years of my life. And even in that early day did his goodness and charity affect me; so that, as well I do mind me, once when I passed the dried body of the bosun, I must stop and loose off my cap, and set up a prayer to God for him, for I knew that Monsieur Jeynois would so have wished it.

THE BURNING DECK

Peter T. Garratt

Until Peter Garratt reminded me I had forgotten that the poem "Casabianca", which begins with the well-known line, "The boy stood on the burning deck . . .", was based on an episode at the Battle of the Nile. Also known as the Battle of Aboukir Bay (or Abu Quir as the author more accurately spells it here), this was the first fleet action in which Nelson was in command. It took place on 1 August 1798. Nelson was still two months short of his fortieth birthday, but the outcome made him a national hero.

Peter Garratt (b. 1949) is a clinical psychologist and the author of many mystery, fantasy and science-fiction stories. He has a taste for major battles, however, as he has also cast a new perspective on the Charge of the Light Brigade in my anthology The Mammoth Book of Sword and Honour.

For those interested I have appended the poem "Casabianca" after this story.

"There's a sail there, look! North-north-west, heading this way!" The boy, our youngest aspirant, was full of excitement. He was jumping up and down in the crow's nest, a most dubious procedure, as even on the biggest ship in the fleet the observation station was little more than half a large barrel with the mizzen running through it like a giant spile. I told him sharply to sit and offered him the glass.

"So, you've seen a sail, but what is it? Is it a man-o'-war, a barque, a brigantine or a fishing smack? Is it French, English, Turkish or Marmaluke?"

When I served in the navy of the former regime, I sometimes taught the aspirants (or midshipmen as we used to call them), though that was more often done by the ship's chaplain. Once this modern age began, it would have been absurd to have a chaplain aboard: when I returned to the navy under the influence of the two Corsicans, Captain Louis Casa Bianca and General Bonaparte himself, I resumed teaching, though my official post was secretary to Admiral Brueys.

There were a lot of aspirants on the ship, for parents knew promotion would be rapid at sea, many traitor officers having deserted the republic. Of all the lads I had taught, this son of Casa Bianca was the most promising. He extended the glass, aligned it on the sail he had called out for, focused and said, "It's quite small. One mast, no topsails or topgallants. I think the sail is a triangle . . . lateen sail."

"So?"

"I think it's a caïque. Or a dhow. That's it, an Egyptian dhow."

"It's probably just a local coaster. Any flag?" I didn't tell him that these lateen-sailed boats had been sighted daily since we arrived at Abu Quir a month before.

However, young Giacimo Casa Bianca was saying excitedly, "I can't see any flag. Could it be a dhow the English have taken to use for spying?"

"Well, how could you tell? What would a spy ship do?"

"Look at us and count our ships? Try to sneak aboard and steal our plans!"

"You've been reading too many romance books, and not enough of the texts I set you! Now, what ships do the English use for scouting?"

"Frigates of course!" He swung the telescope back to the horizon, in case frigates had suddenly appeared. I doubted he knew that just before we reached Alexandria an English fleet had passed by without any frigates.

I said, "So, how do we know if this is a spy dhow? Without sending one of our own frigates to check?" I glanced anxiously downward, and to port. None of our frigates, anchored safely inside our strong defensive line, was showing any sign of putting to sea. I tried not to worry. I doubted the dhow was an English scout, and I knew Brueys's priority was to refit and resupply the whole fleet as soon as possible, but it didn't seem right not to have a single scoutship at sea.

The boy was studying the dhow through his glass. "I don't see any signal flags!"

"Which way would a spy need to go, to start a chain of signals back to his fleet?"

He considered seriously, started to draw a little map in the air with his finger. "Let's see, they've been to Alexandria, that's where the general landed, so they may have gone back there. That's west . . . to the left. So, they'll turn round and go left – if their ships are at Alexandria and they want to signal that ours are here!"

"That's most likely, isn't it. Well done, Giacimo! Now, let's see what they do."

We were looking almost due north, across the spit of sand that connects Abu Quir island to the mainland. It's so low that in tidal waters it would often be submerged. As it was, we could see the dhow clearly. It was starting to pass us. Soon it would be obscured at least briefly by the island. He volunteered: "I reckon with the wind in the north they could ware and sail back the way they came, so it doesn't look as though they are English spies!" He sounded regretful. I was proud of his progress, but still wondered if he had any idea of what would happen if the enemy fleet did return to Egypt. But then at his age, I had been glumly preparing to go to *lycée*, and full of the same dreams of action and adventure, even with no great cause or leader to inspire.

I said gently, "Time for classes."

"Oh. Thank you for letting me up here, Citizen Lieutenant Dumarille." He was polite as well as advanced. He clambered, almost vaulted, over the edge of the nest and scampered rapidly down the ratlines. I followed at a more sedate pace, realizing that this trip to the top observation point, far from being a bit of a treat, was something he was almost certainly as used to as the older aspirants.

It was nine on a fine morning, early in Thermidor in a warm climate, still eased by the fresh Meltemi from the north. The air was so clear I felt I could have seen the English fleet if they had scarcely left England. It was the sort of clear-air morning on which I yearned for the day when I would be able to bring a group of boys, and perhaps some rather older girls, to these latitudes for a study trip which would also be a holiday. I cursed the stubborn English with their pig-headed loyalty to their gross German King! Without them, these youths I was teaching would have so much more to look forward to than I had had, a quarter century ago!

I reached the bottom, made to jump back to the deck, then had to stop. One of the water-boats had already completed its first run of the day – surprisingly, in view of the difficulties the local people made when we went ashore for essential supplies – and had already loaded its barrels on to the deck and set off again. No one had started to get them below, and they stood on end, in an irregular row like recruits trying to parade, from the davit to the shroud I had just descended. I picked my way gingerly over the obstruction, noticing it would be impossible to work a couple of the guns till the barrels were moved. Those guns pointed over the inshore shallows into which the enemy could hardly be expected to venture: but though it burned my stomach to admit it, it was the kind of sloppy work which would never have been tolerated in former times, and was getting more common.

As I reached the deck young Giacimo hurried, almost scampered back to me, stiffened, gave a rather smart salute, and said, "Citizen Lieutenant Dumarille, no classes this morning. You're to report to the admiral at once!"

The boats I could see around the ship were not supply boats but barges which had brought senior officers from other ships. Rear-Admiral Blanquet-Duchayla, who commanded the front of the line, was just arriving. I saw Brueys greet him and then they went below to the Great Cabin. I was about to go for my uniform jacket when the boy said, "If there are no lessons, can we go ashore? Can we?"

"If there's a boat. Mind you, I hear it's quite dangerous. The local people are causing trouble for some reason. You'd better ask your father."

Captain Louis Casa Bianca was still on the quarterdeck, preparing to go below to the council of war. His son ran over to him and gave him a salute of sorts, which he didn't return, but instead affectionately chucked the lad's head. As I came up he was saying, "No no, it's painting duty for you lads if you're planning to skip your homework! Besides, there won't be any more boats to the shore today!"

I saluted and said, "I saw a water-boat just leaving."

I meant to complain that the barrels hadn't been stowed, but Captain Casa Bianca interrupted me: "That was yesterday's boat! The damned Egyptians wouldn't give access to the wells, and they had to dig. This country's no place for boys, until the general wins the locals over! Then you can take your class to Alexandria and give them a lesson on Egyptian history, ending of course with liberation and revolution! Now, get painting! Nothing fancy, mind, none of your mother's fiddly things!"

I never knew if Casa Bianca's frequent references to his wife were proprietorial jibes in my direction, or merely blindly uxorious. He had been at sea when I courted the Lily of Toulon, as I was when he married her. He never referred directly to knowing we had met, but though I had rejoined on his request, his attitude to me seemed more hostile than before. I showed no emotion as my captain said "*Au revoir*" to the boy who was so like his mother, and so little like him. The lad was tall for his age and very slim. He had his mother's elfin, pale-complexioned face and water-blue eyes, even her peach-red cheekbones. Only his hair was Corsican, dark and rebellious, not quite long enough for the seaman's pigtail he was attempting. Captain Casa Bianca was stocky, and though not so short as his general, he had something of the great leader's strut and charisma.

We went below. I would normally enjoy a visit to the main cabin of a great ship, and no ship ever built was bigger or had finer cabins than the *Orient*. This time I screwed up my nose. Certain of the academic citizens who had accompanied General Bonaparte had sailed with him on the flagship, and stowed the supplies for their chemical research in the cabin area. My efforts to persuade these great scholars that I too was a man of learning had not been very successful, but one of them confided that his purpose was to analyze the substances used by the Egyptians in former times to preserve and embalm. The academics had gone ashore in Alexandria, and had not yet removed their jars of chemicals, which had started to leak. The stench was no pleasanter than that of the turpentine the painting crew were using to clean their brushes. For that reason, plus the heat, the windows of the Great Cabin were permanently thrown open, so we could also smell dry salt air and fairly cool water, and in the distance, the mud of the delta.

Brueys told me to spread out a newly prepared chart of Abu Quir and a map of the Mediterranean. Captains were still arriving, and coffee was being served. The chef made it a bit strong for my taste, but at least it helped mask the chemicals. I displayed the maps, and had a minute to look at the new chart. Our defensive line of thirteen anchored ships, ranging from the usual 74s to our mighty 120-gun *Orient* were sketched on to it. We were anchored near the edge of the shoals that made the western part of the bay treacherous. To the north, our van was protected by the battery on Abu Quir island. The ships most in need of refit were stationed there. I was disturbed to see that the shoals were not quite so shallow as we had assumed. In theory, if the enemy had such a chart, we could be attacked in the van or even outflanked and taken on the inshore side, where our guns were largely unmanned. But no chart could be more up to date than ours, and few had ever been made. To venture into these waters without one would be suicide, so if they came, they would have to attack the strongest part of our line.

Brueys called the meeting to order. Instead of the chart I had been studying, he focused on the map of the whole Mediterranean. His summary of the situation I had heard and made notes on before. Still, I liked Brueys. He was an aristo, but had stayed loyal to France when the tide of revolution was perhaps too high. He was tall, pale, prematurely white-haired, and looked every inch a man who didn't want to be where he was. If it had been up to him, we would never have left Toulon without more supplies, and more experienced seamen, officers and gunners.

He hinted we should make for the nearest French base, the island of Corfu. We now had supplies to get there, and might be able to recruit, which was impossible in Egypt. At Abu Quir, our defensive position would be almost impregnable if the English were rash enough to attack us. However, Alexandria was their more logical target. They might decide to blockade it, cutting the great French expedition to the Orient off from home. The harbour mouth was narrow and easy to blockade: we dared not risk getting trapped inside. But if the enemy could draw us out to sea they would have a distinct advantage, for half our guns would be unmanned.

I started writing the minutes, one of my duties as Brueys's secretary. Privately, I was all in favour of Corfu: I felt the hot sun and air of romance we had found in Egypt had induced the wrong spirit in the crew, not that we were seeing any of the great sites in this unfriendly part of the delta. Others disagreed, most notably Casa Bianca, who contributed before any of the rear-admirals had a chance to speak: "Has Citizen General Bonaparte given specific instructions about Corfu?"

Brueys replied stiffly, as he always did when reminded that a young Corsican landsman was his superior: "Not specific. We are to await news of his progress. No word has come after nearly a month."

Casa Bianca replied jovially: "So, you're not saying we should abandon the general! We all know there are only two possible outcomes to this campaign. One, a swift and brilliant victory for the general, putting all the resources of Egypt at our disposal. Or, a more difficult campaign. It looks like these Egyptians are so used to being ruled by Turkish slaves that they're slow to recognize liberty. So, progress is slow! Withdrawing the fleet would be exactly the wrong impression to give!"

Most of the captains nodded. They were fast-promoted, or men brought in from the merchant service after the revolution. They were good seamen, but few had fought in a battle, let alone planned one. The junior admirals were less impressed, but did not look keen to speak. Brueys said, "As we are not speaking in order of seniority, I fancy asking Citizen Lieutenant Dumarille to contribute."

He glanced at me sidelong. He valued my opinion as a sailor. I had joined the navy at the same time as Casa Bianca, though I left when the American war finished and we returned to find the former regime still in place. He also seemed to think of me as a politician. He knew I had tried life in America during the Terror, and returned when the republic was saved by the Directors. No doubt he thought I watched him for the Directors as Casa Bianca did for Bonaparte.

I pointed to the large map. "The question is, where are the enemy? If they are returning, we need to be on full alert, stop long-term projects like painting . . ."

Casa Bianca pointed to Gibraltar on the map. "Here they are. When Napoleon Bonaparte's good fortune énabled us to avoid them earlier, they'll have panicked. They must be afraid he was sailing for the Straits, then the Channel, to attack England. That'll be their big fear, Napoleon in England! That's where they'll be!"

Everyone seemed to want to agree with him except Blanquet-Duchayla, who said, "By my calculations of distances and observed wind speeds, they could still be searching for us all round the eastern Mediterranean. If they are planning to return here, they haven't quite had time yet, but they could be close."

I nodded, having made similar calculations at Brueys's request. Before anyone could comment, we heard a shot in the distance. Someone said, "What was that?" then there were three or four more reports, very definitely shots, muskets probably.

We sprang to our feet. Casa Bianca hurried to the open

window. He exclaimed, "As I thought! One of our shore parties has run into trouble again! Citizens, all my boats are out, and I'll need to borrow some of your barges to take reinforcements!"

Of course, it was totally inappropriate for a flag captain to interrupt a council of war in order to requisition barges for a shore party, let alone to lead it himself, but that was the kind of man Casa Bianca was. He had always been a leader, but was never noted as a strategist. He was older than Bonaparte, but had recently started to model himself on his fellow Corsican. So when he departed shoreward with his requisitioned barges, no one objected, and the conference broke up, as if the ship itself had been attacked. The officers departed two to a barge.

In fact there was no more firing that day. All our boats and barges eventually returned with tales of harassment from the locals, but no full-scale attack. Brueys dictated a letter to Bonaparte, bitterly complaining that the treasury for the whole expedition was still aboard the *Orient*, but he was not permitted to spend any of it on supplies. The natives were expected to contribute to their liberation as willingly as they would if already part of the French Republic.

The next morning was fine, as it always is in Egypt, though light came later than a summer morning at home. Unable to forget that the enemy might soon arrive, I went alone to the mizzen top and scoured the horizon. The boys were still at breakfast. It was cool there in the crow's nest, and the sea was still the dark wine of Homer; at least in the east, where an unusually red sunrise gave it the shade of a nice claret. The west, where they would appear, was just dark. Strain as I did through the glass, I saw no sail of any kind by the time the sun was up.

Relieved, I went down, to find supply boats, rather overloaded with armed men, already setting out for the shore. Casa Bianca was on the quarterdeck, allowing, in his informal way, the boys to surround and pester him for leave to adventure on shore. Some had armed themselves with dirks or pistols. The captain was talking to them genially: "Haven't I told you how expensive ships are, and how more are lost to rot and worm than the guns of the English?" They made disparaging sounds about the enemy, but shut up as he said; "Paint and polish will stop that!"

While they painted, I took more dictation. Brueys was compiling a report for Bonaparte which listed the shortages he faced at great length; perhaps he hoped the landsman would be intimidated by weight of detail into agreeing Brueys's demands, for money to buy supplies locally and army gunners to fire our unmanned pieces. He also ordered a copy sent to the Directors in Paris.

This work took most of the morning. I dined with the admiral, venturing to ask if we would soon send the frigates out on patrol. He replied that they had even more need of resupply than the other ships, and could be longer at sea: that afternoon I should take the barge and visit each of the frigates, compiling a list of who was short of what. The next day, the best supplied could set out.

While I was waiting for the barge, the boys having been given a break from painting for the heat of the day, I was again implored by young Giacimo Casa Bianca for a visit to the mizzen top. I think he would have preferred the main crow's nest, but that was the official lookout, and he knew better than to try there.

I agreed without thinking; but although I liked the boy very much, and was proud he had learned so fast, I found once we were aloft that I was awkward in his company. This wasn't because of his minimal resemblance to his father, who had once been a friend also, and who had persuaded me that the republic needed me in the navy. The truth was he was getting too like his mother, whom I had once loved, and who had offered her heart to me, but her hand to Louis Casa Bianca, who was more senior and under the former regime had much better prospects.

It was very hot, but at least there was a good breeze from just west of north. A couple of single-masted dhows were cruising slowly, apparently fishing, but there was nothing worrying to be seen. The boy studied them eagerly through the glass, then said abruptly, "Citizen, is it true that you don't like General Bonaparte?"

"He's a good general," I replied automatically. "But he isn't an admiral!"

"But General Bonaparte is the great leader whose star is rising!"

I tried to explain, in simple words, the difference between military and political leadership, but I could see he was not listening. I changed tack: "This star. You know I told you the bright star we can see before it's dark in the evening is the same star we see at other times after dawn?" He nodded reluctantly. He was knowledgeable about stars. "Well, I once heard a Bonaparte supporter point to the morning star and say it was the general's star, it would somehow bring him luck. The same evening, he said the same thing about a different star!"

The boy did not respond, instead turning the glass towards the horizon. I did not tell him I had been disparaging his father. Suddenly he said, "Look! Topsails! Over there, just north of west!"

I almost snatched the telescope. "Yes. Technically, all we can see so far are topgallants—"

"No, *No*! Look . . . look there!"

I trained the telescope carefully along the horizon. There were topsails, but they belonged to another ship, rather closer, so all but the lowest course of her sails were visible. She was a three-master, possibly a man-o'-war.

The *Orient* was almost silent. I could hear the low creak of the rigging, almost the slap of small waves against the bow. It seemed everyone was sleeping off their lunch, probably including the official lookout in the main crow's nest. I yelled in his direction: "Two ships! West-north-west!" and saw him jump into action.

The boy was looking scared for once. "Is it the enemy?"

"We don't know yet. Let's see what they do!"

As the lookout started to shout about the sighting, I aligned the telescope on the leading ship. I said, "We can see his whole rig now. What we have to watch for is a lot of small flags going up."

"Signal flags?"

"That's it. I can't see any yet. Have a look."

He looked for a while then said, "Can they see us?"

"We'll be less visible, because we're behind the sandspit, and we've no sails set. But before long they'll see this many masts, if that's what they're looking for."

"There's something going up. Are those signal flags?"

I took the telescope. Strings of small flags were indeed running up. I turned to the second, more distant ship. By now I could see most of her rig, and after what felt like a long wait she too raised extra flags.

"That's it! They're signalling back to the main fleet. I must go to the admiral!" I hurried down to the deck. This time, the boy came more slowly. I found Admiral Brueys on deck. He was ordering the "Prepare for Action" signal to be flown, and one to call another council of war. Casa Bianca was bustling round arranging for the guns to be cleared, though mainly on the starboard side: to port, unstowed supplies and even pots of paint, varnish and turps created an unsightly clutter.

That council of war was a grim affair. There were no recriminations about the repeated decision to not leave for Corfu. Though we were in greater personal danger at Abu Quir, we knew we were needed there by the revolution. (Or by Bonaparte, depending on which received our loyalty.) The key issue was whether to remain in our defensive position adjoining the shoals, or to seek the greater flexibility we would gain by putting to sea.

By that time the main enemy fleet had been sighted, at least a dozen big ships. At sea, they would probably try to break our line and surround a part of it. If that happened, our inability to man both batteries on most of the ships would be a disadvantage. Because the wind was against us, we would have to beat painfully out of the anchorage, and would be lucky to get the whole fleet out before they were in line-breaking range. Besides, many men were still ashore.

Blanquet-Duchayla was the only one to disagree. He commanded the front of the line, old ships in poor repair. He was afraid the enemy might have charted the bay on their previous visit a month before. If that had happened they would be able to take advantage of our weakness by attacking the van, not the centre or rear.

No one else voted to move. After all, as Casa Bianca pointed out, the English had left Alexandria in a great hurry, scarcely bothering to drop anchor before setting sail. It was clear they were in a funk, had no idea where to look for the French fleet, and were rushing wildly around without taking the time to do anything so methodical as make a chart. Probably they would not dare enter the bay at all, but if they did, French gunnery would make them regret it!

Brueys summed up. There were tactical arguments both ways, but the wind direction made the option of fighting at sea the more difficult one. Therefore we would stick to our plan and fight at anchor. To stop them breaking the line, our ships would be double-anchored and connected by cables.

The meeting ended by late afternoon. The enemy fleet was now visible from the quarterdeck, close-hauled to the north wind and making due east. The ships were strung out in no kind of order, certainly not a line of battle. Our supply boats were returning, with supplies as well as men, then setting out again for the shore. I asked Brueys if the boats would not be better employed joining the ships by cable, as he had planned.

He glanced at the direction of the sun, then at his watch. "It's getting late. It'll be an hour till they can even think about turning into the bay. Soon after that it'll start to get dark. They may come in tomorrow, but they can hardly be mad enough to try a night battle without a chart. Let's get all the men back; as it is some of them won't be back till morning. Cabling can be done after dark."

At that moment, I saw the boy, the young Casa Bianca. He was standing near the davits where the latest boat was being unloaded. He was bigger than most boys his age, but at that moment he looked smaller. All the confidence had gone from him, his face was absurdly white for that climate, and he was looking longingly at the boat, not as a conveyance to adventure, but to escape. I had never seen him look more like his mother, not as she was when happy and loving, but as she had looked on a certain day thirteen years ago, or on another, nine years later, when she had come to Paris in an earlier Thermidor, after our second liberation. She had intended to take advantage of the heady atmosphere of those days, libidinous as well as liberated, but had all too soon returned to her husband.

Young Casa Bianca came over to me. Though he was the youngest, there were a few other boys trailing behind him. He said quietly, "What should we do?"

I looked at his ghost-like face, at the boat, and across the spit of sand at the English fleet. I could now count fourteen ships, mostly 74s by the look of them. Their hulls were all painted in black and amber stripes, and all had crammed on maximum sail, skysails even. They looked in a hurry as they swept past, hurrying for the point where they could turn inward and engage us; looking indeed like a swarm of angry hornets buzzing to attack.

I said to the boy, "Perhaps this is a time to get some onshore experience. Go on the boat, make sure all the shore parties are assembled and on their way back here, and don't come back till the last boat, even if it's tomorrow morning!"

He turned to go, still looking very subdued, then I heard a step behind me, and Casa Bianca the father strutted up: "What the devil's this! Where are you sending my boys? My boy!"

"Ashore. I think it'll be safer there."

"Safer! With the English cowering out to sea, and the land swarming with ungrateful Egyptian pirates? This ship has sides thicker than the Bastille; she'll never be sunk by the English and she'll certainly never surrender to them!" He paused. The boy was nodding, looking oddly grateful. The issue seemed closed, but he could not resist saying, "And if she did, if there's one thing for a young boy that's worse than falling into English hands, it'd be to be enslaved by these" – he gestured wildly towards the shore – "degenerates!" He pointed at me threateningly: "Or is that what you want, you with your Greek fancies and perverse universities!"

He wheeled away abruptly, without forcing from me a response which in the old days would have been bound to be thought insubordinate, and probably still would. He often made similar comments about my single state and near-monastic scholarly lifestyle. I wondered if he assumed that I was a sad fellow who could never aspire to sleep with a beautiful woman like his wife; or if on the contrary he was too aware that that was not the case.

Someone shouted, "Signal, English flagship!" I ran up the steps to the quarterdeck and focused my glass. There was an admiral's pennant on a ship halfway down the enemy line, and signal flags were running up the masts. I took up a position where Brueys was between me and Casa Bianca, and watched as the English ships continued to sail east. They did not appear to change course or speed, until one started to disappear behind the small island at the end of the sandspit. I said to the admiral, "Do you think they'll come in tonight?"

It was late, but still over an hour to sundown. He replied, "He's made a signal and no one's doing anything we can see as new or different. It could be an order to carry out some preconceived plan."

Casa Bianca heard this, and gave the word for all gunners to go to their stations. They did, including some who had been working on stowing gear away. Meanwhile, we watched the topgallants of the lead enemy ship go past the island till she emerged. The sun was low in the west now, and she cast a long shadow over the ripples on the cool, shining blue water ahead of her. More ships started to pass the island, then we saw the sails of the lead ship moving, being pulled round to turn her full into the wind. Very soon she was turning on to a southerly course that would bring her right into the bay. Casa Bianca said, "My God! If he does exist! What was it Cromwell said: 'God has delivered them into our hands!'"

Many of the men in hearing cheered, and one or two said a mocking, "Amen!" For myself, I reflected that the English had kept their God even when toying with revolution, but we French had abolished Him, and would have to prevail without

His help. For myself, I wondered what had possessed me to rejoin the navy. Of course, I still admired Bonaparte and like every Frenchman was grateful for his military skills. And at one time I had been under the spell of Casa Bianca, despite our rivalry. If people were seeing Bonaparte as a demigod, Casa Bianca was his representative at sea. But Bonaparte was only half a god: he was a land god.

More and more of the English ships had passed the island and swung round, the red evening sun on their white sails creating a vast shadow on the sea. Now there came the first gunfire: not theirs, but ours, the battery we had placed on the island. A wild, ragged cheer rose from our ships, but it didn't last. The shots all fell short and the enemy proceeded without bothering to return fire. Instead, we heard a bizarre thing: the men on the English ships seemed to be cheering themselves: not spontaneously, but a regular hip-hurrah.

This had a strange effect on our men. Some tried a return cheer, but they weren't used to it. It was Casa Bianca who seized the moment. He shouted, "Come on, lads! Don't listen to that nonsense! How about the Marseilles Song? Let 'em have it!"

And we did, chorus after chorus of "To arms Citizens! Form your Battalions!" echoing out and largely drowning the hoarse English cheering.

But no song could disguise the fact that the enemy were heading directly for the weak front of our line. The ships there tried a few shots, but sail-less and at anchor they couldn't get the angle right. The English were on a tight path heading directly for the bow of our leading ship. Brueys muttered, "Damn them! They must have got a chart from somewhere!" I supposed they had, though through my glass I could see leadsmen taking soundings from the bows of some of the ships.

Then a terrible thing happened. The leading ship turned slightly to the west, and as she did so, fired a broadside directly into the poorly protected bow of our lead ship, *Guerrière*. A few of ours again tried firing, but couldn't get the angle.

Everyone on the quarterdeck of the *Orient* was silent. The English were sailing across the front of our line to attack the scarcely defended inshore sides of our ships. In theory they should have been in severe danger of running aground, but in practice I knew that wouldn't necessarily happen. The English strategy was to sail inshore of our line, so close they could have fired pistols, but instead discharging full broadsides into ships that were completely unprepared. The leader was followed by three or four more Englishmen; there was already so much smoke that I could not see quite how many.

Inside our line were anchored our four frigates. Up to that point, both sides had obeyed the convention that massive ships-of-the-line and flimsily built frigates ignored each other during a fleet action. However, the captain of our nearest frigate, the *Sérieuse*, bravely decided that if no one else could return the fire of the English attackers, he must do so, and at last the roar of a French broadside joined the thunder of the English.

Meanwhile, Casa Bianca was yelling out orders to get as many of the inshore-facing guns as possible ready for action. Men started running across the deck, or down from the rigging. I tried not to imagine the infinitely worse things that must be happening on the *Guerrière* and the other ships, where men would be hurrying to open their inshore gunports under continuous enemy fire.

The English had no such problem. The leading ship, the one just attacked by the frigate *Sérieuse*, started firing broadsides from both batteries almost at once. I saw shot smashing into the side of the brave frigate, even on the waterline, with splinters and cascades of water flying into the air.

Some of the *Orient*'s inshore guns were now loaded and run out, but it was plain we were desperately short of crews for all the 120, and many men had yet to return from shore. Casa Bianca turned to me. "Round up your aspirants and get them on to powder-carrying duties with the rest of the boys."

It wasn't difficult. The lads were all still on deck, or perched in the lower part of the ratlines, watching the action. I could see fascination and excitement, but also terror. By that time the wind was carrying down the smell of gunsmoke. Young Giacimo, who was regarded as a leader by the slightly older boys, for his character and intelligence as much as his connections, was standing like a little ramrod. I saw him fighting a tear as he gestured to the enemy and said, "I though they weren't supposed to be able to do this!"

"Well they have!" I snapped, then more gently, "Look! the ships that have outflanked us seem to be anchoring. If any more try it, they have to go round them, and they'll be bound to run aground!" I tried to sound as optimistic as I could. It was difficult, because the boy's eyes were now on the *Sérieuse*. She was listing badly to starboard, and I could see she would soon have to cease firing or take in water through her gunports; in fact several guns had stopped firing and the ports were being closed. I could not push from my mind the horrible scene as the men desperately struggled to push already hot guns up the sloping deck, secure them, and then close the ports. I yelled at the boys to report to the battery officers to be assigned stations. I noticed young Casa Bianca report to the officer commanding the guns nearest the quarterdeck.

I hurried back to the admiral. By this time, the sun was nearly at the horizon, bathing the scene in bloody light, though we ourselves had yet to see blood. I was right about one thing. No more English ships were trying to outflank us. Instead, a ship which I recognized as the flagship was coming down the outside of our line. Of course, she was attracting broadsides, but these were enfeebled by the need to try and activate the inshore guns. About five of the enemy were anchored inshore of our van, and the next few now took the safer course and anchored on the offshore side, so that each of our ships was being bombarded by two of theirs.

There were many, many terrible things on that awful night, but I think the worst feeling of all was standing there facing into a stiff breeze, one that carried the stench of gunsmoke to us, but could not take us to the rescue, watching the massacre of a third of our fleet, unable to move or offer help. The struggle to save the *Sérieuse* was almost over. The sun was now on the western horizon, and as it set, she keeled slowly over to starboard and sank. The enemy had long ceased wasting ammunition on her.

But at least the water was warm, and the wreck was close to the shore.

As the very last rays of the sun angled over the water, creating weird and horrible shades of red in the interconnected clouds of smoke rising from the battle in the van, an enemy warship sailed round the outside of the engagement heading towards us. I thought she was aiming for the ship in front of us, the eighty-gun *Franklin*, but they exchanged broadsides only once and then she overshot and dropped anchor directly opposite the *Orient*, close enough that I could see through my glass that she was the *Bellerophon*. No ship approached us on the other side, so Casa Bianca ordered all the gunners from the port back to the starboard side. The *Bellerophon* had already opened fire, and we needed every gun of the sixty on that battery. Shots were crashing into the *Orient*'s mighty side, and for the first time I heard clearly the screams of dying men.

For some reason, the starboard gun nearest us remained unmanned. I never found out what happened to the original crew. Casa Bianca turned to me: "You! You've handled a gun! It's only an eighteen-pounder! Get to it!"

Though in theory answerable only to Brueys, I was pleased to obey. There would be little for a secretary to do, plenty for a gunner. From somewhere Casa Bianca found men to load and haul the gun which I aimed and fired. His own son, young Giacimo, he set to carrying our powder. *Bellerophon* was firing fast and well, and for a while it was an even conflict, but it was sixty guns against thirty-seven, and we Frenchmen were very eager to avenge our doomed countrymen in the leading ships. At first we aimed mainly at her rigging, and soon brought down all three of her masts, some sails still set, cracking and keeling gracefully over the side in the dark-blue twilight like diving swans. She showed no sign, however, of striking her flag, and the order came to fire into the hull. Now at last came a true French victory. Our wonderful ship, even with some very scratch gun crews, was too good for them. Mind you, there was no science or tactics in it: it was who could load, haul, fire, swab and load most quickly and energetically.

That time it was we French. The fight had begun at sunset, and by the last gleam of twilight I saw the enemy cut their cables and try to escape by hoisting spritsail and drifting down the line.

Unfortunately, she did escape: I heard ships further down starting to fire, and then I felt a tug at my sleeve. It was Giacimo Casa Bianca. "Come quickly! It's the admiral! He's been hurt!"

I ran to the quarterdeck. Admiral Brueys had fallen and was lying on the planking. Both his legs had been broken by a single ball and were hanging by red threads of flesh. I could see it did not have to be a fatal wound, but the bleeding needed to be stopped well before we could get him to the surgeon. I whipped off my belt, and Casa Bianca, seeing what was on my mind, did the same. We knelt over him, Casa Bianca putting a tourniquet on one devastated leg, I on the other. We did our job well: the dreadful flood of blood slowed to a trickle, then stopped.

By this time, we were again under fire. More ships had appeared out of the near-dark, three of them this time. One was sailing through the gap between ourselves and the *Franklin*: the gap that should have been cabled, had we expected such a desperate night attack. She fired simultaneous broadsides into our bow and *Franklin*'s stern. I heard shot whistling overhead, but most of it crashed into *Orient*'s bow, creating a shudder like an earthquake as the great ship rocked.

Casa Bianca said, "Citizen Admiral, you'd better get below!"

But Brueys replied, "No! I have to stay here." He turned to me: "Go to my cabin, get my favourite chair. You know the one, with the long seat. I can command from that."

Another ship was taking *Bellerophon*'s place to starboard. Casa Bianca ran to the gun I had been firing and started to aim it himself. I ran down into the cabin area, as yet not badly damaged, but one of the scholar's infernal jars of chemicals had cracked and was spreading its stench more vilely than ever. It was very dark in that part of the ship; minimal light was allowed, for fear of fire. The cabin was was lit only by enemy gunflashes. I found the chair and dragged it to the companion-way, then ran up with it. The sky was quite dark, but I could see by gunfire. Fresh ships were anchored on either side of us, blazing away; and a third was across our bows, raking us without reply. Nevertheless, our guns were firing too, an odd mixture from varying parts of the ship.

I carried the chair to Admiral Brueys, then the signal lieutenant and I gently lifted him into it. Up to then he had been silent, bearing his wounds with incredible fortitude, but now he gave a loud groan, then said, "I can't command like this. Listen! In my bureau, in one of the inner drawers, third from the left, you'll find a bottle marked with a poppy. It contains a special derivative of laudanum, one that doesn't cloud the mind as it eases pain. Get it for me!"

I hurried back below. There was a crash as more shots went into the ship. There was more light than I had expected: there were holes in the inner cabin walls, where shots had gone right through, and I saw to my horror that a small fire had started, possibly from a lamp knocked over. Men were yelling and seemed to be trying to stamp it out, while moving all powder away.

I ran by this evil light to the bureau. There was danger here, but there was danger everywhere on the *Orient*. All the cabin windows had been shot out, and it would be an easy dive from there to the water.

But the admiral was at his post, in pain, and the least I could do was get his laudanum. I rummaged through the bureau; there were several bottles, and at first I could not see which it was. Then the crackling light got brighter, and I found the one with the poppy. I ran back to the companionway. I saw to my horror that flames were spreading under the wrecked partition. I hesitated, tempted to try a solitary firefight, then the fire reached the scientist's spilled chemical. With a roar it ignited, far more powerfully than before. A wall of flame spread across the bottom of the companionway. I thought of diving off the ship: but instead took a running jump to the third or fourth step up, hardly felt the heat at first, ran up the steps shouting, "Fire below! Fire below!"

I gave the admiral his bottle. He drank half of it at a gulp, then there was a crash in front of us and he doubled over with a second wound. I raised him, not gently enough, and saw that a huge splinter like a wooden dagger had gone into his stomach. I knew that people seldom survive such wounds, but I said, "I'll get you to the surgeon!"

"No! No point!" He drained the rest of the bottle, said, "I'm a French admiral. I may not be much of one, but at least I can die on the quarterdeck!" He still had the use of his lungs, and he yelled at Casa Bianca, "Fire! Fight the damn fire! That's the priority!"

The captain left his gun and ran to organize the fire crews. We had held few proper drills, and many of the guns on the upper decks were left unmanned, though those below were still blazing away as if on this vast ship the lower gun crews were unaware of this impending disaster.

I ran down to join the fire crew. Men were getting hoses on to it, and it looked as though the pump crew were working well. A steady stream of water was flowing at the blaze, but the accursed chemicals were burning fiercely. Men ran forward with buckets. I grabbed one and joined the chain. Then there was a terrible crash and the whole cabin area seemed to be disintegrating. Firemen were collapsing in heaps, some ripped to pieces by shot, others falling into the flames, which burned far more fiercely. It seemed the enemy had trained an entire salvo at the area where we were trying to extinguish the blaze. More men ran forward, but shots kept crashing through, sending partitions and bits of furniture into the fire. I saw my book of minutes burning away.

Men were hovering in terror, realizing they were in less immediate danger away from the fire and the English guns, but that if it got further out of control, the ship was doomed, and would certainly blow up if the flames reached the magazines. The enemy were still firing steadily into that area. I ran back to the quarterdeck. Brueys was immediately above the worst conflagration, not that that would matter to him for long. Men were pouring up from the middle decks, some already leaping over the side, though far below, guns were still firing.

I found the admiral and reported what was happening. He said in a faint but very firm voice, "Fight the fire as best you can. As long as I last, but when I'm gone, if you still can't put it out, tell Casa Bianca to strike his colours!" He collapsed sideways in his seat. I shook him, he opened his eyes and mouth, but said nothing. He slumped forward: I could not tell if he was already dead, and it hardly mattered. I looked wildly around for Casa Bianca, but could not see him. I started running through the panicking crowd on the deck. The light of the fire was now clearly visible through cracks and shotholes. More and more were diving or jumping off, though the crew were such raw recruits I doubted many of them could swim.

I could not see the captain, but I found his son, throwing gunpowder over the side. I shouted above the roar of ordnance and the crackle of flames, "Where's your father?"

"Below, fighting the fire. Where you should be!"

To my despair, he followed me as I raced below decks. I hoped the rest of my boys had the sense to get off the ship. We found Casa Bianca dragging a hose forward, almost single-handed. The enemy were still using shot to stoke the fire, and no one could get close enough to dampen it. To make matters worse, the deck was filling with the foulest smoke from the chemicals. Only the shotholes and open gunports saved us all from suffocating there and then. I do not know if God and heaven exist, but I knew then that hell is possible, that either the devil was at work, or the old gods of the Egyptian underworld, poisonous and vengeful.

Choking though I was, I explained Brueys's last orders to Casa Bianca, finishing, "There's no choice. You have to sur-render!"

"For one of Napoleon's men, there's always a choice!" He ran forward, dragging the hose, into the light of the flames. The boy followed, helping with the hose, and, amazingly, so did I. Ahead of us, Casa Bianca stood trying to extinguish the flame, like a child pissing into a volcano. Then there was the crunch of yet another salvo hitting, yet more bits of wreckage flew about, many already blazing, and he staggered back and dropped the hose. At that moment it stopped gushing water, as though the men on the ship's pumps were giving up.

The boy shouted, "Help my father!" and ran forward. I followed him to the edge of the inferno, grabbed Casa Bianca and dragged him away, he groaning in pain, I almost screaming with the heat. With desperate strength, I found a companion-way amidships and dragged him up it, the boy helping as best he could. There was no point in going to the quarterdeck. I dumped him beside a davit, to which was attached by its rope the remains of his captain's barge.

To my amazement, he staggered to his feet. He had a terrible wound, a great splinter stuck in his intestines. It was a far worse wound than the one that had finished Brueys. I said, "You have to surrender! Strike your colours! Get them to stop firing! It's the only hope; otherwise she'll blow up and take us with her!"

"Surrender! We've almost won! Listen, they're ceasing fire already!"

It was true that the racket of gunfire was getting less. I looked at the nearest English ship. By the light of the blazing stern of the *Orient*, I could see she was the *Alexander*. She was moving slowly, cables evidently cut. Men were batting the hatches and closing the gunports. Her own pumps and hoses were working, sluicing the decks, the sails and the rigging. I yelled, "They're getting out of here! They can see we're about to blow! We have to—"

"No! Fight to the end! For the republic! For Bonaparte!" Exhausted, he slumped back down on to the deck. The boy rushed to him. I looked over the side again. The *Alexander* was making way, and would soon be past us. The water was full of our men, mostly drowning rather than swimming. I had no fear on my account; I had always been able to swim well, and made sure the boys could do the same. Further off, another English ship, the flagship I thought, was battening down but not moving. Even so, the odd chivalry of the sea meant they were actually lowering rescue boats, although further off many ships were still firing.

I kicked off my boots and turned to the boy. "Come on! We have to dive, like I taught you, and swim for it."

"No. My father ordered 'No surrender!'"

"But Admiral Brueys said we could surrender, once he was gone!"

I looked towards the quarterdeck. By some weird fate, at that moment flames burned through from below. The whole quarterdeck caught quickly, and fire shot up the mizzen, as though it were the stake of Joan of Arc. Clearly, Brueys had had his last wish and perished there. I said to the boy, "Admiral's orders. We have to go!"

"You go then. I won't leave my father!"

"He's—"

"He's still alive!" It was true. The captain was still just breathing, slumped in the arms of his son, who looked at me imploringly, I saw his mother's eyes. I wanted to tell him that I had been his mother's first lover, that I should have been his father. I even thought of saying that I was his father, but he would not have believed that lie.

Instead, I grabbed a mooring rope from the remains of the barge. The bow section had been broken clear from the rest, but was still attached to the davit. I put a bowline round Casa Bianca, then tied him roughly to the bow of his barge. The boy gave a little gasp of relief. Between us, we raised the dying man on his barge-stretcher and hoisted him over the side, then lowered him as gently as we could to the water. I let the rope run out of the davit: the boy dived over the side as soon as he saw his father hit the water.

Firing continued further off, but not around the *Orient*. It was bright as day, flames shooting right up the mizzen to our crow's nest. The other masts were down. I dived over the side, taking care to avoid the boy and his dying father.

I had hoped the shock of the water would bring him to his senses. Oddly, it did not seem unpleasantly cold: indeed, it was absurdly refreshing. Invigorated, I called to the boy, "Let's swim for it. Like I showed you. We can still make the English boats!"

He was treading water beside the wreck of the barge, trying to push it away from the ship and keep his father's head above water. He said, "Help me!"

"I'll help you. But I can't help him. He'll die even if we get him to a surgeon. Now come."

"He's my father!"

I actually shouted, "It should have been me!" but my words were drowned. Firelight was flickering in odd, square beams of light from all the gunports. As I spoke, there was an explosion. Not the big explosion I had been dreading, just a few rounds of powder, but enough. In despair I yelled, "Follow me!" and struck out with all my strength towards the English boats. I looked back once, like Lot's wife. He was not following me, but still trying to save his dying father, the father from whom he had inherited little but too much courage.

The square beams of light were shining from all of the sixty gunports on that side of the *Orient*, and they were getting brighter. Fear chilled me, as though I were sweating into the warm water, and I swam on as hard as I could, steering through a field of drowning or exhausted men by the light of the *Orient*. I could not bring myself to look back again. Just as my strength was about to give out, I saw a boat ahead of me. It was already nearly full, turning away, turning back. I cried as loudly as I still could, *"M'aidez! M'aidez!"* then: "Help! Help!"

They stopped rowing, and from somewhere I found the strength to swim up to them. Strong hands pulled me in: at once they rowed on, as if they were on the Styx, and the Grim Boatman was after them.

We reached the ship. I was recovered enough to climb without help to the deck, where I collapsed. They had other half-drowned French prisoners, who were being herded below. Indeed, I thought everyone was going below, till I saw a wounded man standing with a few other officers. His head was bandaged, but he wore a magnificent uniform jacket. One sleeve was empty, so he had lost an arm in action. I realized this must be the admiral who had orchestrated our defeat, and my rescue. I asked him in English if I could watch the end with him, and he politely agreed.

It came soon. The *Orient* was blazing from stem to stern. At last the fire reached the magazine in the depths of the ship. I am told the explosion was heard in Alexandria, 20 miles away. A fountain of flame shot into the night sky like a giant waterspout of light. It was an awesome moment, as though some God — English, Egyptian, it didn't matter — had created a great firework to mock the efforts of the French to do without him and live by reason.

The English admiral and I ducked instinctively below the boat which had just been hauled back up its davits. We were lucky. The showering wreckage which finished off so many who were struggling in the water did not hit us.

Firing stopped for many minutes. Later it began again, but without the earlier fury. Everyone knew who had won. At dawn all was silent. Boats put out in search of more survivors, but they did not find the Casa Biancas, the wounded father or his brave son.

On the morning after the battle, the enemy gave thanks to the God I had almost forgotten. I did not know whether to give thanks. I did not know if I would ever return to France. I did not know if I would look for my widowed love, and if I did, I did not know what I would tell her. I had always wanted to give her a son of my own, but if I ever did so, I hoped I would endow him with something other than Casa Bianca's mad courage. But perhaps that was what she wanted, and what a revolutionary's son needed.

CASABIANCA

Felicia Hemans

I doubt that many remember the name of Felicia Hemans (1793–1835) today, and not many will remember the title of this poem, published in The Forest Sanctuary *(1829), even though its opening line is oft quoted, usually in parody. She was the daughter of a Liverpool merchant and married Captain Hemans in 1812, though they separated in 1818. She was a renowned beauty in her day and friends with Walter Scott and William Wordsworth. She was also responsible for the phrase "the stately homes of England".*

Despite the romantic power of the following poem the actual fate of the young Casabianca is not known and the version recreated in Peter Garratt's story may be closer to the truth. There is another account that maintains that it was the young boy who was injured and that his father stayed with him on the Orient *until it exploded. We will probably never know the truth but, as someone once remarked, when faced with printing either the truth or the legend, always print the legend!*

> The Boy stood on the burning deck,
> Whence all but him had fled;
> The flame that lit the battle's wreck
> Shone round him o'er the dead.

Yet beautiful and bright he stood,
As born to rule the storm;
A creature of heroic blood,
A proud though childlike form.

The flames rolled on; he would not go
Without his father's word;
That father, faint in death below,
His voice no longer heard.

He called aloud, "Say, Father, say,
If yet my task be done."
He knew not that the chieftain lay
Unconscious of his son.

"Speak, Father!" once again he cried,
"If I may yet be gone."
And but the booming shots replied,
And fast the flames rolled on.

Upon his brow he felt their breath,
And in his waving hair,
And looked from that lone post of death
In still yet brave despair,

And shouted but once more aloud,
"My father! must I stay?"
While o'er him fast, through sail and shroud,
The wreathing fires made way.

They wrapt the ship in splendour wild,
They caught the flag on high,
And streamed above the gallant child,
Like banners in the sky.

There came a burst of thunder sound;
The boy, Oh! where was he?

Ask of the winds, that far around
With fragments strewed the sea,

With shroud and mast and pennon fair,
That well had home their part,
But the noblest thing that perished there
Was that young, faithful heart.

THE TRAP

Kenneth Bulmer

The following is another episode in the turbulent and troubled life of George Abercrombie Fox, the hero of fourteen novels penned by Kenneth Bulmer under the alias Adam Hardy in the mid-seventies. This episode takes place not long after the siege of Acre in the spring and summer of 1799. Until a few years ago Kenneth Bulmer (b. 1921) was a prolific writer of science fiction and fantasy, but his historical novels, of which the Fox series was the most popular, may yet be his most lasting testament.

I

Lieutenant Fox felt that confounded ring of purple and black closing in on the sight of his left eye – and here he was simply standing on the quarterdeck of *Raccoon* safely anchored off Gibraltar. The immediate cause for that defect of vision, which, occasioned by a long-forgotten wound, inflicted itself on Fox usually only in moments of passion or stress or lust, swung up from the lighter overside.

A four-pounder.

The lighter was broad-beamed and capacious and Fox, standing with his ugly face rigidly composed and with his hands tucked up into the small of his back and grinding together like the icebergs of the northern seas, could look down with an uninterrupted view. He wanted to take a last look at those nine-pounders of his. His! Hadn't he taken them from Bonaparte himself? Hadn't he cap-a-barred a battery of nine-pounder field guns from old Boney and proudly set them around *Raccoon*'s deck to bare their teeth and grin back balefully upon their former owners? Yes, bigod, he had!

And now this bumbling idiot Sanders with a bullion swab flaunting on his left shoulder, his face all red and puffed up and delighted with life and all the good fortune heaped upon him, had ordered them sent ashore. In their places he was resurrecting the four-pounders that had given Fox so much affront when he had commanded *Raccoon*. Of course these weren't the same four-pounders – they'd gone God knew where after Acre – but they were still pop-guns to George Abercrombie Fox.

He had to do some fine and fancy talking to explain how he'd gone to sea equipped with fourteen four-pounders and returned with six nine-pounders – and those French guns, into the bargain.

"We go by the book of regulations aboard my ship, Mr Fox," Sanders had said, his bloated face puffing so that his eyes, of that infuriatingly insolent blue, all but disappeared. "You will do well to remember that."

All Fox could reply, of course, was: "Aye aye, sir."

Mediterranean sunshine poured blithely down all around. The Rock heaved itself up out of the sea like the dorsal fin of the ancestor of all the fish in the world. The sounds of men working, of hands tailing on lines, the scuffle of bare feet on holystoned planking, the squeal of ropes through blocks, all the familiar sounds of naval life blended into Fox's mind and, in other circumstances, might have soothed him.

Now he opened his mouth to yell a blistering order and then closed it again as the bosun, Lassiter, vented his own gargantuan yell.

"Handsomely there, you swabs!" With a swish and a crack Lassiter's rattan backed up his order. In immediate sycophantic echo the petty officers' starters cracked down. "Heave, you bastards, heave!"

The four-pounder swung over the knot of hands waiting for it on deck. Fox peered through his right eye, for his left had now resolutely refused to see any more of this dentistry. That was how he saw this, taking the teeth out of the brig and replacing them by gums. He could think of other and more picturesque ways of describing this castration of the vessel he had but so lately commanded. Now he was the first lieutenant. Life, as always, was unfair; and, inevitably, unfair most of all to George Abercrombie Fox.

He could understand quite clearly that it was necessary for Lassiter to display his seamanlike qualities for the new commanding officer. The run to Gibraltar to effect the necessary repairs to their foremast had not, it seemed from Sanders' viewpoint, been long enough. Also, Fox saw, it was necessary that Lassiter emphasize the fact he was the bosun before Grimes, the new gunner brought aboard by Commander Sanders. Sanders had brought a number of his own men with him, and the old Raccoons were very conscious of criticism.

Joachim, the gunner's mate, a steady and reliable hand whom Fox had every reason to be satisfied with – not that he would ever reveal that fact – no doubt resented not receiving his rate and being passed over for the post of gunner. He had discharged his duties efficiently. But Sanders had come the heavy-handed commander and had stamped his desires on *Raccoon* with all the authority his command conferred, without caring how he unbalanced the careful arrangements made by Fox. There were ways and ways of running a King's ship, and Fox had experienced most of them so that by this time in his career – his career! That was a laugh! – he knew exactly what he wanted from a crew and the best way of obtaining it. Commander Richard Sanders had other ideas.

The four-pounder swung, was skilfully caught and manhandled by a forest of brawny arms and blunt-fingered hands, lowered to its carriage. Fox looked one-eyed at it and kept his ugly face rock-like.

He'd have a run ashore tonight, bigod, and Sanders would

have to throw that book he was so fond of quoting at him to prevent it.

Mr Midshipman Lionel Grey came on deck. His handsome profile turned towards Fox as he looked down on the activity by the guns. That young rip had been through a scrape or two with Fox, and despite their disparity in age and condition, as well as looks, Fox was aware with an uncomfortable itch between his shoulder blades that Grey bore him some affection. This was so unlikely an eventuality for Fox that he regarded it with the deepest of dark suspicions. But now, feeling the resentment like hot pitch in his guts, he walked over and said, "Mr Grey. You will accompany me ashore this evening."

He made it abrupt.

Grey looked up, straightening his spine, his frank face and clear eyes taking on that strange look he sometimes adopted when Fox spoke to him.

"Aye aye, sir."

Nothing more. No questions, no hints that he would like to have more information; just that careful acknowledgment, that almost aloof immediate acquiescence in Fox's plans.

About to turn away in frustration at the turmoil of his own feelings, Fox halted as Grey, in a flat and neutral voice that did not deceive Fox for a moment said, "Sir, might I take the liberty of hoping you will do me the honour of accepting the loan of a hat?"

Thankfully he did not enlarge on the woeful inadequacies of Fox's own shapeless headgear that necessitated the offer in the first place.

Fox hesitated. His own hat was a mess, there was no doubt of that. Ruined by weather, sodden in that mad sea-rescue in Palermo harbour, sliced down to the fold over his right eye and clumsily cobbled together by Parsons, his hat was an offence under the sun. Parsons, who had been his steward, was now rated back as an able seaman, for Sanders had replaced all Fox's arrangements with his own people. That hat now, Fox refrained from reaching up and pushing it unnecessarily straight, had taken that sabre cut in the fight at the mine-shaft outside the besieged walls of Acre. It was his hat. As soon as he could afford to spend some of his ill-gotten gold he would buy another. As it was every single penny he earned or won or stole, now that he was no longer responsible for *Raccoon*, could be sent back to that family of Foxes by the Thames.

Fox – uncharacteristically – hesitated.

Of course, he should refuse the offer. Grey had the run of the wardrobes of his peers, and between them they could rig out one of their number respectably. But – but the offer was made in a genuine spirit. It irritated Fox. He ought to accept – the offer was made in good faith. But . . . .

He stared straight at Grey. He tried to make his words friendly. As always, they came out in a kind of grating roar more suitable to hailing the foretop in a gale.

"Thank you, Mr Grey. That will not be necessary."

For an instant, Grey hesitated, his mouth half open, clearly on the verge of being insubordinate.

Then, to Fox's inexpressible relief, the midshipman touched his hat. "Aye aye, sir."

Immediately Fox swung away and reeled out a string of foul and obscenity-punctuated orders to the men labouring over the guns. If *Raccoon* was to be gunned with pop-gun four-pounders then George Abercombie Fox would make damn sure they were used to the best possible advantage.

He had to keep himself occupied. He had been too conscious of the lurking amusement in Grey's eyes. That young rip of Satan had a wonderfully acute way of drilling beneath Fox's calloused skin.

Probably Grey, whose parents wrote him regularly and who appeared to have money and was, in all the best senses of the word, a gentleman, still believed a special relationship existed between them. Certainly Fox liked the lad. And that was a strange business, if you liked. But his period in command of *Raccoon* had, in Fox's eyes, softened him. He had become barnacled over with command. He had changed from that old Fox who would as soon spit in a lord's eye. That brought up memories of Lord Kintlesham and Sophie too painful for him, and he went roaring forward as a four-pounder swung inboard and threatened to carry away a major portion of the standing rigging.

Raccoon was a tight, handy, neat little quarterdeck brig and her normal complement when in British hands was ninety men. After the siege of Acre they were now critically short of hands. This situation held nothing novel in it, for the Royal Navy was perennially short of men; but Fox could hope that Commander Sanders had used some of that influence that had gained him this command to acquire fresh men. A boat slopped over the chop to them now and already Grey had a glass trained on it.

"Well, Mr Grey?"

"About twenty of 'em, sir." Grey half lowered the glass. "Lay me horizontal, sir, but half of 'em look green!"

"Half!" said Fox. "We're in luck."

When the men came over the side chivvied and bullied by the bosun's mates with their cunningly cruel starters, Fox stared at them with the detachment twenty-five years in the navy gave to a man.

"Mr Lassiter!" he roared at the bosun. "Get them under the pump right away. And be prepared to stamp on any little things that scuttle way from 'em!"

"Aye aye, sir!" shouted back Lassiter, and someone in the old crew laughed. Fox turned his back. Damned insubordinate crew of cut-throats he had trained up in *Raccoon*, bigod! Laughter, on the deck of a King's ship! It was unheard of.

The pump was plied willingly by the old hands and the newcomers stripped and gyrated beneath the jet of water. They wore slops, clothes parsimoniously doled out from the purser's slop-chest of whatever ship it had been that had brought them out to the Rock from England. Pressed men, they were, men scooped up from their quiet occupations in England and forced willy-nilly into a King's ship to serve and be flogged until they were dead. If they were lucky and survived they might never see shore again for ten or more years. The war looked as though it would last that long. Nothing good seemed to be heard of the war's progress, although as to that, Fox had to rely on hearsay, for any letters for him had still not caught up with him.

The men's scrawny bodies gleamed in the water jet. A foul-looking lot they were, and no mistake. Fox's eye was caught by one of the newly arrived men, a man who stood apart from his fellows, a man unlike them in almost every possible way.

This man's physique bulged with muscle as he stripped off his white trousers and frock. He had a tufty red beard and his hair glowed with the same arrogant colour. His nose had been broken and set with a tilt to larboard. There were tattooes on his arms and they rolled and danced as he flexed his biceps. He looked tough and competent and – the clinching argument proving what he was – in his left ear swung a tiny gold ring.

One of the bosun's mates cracked his colt down on this man's bare rump. The man started and half turned, and Fox saw his face. Congested with rage, ferocious, malign, that face stared at the bosun's mate as the jet of water gushed to run in rivulets down that massive chest with its plates of muscle and matted reddish hair.

Fox leaned a little forward. He gripped the quarterdeck rail. All kinds of memories floated up in his mind. Some officers would welcome a flogging now as a way of impressing the new arrivals with the awful power and authority of their new captain. As pressed men they would have gone through the dreadful ordeal of impressment, through the receiving ship and the slop ship, signed on, rated, and then battened down in some stinking hold to be shipped 1,000 miles from home, reeking in a foul environment of vomit and puke and excreta and the ever-present dampness inherent in a wooden ship.

They were like sheep prepared for the slaughter.

The bosun's mate lifted his starter again, clearly not relishing the look in the red-headed giant's eye.

"Belay that!" roared Fox. "Get the pump-work finished and then clear away! Jump to it!"

"Aye aye, sir!" yelled back the mate. His lifted colt lowered.

The red-headed man looked up at the quarterdeck along the length of the brig. Fox's eye disclosed a little light; but it was with his right eye he saw the hard and calculating look on the giant's face and he wondered if, once again, he had made a mistake.

He thrust his hands up into the small of his back and stumped aft. There were plenty of other things to think about. Their new foremast had been stepped, they had a new suit of canvas, fresh spars, they were fully stored and provisioned, their powder and shot filled the magazine – damned stupid four-pounder shot! – and they had watered. Watering was the last operation before a vessel sailed. Fox tried not to wonder if he would, after all, get that run ashore he had promised himself for tonight.

Grey called again.

Fox looked over the side. Yes, here came Commander high and mighty Sanders himself.

The bowman of his boat shouted, *"Raccoon!"* as though aboard the brig they couldn't see their captain was coming aboard. A bustle and a scurry boiled and was still as the marines, the side boys and the bosun's mates readied themselves for the evolution of piping the side.

As Sanders touched the deck Fox saluted. He kept that ugly, lined, demoniac face of his expressionless.

Amid the twitter of the pipes and the solid crash as Sergeant Cartwright's marines presented arms, Commander Sanders returned to his kingdom.

He summoned Fox to the aft cabin which, however small and box-like it might appear after the Great Cabin on a 74 was still immeasurably larger than the canvas booth now occupied by Fox. The marine sentry saluted as Fox pushed through.

Sanders looked up, his bloated face flushed, those insolent blue eyes floating as it were on seas of red cheeks, his whole demeanour one of animation and joy.

"Mr Fox. Prepare the vessel for sea immediately."

Fox could not argue. His run ashore with Grey was now merely a pipe dream. He said, "Aye aye, sir."

"I'll lay the course with Mr Macbridge. I want to be clear by nightfall." There was no doubt about it, Sanders was as pleased as a foretopman with a doxy on each arm. "Mr Fox, I am happy to be able to tell you I have a cruise!"

Which, considered Fox as he went back on deck to see to all the pettifogging details that fell to the lot of a first lieutenant, was the justice of the gods. He, Fox, had never had a cruise. But Sanders was handed one on a plate. Well, there was always the treasure of Captain Louis Lebonnet.

II

Commander Richard Sanders possessed the luck of the devil.

The Spanish persisted in their use of coasters and this, surmised Fox, they were forced to do owing to the poor condition of the Spanish roads. Whatever the cause, there were prizes going for a commander anxious to press in close to the coast and take all the chances such a course necessarily predisposed.

There was no gainsaying the willingness of Sanders to take chances, nor of his eagerness to press close in and sweep up whatever fates offered. Most of the coasters were small craft, clumsy sailers, and manned usually by a crew consisting of old men and boys. Their first action on sighting a British ship-of-war was to lower their boat and row for the shore.

Fox experienced familiar sensations of envy and greed as the process went on. As to envy, he tried to quash this emotion as being unworthy; but being Fox he couldn't help gnashing his teeth – as the book would have it – over the way in which Sanders seemed able to conjure prizes from the very sea itself. They took a number of coasters, burning those vessels of no worth after removing any cargo of value, sending others back to Gibraltar with tiny prize crews. Midshipman Prentiss took one prize in, and John Carker another.

Fox was disturbed to see Carker go, for the master's mate was the solid, reliable and conscientious type of warrant officer on whom much of the power and efficiency of the Royal Navy depended. And here, with the master, Macbridge, as useless as ever, all the work fell on the shoulders of Fox and Grey.

When Grey, too, was sent back in a prize, Fox had to brace himself to a future of almost unceasing work. That was no novelty; but he just wished sometimes that all this labour resulted in personal profits for himself and his family commensurate with the efforts involved. A lieutenant's share, after all, bore no comparison with the share of the captain.

During these days when they snapped up the abandoned coasters Fox saw no reason to let his knowledge of Spanish be known. His Castilian, the prevailing language of Spain, was perfect and his Catalan was almost as good, whilst his command of Aragonese was sufficient to get by.

"A fine cruise, Mr Fox," observed Sanders as they stood in towards the coast of Spain. The day was fine, with light airs from the north, and *Raccoon* would have no trouble ghosting to the westward to pick up the coasters Fox, resignedly, knew would sprout from the sea immediately on the arrival of this golden boy Sanders. Then the same breeze would waft them as easily to the eastward to stand off until their next run in.

"Aye aye, sir," said Fox.

"The hands are keeping happy." Sanders tucked his hands up into the small of his back, as though in unconscious imitation of the way he liked hands to behave. "And so they should be, the devil take 'em! They'll have prize-money to buy doxies and whatever else when we get back."

"Aye aye, sir."

Fox, so far, had signally failed to keep this man Sanders under his thumb as he had done so often before – as he had done on this very brig with that poor devil Mortlock.

"One more, Mr Fox, one more, and then Mr Macbridge can lay us a course for Gibraltar."

That lowering, ugly, powerful face of Fox's remained immobile, the lips thin and firmly closed. He wouldn't trust Macbridge to navigate a coster's cart over London Bridge.

"Deck!" The yell screeched from the foretop. That was Wilson up there, the man reputed to have the sharpest eyes in *Raccoon*. "Coaster, sir. Fine on the larboard bow. Two – no three – on 'em!"

The very unfairness of it all took Fox then and shook him speechlessly by the throat. When he'd commanded *Raccoon* they'd spotted one French sail and had been unable to catch her. The brig was foul underneath now and her speed severely reduced; but Sanders didn't need speed. All he needed for success was to be seen by the Spaniards. Then, as soon as they had quitted their vessel, he could calmly send a boarding party across and chalk up another handsome payment from his prize agent.

Damned unfair!

But – since when had life – and the Royal Navy in particular – ever been fair to anyone, including George Abercrombie Fox?

The coasters were quite unable to elude their pursuer; long before they could reach the coast *Raccoon* would be up with them. Even four-pounders in this situation with the thin scantlings and hulls of coasters to smash were effective. Fox admitted that without changing the grounds of his objections. *Raccoon* glided on and soon the masts of the coasters appeared over the horizon, and then their clumsy black hulls. There was no sign of life aboard. Fox wondered if his reading of the minds of the Spanish crews were correct; in their position he would have set his vessel aflame and damn the enemy. But no sailormen liked to burn a vessel. They were superstitious about that kind of behaviour.

The sea heaved and the wind blew and the sun shone and, conjoined with that altogether natural order of things, Sanders in *Raccoon* sailed calmly onward to take his newest prizes. Nature ordained that Sanders should be successful. Fox knew already that nature had condemned him; but being Fox he cursed and struggled and fought against that condemnation and would never resign the conflict.

The little group of three coasters tended to sag together as though for mutual support. The combined action of their sails in the light northerly breeze pushed them at a sharply subtended angle to the coast, heading for a bold promontory that jutted, purple and grey against the light, across their course. Without any conscious directive from his mind Fox's analytical brain was already sorting out the angles, the courses, the wind, the run of the sea, glancing aloft at the scattered cloud formations, estimating what conditions might be like in two hours or so.

That they could reach the coasters and board them on the course on which they now stood was clear. *Raccoon* burbled gently along on the starboard tack, and at a word from Sanders her head fell off three points to bring the wind on her quarter. Immediately she heeled less and picked up speed. Fox frowned. Sanders was aiming to make a faster run down to the coasters by circling wide of them and then hauling up to them as they drifted down from windward. That he would reach the coasters faster this way was indisputable; but Fox wondered. He felt an itch between his shoulder blades. His stomach displeased him, for he had been eating shore-side food just lately, and he rubbed the first two fingers of his left hand across that stomach, back and forth, back and forth.

The Spaniards had left all their sails set. The wind blew against that stained and dirty canvas. The sails bulged. They bulged with an altogether too purposeful way for the liking of Fox.

If he said anything to Sanders he would be snubbed for his pains.

That lucky individual was striding up and down his quarter-deck, a pleased smile making his red and bulbous face glow like a larboard light.

"We'll keep these in company, Mr Fox," Sanders said, in high good humour. "'Pon my oath, they do look a lovely sight!"

He sounded, Fox thought without overmuch rancour, just like a kid from one of these fancy colleges his kind went to staring at sticky sweets in a shop window. Fox understood well enough the emotions of pleasure and happiness suffusing the mind of Commander Sanders. Prizes!

"Aye aye, sir," Fox said. Then: "We'll be running down tidily close to that headland."

Sanders could not be diverted.

"Mr Macbridge will see us safely out, eh, Mr Macbridge?"

The master came forward from the traverse board, his face smirking with his own pleasure. Fox had no doubts as to the feelings of Macbridge. He had been sucking up to Sanders in a way that would have made Fox sick if he spared time to become emotional over anyone else's problems.

"Oh, aye, sir. There'll be steep water under yon cliff."

"The coasters are pulling with all sail, sir," Fox said. Now the conversation had been opened he not only could go on; he would have to go on. That damned itch between his shoulder blades worried him. He was still seeing well with both eyes; if his left eye packed up on him he would be seriously worried. "They'll be very close. We'll have to tack—"

"Yes, yes, Mr Fox!" Sanders interrupted him brusquely. Captains could do that, of course. They could interrupt a man when he was speaking, without bad manners coming into it. Captains could do damn nigh anything they liked, come to that.

Fox looked up at Wilson perched in the foretop. His banshee bellow lifted clearly to the lookout.

"Keep your eyes skinned to all points of the compass up there!"

"Aye aye, sir."

Still that light dry northern air persisted.

Raccoon eased along. Fox felt the wind on his cheek, watched the shadows of the masts and yards and canvas on the deck and water, felt his chunky body moving with the pitch and roll of the brig, listened to the chuckle of the water as it parted by the cutwater and tinkled and splashed away along the sides, heard the creak of blocks and the slap of tackle, heard, too, all the murmurous creaking from the brig's timbers.

Too damned much freeboard with those four-pounders aboard. *Raccoon* might possess a fantastic turn of speed; that speed had been drastically reduced by weed and barnacles and other maritime filth on her bottom.

And still those coasters surged on with the wind.

They were holding course with a remarkable sureness.

Their canvas did not slat.

If they had been abandoned and no hand lay on the tillers, then how come they sailed so tightly?

"Mr Fox!" Sanders was speaking with the air of a long-suffering man anxious to have a lunatic incarcerated. "Have the boat readied, if you please."

"Aye aye, sir."

Fox marched himself away. The boat was all ready to be swung overside. Did that dolt Sanders think him deficient in intellect?

The coasters were appreciably nearer now. Fox detested the feeling of tension creeping over him. He tried to be honest with himself, and to give Sanders some kind of credit. If he was in command now, what would he be doing? Would he not be doing just the same as Sanders?

George Abercrombie Fox was a hard man. He had to be. He knew he would not be acting in the way Sanders was acting. The knowledge simply made him that much more tough and uncompromising and ready to bear down on anyone for the slightest dereliction of duty.

Now was the time to back the foretopsail—

"Back the fore-tops'il!" came Macbridge's roar. Sanders looked pleased and stomped over to the starboard rail to stare across the water at the three coasters bearing down. They were moving through the water at a fair rate of knots. Fox, as the senior officer after Sanders with Macbridge as the master, would have to look very carefully indeed at the not-so-simple evolution of boarding.

Lassiter had everything ready. Phillips, who had been coxwain when Fox commanded, came up and knuckled his forehead.

"Beg pardon, sir. Jimmy Croker's got a pain in his guts, sir. Bad 'un. He's spewing something terrible – 'e'll bring his ring up next, like as not."

"I'll get him an extra tot, Phillips." Fox felt as confident over the genuineness of Jimmy Croker's bad inside as he could about anything. Croker had been one of the men who had pulled in the Sicilian boat when they'd taken those doomed souls from the wreck in Palermo harbour, when they'd picked up Ben Ferris and Ben's mother had died.

"Begging your pardon, sir," went on Phillips. "I'd like to take Barnabas, sir."

Barnabas was the giant red-head man who had joined the

vessel at Gibraltar, along with a miserable gaggle of pressed men. There had been a certain air about the man, something intangible and quite apart from the obvious fact that he was a seaman, that had impressed Fox.

"Very well," he said. "He looks as if he can pull an oar handily."

"Oh, aye, sir. He's a right seaman, sure enough."

Fox did not wish to bandy words any more with his excox-wain. He experienced a strange and pleasurable jolt of surprise at his own feelings when he stepped down into the cutter and found the familiar bronzed faces staring at him as he took his place in the sternsheets. The only face that might have appeared out of place was that of this Barnabas, and he sat with the relaxed yet lithely alert poise of the master-oarsman.

The powerful figure of Josephs was, as usual, at stroke oar. For a betraying moment Fox remembered how it had been when he commanded *Raccoon*.

Then, with his usual harshness, he gave the order and the oars fell as one and the cutter surged powerfully away from the brig.

Fox took the tiller himself.

He allowed himself plenty of searoom.

The cutter surged up to the leading coaster. White water burst away from her forefoot, and she pitched up and down with some force. Rapid calculations flitted through Fox's mind. He handled the cutter with the practised ease habitual to him, a confidence in small boats he had acquired as a very small child on the Thames and which had never deserted him, allowing him to con the boat and let his mind work on all the myriad other details pressing in for solutions.

The bowman – it was young Ben Ferris, as agile as a monkey – hooked on and the cutter swung in the wash. The starboard side oars came in, the hull touched, and Fox was out of the boat and handing himself up the rudimentary constructions that passed as channel and main chains for the mast.

He leaped over the rail and landed cat-like on deck.

If he lowered the sails the following coasters would be held by this one and an agile man could swarm across to them, one after the other, and lower their sails in turn.

Already Josephs and Ferris and the new man, Barnabas, had followed him on to the deck.

The coaster was deserted.

All Fox's fears seemed to him now no more than fever-dreams, stupid, unworthy of a fighting sea-officer.

At that moment Ferris let out a shout.

"Sail ho! Look, Cap'n! A Spanisher!"

Fox let rip a curse and leaped to the rail. He stared across the sea that danced with mocking silver gleams.

A Spanish corvette! Sneaking out of a cove, boring down on the larboard tack to gain the offing of *Raccoon*. *Raccoon* was heading for that damned headland, and the corvette sped down to hem her in against the cliffs with the wind driving her steadily down on to them.

The Spanish ship would have twenty twelve-pounders, like as not, and she would make short work of the brig and her puny four-pounders and her depleted crew. Fox scarcely noticed that in the excitement of the moment Ben Ferris had reverted to the old form of address, and had called him cap'n. All that mattered now was that *Raccoon* was trapped.

III

"She'll cut us close alongside, sir," said Phillips, leaning over the rail and staring hardly at the oncoming corvette.

Fox yelled back at him, "Get below and make sure no one is aboard."

"Aye aye, sir."

"Take Josephs and Barnabas with you. Don't stand any nonsense, mind."

Since the moment he had leaped over the rail until the first glimpse of that Spanish corvette sneaking out of that misbe-gotten concealed cove only a few minutes had passed. If anyone was concealed below they might still be gathering themselves for the rush on deck.

Concealment – that was the key here.

Fox tried to imagine if this whole affair was a gigantic trap. The flock of coasters huddling down with all sails set towards that spurred headland. The corvette ready to leap outside once the British vessel had passed to leeward. It all fitted. But, somehow, in the turmoil of the moment, he fancied that everything had fallen into shape by chance.

There could be no doubt the Spanish had been waiting for *Raccoon*. The Spanish authorities were bound to be weary of the depredations along their coasts. This corvette was their retribution.

He looked again across the water. Still only moments had passed.

Alarm was clearly evident on *Raccoon*'s deck. He could see the dark agitated figures of men running. They clambered up the main and forward shrouds and immediately the royals dropped . . . When they were sheeted home *Raccoon* might be able to show a clean pair of heels to the Spaniard – if she could weather the point.

That meant, of course, that he was left in command of three captured prizes.

The corvette looked a striking vessel, painted after the fashion and, without a doubt, crowded with men.

To get at *Raccoon* she would have to pass close by the three prizes, as Phillips had said.

He glanced about the decks, wrinkling his nose at their state of filth. The other two coasters were now nuzzling his quarters and in a moment would scrape by. If they did not do extensive damage to his rigging he would be lucky. If he let them past they'd sail on, alone and untended, until they piled up against the cliffs.

Phillips popped back on deck.

"All clear below, sir."

Barnabas, looking huge and ruffianly with his red beard and whiskers flaming, his red hair angry, started aft. He thrust his cutlass into his belt.

"Permission to get across to the other prizes, sir?"

Fox stared at him in an amazement that quickly broke into a solid feeling of satisfaction.

"Good man, Barnabas. Cut along as soon as you like." He lifted his voice. "Josephs, Hampton – go with Barnabas. Get the sails off them."

He swung back to Phillips.

He pointed.

"That's a four-pounder, Phillips. It's brass and it's Spanish. But, I've no doubt it will fire. Get powder and see what kind of shot is in the lockers. I want bar, chain – jump to it, man!"

"Aye aye, sir."

Phillips jumped.

Ben Ferris ripped open a shot locker – the coasters did not extend to garlands – and exclaimed in delight.

"Plenty of shot here, sir!"

"Ben, Ben! Bar, chain—"

"Aye aye, sir – all here!"

Trust the Spaniards to keep that kind of ammunition handy.

He had to work fast now, like a tinker's elbow. He'd get one shot in and then the corvette would pulverize him with her broadside.

That one shot must count.

He personally loaded the gun. It was unloaded with the tompion in, and that pleased him. He stared at the offerings Ferris displayed for his inspection.

"That one, I think," he said.

Grabbing the chain shot, Ferris brought the two hemispheres together. Like that it looked like a normal roundshot. Chain had more spread than bar. It had to do the job. Bar had more force than chain. But it would have to do. The thick links lay in the barrel up towards the muzzle.

They spiked the gun around and Fox prepared to take aim.

A furore of shouts and the banging of a pistol broke out from the two prizes astern.

Fox looked, cursing.

Phillips let rip an oath.

Over there, with the first coaster's sails down in untidy heaps, men were fighting.

The flash of a raised cutlass, a man's shriek – it was all confused.

"They hid 'emselves, sir, the blagskites!"

Fox yelled.

"Ferris, remain here with me to man the gun. All you men, get across there! Chuck those Dagos into the drink! *Jump!*"

With wild whoops the cutter's crew leaped towards the fight. Fox had no idea how many Spaniards there were; but the smell of trap was now unmistakable.

All his previous calculations had been wrong.

But – he felt he had reacted correctly; and time was running out.

The corvette surged up alongside. White water crashed away from her forefoot and her bowsprit dipped and rose as she strained on under full canvas.

She presented a fine spectacle.

Fox and Ferris manhandled the little brass gun around and Fox looked along the barrel. Now was the time to prove just how wonderful a shot he was. The story of how he had stolen a whole battery of nine-pounder field guns from Bonaparte had gone around the fleet, if he was not mistaken, and also the story of how he had blown up the battery's limbers with a single shot.

Well, he had known the gun he was using then. That had been a British nine-pounder, reckoned the most accurate of guns. Now he was handling a Spanish brass four-pounder and no doubt the bore was as straight as a corkscrew, to put it mildly.

He let his body take over, feeling the pointing barrel as an extension of his brain. Long hours on the Thames marshes as a boy had given him a perfect eye and arm with a slingshot, so that he could knock his supper out of the air ten times out of ten. This was a little different.

The noise of fighting continued on the trailing vessels.

He had not time for them now.

This corvette would knock *Raccoon* out of the water if she got at the brig.

He felt the swing and sway of the coaster. He watched the rise and fall of the corvette. He was aware of men in her pointing and then he lifted his eyes – both of them, thank the good Lord – to the fine mass of her rigging and spars.

Somewhere around the foretop. Yes, that would be the best place. He knew he was going to be lucky. He knew that with a conviction that would not be shaken. He knew, even as he applied the match, that he was going to strike.

The brass gun roared and heaved back on its trucks.

The smoke billowed and irritably he cuffed tendrils of it away from his face.

Ben Ferris let out a shriek; but Fox was bending to the powder again.

"A hit!" Ferris screamed. He started to dance and Fox roared in as malevolent a tone as he'd ever used to the boy, "Bring the next shot, you confounded idiot!"

Ferris leaped for the locker, dragging out the next shot. Fox had sponged out and loaded and now he carefully slid the chain shot in and rammed down. The fit was a trifle loose and he would have to figure that windage into his next shot. With a straining heave they ran the gun up.

He looked along the brass barrel again and – and saw the foremast of the corvette swaying forward and then, even as he stared, the lighted match ready, it folded backwards and smashed into the maintop.

A great billowing mass of sails and spars tangled and tumbled aloft over there.

He thrust the match down. The gun bellowed and bucked.

This time he stood to watch.

The corvette was crippled; no doubt of that.

And that meant . . .

"Ben! Get aft! Jump across to the next coaster—"

Ferris obeyed with the quick instinctive reaction of the trained sailor.

The smoke puffs, when they came, looked as ever more pretty than deadly.

Fox leaped.

He dived full length and the side of the coaster burst about him in splinters and whining death.

No doubt most gallant bone-headed naval officers would have stood proudly to receive the broadside. But Fox wanted to stay alive, and dignity meant nothing beside that. He saw the gun lifted and flung spinning backwards. A huge chunk of the bulwark was torn away and span crazily through the air, a giant rip-saw of destruction. Bits and pieces of spars and blocks and tackle fell on to the deck.

But he was not struck.

He breathed out and got to his feet.

Knowing when to make oneself scarce was a discipline hardly ever used in the navy. It had saved Fox's life before and, being Foxey, he devoutly hoped it would continue to do so in the future.

The fight was still going on aboard the other coaster.

The corvette had flown up into the wind and was falling off. Men were racing about aboard her. He let a grim and altogether unlovely smile twist his lips. Fox never smiled – except in circumstances of like nature. Let 'em stew!

He ran aft and clambered across to the second coaster.

As soon as he hit the deck he jerked out one of his pistols. A standard navy-issue pistol, it was still dry, having been carefully covered by a flap of tarpaulin cloth. He cocked it.

Men reeled about the deck. Two Spanish sailors lay face down by the rail, their blood running across the deck.

Ben Ferris was herding two Spaniards before him, emitting wild whoops, thrusting with his cut-down boarding-pike. That was a favourite weapon with young Ben Ferris. Barnabas had lost his cutlasses and now swung a tomahawk with such ferocious swings that the three Spaniards who were trying to get at him with cutlasses and knives had to skip out of the way or be cut into mincemeat. Phillips, Josephs, Hampton, the other members of his cutter's crew, were laying into the Spaniards.

"They were waiting for us, bigod!" yelled Fox, outraged at having walked into the trap. He pistolled a man with some fancy gold lace proclaiming him an officer and then yanked out his cutlass and pitched in.

The fight was a merry one – or as merry as a fight ever could be – and did not last long. In a few moments the British had overawed the Spaniards, disarmed them, and Phillips and Barnabas were herding them below into the tiny cramped cabin.

Fox looked out at the corvette.

Then he cursed, and cursed again, and the ring of devilish purple and black that had left him free all during the fight up to now formed treacherously around his left eye, barring off the sight that so infuriated him.

The Spanish corvette lay hove-to and judging by the amount of activity visible her captain must be rapidly going mad trying to sort out the raffle of wrecked spars and canvas that trailed all across his decks. He'd lost his foretopmast and his main topmast might come down at any moment and Fox hoped with keen malevolence that it would not go by the board but come down square across the deck and add to the confusion. And, in all that confusion, what he had expected to see – what any right-minded fighting sailor had every expectation of seeing – just was not taking place.

"The blagskites!" Fox said, hardly caring that his men could hear him. "What the devil does he think he's up to?"

For *Raccoon*, commanded by Richard Sanders, which should have been surging around to let fly with all her broadside at the corvette's quarter, and then coming round to let rip with the other, was tamely bearing away with the wind, aiming to clear the gap between the disabled corvette and the headland.

All his men and that included Barnabas now, had the sense to make no comment, even among themselves.

Phillips came running up, touching his forehead.

"Begging your pardon, sir. The leading coaster's going down, sir. Going fast."

"The devil she is!"

Fox jerked his one good eye away from that incredible sight of a British man-of-war meekly sidling past a disabled but still fighting-fit adversary, and looked forward.

The leading coaster must have been hulled by the corvette's

broadside. Typical Spanish gunnery, that had been, a broadside with a wide spread. Some of the shots had been good and some bad. Mind you, Fox thought as he ran forward, there were advantages as well as disadvantages in uncontrolled shooting of that nature.

He eyed the coaster. Water must be making fast. Already the hull was appreciably lower. There was no profit in thinking any more of the vessel. Whatever she contained would soon join the cargoes of all the other ships that littered the bed of the Mediterranean.

He rounded back on what there was left to him.

"We're taking these two prizes into Gibraltar!" he said to his men. His tone of voice was such that the arch-angel Gabriel himself would have knuckled his forehead and tailed on to a brace. "Clear all the raffle away." A boat lay on the third coaster's deck, still in its chocks. Maybe that might have been some kind of clue, although as a rule these vessels trailed their boats astern on a long line, their decks being cumbered enough.

He pointed.

"Ship that boat's gear and drop it overside. Phillips, you and Joseph roust out the Dagoes from below and put 'em in the boat. Any funny business, and . . ." He held up his cutlass significantly.

"Aye aye, sir."

The boat was quickly hoisted overside and the bewildered and miserable Spanish sailors herded in. Their clever scheme had come to nothing. Fox would have expected any kind of behaviour from them now. All the British kept a watchful eye on their prisoners; but the Spanish gave no trouble. They were not, clearly, the regular run of coaster sailormen; for one thing there were too many of them and they were all fit and active men, not the old men and boys usual in the trade now the war had swept up all the men able to fight.

The Spanish authorities had set a trap, and it had nearly worked.

The foretopsail had been cleared on the corvette and men were frantically at work cutting away the loose raffle. Fox eyed the maintop; but his hopes were not to be realized. After all, he had done tremendous damage with just one shot from a little four-pounder.

The corvette would be a cow to manoeuvre; but it could be done. Fox could do it, as could any anywhere-near competent captain or master in the service. If the Spaniard was a sailor he would bear away with what he had and go in chase of the brig. He might believe that the trap had worked in the coasters and leave them, as he would think, safely in Spanish hands.

Then again, he might not.

He might decide he could not hope to catch the brig and turn his attention to the coasters. He would have heard the sounds of the fighting. The boat with the prisoners was still hidden from him by the coasters themselves; but as soon as he spotted that he would know. Fox cursed his own thoughtless action. To have battened down the Spanish would be to invite trouble; to have killed them all and solved the problem that way, that would have been the best solution.

Fox glared at that corvette. He was getting soft in his old age.

"Phillips. Take half the men and get aboard the other coaster. Make sure you conform exactly to my movements. Set what we do. With this rig we can keep to windward of the Dagoes. I'm going out to wind'ard of 'em. Understood?"

"Aye aye, sir. I'll do the same as you, sir."

"Right. Get moving."

Fox quelled instantly the pang that struck him as he saw Phillips select Barnabas. The big red-head was a useful man, no doubt of that; but Fox had got along without him before and no single man made all that difference. He told Ben Ferris to take the tiller.

Old men and boys crewed these vessels and the rigging arrangements and sail plan were crude in the extreme, although Fox would have been the first to point out its effectiveness hammered out under practical conditions for hundreds of years. For sailormen of the Royal Navy there were no problems in setting the canvas and getting under way. The first coaster was now gunwale awash and would be gone in a few moments. Fox stared at her, bleakly, for only a moment. He did not like the thought of ship's endings – no matter whose ship she might be.

Something was going on aboard the corvette; but just what they were up to over there Fox couldn't be sure. The corvette hauled her wind and moved forward for a minute or so; then the yards went around and she dashed off south-eastwards, making Fox think she was after *Raccoon*. The brig, too, was beginning to beat back and keeping her offing. Fox consigned both vessels and their respective captains to Hades and got on with bringing his squadron – how grand that sounded! – out to windward.

"Watch your lee-helm, Ben," he growled. "Steer small, confound it, lad!"

"Aye aye, sir."

Ben Ferris, who was a silent lad, as far as Fox could tell given the enormous gulf that separated them within the hierarchy of the navy, knew how to handle a vessel. No doubt he had had plenty of experience in his merchantman days. His father, who had been drowned in that wreck in Palermo harbour, had made the decision to take his wife and boy to sea with him. Fox knew with an instinctive flash of revulsion that he would hesitate long and agonizedly before he took on himself the charge of taking a woman to sea.

The corvette, for whom he spared the sight of his good eye at regular intervals, appeared undecided. She seemed to be hovering out there. The two coasters sailed close-hauled. They clawed up into the north-east. Fox began to think he might get away with this after all.

"Ease off two points, Ben."

"Aye aye, sir."

He wanted to put as much room as possible between himself and the coast and now that he had weathered the corvette was the time to extend into the east. He checked that Phillips was conforming. As he did so, feeling the wind brisking up his neck, he realized he was seeing with both eyes again.

Gradually they were making searoom for themselves. An hour went by, two, and the corvette was a mere white triangle visible only from the masthead. Now was the time.

"Put your helm up, Ben."

"Aye aye, sir."

The coaster's head came around, the necessary orders, already given in preparation and now in execution, brought the canvas taut once again and the coaster picked up a lively turn of speed into the south-east. Fox took a turn up and down the deck, cursed as he saw a loosely piled raffle of rope and bawled a foul-mouthed and intemperate order, whereupon one of the hands leaped on the line as though it was an anaconda and rapidly and carefully flemished it down. Tucking his hands up into the small of his back, Fox marched back to the tiller.

Phillips had matched his turn exactly and now lolloped along on Fox's starboard quarter.

Being the man he was Fox never really thought he'd get away with that kind of saucy behaviour without a further fight. As the masthead yell reached him he felt a weary, almost indifferent flash of resignation sweep over him. The corvette had made up her mind and had clapped on what sail she had in pursuit. Now she was haring in, crojack only set on her mizzen to balance out the unequal thrust caused by the loss of her foretopsail, plunging along to shred him into little pieces of driftwood and bloody flesh if he did not strike.

He stared across and waited. Soon the Spaniard was hull up and gaining fast. Fox did not believe in striking his colours. He was a hard man, iron-hard, and whilst he recognized the irrationality of that kind of behaviour, so far he had seen no reason to mollify his beliefs. He gave the orders that set the men scurrying to break out powder and shot and train the brass four-pounder around. If this example shot as well as the one with which he'd crippled the corvette he would be satisfied.

"*Raccoon* ahoy!" yelled the masthead.

Fox waited, in a fever of impatience he concealed behind an iron and indifferent mask. He climbed halfway up the ratlines and stared carefully through the coaster's telescope he'd taken from the beckets on the deck-house bulkhead. Yes, bigod, *Raccoon*! Bowling along directly for them. Now what did Sanders think he was up to?

Once more the masthead hailed.

"Sail ho! Tops'ils, sir. Three on 'em – a frigate–"

Fox waited.

"British sir!" Then: "I think she's the old Nicky!"

By which he meant *Nike*. An eighteen-pounder thirty-two-gun frigate. It looked as though G.A. Fox had squeaked through again.

THE REVENGE

Frederick Marryat

More than anyone, Frederick Marryat (1792–1848) was respon-
sible for initiating the interest in stories of maritime action. He
wasn't quite the first. The grandfather of all naval action novels (if
we ignore such obvious predecessors as Defoe's Robinson Crusoe *or*
Swift's Gulliver's Travels*) is* The Adventures of Roderick
Random *(1748) by Tobias Smollett. But Marryat made a career*
out of them. He had a most distinguished naval career himself. He
joined the Royal Navy in September 1806, just a few weeks after
his fourteenth birthday, and he served with distinction under the
famous Captain Lord Cochrane in the frigate Imperieuse*. He*
remained in the navy until 1830, being promoted to commander in
1815. He then settled down to a literary career, having already
achieved success with The Naval Officer, or Scenes and Adventures in the Life of Frank Middlemay *(1829), a thinly disguised*
autobiographical novel. It was followed by The King's Own
(1830), about the Nore Mutiny, and the books that solidified
his reputation, Peter Simple *(1834),* Mr Midshipman Easy
(1836) and Masterman Ready *(1842). The last named was*
written more for younger readers and today Marryat is probably
better remembered for The Children of the New Forest *(1847)*
and tends to be dismissed as a writer of boys' adventures. As a
consequence one of his last books, certainly not intended for young
readers, The Privateersman *(1846), has become forgotten. It is*
the personal memoir of Alexander Musgrave, a privateer turned
adventurer, whose exploits take him from Europe to America and

*to Africa. The following episode is from the start of the novel and
recounts Musgrave's adventures in the West Indies and the Atlantic. Although undated, Marryat was almost certainly drawing
upon the exploits of the privateer schooner, the* Revenge, *under the
command of Robert Hosier which, in December 1799, was attacked
by four Spanish privateers off Vigo Bay.*

I

To Mistress———.

RESPECTED MADAM,

In compliance with your request I shall now transcribe from
the journal of my younger days some portions of my adventur-
ous life. When I wrote, I painted the feelings of my heart
without reserve, and I shall not alter one word, as I know you
wish to learn what my feelings were then, and not what my
thoughts may be now. They say that in every man's life,
however obscure his position may be, there would be a moral
found, were it truly told. I think, madam, when you have
perused what I am about to write, you will agree with me,
that, from my history, both old and young may gather profit,
and, I trust, if ever it should be made public, that, by divine
permission, such may be the result. Without further preface, I
shall commence with a narrative of my cruise off Hispaniola, in
the *Revenge* privateer.

The *Revenge* mounted fourteen guns, and was commanded by
Captain Weatherall, a very noted privateersman. One morning at
daybreak we discovered a vessel from the masthead, and immediately made all sail in chase, crowding every stitch of canvas.
As we neared, we made her out to be a large ship, deeply laden,
and we imagined that she would be an easy prize, but as we saw
her hull more out of the water she proved to be well armed, having
a full tier of guns fore and aft. As it afterwards proved, she was a
vessel of 600 tons burden, and mounted twenty-four guns,
having sailed from St Domingo, and being bound to France.

She had been chartered by a French gentleman (and a most gallant fellow we found him), who had acquired a large fortune in the West Indies, and was then going home, having embarked on board his whole property, as well as his wife and his only son, a youth of about seventeen. As soon as he discovered what we were, and the impossibility of escape from so fast a sailing vessel as the *Revenge*, he resolved to fight us to the last. Indeed, he had everything to fight for; his whole property, his wife and his only child, his own liberty, and perhaps life, were all at stake, and he had every motive that could stimulate a man. As we subsequently learnt, he had great difficulty in inspiring the crew with an equal resolution, and it was not until he had engaged to pay them the value of half the cargo provided they succeeded in beating us off, and forcing their way in safety to France, that he could rouse them to their duty.

Won by his example, for he told them that he did not desire any man to do more than he would do himself, and perhaps more induced by his generous offer, the French crew declared they would support him to the last, went cheerfully to their guns and prepared for action. When we were pretty near to him, he shortened sail ready for the combat, having tenderly forced his wife down below to await in agony the issue of a battle on which depended everything so dear to her. The resolute bearing of the vessel, and the cool intrepidity with which they had hove-to to await us, made us also prepare on our side for a combat which we knew would be severe. Although she was superior to us in guns, yet the *Revenge* being wholly fitted for war, we had many advantages, independent of our being very superior in men. Some few chase guns were fired during our approach, when, having ranged up within a cable's length of her, we exchanged broadsides for half an hour, after which our captain determined upon boarding. We ran our vessel alongside, and attempted to throw our men on board, but met with a stout resistance. The French gentleman, who was at the head of his men, with his own hand killed two of our stoutest seamen, and mortally wounded a third, and, encouraged by his example, his people fought with such resolution, that after a severe struggle we were obliged to give it up, and retreat precipitately into our own vessel, leaving eight or ten of our shipmates weltering in their blood.

Our captain, who had not boarded with us, was much enraged at our defeat, stigmatizing us as cowards for allowing ourselves to be driven from a deck upon which we had obtained a footing; he called upon us to renew the combat, and leading the way, he was the first on board of the vessel, and was engaged hand to hand with the brave French gentleman, who had already made such slaughter among our men. Brave and expert with his weapon as Captain Weatherall undoubtedly was, he for once found rather more than a match in his antagonist; he was slightly wounded, and would, I suspect, have had the worst of this hand-to-hand conflict, had not the whole of our crew, who had now gained the deck, and were rushing forward, separated him from his opponent. Outnumbered and overmatched, the French crew fought most resolutely, but notwithstanding their exertions, and the gallant conduct of their leader, we succeeded in driving them back to the quarterdeck of the vessel. Here the combat was renewed with the greatest obstinacy, they striving to maintain this their last hold, and we exerting ourselves to complete our conquest. The Frenchmen could retreat no further, and our foremost men were impelled against them by those behind them crowding on to share in the combat. Retreat being cut off, the French struggled with all the animosity and range of mingled hate and despair; while we, infuriated at the obstinate resistance, were filled with vengeance and a thirst for blood. Wedged into one mass, we grappled together, for there was no room for fair fighting, seeking each other's hearts with shortened weapons, struggling and falling together on the deck, rolling among the dead and the dying, or trodden under foot by the others who still maintained the combat with unabated fury.

Numbers at last prevailed; we had gained a dear-bought victory – we were masters of the deck, we had struck the colours, and were recovering our lost breaths after this very severe contest, and thought ourselves in full possession of the ship; but it proved otherwise. The first lieutenant of the privateer and six of us had dashed down the companion, and were entering the cabin in search of plunder, when we found opposed to our entrance the gallant French gentleman, supported by his son, the captain of the vessel, and five of the French sailors; behind them was the French gentleman's wife, to whose protection they had devoted themselves. The lieutenant, who headed us, offered them quarter, but stung to madness at the prospect of the ruin and of the captivity which awaited him, the gentleman treated the offer with contempt, and rushing forward attacked our lieutenant, beating down his guard, and was just about to pierce him with the lunge which he made, when I fired my pistol at him to save the life of my officer. The ball entered his heart, and thus died one of the bravest men I ever encountered. His son at the same time was felled to the deck with a pole-axe, when the remainder threw themselves down on the deck, and cried for quarter. So enraged were our men at this renewal of the combat, that it required all the efforts and authority of the lieutenant to prevent them from completing the massacre by taking the lives of those who no longer resisted. But who could paint the condition of that unhappy lady who had stood a witness of the horrid scene – her eyes blasted with the sight of her husband slain before her face, her only son groaning on the deck and weltering in his blood; and she left alone, bereft of all that was dear to her; stripped of the wealth she was that morning mistress of, now a widow, perhaps childless, a prisoner, a beggar, and in the hands of lawless ruffians, whose hands were reeking with her husband's and offspring's blood, at their mercy, and exposed to every evil which must befall a beautiful and unprotected female from those who were devoid of all principle, all pity, and all fear! Well might the frantic creature rush, as she did, upon our weapons, and seek that death which would have been a mercy and a blessing. With difficulty we prevented her from injuring herself, and, after a violent struggle, nature yielded, and she sank down in a swoon on the body of her husband, dabbling her clothes and hair in the gore which floated on the cabin deck.

This scene of misery shocked even the actors in it. Our sailors, accustomed as they were to blood and rapine, remained silent and immovable, resting upon their weapons, their eyes fixed upon the unconscious form of that unhappy lady.

The rage of battle was now over, our passions had subsided, and we felt ashamed of a conquest purchased with such unutterable anguish. The noise of this renewed combat had brought down the captain; he ordered the lady to be taken away from this scene of horror, and to be carefully tended in his own cabin; the wound of the son, who was found still alive, was immediately dressed, and the prisoners were secured. I returned on deck, still oppressed with the scene I had witnessed, and when I looked round me, and beheld the deck strewed with the dead and dying – victors and vanquished indiscriminately mixed up together – the blood of both nations meeting on the deck and joining their streams – I could not help putting the question to myself, "Can this be right and lawful – all this carnage to obtain the property of others, and made legal by the quarrels of kings?" Reason, religion, and humanity, answered, "No."

I remained uneasy and dissatisfied, and felt as if I were a murderer; and then I reflected how this property, thus wrested from its former possessor, who might, if he had retained it, have done much good with it, would now be squandered away in riot and dissipation, in purchasing crime and administering to debauchery. I was young then, and felt so disgusted and so angry with myself and everybody else, that if I had been in England, I probably should never again have put my foot on board of a privateer.

But employment prevented my thinking; the decks had to be cleaned, the bodies thrown overboard, the blood washed from the white planks, the wounded to be removed, and their hurts dressed, the rigging and other damages to be repaired, and when all this had been done, we made sail for Jamaica with our prize. Our captain, who was as kind and gentle to the vanquished as he was brave and resolute in action, endeavoured by all the means he could think of to soften the captivity and sufferings of the lady. Her clothes, jewels, and everything belonging to her, were preserved untouched; he would not even allow her trunks to be searched, and would have secured for her even all her husband's personal effects, but the crew had seized upon them as plunder, and refused to deliver them up. I am almost ashamed to say that the sword and watch of her husband fell to my lot, and whether from my wearing the sword, or from having seen me fire the pistol which had killed him, the lady always expressed her abhorrence of me whenever I entered her presence. Her son recovered slowly from his wound, and, on our arrival at Port Royal, was permitted by the admiral to be sent to the King's Hospital, and the lady, who was most tenderly attached to him, went on shore and remained at the hospital to attend upon him. I was glad when she was gone, for I knew how much cause she had for her hatred of me, and I could not see her without remorse. As soon as we had completed our repairs, filled up our provisions and water, we sailed upon another cruise, which was not so successful, as you will presently perceive.

For five or six weeks we cruised without success, and our people began to grumble, when one morning our boats in shore off Hispaniola surprised a small schooner. A negro who was among the prisoners offered to conduct us through the woods by night to the house of a very rich planter, which was situated about 3 miles from a small bay, and at some distance from the other plantations. He asserted that we might there get very valuable plunder, and, moreover, obtain a large ransom for the planter and his family, besides bringing away as many of the negro slaves as we pleased.

Our captain, who was tired of his ill-success, and who hoped also to procure provisions, which we very much wanted, consented to the negro's proposal, and standing down abreast of the bay, which was in the Bight of Lugan, he ran in at dark, and anchoring close to the shore, we landed with forty men, and, guided by the negro, we proceeded through the woods to the house. The negro was tied fast to one of our stoutest and best men, for fear he should give us the slip. It was a bright moonlight; we soon arrived, and surrounding the house, forced our way in without opposition. Having secured the negroes in the outhouses, and placed guards over them, and videttes on the lookout to give timely notice of any surprise, we proceeded to our work of plunder. The family, consisting of the old planter and his wife, and his three daughters, two of them very beautiful, was secured in one room. No words can express their terror at thus finding themselves so suddenly in the power of a set of ruffians, from whose brutality they anticipated every evil. Indeed the horrid excesses committed by the privateersmen, when they landed on the coast, fully justified their fears, for as this system of marauding is considered the basest of all modern warfare, no quarter is ever given to those who are taken in the attempt. In return, the privateersmen hesitate at no barbarity when engaged in such enterprises.

Dumb with astonishment and terror, the old couple sat in silent agony, while the poor girls, who had more evils than death to fear, drowned in their tears, fell at the captain's feet and embraced his knees, conjuring him to spare and protect them from his men.

Captain Weatherall, who was, as I have before stated, a generous and humane man, raised them up, assuring them, on his word, that they should receive no insult, and as his presence was necessary to direct the motions of his people, he selected me, as younger and less brutal than most of his crew, as a guard over them, menacing me with death if I allowed any man to enter the room until he returned, and ordering me to defend them with my life from all insults. I was then young and full of enthusiasm; my heart was kind, and I was pure in comparison with the major portion of those with whom I was associated.

I was delighted with the office confided to me, and my heart leaped at having so honourable an employment. I endeavoured by every means in my power to dissipate their terrors and soothe their anxious minds; but while I was thus employed, an Irish seaman, distinguished even amongst our crew for his atrocities, came to the door, and would have forced his entrance.

I instantly opposed him, urging the captain's most positive commands; but, having obtained a sight of the young females, he swore with a vile oath that he would soon find out whether a boy like me was able to oppose him, and finding that I would not give way, he attacked me fiercely. Fortunately, I had the advantage of position, and supported by the justice of my cause, I repelled him with success. But he renewed the attack, while the poor young women awaited the issue of the combat with trembling anxiety – a combat on which depended, in all probability, their honour and their lives. At last I found myself very hard pushed, for I had received a wound on my sword arm, and I drew a pistol from my belt with my left hand, and fired it, wounding him in the shoulder. Thus disabled, and fearing at the same time that the report would bring back the captain, whom he well knew would not be trifled with, he retired from the door vowing vengeance. I then turned to the young women, who had witnessed the conflict in breathless suspense, encircled in the arms of the poor old couple, who had rushed towards them at the commencement of the fray, offering them their useless shelter. Privateersman as I was, I could not refrain from tears at the scene. I again attempted to reassure them, pledged myself in the most solemn manner to forfeit my life if necessary for their protection, and they in some degree regained their confidence. They observed the blood trickling down my fingers from the wound which I had received, and the poor girls stained their handkerchiefs with it in the attempts to staunch the flow.

But this scene was soon interrupted by an alarm. It appeared that a negro had contrived to escape and to rouse the country. They had collected together from the other plantations, and our party being, as is usually the case when plunder is going on, very negligent, the videttes were surprised, and had hardly time to escape and apprise us of our danger. There was not a moment to be lost; our safety depended upon an immediate retreat. The captain collected all hands, and while he was getting them together that the retreat might be made in good order, the old planter who, by the report of the firearms and the bustle and confusion without, guessed what had taken place, pressed me to remain with them, urging the certainty of our men being overpowered, and the merciless consequences which would ensue. He pledged himself with his fingers crossed in the form of the crucifix, that he would procure me safe quarter, and that I should ever enjoy his protection and friendship. I refused him kindly but firmly, and he sighed and said no more. The old lady put a ring on my finger, which she took from her own hand, and kissing my forehead, told me to look at that ring, and continue to do good and act nobly as I had just done.

I waved my hand, for I had no time even to take the proffered hands of the young ones, and hastened to join my shipmates already on the retreat, and exchanging shots with our pursuers. We were harassed by a multitude, but they were a mixed company of planters, mulattoes, and slaves, and not half of them armed, and we easily repelled their attacks, whenever they came to close quarters. Their violent animosity, however, against us and our evil doings, induced them to follow close at our heels, keeping up a galling irregular fire, and endeavouring to detain us until we might be overpowered by their numbers, every minute increasing, for the whole country had been raised, and were flocking in. This our captain was well aware of, and therefore made all the haste that he could, without disturbing the regularity of his retreat, to where our boats were lying, as should they be surprised and cut off, our escape would have been impossible. Notwithstanding all his care, several of our men were separated from us by the intricacies of the wood, or from wounds which they had received, and which prevented them from keeping up with us. At last, after repelling many attacks, each time more formidable than the preceding, we gained our boats, and embarking with the greatest precipitation, we put off for the schooner. The enemy, emboldened by our flight, flocked down in great numbers to the water's edge, and we had the mortification to hear our stragglers, who had been captured, imploring for mercy; but groans and then silence too plainly informed us that mercy had been denied.

Captain Weatherall was so enraged at the loss of his men that he ordered us to pull back and attack the enemy on the beach, but we continued to pull for the schooner, regardless of his threats and entreaties. A panic had seized us all, as well it might. We even dreaded the ill-aimed and irregular fire which they poured upon us, which under other circumstances would have occasioned only laughter. The schooner had been anchored only 200 yards from the beach, and we were soon on board. They continued to fire from the shore, and the balls passed over us. We put a spring upon our cable, warped our broadside to the beach, and loading every gun with grape and cannister, we poured a whole broadside upon our assailants. From the shrieks and cries, the carnage must have been very great. The men would have reloaded and fired again, but the captain forbade them, saying, "We have done too much already." I thought so too. He then ordered the anchor to be weighed, and with a fresh land-breeze, we were soon far away from this unlucky spot.

II

About six weeks after the unlucky affair before described, we met with a still greater disaster. We had cruised off the Spanish Main and taken several prizes; shortly after we had manned the last and had parted company, the *Revenge* being then close inshore, a fresh gale sprung up, which compelled us to make all sail to clear the land. We beat offshore during the whole of the night, when the weather moderated, and at daybreak we found out that we had not gained much offing, in consequence of the current; but what was more important, the man who went to the lookout at the masthead, hailed the deck, saying there were two sail in the offing. The hands were turned up to make sail in chase, but we found that they were resolutely bearing down upon us; and as we neared each other fast, we soon made them out to be vessels of force. One we knew well – she was the *Esperance*, a French schooner-privateer of sixteen guns, and 120 men; the other proved to be a Spanish schooner-privateer, cruising in company with her, of eighteen guns, and full manned.

Now our original complement of men had been something

more than one hundred, but by deaths, severe wounds in action, and manning our prizes, our actual number on board was reduced to fifty-five effective men. Finding the force so very superior, we made every attempt with sails and sweeps to escape, but the land to leeward of us, and their position to windward, rendered it impossible. Making, therefore, a virtue of necessity, we put a good face upon it, and prepared to combat against such desperate odds.

Captain Weatherall, who was the life and soul of his crew, was not found wanting on such an emergency. With the greatest coolness and intrepidity, he gave orders to take in all the small sails, and awaited the coming down of the enemy. When everything was ready for the unequal conflict, he ordered all hands aft, and endeavoured to inspire us with the same ardour which animated himself. He reminded us that we had often fought and triumphed over vessels of much greater force than our own; that we had already beaten off the French privateer on a former occasion; that the Spaniard was not worth talking about except to swell the merits of the double victory, and that if once we came hand to hand our cutlasses would soon prove our superiority. He reminded us that our only safety depended upon our own manhood; for we had done such mischief on the coast, and our recent descent upon the plantation was considered in such a light, that we must not expect to receive quarter if we were overcome. Exhorting us to behave well, and to fight stoutly, he promised us the victory. The men had such confidence in the captain that we returned him three cheers, when, dismissing us to our quarters, he ordered St George's ensign to be hoisted at the mainmast head, and hove-to for the enemy.

The French schooner was the first which ranged up alongside; the wind was light, and she came slowly down to us. The captain of her hailed, saying that his vessel was the *Esperance*, and our captain replied that he knew it, and that they also knew that his was the *Revenge*. The French captain, who had hove-to, replied very courteously that he was well aware what vessel it was, and also of the valour and distinguished reputation of Captain Weatherall, upon which, Captain Weatherall, who stood on the gunnel, took off his hat in acknowledgment of the compliment.

Now Captain Weatherall was well known, and it was also well known that the two vessels would meet with a severe resistance, which it would be as well to avoid, as even if they gained the victory, it would not be without great loss of men. The French captain therefore addressed Captain Weatherall again, and said he hoped, now that he was opposed to so very superior a force, he would not make a useless resistance, but as it would be no disgrace to him, and would save the lives of many of his brave men, his well-known humanity would induce him to strike his colours.

To this request our commander gave a gallant and positive refusal. The vessels lay now close to each other, so that a biscuit might have been thrown on board of either. A generous expostulation ensued, which continued till the Spanish vessel was a short distance astern of us.

"You now see our force," said the French captain. "Do not fight against impossible odds, but spare your brave and devoted men."

"In return for your kind feeling towards me," replied Captain Weatherall; "I offer you both quarter, and respect to private property, upon hauling down your colours."

"You are mad, Captain Weatherall," said the French captain.

"You allow that I have lived bravely," replied Captain Weatherall; "you shall find that I will conquer you, and if necessary I will also die bravely. We will now fight. In courtesy, I offer you the first broadside."

"Impossible," said the French captain, taking off his hat.

Our captain returned the salute, and then slipping down from the gunwale, ordered the sails to be filled, and, after a minute to give the Frenchman time to prepare, he fired off in the air the fusee, which he held in his hand, as a signal for the action to begin. We instantly commenced the work of death by pouring in a broadside. It was returned with equal spirit, and a furious cannonading ensued for several minutes, when the Spaniard ranged up on our lee quarter with his rigging full of men to board us. Clapping our helm a-weather and hauling our fore-sheets to windward, we fell off athwart his hawse, and raked him with several broadsides fore and aft; our guns having been loaded with langridge and lead bullets, and his men being crowded together forward, ready to leap on board of us, her deck became a slaughterhouse. The officers endeavoured in vain to animate their men, who, instead of gaining our decks, were so intimidated by the carnage that they forsook their own. The Frenchman, perceiving the consternation and distress of his consort, to give her an opportunity of extricating herself from her perilous condition, now put his helm a-weather, ran us on board, and poured in his men; but we were well prepared, and soon cleared our decks of the intruders. In the meantime the Spaniard, by cutting away our rigging, in which his bowsprit was entangled, swung clear of us, and fell away to leeward. The Frenchman perceiving this, sheered off, and springing his luff, shot ahead clear of us. Such was the first act of this terrible drama. We had as yet sustained little damage, the enemy's want of skill and our own good fortune combined, having enabled us to take them at such a disadvantage.

But although inspirited by such a prosperous beginning, our inferiority in men was so great that our captain considered it his duty to make all sail in hopes of being able to avoid such an unequal combat. This our enemies attempted to prevent by a most furious cannonade, which we received and returned without flinching, making a running fight of it, till at last our fore yard and foretopmast being shot away, we had no longer command of the vessel. Finding that, although we were crippled and could not escape, our fire continued unabated, both the vessels again made preparations for boarding us, while we on our part prepared to give them a warm reception.

As we knew that the Frenchman, who was our most serious opponent, must board us on our weatherbow, we traversed over four of our guns loaded to the muzzle with musket balls to receive him, and being all ready with our pateraroes and hand-grenades, we waited for the attack. As he bore down for our bows, with all his men clinging like bees, ready for the spring, our guns were discharged and the carnage was terrible. The men staggered back, falling down over those who had been killed or wounded, and it required all the bravery and example of the French captain, who was really a noble fellow, to rally the remainder of his men, which at last he succeeded in doing, and about forty of them gained our forecastle, from which they forced our weak crew, and retained possession, not following up the success, but apparently waiting till they were seconded by the Spaniard's boarding us on our lee quarter, which would have placed us between two fires, and compelled us to divide our small force.

By this time the wind, which had been light, left us, and it was nearly a calm, with a swell on the sea, which separated the two vessels; the Spaniard, who was ranging up under our lee, having but little way and not luffing enough, could not fetch us, but fell off and drifted to leeward. The Frenchmen who had been thrown on board, and who retained possession of our forecastle, being thus left without support from their own vessel, which had been separated from us by the swell, or from the Spaniard, which had fallen to leeward, we gave three cheers, and throwing a number of hand-grenades in among them, we rushed forward with our half-pikes, and killed or drove every soul of them overboard, one only, and he wounded in the thigh, escaped by swimming back to his own vessel. Here, then, was a pause in the conflict, and thus ended, I may say, the second act.

Hitherto the battle had been fought with generous resolution; but after this hand-to-hand conflict, and the massacre with which it ended, both sides appeared to have been roused to ferocity. A most infernal cannonade was now renewed by both our antagonists, and returned by us with equal fury; but it was now a dead calm, and the vessels rolled so much with the swell, that the shot were not so effective. By degrees we separated more and more from our enemies, and the firing was now reduced to single guns. During this partial cessation our antagonists had drawn near to each other, although at a considerable distance from us. We perceived that the Spaniard was sending two of his boats full of men to supply the heavy loss sustained by his comrade. Captain Weatherall ordered the sweeps out, and we swept our broadside to them, trying by single guns to sink the boats as they went from one vessel to the other. After two or three attempts, a gun was successful; the shot shattered the first of the boats, which instantly filled and went down. The second boat pulled up and endeavoured to save the men, but we now poured our broadside upon them, and, daunted by the shot flying about them, they sought their own safety by pulling back to the vessel, leaving their sinking companions to their fate. Failing in this attempt, both vessels recommenced their fire upon us, but the distance and the swell of the sea prevented any execution, and at last they ceased firing, waiting till a breeze should spring up which might enable them to renew the contest with better success.

At this time it was about eleven o'clock in the forenoon, and the combat had lasted about five hours. We refreshed ourselves after the fatigue and exertion which we had undergone, and made every preparation for a renewal of the fight. During the engagement we were so excited, that we had no time to think; but now that we were cool again and unoccupied, we had time to reflect upon our position, and we began to feel dejected and apprehensive. Fatigued with exertion, we were weak and dispirited. We knew that our best men were slain or groaning under their severe wounds, that the enemy were still numerous, and as they persevered after so dreadful a slaughter, that they were of unquestionable bravery and resolution. Good fortune, and our captain's superior seamanship had, up to the present, enabled us to make a good fight, but fortune might desert us, and our numbers were so reduced, that if the enemy continued resolute, we must be overpowered. Our gallant captain perceived the despondency that prevailed, and endeavoured to remove it by his own example and by persuasion. After praising us for the resolution and courage we had already shewn, he pointed out to us that whatever might be the gallantry of the officers, it was clear that the men on board of the opposing vessels were awed by their heavy loss and want of success, and that if they made one more attempt to take us by the board and failed, which he trusted they would do, no persuasion would ever induce them to try it again, and the captains of the vessels would give over such an unprofitable combat. He solemnly averred that the colours should never be struck while he survived, and demanded who amongst us were base enough to refuse to stand by them. Again we gave him three cheers, but our numbers were few, and the cheers were faint compared with the first which had been given, but still we were resolute, and determined to support our captain and the honour of our flag. Captain Weatherall took care that this feeling should not subside – he distributed the grog plentifully; at our desire he nailed the colours to the mast, and we waited for a renewal of the combat with impatience. At four o'clock in the afternoon a breeze sprang up, and both vessels trimmed their sails and neared us fast – not quite in such gallant trim as in the morning it is true – but they appeared now to have summoned up a determined resolution. Silently they came up, forcing their way slowly through the water; not a gun was fired, but the gaping mouths of the cannon, and their men motionless at their quarters, portended the severity of the struggle which was now to decide this hitherto well-contested trial for victory. When within half a cable's length, we saluted them with three cheers, they returned our defiance, and running up on each side of us, the combat was renewed with bitterness.

The Frenchman would not this time lay us on board until he was certain that the Spaniard had boarded us to leeward – he continued luffing to windward and plying us with broadsides until we were grappled with the Spaniard, and then he bore down and laid his gunwale on our bow. The Spaniard had already boarded us on the quarter, and we were repelling this attack, when the Frenchman laid us on the bow. We fought with desperation, and our pikes gave us such an advantage over the swords and knives of the Spaniards, that they gave ground, and appalled by the desperate resistance they encountered, quitted our decks strewed with their dead and dying shipmates, and retreated in confusion to their own vessel. But before this repulse had been effected, the French had boarded us on the weatherbow, and driving before them the few men who had been sent forward to resist them, had gained our main deck, and forced their way to the rise of the quarterdeck, where all our remaining men were now collected. The combat was now desperate, but after a time our pikes, and the advantage of our position, appeared to prevail over numbers. We drove them before us – we had regained the main deck, when our brave commander, who was at our head, and who had infused spirit into us all, received a bullet through his right wrist; shifting his sword into his left hand, he still pressed forward encouraging us, when a ball entered his breast and he dropped dead. With his fall, fell the courage and fortitude of his crew so long sustained – and to complete the mischief, the lieutenant and two remaining officers also fell a few seconds after him. Astonished and terrified, the men stopped short in their career of success, and wildly looked round for a leader. The French, who had retreated to the forecastle, perceiving our confusion, renewed the attack, our few remaining men were seized with a panic, and throwing down our arms, we asked for quarter where a moment before victory was in our hands – such was the finale of our bloody drama.

Out of fifty-five men twenty-two had been killed in this murderous conflict, and almost all the survivors desperately or severely wounded. Most of the remaining crew after we had cried for quarter jumped down the hatchway, to avoid the cutlasses of their enraged victors. I and about eight others, having been driven past the hatchway, threw down our arms and begged for quarter, which we had little reason to expect would be shown to us. At first no quarter was given by our savage enemies, who cut down several of our disarmed men and hacked them to pieces. Perceiving this, I got on the gunwale ready to jump overboard, in the hopes of being taken up after the slaughter had ceased, when a French lieutenant coming up protected us, and saved the poor remains of our crew from the fury of his men. Our lives, however, were all he counted upon preserving – we were instantly stripped and plundered without mercy. I lost everything I possessed; the watch, ring, and sword

I had taken from the gallant Frenchman were soon forced from me, and not stripping off my apparel fast enough to please a Mulatto sailor, I received a blow with the butt-end of a pistol under the left ear, which precipitated me down the hatchway, near which I was standing, and I fell senseless into the hold.

III

On coming to my senses, I found myself stripped naked, and suffering acute pain. I found that my right arm was broken, my shoulder severely injured by my fall; and as I had received three severe cutlass wounds during the action, I had lost so much blood that I had not strength to rise or do anything for myself. There I lay, groaning and naked, upon the ballast of the vessel, at times ruminating upon the events of the action, upon the death of our gallant commander, upon the loss of our vessel, of so many of our comrades, and of our liberty. After some time the surgeon, by the order of the French commander, came down to dress my wounds. He treated me with the greatest barbarity. As he twisted about my broken limb I could not help crying at the anguish which he caused me. He compelled me to silence by blows and maledictions, wishing I had broken my rascally neck rather than he should have been put to the trouble of coming down to dress me. However, dress me he did, out of fear of his captain, who, he knew well, would send round to see if he had executed his orders, and then he left me with a kick in the ribs by way of remembrance. Shortly afterwards the vessels separated. Fourteen of us, who were the most severely hurt, were left in the *Revenge*, which was manned by an officer and twenty Frenchmen, with orders to take her into Port-au-Paix. The rest of our men were put on board of the French privateer, who sailed away in search of a more profitable adventure.

About an hour after they had made sail on the vessel, the officer who had charge of her, looking down the hatchway, and perceiving my naked and forlorn condition, threw me a pair of trousers, which had been rejected by the French seamen as not worth having, and a check shirt, in an equally ragged condition,

I picked up in the hold; this, with a piece of old rope to tie round my neck as a sling for my broken arm, was my whole wardrobe. In the evening I gained the deck, that I might be refreshed by the breeze, which cooled my feverish body and somewhat restored me.

We remained in this condition for several days, tortured with pain, but more tortured, perhaps, by the insolence and bragging of the Frenchmen, who set no bounds to their triumph and self-applause. Among those who had charge of the prize were two, one of whom had my watch and the other my ring; the first would hold it to me grinning, and asking if monsieur would like to know what o'clock it was; and the other would display the ring, and tell me that his sweetheart would value it when she knew it was taken from a conquered Englishman. This was their practice every day, and I was compelled to receive their gibes without venturing a retort.

On the eleventh day after our capture, when close to Port-au-Paix, and expecting we should be at anchor before nightfall, we perceived a great hurry and confusion on deck; they were evidently making all the sail that they could upon the vessel; and then hearing them fire off their stern-chasers, we knew for certain that they were pursued. Overjoyed at the prospect of being released, we gave three cheers. The French from the deck threatened to fire down upon us, but we knew that they dared not, for the *Revenge* was so crippled in the fight, that they could not put sail upon her so as to escape, and their force on board was too small to enable them to resist if overtaken – we therefore continued our exulting clamours. At least we heard guns fired, and the shot whizzing over the vessel – a shot or two struck our hull, and soon afterwards a broadside being poured into us, the Frenchmen struck their colours, and we had the satisfaction of seeing all these Gasconaders driven down into the hold to take our places. It was now their turn to be dejected and downcast, and for us to be merry; and now also the tables had to be turned, and we took the liberty of regaining possession of our clothes and other property which they carried on their backs and in their pockets. I must say we shewed them no mercy.

"What o'clock is it, monsieur?" said I to the fellow who had my watch.

"At your service, sir," he replied, humbly taking out my watch, and presenting it to me.

"Thank you," said I, taking the watch, and saluting him with a kick in the stomach, which made him double up and turn round from me, upon which I gave him another kick in the rear to straighten him again. "That ring, monsieur, that your sweetheart will prize."

"Here it is," replied the fellow, abjectly.

"Thank you, sir," I replied, saluting him with the double kick which I had given to the former. "Tell your sweetheart I sent her those," cried I, "that is, when you get back to her."

"Hark, ye, brother," cries one of our men, "I'll trouble you for that jacket which you borrowed of me the other day, and in return here are a pair of iron garters (holding out the shackles), which you must wear for my sake – I think they will fit you well."

"Mounseer," cries another, "that wig of mine don't suit your complexion, I'll trouble you for it. It's a pity such a face as yours should be disfigured in those curls. And while you are about it, I'll thank you to strip altogether, as I think your clothes will fit me, and are much too gay for a prisoner."

"I was left naked through your kindness the other day," said I to another, who was well and smartly dressed, "I'll thank you to strip to your skin, or you shall have no skin left." And I commenced with my knife cutting his ears as if I would skin them.

It was a lucky hit of mine, for in his sash I found about twenty doubloons. He would have saved them, and held them tight, but after my knife had entered his side about half an inch, he surrendered the prize. After we had plundered and stripped them of everything, we set to to kick them, and we did it for half an hour so effectually that they were all left groaning in a heap on the ballast, and we then found our way on deck.

The privateer which had recaptured us proved to be the *Hero*, of New Providence; the Frenchmen were taken out, and some of her own men put in to take us to Port Royal; we being wounded, and not willing to join her, remained on board. On our arrival at Port Royal, we obtained permission to go to the King's Hospital to be cured. As I went upstairs to the ward allotted to me, I met the French lady whose husband had been killed, and who was still nursing her son at the hospital, his wounds not having been yet cured. Notwithstanding my altered appearance, she knew me again immediately, and seeing me pale and emaciated, with my arm in a sling, she dropped down on her knees and thanked God for returning upon our heads a portion of the miseries we had brought upon her. She was delighted when she heard how many of us had been slain in the murderous conflict, and even rejoiced at the death of poor Captain Weatherall, which, considering how very kind and considerate he had been to her, I thought to be very unchristian.

It so happened that I was not only in the same ward, but in the cradle next to her son, and the excitement I had been under when we were recaptured, and my exertion in kicking the Frenchmen, had done me no good. A fever was the consequence, and I suffered dreadfully, and she would look at me, exulting in my agony, and mocking my groans, till at last the surgeon told her it was by extreme favour that her son had been admitted into the hospital instead of being sent to prison, and that if she did not behave herself in a proper manner, he would order her to be denied admittance altogether, and that if she dared to torment suffering men in that way, on the first complaint on my part, her son should go to the gaol and finish his cure there. This brought her to her senses, and she begged pardon, and promised to offend no more; but she did not keep her word for more than a day or two, but laughed out loud when the surgeon was dressing my arm, for a piece of bone had to be taken out, and I shrieked with anguish. This exasperated one of my messmates so much that, not choosing to strike her, and knowing how to wound her still worse, he drove his fist into the head of her son as he lay in his cradle, and by so doing reopened the wound that had been nearly healed.

"There's pain for you to laugh at, you French devil," he cried.

And sure enough it cost the poor young man his life.

The surgeon was very angry with the man, but told the French lady as she kneeled sobbing by the side of her son, that she had brought it upon herself and him by her own folly and cruelty. I know not whether she felt so, or whether she dreaded a repetition, but this is certain, she tormented me no more. On the contrary, I think she suffered very severely, as she perceived that I rapidly mended, and that her poor son got on but slowly. At last my hurts were all healed, and I left the hospital, hoping never to see her more.

THE NIGHT ATTACK

Richard Woodman

I am delighted to present this brand-new story featuring Nathaniel Drinkwater, which has been specially written for this book. Set in August 1801, it fits chronologically between the fourth and fifth books of the fourteen titles in Richard Woodman's Drinkwater series. It therefore follows The Bomb-Vessel, *which ends with the newly promoted Commander Drinkwater returning from the Baltic where he was present at the Battle of Copenhagen, and takes place before Drinkwater's departure for the Arctic as master and commander of the sloop* Melusine, *described in* The Corvette. *There is a reference in an early chapter of* The Corvette *to Drinkwater having acquired a second wound as a result of taking part in Lord Nelson's abortive attack on French invasion forces assembling at Boulogne. Drinkwater had sustained an earlier wound in the right arm as a result of a sword-fight in an alleyway in Sheerness related in* A King's Cutter. *Although this second compounding disfigurement is alluded to on several occasions in the subsequent novels, the action in which Nathaniel Drinkwater received it is here told for the first time.*

I

Commander Nathaniel Drinkwater stood poised expectantly in the stern of the cutter. He closed his watch as the first flowery plumes of smoke rose from the waists of the bomb-vessels anchored to the west of him and fished in his tail pocket for his Dollond glass. He caught sight of the thin line of one of the shell's trajectories as it rose overhead, culminated and then descended somewhere amid the forest of masts crowded in Boulogne harbour. The brief orange glow of explosions told where the shells burst, throwing up clouds of grey and, Drink-water fancied as he focused the telescope, the small and distant evidence of destruction.

"Give way if you please."

Beside him Midshipman James Quilhampton marked the drift of the cutter by the altering transit of his shore marks. The coxswain, a man named Hathaway, ordered the seamen to ply their oars, maintaining station in advance of Vice-Admiral Lord Nelson's squadron in an attempt to mark the fall of the shells. As the thunderous booms of the 10- and 13-inch mortars rolled across the rippled sea, Drinkwater felt a distinct lack of enthusiasm for his task. A better vantage point was to be had from the tops and mastheads of almost any one of Lord Nelson's men-of-war, including his own sixteen-gun brig-sloop *Wolf*, which lay at anchor offshore beyond the bomb-vessels. But Drinkwater, obedient to his lordship's command conveyed by a letter signed by Nelson's flag-captain, John Gore, had boarded the cutter sent from the flagship, taking Midshipman Quil-hampton with him. Hence he now occupied his advanced station close off the target of the mortars: the huge assembly of flat-boats, barges, *péniches*, *radeaux*, corvettes, luggers, gun-dalows and God knew what besides, assembled by General Bonaparte for the invasion of England. With peace between France and Austria, the war on the European continent had been won by the French. Great Britain was now isolated, the only hostile obstacle to the ambitions of revolutionary France.

The tone of Gore's note reflected the hurried, piecemeal assembly of the so-called "Anti-Invasion Flotilla". It was under this grandiloquent name that the Admiralty had scratched together an opposing collection of frigates, sloops, bomb-vessels, gun-brigs and gunboats. Their instructions to harry and deter the French forces had been issued by the First Lord of the Admiralty, Earl St Vincent. These orders had been intended to assuage the extreme public anxiety caused by the collapse of Britain's last continental ally, Austria. St Vincent had placed his favourite, Lord Nelson, in command of the flotilla partly to pacify his own political critics, but also to dissipate Nelson's immoral notoriety, acquired by his continuing scandalous liaison with Emma Hamilton. St Vincent's true strategic appreciation had been summed up in the House of Lords when the old man had risen to his feet to reassure their lordships that he did not say that the French would not invade, only that they would not invade by sea.

This witty remark was held in many quarters to be too clever a sophistry. Only the appointment of Nelson, the victorious hero of the battles of the Nile and Copenhagen, satisfied those who considered all that could be done, should be done.

As for Commander Drinkwater, he was not at all sure that the appointment of Nelson to the command of this odd assembly of men-of-war was entirely wise. While he shared St Vincent's conviction that an attempt by the French to throw a vanguard of 40,000 soldiers across the Channel to effect a beachhead was far more difficult than Bonaparte and his staff appreciated, he was anxious about Nelson's own intentions. Although there was nothing wrong with throwing explosive carcasses into a crowded anchorage as a means of interfering with whatever preparations the French had in train, Drinkwater, in common with most of the officers in the squadron, guessed that this was only a prelude to what Nelson had in mind. The entire British flotilla knew the admiral was a glory-hunter, often careless of the men he commanded in his ruthless desire to annihilate the enemy. Everyone had heard of the disastrous boat attack made on Tenerife one dark and blustery night four years earlier. Nelson himself had lost an arm in the affray, and this severe wound had somehow caught the sympathy of the public, obscuring the serious losses of other men and conveniently burying the accusations of foolhardiness and even bungling that were whispered in certain heretical corners.

Drinkwater was no coward, but was worried about this present enterprise against the invasion fleet of the French. After the careful, comprehensively plodding preparations and the final painstaking execution of the attack on Copenhagen earlier in the year, this new operation had all the hallmarks of hurried expediency. Were there not other flag-officers charged with the defence of the shores of Kent, Sussex and the Thames Estuary? Graeme commanded at The Nore and Lutwidge was in The Downs not fifteen miles away. It seemed clear that the firebrand Nelson had hoisted his flag at the main truck of the frigate *Medusa* with one objective in mind: to make a quick and major attack upon Bonaparte's invasion fleet at any cost. This haste was echoed in Drinkwater's own appointment to the *Wolf*, an order to transfer his crew from the bomb-vessel *Virago* to the brig-sloop and to commission her "with all despatch". Initially he had embraced the order with his customary energy, for the *Wolf* was bound upon "a particular service" which seemed to hold the promise of personal opportunity, but the process of disillusionment had begun when he had set eyes upon the dismantled *Wolf*. The appearance of *Virago* laid up in ordinary had been depressing enough, but that of *Wolf* had been far worse. Even now she bore all the marks of neglect about her hull and only her rigging displayed the diligence of men hard pressed to get her fit for war.

Perhaps there would be more time after this particular service had been executed to complete her paintwork and better organize her interior arrangements. Fortunately the Viragos were well acquainted with the business of storing and stowage, their old ship having been in her original form nothing more prestigious than a bomb-tender, but Drinkwater would have liked to make his debut as a sloop commander in a vessel in which he could have taken a little more pride. Not that the *Wolf* was not a smart enough craft under her patina of neglect; on the contrary she had been French-built only four years previously, a privateer of sixteen six-pounder guns fitted out for an *armateur* of Nantes. But since being captured by the British frigate *Magnanime* she had been languishing in the Medway with a few scandalously idle hands assigned to maintain her.

"Very well . . ."

Quilhampton's voice brought Drinkwater back to the present with a jerk. He had been about to embark on another train of thought, that of his wife's new pregnancy, but threw his anxieties on Elizabeth's behalf aside. That too was clouding his judgment these days, and he could not admit so personal an intrusion into the afternoon's business. He coughed to clear his mind as much as his throat, lowering his glass and turning to stare down at the midshipmen in the stern.

Mr Quilhampton looked up expectantly. The young man's gangling figure, with its incongruous wooden fist in which he held a writing tablet, seemed oddly out of sorts with the popular image of the Royal Navy's midshipmites. The boy next to him was more in keeping with the public notion, a small blond child whose parents should be horse-whipped for sending so delicate a creature aboard a man-of-war. He, like the cutter, her coxswain and her oarsmen, belonged to *Medusa*, though unlike them he looked sadly inexperienced on this warm August afternoon. Drinkwater smiled at the boy.

"Mr, er . . . ?"

"Fitzwilliam, sir," the boy squeaked nervously as he eyed the standing figure with the scarred cheek, the long queue down his back and the odd blue marks on one eyelid. Mr Fitzwilliam was as yet unable to stand up in a boat; as for the figure of the strange commander with his single epaulette, it seemed to the boy that the remote persons who bore such gold embellishments were an odd, disfigured breed. This Commander Drinkwater, though not quite so knocked about as Admiral Lord Nelson, seemed to have something wrong with his right arm. As for the timber fist of his adjacent colleague, Midshipman Quilhampton, poor Mr Fitzwilliam could not bring himself to look at so horrible a thing! The wretched boy kept his eyes steadfastly on the commander and thought he did not look so forbidding when he smiled.

"Mr Fitzwilliam," Drinkwater was saying kindly, "I desire that you take the cutter in a little closer. I fear we are going to disappoint his lordship at this remove."

Drinkwater nodded encouragingly. The greenhorn midshipman had been told to repeat all orders so that they were known to be comprehended by both parties and he did so now with a certain diffidence.

"T . . . take the cutter in a little closer, sir. Aye aye."

Next Fitzwilliam turned to the grizzled coxswain who, Drinkwater guessed, had been appointed by Gore or his first luff to be sea-daddy to the tow-haired infant.

"Hathaway, take the cutter in a little closer, if you please."

"Aye aye, sir," Hathaway responded with a dry and solemn dignity. "Stand by . . ." The oarsmen leaned forward and their oar blades flashed in the sunshine as they held them poised above the glassy surface of the Strait. "Give way . . . tooogether!" At Hathaway's last syllable they stabbed at the water, the grunting seamen leaning back while the cutter laid her clinker strakes to the tide and sent the water chuckling away from her cut-water.

"Keep her on this transit, Mr Q," Drinkwater said to his own acolyte as he braced himself against the sudden surge of the boat. "Oh, and you had better explain to Mr Fitzwilliam what a transit is and how he will need to crab across this damned tide to maintain it."

"Aye aye, sir."

Drinkwater raised his glass again, satisfied with Quilhampton's explanation as the older midshipman coached the younger in the business of allowing for the set of the tide, pointing out the two marks they had selected to keep in line as they swept in closer to the French anchorage.

II

"I think, my lord, that we certainly hit several of their lugger-rigged gundalows, and we may have sunk two or three of 'em. One was most positively driven ashore, for I did see a shell explode forward and shortly afterwards noted her drifting out of the line—" Drinkwater ceased speaking as Lord Nelson cut him short.

"Thank you. So, out of the two dozen corvettes, gundalows and a schooner, we sank two or three, and perhaps drove another ashore." The admiral stared around the group of officers gathered in the *Medusa*'s stern cabin which did duty as his headquarters. The candlelight sparkled on their gilt buttons and their single epaulettes, for all except Gore, *Medusa*'s captain, were mere masters and commanders. The admiral's good eye raked each in turn, his wide mouth mobile with his suppressed disappointment.

"I saw a brig-corvette in trouble, my lord, at the tail of the line . . ."

"Did anyone else other than Captain Cotgrave witness a corvette in trouble?"

"Yes, my lord," confirmed Commander Somerville, "I did, though my first lieutenant initially spotted her predicament. I think she too drifted out of the line and may have got ashore."

"You did not see this from your advanced position, Captain Drinkwater?"

Drinkwater shook his head. "I did not, my lord, but it seems quite possible since she could have been obscured, my horizon being somewhat limited by my height of eye and the arrangement of the French line."

"Quite so. Then we must have effected some damage within the pier, judging by the amount of shells thrown into the place and the crowded state of the anchorage. Confound it, we lost three men ourselves as a consequence of a mere handful of shells the enemy fired back at us!" The admiral's tone of voice made the lilt of his Norfolk accent rise as he expressed his exasperation. "I think therefore that ten is a not impossible number by way of losses of flat-boats and the like, but I had hoped for more, damn it!" Nelson stared down on the table where a sheet of notes lay over a chart of the Strait of Dover. After a moment he looked up and his whole body stiffened with resolve, the movement making the stars upon his breast glitter in the candlelight and drawing attention to the empty, gilt-braided cuff pinned across his chest. "Well, gentlemen, it ain't much of a haul for the expenditure of powder and shells! Over 900 carcasses were thrown at the enemy, but it shall have to suffice for the moment."

"It has proved useful as a reconnaissance, my lord," enthused the young Edward Parker, catching the admiral's mood.

"That may be so, Edward, but if we have but tapped at the door, they will be the readier when we next pay them a call."

A low murmur of assent greeted this remark. Drinkwater, waiting in silence as behove the most junior commander, felt the worm of anxiety uncoil in his belly. There was something vaguely posturing about the gallant admiral, and something disturbing about the response it evoked among the young officers surrounding him as he assiduously plied them all with the courtesy title of "captain".

"And might we know when that might be, my lord?" Parker asked, presuming on his friendship with the admiral, but asking the question that was almost palpably springing up all around the table.

"Well, I shall need to consult the almanac, gentlemen, but I can tell you now that it will be a night attack."

III

"We should be concentrating against Flushing," Lieutenant Rogers said firmly. He and Drinkwater paced the *Wolf*'s tiny quarterdeck as the brig-of-war lay under her topsails, stemming the ebb as it ran fast through the Strait of Dover. "That is where the greater number of flat-boats lie."

"I heard aboard *Medusa* that Nelson is all for striking Flushing but that we lack the resources or the time for such a move. Moreover, St Vincent is the more eager for a blow against Boulogne."

Drinkwater broke off and cast a glance about the horizon. To the north-west, dark against the afterglow of the sunset, the cliffs of Dover stood sharp against the sky. To the east only a smear of grey marked the cape of that name, as Cap Gris Nez faded into the night, so insubstantial that it seemed impossible that a few miles inland an army massed to invade England. But then in the twilight even Rogers's face was growing indistinct as Drinkwater and his first lieutenant discussed the situation.

"I presume St Vincent wants to strike directly at France, hence his desire to attack Boulogne," Drinkwater went on after satisfying himself no hostile sail was in sight.

"Aye," added Rogers, "'tis the nearest port and that from which the first assault would come."

"Perhaps," responded Drinkwater, unconvinced. "Anyway," he added, "we shall have to wait a day or two, I suppose. His lordship has gone to Harwich, though for what purpose I do not know."

"To throw one arm and both legs about La Belle Hamilton, I'd say," Rogers said in his coarse way.

Drinkwater ignored the crude reference to Nelson's mistress. "Well, if it is to be Boulogne again, I think we shall find the French have not been idle. They were active enough this afternoon."

"Quilhampton said that you thought they were laying out chain moorings . . ."

"No doubt about it," Drinkwater said promptly. "I have done the same myself sufficient times to know what they were up to," he said, referring to his own years as mate of a Trinity house buoy-yacht. "They have clearly protected the invasion craft in the inner harbour with that cordon of moored vessels outside the mole. Such a boom constructed by mooring their corvettes and outer gundalows head-and-stern with chain will prove most effective. The Elder Brethren of the Trinity House have long had such a contingency in mind for blocking the Thames. If the French stuff those outer vessels full of infantrymen and marines as well as their regular seamen, then cover the cordon with fire from batteries ashore, we shall have as a warm a reception as met his lordship's last such assault on Tenerife."

"Good God Almighty, I had forgot that fiasco!" Rogers exclaimed.

"And you should recall the strength of the tides hereabouts," Drinkwater added gloomily. "I fear Lord Nelson, with his greatest triumphs in the Mediterranean and the Baltic, has too little appreciation of the tides.''

It was a conviction that had been growing for some time in Drinkwater's mind. He was familiar with these waters, for it had been here that he had cut his teeth as a young man in the buoy-yachts of Trinity House when, after the American War, the Royal Navy had had no use for him. And here too, not so very long ago when the revolution convulsed France and first precipitated war with Britain, Drinkwater had rejoined the Royal Navy and, as master's mate aboard the man-of-war cutter *Kestrel*, had carried out the cloak-and-dagger orders of the Admiralty's Secret Department. He knew well that operations conducted in these waters had to be precisely planned, that delays compromised success and that it was better to abandon an enterprise rather than have it miscarry to the enemy's advantage. The bombardment of the invasion craft at Boulogne on 4 August had been a lacklustre affair, and any repetition seemed doomed now that the French had had due warning. It was inconceivable that they had not reinforced their defences.

On the 14th a lugger appeared, recalling to the admiral's anchorage in The Downs the *Wolf* and the two hired revenue cutters left to watch Boulogne. That evening Drinkwater found himself again in *Medusa*'s Great Cabin as the extempore flagship swung to her best bower, under the lee of the Kent coast. As he listened to Nelson summing up his plan and impressing upon the assembled commanders the necessity of keeping in close contact, Drinkwater felt his gloomiest forebodings coming true, for Nelson proposed nothing less than a grand cutting-out expedition. The boats of the squadron, supported by howitzer-armed launches, were to seize all the craft lying at anchor outside the pier of Boulogne, cut them loose from their moorings, and bring them out under the guns of the frigates *Medusa* and *Leyden*, the sloops and the gun-brigs.

During the discussion, Drinkwater had emphasized his belief that the enemy had formed a defensive cordon of their own vessels anchored not by rope cables, but moored head-and-stern by chains. Somerville, who would lead the first division of boats in his capacity as senior commander, buried any anxieties under a cheerful response. He had some reason for this, for if he succeeded and survived, he would undoubtedly be promoted to post captain.

"Well," Somerville had concluded to Nelson's obvious approval, "once we have taken their decks, we shall be put to the trouble of casting them off from these chain moorings you so apprehend, Captain Drinkwater. However, I think this will prove but a trifle." Nelson agreed with Somerville, and Drinkwater felt stung by the admiral's quick glance in his own direction. He coloured accordingly and was still flushed as the commanders took their written orders from Nelson's secretary and walked out on to *Medusa*'s twilit quarterdeck, unaware that there was any concern in the minds of others until John Conn, a man whom Drinkwater did not know and under whom Drinkwater would serve with a division of howitzer boats, plucked his sleeve and drew him to one side.

"Drinkwater," Conn began, "you clearly perceive the difficulties of this night's work."

"Indeed, I do and it runs to more than mere anxiety about the strength of the enemy's moorings. I am very concerned about the ability of the boats to act in concert, for the tides are devilish strong and at night separation is all too likely."

"Perhaps, but the admiral is determined. Besides, who are we to question the affair until our blood is spilled in sufficient quantity to appease the public appetite for gore? No pun is intended, I assure you, but it strikes me that our role of giving covering fire may place us in a position of attracting more attention than we warrant. However, I want to assure you that I shall support Somerville to my utmost and that I shall expect you to be of similar mind."

"What precisely are you saying, Commander Conn?" A horrified Drinkwater, aware that he had misunderstood Conn, confronted his colleague. "That you share Lord Nelson's doubt as to my courage because I report a strengthening of the French defences?" Drinkwater's blood ran icily cold now. He felt his fists clenching and he longed for the mad catharsis of action to put an end to this shilly-shallying. "Have a care, sir," he said as he turned on his heel and went to seek his boat.

IV

A little over twenty-four hours later, at half past eleven on the evening of 15 August 1801, the assembled fleet of boats bobbed in the darkness alongside the *Medusa*. The squadron lay all around them in mid-Channel, well to the east of the Varne shoal and about a league off Boulogne. The night was moonless and dark, with a light breeze from the east and a low swell from the west, the one bringing the pleasant scent of the land, the other warning of a gale far out in the Atlantic. The tide was flooding, running north-east past Boulogne, with a greater strength on the French coast than on the opposite English shore.

Somerville's division led off, his boats loosely roped together, followed by those of Parker, Cotgrave and Jones. Conn and Drinkwater's howitzer boats, consisting of launches from Chatham and Sheerness dockyards, each of which bore a small mortar, departed last.

"Keep close up with Somerville, Captain Conn, and good luck to you." Drinkwater heard Nelson's East Anglian accent cut the night air with its characteristically slightly high-pitched diction.

"Aye aye, my lord, and thank you," Conn responded. No word of encouragement or instruction came from *Medusa*'s rail for the last division to leave. Commander Nathaniel Drinkwater felt the omission keenly; it was as if his part in this night's enterprise was of no consequence, and he was already forgotten.

Sitting in the stern of the big launch Drinkwater brooded on his misfortune. Not to have reported the strengthening of the French line would have been a dereliction of duty, so the attracting of vague suggestions of cowardice were unjust. But the inner conviction that matters augured ill had undoubtedly engendered a lack of enthusiasm, and he regretted revealing this to Conn. The man's odd turn of phrase had misled him into thinking he shared Drinkwater's misgivings, but there was nothing he could do about it now, except avoid any further possibility of such accusations during the attack, which meant he must now thrust himself forward to avoid the slightest chance of such a charge. To this end he had sent Quilhampton forward, to keep an eye on the boats ahead, taking a seat in the sternsheets beside Tregembo and alongside the artillery bombardier and two artillerymen who would man the mortar when they closed the enemy. Following astern of Drinkwater's launch came the other four boats in his division, but the night was so dark that already there was no sign of *Medusa* or her consorts, though they could not yet be far away.

"This is likely to go very ill with us," Drinkwater muttered, lowering his glass and sitting down in the sternsheets and instantly regretting giving voice to his misgivings.

"Do you know where we are, sir?" a voice asked in the darkness and Drinkwater made out the face of the bombardier, clearly a man mystified as to how they knew their way over the black water. The man's nervous curiosity drew a brittle laugh from Drinkwater, but he said nothing to assuage the fellow's anxiety, merely bending to uncover the shuttered lantern so that, for a brief moment, the candlelight fell upon the boxed compass lying on the bottom-boards.

"Ah," the bombardier sighed, none the wiser.

"Can you see the next ahead, Mr Q?" Drinkwater called.

"Just about, sir."

Drinkwater grunted and looked astern to where a faint white feather showed the second boat in his own division. The rhythmic sway of the oarsmen and gentle knocking of the muffled oar-looms on their thole-pins was accompanied by the faint grunts of the labouring oarsmen. From time to time the bright glow of phosphorescence was stirred up by the dipping blades and with every stroke those in the stern swayed forward and back in a curious motion that induced a state of somnolence in those not actively employed. Drinkwater's mind wandered obsessively back to the council aboard *Medusa*.

Had Nelson really glared at him, or had he imagined it? True, he had got off to a bad start with his lordship months earlier when they had met in Great Yarmouth, but the misunderstanding had been cleared up and he had been in no doubt that his conduct under fire at Copenhagen had attracted Nelson's notice. Moreover, the little one-armed admiral had commended him to the commander-in-chief for promotion. But Conn's unpleasant comment seemed to lend credence to Drinkwater's view that his own assessment of the French preparations had been taken, not as a professional judgment, but an indication of his lack of personal courage.

Many men lost their appetite for danger if they did not lose their nerve altogether and, it occurred to Drinkwater, he was the oldest among the commanders, a fact emphasized by his unfashionable queue, his shabby uniform and his several disfigurements. This would not be lost on his younger colleagues. Conn, Parker, Somerville and the rest were as eager as puppies, and he would have to put up with his present circumstances as with so much else in this unfair and unfathomable life. At this point in his philosophical deliberations Quilhampton's voice jerked him back to reality.

"Sir! I can't see the boat ahead!"

"God's bones!" Drinkwater blasphemed and bent to uncover the lantern and check their course. They were two points to starboard of it. Why the devil had he fallen prey to foolish daydreaming? "Come to larboard, Tregembo!"

"Larboard hellum, sir." His own coxswain acknowledged the order and the boat heeled slightly as she swung.

Again Drinkwater looked astern. It was bad enough losing touch with Conn, but to lose contact with his own boats would be unforgivable! The white feather was still behind them and he saw it follow them round as they adjusted their course.

"Steady," Drinkwater said, relieved. "Steady as you go . . ."

The launch drove on and Drinkwater relaxed a few minutes later when Quilhampton called out that he could see something ahead, then confirmed it as the transom of a boat. Drinkwater's relief was short-lived, for they rapidly overhauled the stranger and found her lying on her oars, all alone.

"What boat is that?" Drinkwater called out in a low voice.

"Number three in Captain Somerville's division. Who are you . . . sir?" The voice was adolescent and uncertain, but the strange boat got under way again, keeping pace with them as the midshipman in charge answered.

"You say you are with Somerville?" Drinkwater asked, astonished.

"Is that Captain Drinkwater?"

"It is. Is that Mr Fitzwilliam?"

"Yes, sir."

"Have you lost touch with your next ahead, Mr Fitzwilliam?"

"Er, yes, sir; I think I have. Our line parted." The boy was obviously terrified at the consequences of his failure.

"Very well, Mr Fitzwilliam, maintain station on my starboard beam."

"On your starboard beam, sir, aye aye," responded the relieved midshipman.

They pulled on, Drinkwater leaving the compass uncovered and consulting his watch. Another quarter of an hour dragged by and then, quite suddenly, all the uncertainty ended when about seven cables' length ahead they saw a bright flash light up the night. This was followed by smaller, surrounding points of twinkling fire as first the howitzers and then the small arms of what Drinkwater presumed to be Conn's and Parker's divisions encountered the line of anchored French vessels. The boom and crackle of the discharges rolled over the water towards them, accompanied by the flash of the defending gunfire which was startling in its furious concentration. Against the individual flashes of Conn's howitzers and a pair of twelve-pounder boat-carronades in Parker's craft, the low line of a score of cannon stabbed the night with brilliant points of fire. Before the concussion of the French response reached Drinkwater, the whine of shot and even the splash and curious whizzing noise made by a ricochet flew past them.

"Steadeeee, my lads," Drinkwater growled. "Keep the stroke, my boys, keep it going together; that's the way, that's the way." He coaxed them along, keeping their minds on their laborious task.

They could hear the shouting now, and Drinkwater could see intermittently in stark images that lingered on the retinae brief vignettes of the struggle as they drew closer. Conn's boats lay on their oars firing their mortars, while what he assumed were Parker's were already clustered alongside the elegant sheer of a corvette and her flanking neighbours. He could see figures reaching up in an attempt to gain the corvette's decks, saw men clustered on the channels, thrusting inboard with pikes and cutlasses. Among them the sparkle of fire-locks was less intense as men grappled hand to hand, and then the ordered discharge of a volley of musketry betrayed the presence of French infantry or marines.

"Up forrard!" Drinkwater ordered the bombardier and his artillerymen as he motioned Tregembo to ease the stroke and then to hold water. The launch was stopped and then Quilhampton clambered aft and acted as co-ordinator, ordering the oars plied to swing the boat on to target. Like Conn's, Drinkwater's boats were to hold off and throw their shells over the boat attack made on the enemy's cordon largely to intimidate reinforcement from the shore, but also to do whatever execution they could. They were already late getting to their station, a fact that would doubtless be held against him if the night's work went according to Drinkwater's doom-laden prognostications.

A moment later the bombardier expressed himself satisfied and with a great roar and a bucking of the launch, the howitzer threw its first charged carcass high into the air. A faint trail of red soared up as the shell's fuse rose on its high trajectory before it fell beyond the flashing fire-fight of the main assault.

After the sudden momentary blindness that followed the flash of the howitzer's discharge, Drinkwater became aware of Fitzwilliam's adjacent boat. As the artillerymen carefully prepared the next shell, he raised his voice and pointed ahead.

"Mr Fitzwilliam! There is where you should be! Do you go forward directly and lend your support!"

The midshipman's response was drowned in the boom as the next howitzer boat in Drinkwater's own division fired her own mortar, and one by one the rest of his craft reached their positions to bombard the French. Watching Fitzwilliam's boat pull forward, vividly if erratically silhouetted against the gunfire ahead, Drinkwater raised his glass and took stock of the situation. He was aware that Quilhampton had continuously to order the boat's crew to ply their oars, for the north-easterly flood tide was as strong as Drinkwater had predicted and in order to fire the howitzers they had to lie athwart the stream. Their own rate of fire was therefore necessarily slow. Moreover, as a result of this constant manoeuvring the tide was setting them obliquely towards the action. Drinkwater's heavy launch was by now drawing close to a brig-corvette, around which a number of the British boats had clustered. It was clear that the attackers had thus far been unsuccessful in gaining command of her deck, for Drinkwater could see not only a spirited defence being put up by the musketry of soldiers and marines, but the occasional shot from broadside guns still punched the night with flame and fire. Drinkwater observed, amid the shouts, screams, oaths, sputter of small arms, and the general clash of hand-to-hand fighting, the presence of taut boarding nettings leading up from the corvette's rails to her lower yard-arms. The attackers were unable to penetrate this defensive web. As he waited for his own howitzer to fire again, Drinkwater watched horrified as Mr Fitzwilliam's boat was swept by an iron hail. He saw the craft slew round, a mess of splintered oars and planking, the scream of her wounded piercing the night before she drifted inexorably north. God's bones, he had ordered that child into an inferno!

An instant later the air round them too was full of the lethal buzz and whine of projectiles. His own launch shuddered under the impact of shot, while grape and langridge spattered viciously into the water all around them.

"God *damn* the French!" a seaman cried, clapping one hand to his useless arm and relinquishing his hold on his oar-loom. The loss of the oar was only averted by Quilhampton grabbing it while the wounded oarsman, his arm smashed, sobbed in a kind of pathetic rage at his bloody misfortune.

"God's bones!" Drinkwater blasphemed again, as the bottom-boards beneath his feet bucked with the discharge of their own howitzer, then darkened as water ran over them. "Clap a pledget on that man, Mr Q, and tell him to keep his mouth shut! Look for leaks under your feet, men, and stuff your kerchiefs into 'em. Come, look lively!"

As the boat slewed round, her crew bent and checked the planking about them, tearing off their neckerchiefs where the black roil of water betrayed the ingress of water. Drinkwater looked to the right and the left. He could see a struggle similar to that engulfing the corvette taking place alongside other craft to the north; to the south a further attack was being made, though on what Drinkwater could not see as the tide bore them away. Further gunfire flashes were intermittently visible elsewhere, but these were disembodied and confused, lacking the cohesion so essential to the achievement of Nelson's objective. As he stared through his glass Drinkwater was convinced that this was not the mass attack that the admiral intended; it had all the appearance of going off at half-cock. Where in God's name were the remainder of the British boats?

A rumbling of oaths came from near at hand and Drinkwater lowered his glass. "What's amiss?" he growled.

"Mortar's split, sir." It was the bombardier's voice. "We've fired our last shot, I'm afraid."

"Well, thank God for that," Drinkwater said, shutting his glass with a snap. "Now we may be able to do something useful." Aware that Quilhampton had clambered forward and was now working his way aft checking on the stopping of the leaks, Drinkwater asked, "Well, are we fit for further duty?"

"No doubt about it, sir," said Quilhampton, "though we've a man dead forward, as well as Bellings being wounded."

"Who's gone forward?"

"'Tis Jameson, sir," someone piped up. "Shall I pitch him over the side?"

"Aye, if you please, and Bellings, do you move aft and let Mr Q have a look at your wound."

"I'm all right, sir . . ."

"Do as you're told," Drinkwater snapped.

"Aye aye, sir."

As this reorganization took place, Drinkwater peered to the north. Something caught his eye and a quixotic hope leaped in his heart as the oars were once more manned and the boat's crew settled to their wearying task. He ordered Tregembo to give way. "Put the helm over hard a-larboard, Tregembo," he added, conning the boat away from the fight.

Within five minutes they had come up with Fitzwilliam's boat as it lay wallowing, half submerged, its oars wrecked, its crew badly shattered by the full force of two bags of grapeshot. Even in the darkness Drinkwater could see a cold pallor on the features of the young midshipman as he was almost tenderly passed across into Drinkwater's boat and laid down on the wet boards of the sternsheets. Only five or six fit men were able to clamber after their young chief as, leaving the remaining wounded with orders to pull the boat as best they could into the tide, Drinkwater swung his own launch round again.

"Now put your backs into it!" he ordered sharply. "Tregembo, lay me alongside that bloody corvette, and you spare hands change the priming and charges in your pieces."

Fitzwilliam's boat had been intended for the assault and the handful of armed men they had taken out of her might prove useful additions to Drinkwater's own. Ordering the three now unemployed artillerymen to prepare to use their short swords, Drinkwater warned his oarsmen that they should be ready to support their colleagues once they had joined the fray. It took them twenty minutes to regain their position against the tide, during which they spoke with the rest of their division which still threw their howitzer shells at the enemy. Gathering these boats about him, Drinkwater headed directly for the nearest French vessel which now seemed the centre of the fight in their immediate locality.

"I intend to attempt to carry her," he declared with a defiance he was far from feeling as he bowed to the stern demands of duty.

V

As they approached, it was clear that the attack had failed utterly. Conn's launches had become separated, though they still threw their shells over the cordon of gunboats and corvettes that lay moored outside the head of Boulogne mole. Those British boats whose crews had been in the thick of it, which Drinkwater had correctly assumed to be those of Parker's division, lay in complete disarray. They passed through several of these as they drifted aimlessly, a few exhausted and wounded men collapsed within them, the odd figure stoically plying half-heartedly at an oar. A few men splashed through the water, calling out for assistance and moving Drinkwater to order one of his following launches to veer aside and pick up as many of these wretched creatures as possible. Drinkwater pressed forward himself to where a few boats still lay alongside a large ship-corvette and, he could see clearly now, a large *chasse-marée* astern of her.

It was quite obvious that the preparedness and fury of the defence had overwhelmed the attack, for at the first sign of Drinkwater's approaching launches, the *qui vive* went up with a shout and a fusillade of musketry burst all along the corvette's sheer. This was followed by a broadside which, though it left Drinkwater's launch unscathed, landed a roundshot squarely into the bow of his third boat, smashing in the bow and sending her to the bottom in a matter of minutes. It seemed to Drinkwater that those British craft remaining alongside the corvette were filled with dead or wounded, such had been the intensity of the French fire.

It was now equally clear that little advantage could be wrung from pressing the attack further. Their only duty now lay with recovering the wounded. As the French reloaded, Drinkwater stood and shouted to Quilhampton.

"Put her about, James!"

Bracing himself, he cupped his hands and, as they swept across the bows of the following launches, he ordered them each to fire their howitzers and small arms and then withdraw, rendering assistance wherever possible. There was sufficient confusion in the night to strangle any vainglorious desire to send them to a certain death. Drinkwater was quite unaware that in the diverting approach of his handful of launches, the handful of survivors in Parker's boats had cast themselves adrift and made good their escape. As the tide bore them away, Drinkwater's own crew were dragging the survivors of the stove boat over their own gunwale. All about them the French musket balls pitched, while roundshot whined overhead, making them gasp, half winded in their passing. But the tide was now their ally, so that they attracted only occasional fire from the rest of the French vessels as they were carried along the moored cordon.

Drinkwater's launch was now dangerously overloaded. He was hauling a man out of the water when Quilhampton roared out, "Sir! Under the stern of the lugger!"

At the urgent cry of alarm, Drinkwater twisted round and relinquished his hold on the sodden seaman. The abandoned fellow slithered across his lap to lie gasping in the bottom of the launch alongside Fitzwilliam.

At that moment they were sweeping past a large *chasse-marée*. Her topsides were so close that Drinkwater could see the ironworks strapping her wide channels to her topsides, and the dead-eyes and lanyards of her shrouds as they vanished upwards into the impenetrable night. It was the appreciation of an instant, for the next thing he was aware of was the flurry of water at the bow of a wide flat-boat and the faint gleam of vigorously plied oar blades: a counter-attack, by God!

"Watch there, my lads!" he bellowed. "The enemy are upon us!"

The words had scarcely left him before there was a succession of shouts, a splintering of oars as the colliding flat-boat sheered them off and then her solid bow caught the launch a glancing blow. A moment later the two craft crashed together, bow to stern, the launch heeling under the impact. Drinkwater and his men were suddenly fighting for their lives.

In the struggle to get men out of the water Drinkwater's sword-belt had slipped behind him and he had no time to reach his hanger before a boarding-pike was thrust at him. He twisted away and fell backwards, crashing into Tregembo as the coxswain drew the tiller from the rudder stock and used it as an extempore weapon, reaching over Drinkwater to catch his commander's assailant a glancing blow on the foremost fist with which the French seaman held the weapon.

As the French seaman lost his grasp on the boarding-pike with the agony of a smashed hand, Drinkwater twisted sideways and extricated himself. He rose with a tremendous effort as the launch rocked wildly under the assault of at least a dozen leaping Frenchmen. He drew his hanger. The rasp of the blade against the gilded brass ferrule of the scabbard filled him with a savage determination. He drove the blade into the flank of the French sailor, twisted and withdrew it, leaving the wretch to writhe in agony.

As the man fell, the brief flash of a pistol close by momentarily blinded Drinkwater.

"Watch the young gennelman, zur," Tregembo shouted as Drinkwater unwittingly kicked the small, still form of Fitzwilliam lying at his feet half under the sternsheet benches.

"*Hela!*"

Drinkwater spun round, his eyes clearing. A French officer was poised on the higher gunwale of the flat-boat. Even in the darkness his posture was truculently triumphant, his sword-blade a grey wisp at which Drinkwater struck with a cold and pre-emptive fury. The jar of the contact told him his opponent was a practised swordsman: the enemy's blade wavered not an inch. Then the Frenchman extended and Drinkwater felt his right shoulder pinked by his opponent's blade. He ducked as the French officer's sword-point tore through the fabric of his coat, then he thrust upwards with all his might before his enemy recovered his guard. But the French officer was too quick for him and drew swiftly back as the boats rocked and bumped together.

The launch seemed a seething mass of struggling men; their grunts were punctuated by oaths and howls and sobs and screams, and Drinkwater had not the faintest notion of who, if anyone, was gaining the upper hand.

Where was Quilhampton? Where was Tregembo? Where in God's name were his other boats? For a fraction of time Drinkwater hesitated, his concentration divided between his personal survival and his responsibility as a sea-officer in charge of a division of howitzer launches. In that instant he lost the cold concentration of his fighting instincts; he saw instead the justification of his misgivings, the consequences of Nelson's rashness and his own seesaw relationship with the admiral. He saw too his own successes and failures: the pale face of the wounded Fitzwilliam, the smooth curve of his wife's pregnant belly and again the utter craziness of this night's foolhardy attack.

Then, alerted by some nervous imperative, he was recalled to the dangerous present. The French officer, having caught his own breath and recovered his footing, renewed his attack and flung himself down from his flat-boat's side in a wildly determined lunge intended to kill Drinkwater and to destroy with him the spirit of the British boat's crew. Drinkwater sensed the descending loom of the man and swung to defend himself. He was too late: the French officer's sword-blade stabbed Drinkwater a second time on his right shoulder, passing right through it up to its hilt.

All Drinkwater could do as the French officer fell upon him was to hold his own blade for as long as his right hand did as it was bid. He fell backwards with a sickening jar, his enemy falling on top of him, their common descent broken by a body sprawled over the opposite gunwale. Drinkwater felt the breath driven out of his lungs and gasped at the fire in his shoulder. As the shock and pain robbed him of consciousness, Drinkwater beheld in the gloom his own blade emerging from the small of his enemy's back.

VI

"Well, sir, I see at last that you are cognisant of my presence. May I impress upon you, how fortunate a man you are to have fallen into my clutches at last," said Mr Lettsom. Then, giving way to his muse, the *Wolf*'s surgeon declaimed:

> When people's ill, they come to I,
> I physics, bleeds and sweats 'em;
> Sometimes they live, sometimes they die,
> What's that to I? I let's 'em.

"Lettsom? Is that you?"

"Of course it is I, sir. Who else would it be?"

"Where . . . ? How long have I been . . .?"

"It is the eighteenth day of September, the year is the first of the new century, though there are those who debate this assertion. You are aboard the brig-sloop *Wolf* of which you are somewhat notionally in command and the said brig is lying off the dockyard of Sheerness into which anchorage she was rather creditably carried by Lieutenant Rogers. I refused to allow you ashore into the hospital on the grounds that you were too ill to move and were better left in my care. Fortunately their lordships, having no immediate employment for the *Wolf*, have not seen fit to issue any orders regarding her movement, other than that she is to remain at anchor pending perhaps the outcome of what appear might be peace negotiations—"

"Peace?" Drinkwater interrupted. Then, half sitting up, he asked, "*What* did you say the date was?"

"The eighteenth of September, sir."

"Then I have been . . ."

"In a fever for a month and while Mr Q was convinced you were about to expire, I managed to prevent him alarming your wife. In short, sir, as far as the outside world is concerned, you are recovering from a wound received in hand-to-hand service, as the vicious boat-work such as you were sent upon is so euphemistically called by the powers-that-be . . . or should it be, that-are? Well, well, never mind. You are going to recover now, though it will be some time before you will be waving a sword again." The surgeon smiled, adding, "But then, if rumours of peace come to pass, you will not need to."

Drinkwater was no longer listening. He was trying to recollect the events of that frightful night. He recalled the confusion, the strong, ineluctable sweep of the tide and the terrifying looming nemesis of the French officer. Then, as Lettsom's words made sense to him he remembered Quilhampton. "Then James is all right?"

"Indeed he is, though his wooden arm took more knocks than it could stand."

"And Tregembo?"

"Indestructible as ever."

"And I have been in a fever for a month?"

"More or less; you enjoyed a few lucid moments."

"And my report? Who wrote my report to Lord Nelson?" Drinkwater struggled to sit up.

"Your young friend James Quilhampton submitted his report, countersigned by Samuel Rogers, to Captain Conn. Word came back from the *Medusa* that his lordship was well pleased with the conduct of all the officers and men employed upon that dangerous and regrettably unsuccessful attack. However, all had acquitted themselves as befitted British seamen and were rightly deserving of his lordship's approbation. In short, my dear sir, it was a disaster. There, are you finished your damned catechizing?"

Drinkwater lay back. He felt very weak, though his head was clear now, clearer than it had been for a very long time, he realized.

"It seems I owe my life to you, Mr Lettsom."

Lettsom smiled, then said:

No sword have I, no bayonet,
No Frenchmen do I slaughter,
I serve, dear sir, with my curette,
With sutures, rum and water . . .

"And my shoulder?"

"Ah. Something of a mess, I am afraid. The French officer whom you impaled, spitted you rather well and although you will not lose the articulation of the enarthroidal joint itself since it is intact, damage to the coraco-humeral ligament is sufficient to render you significantly weaker and you will suffer a consequent loss of power in your right arm. The scapula was chipped badly and the surrounding muscles lacerated but I have debrided the wound, removed the debris and" – Lettsom shrugged – "your constitution has fought off the effects of the ensuing fever."

"You almost inspire me with the notion you know your business, Mr Lettsom," Drinkwater said with a wan smile. "I am most grateful to you."

Lettsom inclined his head. "Thank you, sir, you are most kind. It would not, I think, be considered too overweening of me to assume that I knew my business better than his lordship."

"Nelson, d'you mean?" Drinkwater asked. Lettsom nodded. "Then there is talk of what? A bungling?"

"No, not of that, but of an unlucky defeat. Mind you, 'twould have been a bungling had anyone else been its instigator. Nelson continues to ride a popular chariot, but the butcher's bill was high. It included young Parker which has mortified his lordship, I gather." Lettsom paused, then added with a detached disdain for the technicalities of seamanship, "They tell me quite half the boats did not come into action at all on account of the tide."

"It does not surprise me," Drinkwater said reflectively. "I tried to warn his lordship of the dangers inherent in a night attack in those waters, but—" Drinkwater broke off with a groan and an oath. "God's bones, Lettsom, that fellow's sword-blade still bites like the very devil," he gasped.

Lettsom smiled and bent over him. "You should not attempt to shrug your shoulders, my dear sir. 'Tis such a very *Gallic* gesture!"

VII

A week later His Britannic Majesty's brig-sloop *Wolf* lay moored in the trots off Chatham Dockyard. Drinkwater, his right arm in a sling, his face pallidly anaemic, dictated to James Quilhampton as he prepared to leave the little man-of-war. A knock at the door diverted their attention from the Navy Board's bureaucratic demands.

"Come in!" Drinkwater called, expecting Samuel Rogers, his first lieutenant.

A small, thin figure dressed in the uniform of a midshipman entered *Wolf*'s cabin, removing his hat and making a short, courteous bow. The youth had all the hallmarks of coming from a flagship, an admiral's protégé.

Quilhampton recognized the young man before his commander. "Good heavens, Mr Fitzwilliam, how good to see you!" Quilhampton rose and impetuously held out his right hand. Seeing it was of flesh and blood, Fitzwilliam took it with a shy smile.

"Fitzwilliam . . .?" Drinkwater frowned, and then Quilhampton reminded him. "Good God, I thought you were dead!" he said as the youngster smiled and shook his head.

"No, sir, thanks to you I am not yet dead."

"I am damned glad to hear it, young fellow. Did you suffer much?"

"Nothing worse than a severe contusion. I was knocked senseless but, as you see, sir, otherwise unscathed."

"Well, what brings you aboard the *Wolf*?"

"I, er, I wished to express my gratitude, sir, and I am charged to pass a message to you from Lord Nelson."

"Oh?"

"His lordship wishes me to tell you, to tell you personally, sir, that he omitted your name from the list of commanders engaged and that he is most regretful that it slipped his mind but he was most uncommonly disturbed and distressed by the numbers of officers and men killed and wounded in the attack. He wishes me in particular to say that he was well aware that you had not only supported my own boat after it was damaged, but that by pressing on and leading a second attack after the first had failed, you distracted the enemy sufficiently for most of Captain Parker's boats to get away in the confusion. Captain Parker owes his life to you, sir, and if his lordship can be of service to you, Captain Drinkwater, he wishes only to be reminded of it in the future."

"That is most kind of his lordship," Drinkwater replied.

"Please tell him as much when you next wait upon him. Perhaps, Mr Q, you will see that our young Mercury has something to eat and drink before he returns. That is enough letter writing for this morning."

After the two midshipmen had gone Drinkwater poured himself a glass of wine. Staring astern through the windows of the cabin he meditated on the news. It was a damnably unfortunate oversight that Nelson had not mentioned him in his report. On the other hand perhaps, Drinkwater supposed, the admiral was sensible that he had done Drinkwater a double injustice and had at least taken the trouble to admit the fact and send young Fitzwilliam to make amends. Drinkwater smiled wryly; it was typical of Nelson to offer his own influence in the belief that it was of more use to a wretched tarpaulin officer like Drinkwater than a supplementary note to the Admiralty!

Drinkwater shook his head. How could he ever remind Nelson of such an error, let alone seek advancement thereby on some conjectural future encounter? He could never bring himself to do such a self-seeking thing. Although Nelson would not have hesitated to do it for himself, Nathaniel Drinkwater was an entirely different kettle of fish! Drinkwater dismissed the idea as a chimera. It was a kind but misguided notion and, Drinkwater concluded, palliative enough. He stared out over the grey waters of the Medway, watching the young flood tide swirl upstream under the Wolf's transom. There was a dangerous energy in it, he thought ruefully.

He finished his glass of wine and rose to his feet.

KING GEORGE'S
FREE TRADERS

M.B. Warriss

The following story, which is based on a real episode, takes place in the months leading up to the Battle of Trafalgar, when Nelson had the French admiral Pierre de Villeneuve trapped in Toulon. With the navy on full alert it was a golden opportunity for privateers and those otherwise on the wrong side of the law to show their true colours.

Mike Warriss has served in the Navy Reserve and taken part in square-rig sailing. He has been a gunner in the Sealed Knot historical society and has travelled widely. He currently teaches English abroad. He also writes as M.G. Owen.

It could not be said that Midshipman Edward Boscowen depended for promotion only on his famous great-grandfather "Wry Necked Dick", Admiral of that Ilk. It could never be said that the descent was from a bend sinister. Midshipman William Courteney had said it, when the wine was in and the wit was out, and now Boscowen and his shipmate, Dawkins, cast long shadows before them as they walked towards Courteney and his cousin in the lee of a sand-dune. A surgeon was waiting with the Courteneys, his square black bag resting on the sand. George Courteney carried a long bundle, tightly wrapped in canvas.

All this for an over-witty recruiting song in a tavern in Archer Street. The midshipmen had been drinking their prize-money and discussing the limits of the press-gang. With Nelson bottling Villeneuve up in Toulon and flotillas watching every port from Cadiz to Brest, the fleet was at full stretch. It seemed that every sailor in Plymouth was under protection or in hiding.

"Cochrane had the rights of it. He put up posters, saying he would not take landsmen or weaklings, only men who could carry a great sack of pewter without stopping."

"He was a recruiter of looters of pewter," offered Boscowen.

That was a two-glass joke, and Boscowen was proud of it, especially as he was at least five glasses down.

"But Cochrane was a Scot, recruiting Scotchmen. Scotchies can read and write – we have to charm English yokels off the plough."

"A marine drummer, and a recruiting song?"

Somewhere in the tavern a fiddler was sawing out "Ladies of Spain". While his shipmates gossiped, Boscowen hummed quietly and let words tumble over in his head. Then he slammed his hand on the board for silence and sang, in time to the fiddle.

Don't come any landsmen, or weaklings or fearlings,
Come only ye sailors, strong men who can shoot
For if you'd be going with Captain Boscowen
You must have the strength for to carry your loot.

You have heard of the charms of the dark Spanish ladies
Sixteen ounce to the pound, all creamy and soft
But if you'd be the adorer of a buxom señora
You must have the strength for to hoist her aloft

You have heard of the wealth of the city of Panama
More than you'll carry unless you are strong
But if you'd be a looter of silver and pewter
You must have the strength for to carry it along.

You landsmen and weaklings, don't sail with Boscowen;
There's nothing for you, you're safer ashore
But for seamen who're handy, there's hollands and
  brandy
Dark señoritas, gold coins by the score.

A few midshipmen banged glasses. Will Courteney did not move.

"My congratulations on your promotion, Captain Boscowen."

The bad blood between Cornishmen and men of Devon was older than the Civil War, probably older than Drake and Grenville. Courteney was from one of the oldest and richest families in Devon, his cousin was the local magistrate. As soon as he had come ashore he had purchased a new uniform, hat to shoe. Now he was leaning back, his legs stretched out to show his silk stockings and gilt buckles. Boscowen was suddenly conscious of his cotton and brass-covered legs, tucked discreetly under the chair.

"I am a captain in Cornwall, for I own a tin mine." (He omitted to mention that he only held a half share, or that the mine was all but worked out.) " 'Tis a social rank, slightly below esquire."

"Slightly below? A blanket's thickness below?"

That remark hurt, for relations between Boscowen's parents were affectionate but somewhat informal, as was not uncommon in the lonelier parts of Cornwall.

The details of what followed were gone from Boscowen's memory. He could not be sure whether he had thrown the glass or knocked it across the table. If he had been sober he would have remembered the exact words spoken. But then, if he had been sober he would not have been standing here, at dawn, while the seconds negotiated.

Dawkins and Courteney's elder cousin George stepped forward.

"Will Mr Boscowen accept an apology?"

"Yes, in the presence of all those who heard the original words."

"My cousin would be willing to make a private expression of regret."

Dawkins shook his head and returned to his principal.

"They have marked out the place. It's even ground. Do you want north or south?"

"South."

Courteney would have to face south towards the sand-dune and the sea hidden behind it. If a sailor's face is towards the sea his mind is never off it. A sail over the horizon of the dune, even a seagull, might distract Courteney, just an eyeblink, and give Boscowen the edge.

The two men stripped to shirts and breeches and took their places. Boscowen felt as he had before, while waiting for action: an odd sensation of being 10 feet tall and invulnerable. Every stone, every blade of grass became needle-sharp and clear as newly broken glass. Boscowen knew that he would carry the images for the rest of his life, which might be long or short. Courteney seemed to move slowly, like glue. The two men took up positions with their cutlass points just touching. The seconds each held a handkerchief aloft. Boscowen was briefly transfixed by the elaborate lace trimming on Courteney's handkerchief: there was something odd about it. The hankies fell and the swords clashed.

Courteney was taller and better trained, but Boscowen was long of arm. His only chance was to go in low, attacking both sides at once, make Courteney reach for his point and get in a lucky blow before Courteney could wear him out.

Courteney knew how to use his height; he went for Boscowen's head. The two swords locked overhead, hilt to hilt, strength of arm against arm. Suddenly Boscowen gave way, stepped back, sword in a cross-parry. Overbalanced, Courteney's sword swept down in a graceful curve, right shoulder exposed. A quick backhand slash, a backward jump clear of a riposte and Courteney's sleeve was turning red. Someone shouted "Surgeon!"

The sawbones knew his business. Within seconds Courteney's sleeve was in rags, George Courteney pressing on the artery in the armpit, Dawkins sitting astride his hips and holding his arm at the wrist. The surgeon had two curved needles, neatly threaded, and drove each one in turn into Courteney's flesh and out again, reef knot in the thread, point of the needle into what remained of Courteney's shirt, change needles, start again. He worked steadily from each end of the wound towards the middle, so that the edges of the wound would meet up neatly. Courteney bit down on his gag and thrashed his legs about. At a look from Dawkins, Boscowen straddled the writhing legs and immobilized the patient. Boscowen kept low down, out of Courteney's sight – better he did not know that he was being ministered unto by the man who had just cut him open.

The surgeon tidied up his stitches, applied a bandage and put the arm into a sling.

"Help him into his coat – throw it over the shoulder. Gently, now, a chill's the worst thing for a wound. Take his good arm."

Boscowen had mixed feelings as he watched Courteney limp away between his cousin and the surgeon. He had settled a grievance, other midshipmen would be reluctant to cross him, he had added to his reputation for lawless bravery, but the Admiralty might not see things that way. The Courteneys were a rich and old family and had powerful friends in Devon.

In fact, the Admiralty did not see things Boscowen's way. They put him on to half pay, sent him home to Cornwall and gave Courteney a berth on a hulk until his wound should heal. So Courteney could build up sea-time from the comfort and safety of Spithead, while Boscowen's career was literally on the beach. Other midshipmen could put in their six years of sea-time and then form a queue for a lieutenant's epaulette. Boscowen must wait in Helston until his transgression be forgiven, until he could go to the back of the long queue of time-serving midshipmen to enter the ranks of time-served midshipmen lurking at the gates of the lieutenants' examinations. Even if he should win a commission, three months wasted now would be three months' lost seniority for the rest of his career.

Meantimes, Boscowen must keep his seaman's skills sharp.

The navy had discovered his talent for cartography, and developed it. In return, he had given them over fifty charts and sketches of the east coast of Spain. Now, whenever light permitted, he took easel, pens and ink to whichever headland pleased him. He never bothered with colours – his sketches were for the engraver and printer, meticulously accurate tools of the sailor's trade, with a few seagulls and dolphins added, for style.

One afternoon he was sketching the Manacles from the headland (very appropriate for a sailor chained to the land) when he heard a voice behind him.

"Don't look round."

Boscowen went on sketching.

"Keeping watch from the cliffs, were ye? Tha's a two-year crime, or five if ye gives a signal."

"No Cornish court will convict a smuggler unless he is caught sitting on the barrels. I d'aint even know this was a smuggling bay – I thought they came in through Porthbeer Cove. But I know now. I'll buy a keg of brandy from you, if the price is right."

"No, no, young Captain, I'm not a free trader. I'm the preventative. I might put a proposition to you. I'd like you to have a word with Captain Jacob Menhennit. Of course a gentleman like yourself wouldn't know him, but you might have seen his lugger roundabouts."

"Not the one that didn't run into a cove near here, somewhere between the Lizard and Gunwalloe? The *Queen of Hanover*? A very patriotic gentleman is Captain Menhennit."

"Don'ee throw names around like pebbles, they might hit someone. And me being a preventative, I wouldn't know. I don't know anything about six six-pounder guns he's got aboard the lugger, either."

Boscowen was impressed. Thirty-six pounds of shot meant eighteen pounds of powder. Some days back, Trelissick of Wheal Vor, beyond Helston, had hinted at a brandy-for-powder bargain, more powder than a mine captain was likely to want. So Trelissick was dealing with Menhennit, was he?

"What's your bargain?"

"There's a French privateer, a cutter, lurking around the 50-degree line. If Captain Menhennit was to challenge her, we might lose the evidence we found when we took six of his men."

"A privateer carries ten guns at least, maybe more, and not mere pop-bang six-pounders. It's suicide."

"In a close fight, maybe. But if the captain had a young naval officer aboard, who could take note of every detail of her guns and rig, he could take a description, or even a sketch, over to Plymouth, and come back with a King's ship."

"The evidence you might lose – what is it?"

"Four bolts of silk, peachy red, and six reels of Brussels lace."

"Give Menhennit his men back, and his goods, before he goes out against the Frenchman."

"Don'ee trust me?"

"King George obviously can't. But if Captain Menhennit is to go to war then he needs every man he can get. And he might not live to collect his silk and lace after the battle."

"There'll be no battle. Just get close enough to the Frenchie to take her measure, then come away safe. We'll let the men sail with the captain and leave the goods with Parson Mawthy, over to Gweek."

The Reverend Mawthy was a man that preventative men and smugglers could equally trust, since both were in his congregation.

So Boscowen put on plain grey breeches, goatskin waistcoat and knitted cap and took himself off to Poldhu Cove, to eye up the *Queen of Hanover*, and make plans. She carried a foresail and a great mainsail, both dipping lugs. She had less keel than he would have liked – easy to run into a shallow cove, not so handy to windward. She might have better weather-coil with her foresail close-reefed. Boscowen hated lugsails, they were the very devil to gybe. The mainsail would give the foresail a lee, but how in damnation could they dip the mainsail itself, with a strong wind astern? He was too proud to ask, but Jacob Menhennit followed his eyes and answered the question.

"Say you're working up a creek, the wind is light. With a

good crew, who know what they're about, you can gybe. In open water, with strong winds, you have to tack through the wind, or run by the lee."

"How high does she point?"

"Maybe ten points, or twelve at worst."

Boscowen believed the latter figure. A cutter pointed higher than a lugger, he supposed, but the *Queen of Hanover*'s gear was in good order and her bottom clean. By rumour, the Frenchman had been at sea for some time; the barnacles would be starting to grow. He speculated about putting the spare shot in nets, with tackles so that they could be hauled up to the weather gunwales – anything to improve her trim on a beat.

"Just how strong are your guns, Captain Menhennit? How many shots can you fire in, say, a quarter-hour?"

"I amn't rightly sure. We ain't built for a long fight; just a few shots in case of trade disagreements, like, or to advise the preventatives to keep a respectful distance."

This venture was not looking healthy to Boscowen – but he had not joined King George's navy in search of a comfortable life. If he lived through this venture then he would be reinstated, shuffling forward in the long queue of midshipmen seeking to be lieutenants.

Well-crewed, well-stored and with as many shot as her six little guns would need, the *Queen of Hanover* slipped out of Poldhu Cove.

In the next four days, Boscowen learned the reason for her strange rig. With her mainyard sent down to half mast and her mainsail reefed she could lurk below the horizon at three miles. But a man at the maintop could easily see for five – more, since a cutter had a high mast. The Frenchman depended on looking innocent, not on being invisible.

For those four days the *Queen of Hanover* danced the hay around the Lizard, lurking in ambush for the Frenchman who might be lurking in ambush for a homeward-bounder, or who might be north of Cape Cornwall, looking for the Bristol trade. The wind blew steady south-west, on shore, and Boscowen came to dread the sight of Predannack Point; north of it, the

Queen of Hanover would be embayed. Boscowen respected Menhennit's seamanship. He was coming to believe the boast that the *Queen of Hanover* could point within ten points of the wind – he just didn't want to test it, not with a lee shore and a flowing tide.

It was after two bells of the first dog-watch, Boscowen supposed, when the lookout hailed the deck. The square topsail of a cutter proved nothing – the core of the Frenchman's strategy was to look like every other cutter, a wolf in a fleece – but she was clearly chasing a brig.

Heading east with the wind on her starboard quarter, the cutter still had the sea-legs of the square-rigger. She must be well-gunned, Boscowen judged, to attack a larger ship – but owners of merchantmen grudged the expense of arming their ships, or of providing crew to serve the guns.

At a word Menhennit's men shook out the reef, hoisted the mainsail up on the parrels and sheeted it home in the parrel-blocks. Her helm went down, she heeled over to larboard and headed south, keeping the Frenchman on a constant bearing and aiming to cut across her stern.

Menhennit knew his business. The *Queen of Hanover* was on the Frenchman's larboard quarter, where her guns could not bear. He could cross her stern, exchange shots "one for the flag" (his three larboard guns against her two stern-chasers), get Boscowen close enough to note every detail of her rig, then bear off.

Boscowen estimated her scantlings and jotted them down on a slate. She carried a square topsail and a great mainsail hung from a gaff-boom at least 20 feet long, and a free foot, with a running backstay, he supposed, hidden behind the mainsail on the starboard quarter.

She had the lines of a coastal trader, probably Breton-built. She had a very small fo'c'sle and a low after-cabin, almost flush-decked, her hull sleek and black-painted, but at this range Boscowen could make out the four dark squares of gunports. (If she carried a full gun crew they must be cramped, down in the hold.) Eight guns, plus the chasers. How big the guns, how accurate? He had no wish to learn. But if the Frenchie veered to bear her guns on the *Queen of Hanover*, she would lose the chase. The *Queen* could come as close to her stern as she pleased, risk one shot from her chase guns, and veer away.

As in the duel, Boscowen had gone through the fear into a cold, steel calm, as frightening as his morning razor. Everything moved slowly and became sharp and clear, like the cut copper lines on a new engraving. He saw the carving on her stern, the tricolor, her name in gold letters on the black: *Requin* of St Malo (he was right, she was a Breton).

A great thunderclap struck his ears and became a high, constant ringing. The *Queen of Hanover*'s bow gun dropped a shot a few yards to larboard of the *Requin* and sent up a great glittering plume of spray. Too early, nervous shooting. Now the waist guns were bearing and Menhennit was shouting: "Aim low and spoil the Frenchie's aim!"

Two guns roared out together, two white clouds of smoke drifted to leeward, another white pillar of spray to larboard of the *Requin*, another amateur gunner firing early: how could they miss at this range? Thank God they had the weather gauge. Tiny burning rags were still swirling over the lee rail, drifting harmlessly over the sea. What could Menhennit's gunners be using as wads? Boscowen didn't want to know. He only smelled the sharp, bitter smell of burnt saltpetre on metal.

Two clouds of smoke from the *Requin*'s gallery, held back by the breeze. Two red-gold spikes of flame, two shocks of round-shot hitting home and a pale line of new wood where the gunwale had split. Twelve-pounders at least, probably bigger.

As the wind cleared the smoke from the *Requin*'s stern he saw that one of Menhennit's funners had known his business. One shot had gone through the stern gallery and left some splintering behind it.

As the *Requin* held on eastwards, Menhennit headed south, close-hauled, pointing the *Queen* as high as he could. The range opened and the *Requin* was obviously content to have fought off the challenge.

Oh no she wasn't. The cutter put her helm down, heeling

over (Please, God, let her break a gun tackle now!), then
righting as the wind spilled from the mainsail, the great gaff-
boom swung over and she came close-hauled, on a parallel
course to the *Queen*. They exchanged single shots; one struck
the *Queen*'s hull and her timbers cried for mercy, but she still
had the weather gauge, she could not be hit below the waterline.

But the range was inching closer, the cutter pointed higher
than the lugger, as Boscowen had feared. The accuracy of the
shots was increasing. William Carter was lying on the deck,
head and shoulders behind the wreck of the bow gun carriage.
The rest of the gun crew were helping serve the waist gun.
Boscowen went to help Carter.

Carter had no head, only a red mess of neck, and what might
have been a jaw. Boscowen threw up, over the lee gunwale. A
body came out of the *Requin*'s stern gallery, a body wearing a
gaudy maroon jacket and somehow tied to a spar or baulk of
timber. A musket shot hit the gunwale near Boscowen, a chip
flew up and he ducked down.

The *Requin*'s greater firepower, and her more skilled gunners, were beginning to tell. The *Queen* was taking a pounding,
to no good purpose. Menhennit gave the order "Helm down!"

She swung to larboard, almost sweeping her bowsprit across
the *Requin*'s stern. As she passed aft of the *Requin* Boscowen
looked in through what remained of her stern gallery and saw
the dismounted stern-chase gun.

Still the Frenchman would not quit. The *Requin* put her helm
down and made a parallel course, running downwind with the
Queen, towards the cliffs. The *Queen* had somehow gybed her
foresail out to starboard but, as Boscowen had foreseen, gybing
the great mainsail, under fire, was not an option. The crew
would have been mown down. The *Requin* was slowly closing
the range and the *Queen* could alter course no further. The
Requin was aiming her shots at the foremast. As the second ball
struck it split, bent, and then the foreyard, sail and all, came free
as Billy Blake cut the parral ropes.

Still the *Requin* poured down shot. Wisps of brown smoke
from below decks came out of the ports and thickened into a

cloud, heavy tarry smoke that sent the men a-choking. At last the *Requin* bore away. Predannack Point was on their lee, and any Frenchman who came ashore there would invade England on his own, one plank at a time. The point could take care of the rival that had provoked the *Requin* and was now crippled and afire.

The Frenchman was not five cables off when the fire died down. Billy Blake banked down a hasty but ingenious device of a tarred shirt burning in a cooking pot. The splintered mast needed more attention. The yard was quickly fished up to what remained of the foresail yard and the forecourse jury-rigged as a jib.

As Boscowen worked hastily to reeve new lines for the jury-jib, he noticed the skill of the Cornish smugglers. They had done this change of rig before. Set the mainyard all abaft the mainmast with some sort of lightweight square topsail, such as the *Requin* carried, and, behold! the cutter becomes a small brigantine. Set staysails and you would have a slow but very yare fishing-boat, not at all like the famous *Queen of Hanover*. Billy Blake had been very quick to set his false fire in the galley. Menhennit's men were bad gunners but good sailors and good liars. It was a pity King George could not use them more often.

The jury rig made the *Queen* easier to steer but added nothing to her speed. There was no question of working her way round to Looe Bar; her only hope was to run aground in Pentreath Bay.

Menhennit lowered the boat over the *Queen*'s stern, to stop her drifting on to the slabs of rock south of the bay. Boscowen looked out to sea; the *Requin* was hull-down already. But there was something red, closer inshore. What was left of William Carter? No, it was more maroon than red. He remembered the gaudily dressed Frenchman, thrown overboard from the *Requin*. But the maroon coat was moving. Well, everybody knew that frogs could swim.

The cliffs loomed closer. Menhennit clewed up the mainsail, to see better. With the ship's boat for a drag she worked round the point, and there lay the pebbles of Pentreath Bay.

"Shake out the clews!" shouted Menhennit. The ship lurched forward. "Boom her off, larboard!" Two men thrust a spar between what remained of the gunwale and the steep-sloping rock. There was a scrape of keel on stones and the much-abused *Queen* lurched over to larboard; every man grabbed whatever fixed point he could, all the debris of the battle slid over to the larboard gunwale, and the scraping stopped. The *Queen of Hanover* was aground.

Every man cheered, except Boscowen. He had work to do. There was a Frenchman alive out there somewhere. He spoke to Billy Blake and three of the other men. They took the boat and started to row.

They would never have found him if he had been swimming. A head in the water is invisible at more than a cable's length. But he was straddling a spar and a large portion of his bright coat was out of the water, maroon against a blue-green sea. They got him into the boat, alive but too exhausted to talk. That could wait.

Boscowen spoke French two ways. Thanks to the French émigré schoolmasters earning a crust in Chatham, his command of grammar was no worse that the average English schoolboy. But many peasants from Brittany and the Vendée had fled to Cornwall, and even as a boy Boscowen had done his share of free-trading. As such, he could put on a villainous Breton accent.

Boscowen had surmised from the survivor's coat that he was a man of rank. He had first had vague ambitions of ransom. In fact the survivor was the captain, a Monsieur de Frontenac. Boscowen noted the aristocratic "de". Many aristos, more realist than royalist, had joined a revolution that they had no chance of beating, and now King Napoleon was setting up an aristocracy of his own. But there was no love lost between them and the old revolutionaries, and the master of the *Requin*, Jacques Chardin, was one such.

Once inside a warm blanket and outside a glass of rum, Monsieur de Frontenac became talkative. He had been a free-trader and had become a privateer out of social ambition as much as desire for profit. Accepting Chardin as master had been the politically necessary price of his letters-of-marque. There had been bickering about the share of the business proceeds, but de Frontenac's account of what had occurred by the stern-chase guns shocked even Boscowen.

"I am a soldier and adventurer, not a seaman. I worked the guns – the chase guns in this case – and Chardin was at the wheel, when your shot came in through the gallery, and did great execution."

"The fortune of war."

"Quite so. There was little profit in the fight. I was for breaking off the action, but Chardin was bent on destroying a royalist oppressor. As I had taken a bad knock on the head, he assumed command."

"Lawful, by the rules of war."

"It was. But he left me in command of the stern guns and then, in a lull in the battle, sent the surviving gunners on deck and removed me from the scene, through the stern gallery."

"At least he gave you the spar, as a parting gift."

"To live or die, as God should please, thus he had not murder on his conscience."

"A victory for the revolution, and, for the revolutionary, a greater share of the loot – er – the profits of the venture."

"You English! even when you fight, you are still shop-keepers."

The Frenchman gave a dismissive wave of his hand – a hand holding an elegant lace hankie.

"Where did you get that?"

"It is a Brussels pattern, part of a consignment I ran into a certain bay in Devon. We send in so much, I am sure it must hurt the Honiton lacemakers' business."

"But who bought it?"

"Monsieur le Cornishman, you have a long nose. Englishmen east of the Tamar, now, they have short noses." The French-man smirked.

"Short nose" in French is *court nez*. Boscowen knew where he had seen that pattern of lace before. Now he understood why

George Courteney prospered better than the other landowners, how Will Courteney had bought his fine new uniform before anyone had actually received any prize-money.

"Monsieur de Frontenac, would you like a free passage back to France? You have an account to settle with Jacques Chardin, and I have an account to settle with two gentlemen in Devon."

"Your price?"

"What you can give, and still keep – information. Full details of your trading with Monsieur Court-Nez. Harbours, dates of shipments, sale of privateer prizes, capture of empty ships fully insured, everything. If your friend Jacques Chardin gets caught in the net, so much the better for you."

The thought of either or both Courteneys standing trial lived in Boscowen's heart for about ten seconds. The Courteneys would pay for silence. Their influence that had put him on the beach could get him off it, on to the ship of his choice, the Mediterranean perhaps, somewhere warm. Pyramids in Egypt, pillared temples in Greece, or was it the other way round? Perhaps he would find out. How to turn an enemy into a trusty friend? Hold a knife to his throat.

But be very careful when you take the knife away.

THE DESERTER

Guy N. Smith

This story and the next are both set at the Battle of Trafalgar. I hadn't originally planned it that way but, when both stories turned up in the same post (yet another of the odd coincidences associated with this volume) I became fascinated by the depiction of the engagement from two different perspectives. And it seemed to me that what is almost certainly our most famous naval battle deserves at least two stories.

Guy N. Smith (b. 1939) is probably best known for his many horror novels which began with Werewolf by Moonlight *in 1974. But he has written much more besides, including children's books, animal stories, crime thrillers and many non-fiction books on gamekeeping and country pursuits. He has also written over 1,200 stories and magazine features and columns. His mother was the historical novelist E.M. Weale. Guy was inspired to write this story by the renowned painting by Joseph Turner of* The Fighting Téméraire, *a copy of which has hung in his house for as long as he can remember.*

> *Like those beneath whose sightless stare*
> *The sullen smoke-drift rolled*
> *Round her, well-named the Téméraire,*
> *In famous fights of old.*
>
> From a headstone in
> Odiham churchyard, Hants

Tonight nobody would sleep aboard the *Téméraire*, or any of the other twenty-seven ships and four frigates moored off Cadiz. Men would toss restless in their bunks, envying the watch whose duty it was to remain awake. Midshipman Peck had gone up on to the top deck, kept to the shadows, not that his presence there was likely to be challenged but a low profile was preferable. His own unease might serve to unnerve any one of those statue-like silhouettes whose duty it was to be vigilant throughout the nocturnal hours. They would not see him; a veteran of Corunna, he was confident that the battle on the morrow would be won and that he would survive.

Earlier that day Nelson had summoned all his captains aboard the *Victory* to outline his plan of attack. The ships would form two columns, Nelson in command of one, Collingwood the other, and sail towards the centre and rear of the combined French and Spanish fleet as it sailed from Cadiz. This way the British ships would be brought into close action, cutting off the Combined Fleet which would then be delayed in getting back into action.

The *Téméraire* was a fine ship to be aboard, Peck reflected. Only the *Victory* herself with 110 guns and the *Britannia* with 100, equipped them better for warfare. The *Téméraire*, like himself, was a veteran, a survivor that would go on to fight another day.

Peck winced as the twinge in his shoulder reminded him of the ball that had struck him at Corunna. Tall and lean, he made a determined effort not to bow his shoulders, a posture which was a legacy from that musket ball. A widower, he had lost his wife ten years ago in childbirth. He would not remarry; all that was left to him was serving his country, and when he became too old for that then the will to live would flicker and extinguish like a candle in a draught.

He glanced up at the myriad of stars, said a silent prayer for the morrow. There would be casualties; no battle was fought without them, and every man prayed that he would not be among them. You sensed the atmosphere of tension, envisaged men lying awake in their bunks, craving action because until it began there was no possibility of it being over and done with.

A movement to larboard had Peck pressing himself back against a mast, his keen grey eyes penetrating the darkness. Another movement, something that was blacker than the shadows, a flitting shape that checked furtively as though to ascertain that it was not being observed. Nobody on watch would react that way because the danger, if it came, would be from a seaward direction.

Now he saw the other more clearly in a shaft of starlight, a man who bent to loosen his boots, bare-headed and coatless, an urgency about his every movement now. Peck moved forward, treading with the balls of his feet to minimize any sound he might make, instinctively drawing his pistol, for this was some subversive action which no way figured in the admiral's battle plans.

"Halt!"

Peck made it unseen to within a yard of the unknown man, his pistol clicking loudly as he cocked it. The other jerked upright, almost lost his balance as he whirled on a bootless foot.

"What goes on? Let me see your face and recognize you!"

The faint starlight was sufficient for Midshipman William Peck to recognize the other's pallid, deathly white features. A man of twenty-five or so, straggling hair, a hairlip and slight of build.

"James Finter!" Peck spoke the name aloud, his lips curling with contempt. "About to desert, I perceive, contemplating the long swim to the shores of Cadiz where mayhap the Spanish or French would put a bullet in your brain. As, indeed, I would do right now were it not for the fact that tomorrow we need every man to fight the Combined Fleet. With luck, you will die in battle, honoured rather than despised. But, tell me the reason for your intended desertion. Apart from *cowardice*."

Finter was no coward, that was what puzzled Peck. The man was a good rifleman, and had proved himself already in service. It was strange, indeed.

James Finter licked his dry lips, shuffled his booted foot nervously. "My wife, sir, she was close to childbirth when we sailed from England. There had been . . . problems in the early stages. The doctors warned me that . . . that it might be a difficult birth. There has been no word, she has no next of kin. I hope for the best, fear for the worst. There is only one way to know for certain and that is to go to her."

"By deserting." Peck tightened his lips; it was an all too common story which he had heard before. "So you planned to swim to Cadiz. And from there?"

"I had no plans, sir, other than by some means to make my way back to England and hopefully to find—"

"You poor fool." The midshipman slowly lowered the hammer of his pistol, returned the weapon to his belt. "Everything risked, an honourable career, execution. All for a woman who may already have died in childbirth. Or the rest of your life spent as a penniless fugitive *if* you lived."

"I love her, sir." Finter's eyes glinted as they misted; he was trembling visibly. "A decision I made on the spur of the moment, one which I am already regretting. As you say, my desertion would have served no purpose."

"Aye, whatever fate decreed has already passed. Your wife is either dead or alive. Do you think she would welcome you home as a deserter?"

"No, sir." The rifleman shook his head, stared down at his feet. "I planned to tell her that I had been sent home after the battle. For surely tomorrow's encounter would have been history by the time I returned to her."

"I should take you before Captain Harvey, have you tried and executed." Peck spoke with a hoarse, angry whisper. "Indeed, I would do just that did we not need every man tomorrow. So, Finter, return to your bunk, rest and prepare yourself for what lies ahead. After the battle has been fought I will decide what action to take."

"Thank you, sir." The rifleman pulled on his discarded boot, and slunk away into the darkness.

William Peck remained on deck, staring into the night in the direction of Cadiz. History would be made, one way or the other, when the new day dawned.

Shortly after daybreak the French and Spanish fleets were spied, formed in a close line off Cape Trafalgar, some 12 miles to leeward of the British. A count revealed thirty-three sailing ships and seven frigates, outnumbering Nelson's fleet, both in size and weight, as well as in numbers. It was estimated that there were some 4,000 troops on board.

A signal was run up the *Victory*'s halyards on the instructions of Nelson. *England expects that every man will do his duty*. The British ships began to move according to the admiral's plan. Then came another signal on the telegraphic flag.

Engage the enemy more closely.

At midday the first shots were fired at the *Royal Sovereign*, followed by further long-range fire on the *Victory*. The Battle of Trafalgar had begun on 21 October 1805.

Nelson's ship had received some scathing fire and the casualties were heavy. The admiral's personal secretary, John Scott, had died, together with some marines on the poop deck. Thus Captain Hardy came to the decision to take his ship beyond the rear of the *Bucentaure* and the riflemen were ordered to disperse around the deck in an attempt to counter the hail of bullets from the French sharpshooters.

Meanwhile, the *Téméraire* was engaged with both the *Redoubtable* and *Neptune*. The veteran warship already had three topmasts down but continued to pound away at the *Redoubtable* as she drifted down on her, heading towards the *Victory*. Clearly the Combined Fleet had singled out Nelson's ship as an early trophy, for, with that captured or sunk, morale would be low on the other vessels.

William Peck glanced around the *Téméraire*'s deck as he reloaded. Less than 10 yards to his right young Finter was taking aim again; a puff of black powder-smoke; it was impossible to distinguish the report from the salvo all around but a French sniper fell back. The younger man was certainly no coward, the midshipman surmised as he primed his weapon.

Perhaps last night could be forgotten. Right now was not the time to make such decisions.

The *Redoubtable* had closed alongside the *Victory*, and the enemy troops were anticipating the order to board the greatest prize of all, crowding on deck in readiness. That was when the *Téméraire* ground up against the French ship on the opposite side to the *Victory*.

Captain Harvey gave the order to fire and, at close range, the *Téméraire*'s broadside swept the enemy decks. Through the pall of smoke William Peck saw the sickening devastation, enemy troops blasted beyond recognition, others with limbs missing, bleeding profusely, crawling aimlessly in all directions.

Captain Lucas, though, refused to surrender the *Redoubtable* even with a third of his crew either dead or dying. He yelled for the survivors to carry on attacking the *Téméraire* with grenades and a hail of bullets from the tops.

The worst danger came from fireballs, missiles like flaming meteorites designed to create maximum devastation. Peck ducked instinctively as one screamed over his head, heard it crash beyond him. Seconds later flames were licking the wood-work by the after-magazine.

"*Fire!*" he yelled. "Bring buckets."

Men left their posts, struggled with pails of water which had been kept for such an emergency. One of these fire-fighters was James Finter, his features blackened almost beyond recogni-tion, throwing water on the flames then returning for another bucket. The fire sizzled, the flames died down until they were easily stamped and beaten out. Another catastrophe had been averted.

Momentarily Finter's eyes met Peck's gaze, a brief exchange and then both men were back at their posts, firing at the enemy.

Sharpshooters fell from the topmasts of the *Redoubtable* as the British kept up a continuous fire. Still the stubborn Captain Lucas refused to surrender his ship, watched as she was lashed to the *Téméraire*. He and a handful of survivors would defend her until the bitter end. Then both the *Victory* and the *Témér-aire* moved on in search of further conquests.

The *Fougueux* arrived on the scene, bore down upon the *Téméraire*. The latter, showing signs of severe damage, seemed easy prey for the 700 troops aboard the French ship. The captured *Redoubtable* would almost certainly be an encumbrance to the British warship.

The *Téméraire*'s first lieutenant was quick to realize the danger, ordering the men from the larboard batteries to man the starboard side. So far no guns had spoken from there.

"Stand by. *Fire!*"

A cannonade crashed into the approaching *Fougueux*, smashing her side and sweeping troops from the deck. The French had underestimated the *Téméraire* and now one of their best warships floated like a crippled waterfowl. There was no resistance as the *Téméraire* drove up against her and lashed fast to her side. Some thirty men boarded the *Fougueux* and the Union Jack was hoisted above the tricolor of the French jackstaff.

Shots were still coming from the *Redoubtable*. Lucas and his remaining survivors were putting up a token resistance even though their ship was lashed to the *Téméraire*. Then, without warning, the French ship's mainmast, weakened by cannon-fire, came crashing down, bridging the two ships.

"Board the *Redoubtable*." Master-at-arms John Toohig conveyed the order from Captain Harvey.

Peck was one of the first to respond, and led the way across the fallen mast. He coughed as the sulphurous powder-smoke seared his lungs, made his eyes smart. A French trooper barred their way, rifle raised to fire. A shot rang out; Peck braced himself for the inevitable bullet which would smash into his chest. But it was the Frenchman who went down, dropping his weapon as his legs buckled beneath him.

"Good shooting, rifleman." Peck glanced at the man beside him, smoking rifle in his hands. "I thought that bullet had my name on it. Thank you . . ."

His words died away as his bleary eyes met those of James Finter, the man who had planned to desert. Had Finter succeeded in leaving the *Téméraire* then right now Peck would have been lying dead or mortally wounded.

"It was my duty, sir." The other's reply was shouted above the noise of battle. "I shot him because he was an enemy, for no other reason."

"Of course, rifleman." Peck fired as another French trooper showed himself, saw the man crumple to the deck. "Just as I did then."

It was in the heat of that final skirmish aboard the *Redoubtable* that the midshipman made a decision that had no bearing on the battle. Afterwards when, not "if", the Combined Fleet was defeated, he would forget all about what had happened last night between himself and Finter. He would set the younger man's mind at rest with one final reprimand and that would be that. Peck found himself wondering whether or not Finter's wife had survived childbirth. Which was an irrelevant thought as Captain Lucas finally conceded defeat. It was a sure sign that Midshipman Peck was getting too old for warfare.

The capture of the *Redoubtable* was but a brief interlude for the *Téméraire* and those aboard. The *Neptune*, a formidable Spanish warship under the command of Don Antonio Parejo, with eighty-four guns and several hundred troops, began to close in on the much-battered *Téméraire*. Like the *Fougueux* and the *Redoubtable* earlier, it saw the British veteran as easy prey.

Captain Harvey gave the order for his men to move back from the starboard batteries to man the larboard. Around him were more casualties than he had hoped for. Mould and Payne, lieutenants of Royal Marines, were lying badly injured; Brooks, the bosun, had been shot in the shoulder. Midshipman Eastman was dragging his legs as he attempted to crawl to the latest scene of action. Simeon Busigny, captain of Royal Marines, had been carried below deck earlier with what at first seemed a flesh wound. It had been more serious and he had died as the doctor attempted to remove the leaden ball. John Kingston, another marine, and Oades, a carpenter, had been killed outright. The toll was mounting.

Now more men would die; it was a stark fact of battle, whether on land or at sea.

"Man the larboard. *Fire!*"

Cannon- and rifle-fire raked the *Téméraire*. Wood splintered; William Peck felt a trickle of blood on his cheek but he knew it was not serious. There would be much worse before this day was done.

He fired but the drifting smoke pall was too dense for him to see whether or not he had dropped his man. A rifle next to him boomed, a familiar voice yelled, "Got 'im!"

"Good shooting, Finter." Peck spared his companion a glance; it seemed that he and the young rifleman were destined to see this battle through together, comrades of war in the finest battle the English had ever fought.

"Look!" Finter paused in the act of reloading to point out to sea. "Here comes the *Leviathan*; she's going for the *Neptune*. Not as many guns as us but between us we'll give that Spaniard a pounding. See, she's opened fire already; we can catch the *Neptune* in a crossfire."

The Spanish warship had slowed; maybe her captain had already decided to seek safety with her own few surviving ships.

"She's going to retreat!" Finter paused in his reloading, stood upright in his exultation. "Looks like—".

The Spaniards had not yet ordered their sharpshooters to cease firing and spasmodic shots still came from the enemy ship.

"Finter!" Peck turned, went over to the fallen man. He saw at once that it was a chest wound, blood already seeping and saturating the rifleman's tunic. "Here, let me see." His fingers ripped at the material, tugged and tore until he exposed the bloodied flesh. The wound looked nasty, a gaping hole to the left of the heart. Maybe the breastbone had deflected it and it had missed the vital organs. Many had survived such wounds and lived to fight another day.

Finter's eyes flickered open, a trickle of blood came from his thin lips. "You shouldn't be doing this, sir," he whispered faintly. "Your job is to fight the enemy. You could face a court martial."

"That's my worry." Again Peck found himself wondering about Finter's wife, whether or not she had lived after childbirth. It was ridiculous, no business of his. You were taught not to become emotionally involved with casualties of war.

Below deck the doctors were hard-pressed, many of the wounded dying before they reached the treatment table. Perhaps he could get Finter below by himself and if anybody asked any questions he had the answer ready. "This man saved my life. Treat him."

His fingers again explored the wound tenderly. It was bleeding even more heavily as though the release of the tight-fitting garment had removed that which was stemming the flow.

"What's this?" His probing fingers came into contact with something hard and smooth that was neither flesh nor cloth. It had been wedged securely between the man's vest and his body. Peck secured a grip on its smooth, blood-smeared surface, tugging it free.

"*No!*" Finter's eyes opened and there was no mistaking the fear in them. He made as if to snatch the object from the other but his strength was waning fast. His hand fell away, thudded limply on to the deck. "No, please. Throw it overboard, sir. Please, if you think you owe me anything, destroy it."

"Why?" Peck would have opened the small oilskin package there and then but for another bullet that embedded itself in the fallen mast just behind him. He grabbed up his rifle, returned to his dilemma, made a decision that was fitting to a midshipman in the heat of battle.

"They'll take you below shortly, rifleman." It was the tone of a superior who accepted that he must leave a wounded man to die. For had not Nelson ordered that "England expects that every man will do his duty."

Midshipman William Peck had his duty to do. He glanced down at Finter, saw that the other's smoke-grimed features had relaxed, the arms sprawled and unmoving. If James Finter still had a wife somewhere then she was now a widow. It was a stark fact of war and Peck wondered why, momentarily, he had become emotionally involved. He would not let it happen again.

And as soon as the *Leviathan* drove off the Spanish ship then he would examine that package that he had retrieved from Finter's body.

The news of Nelson's death was conveyed to the fleet in the late afternoon, casting a sombre mood over an otherwise sense of exultation at the routing of the Combined Fleet. Flags were lowered to half mast, while aboard every vessel doctors treated the wounded, and corpses were stitched in sailcloth. The full death toll would not be known for some time.

Captain Sir Eliab Harvey sat in his private cabin, glancing alternately from some sheets of paper to the master-at-arms, John Toohig, who stood before him.

"I find this almost unbelievable." Harvey's tone was grave, his lips tightened to a thin bloodless slit.

"You say you found it on Midshipman Peck's body?"

"Aye, sir, tucked in his shirt. The ball that got him missed it by a fraction, pierced his heart."

"And perhaps it is as well it did." The captain leafed through the sheets of paper, stared fixedly at them. A handwritten scrawl, barely legible in parts, together with a map and diagrams. There was no mistaking the Cadiz coastline and Cape Trafalgar. A series of diamond shapes depicted ships, the English ones shaded in. "Nelson's battle plan, the one that worked so admirably. Yet it would have been a disaster for England had Villeneuve and Gravina got hold of this."

"I don't quite understand you, sir. Midshipman Peck, in all probability, recorded the battle plan for his own use."

"There was no need. Every captain had a copy, given to them in strict secrecy, only to be opened at daybreak. There can be no doubt concerning Peck's intentions, which were to swim out to the Combined Fleet and sell Nelson's strategics to them. Had he managed to do so, then undoubtedly he would have been handsomely rewarded and lived out the rest of his days on Spanish soil. He would have been known throughout history as the man who defeated Nelson at Trafalgar."

"Then why did he not leave the *Téméraire*, sir?"

"Because the enemy moved too quickly for him. Doubtless he

intended to desert before dawn, only the Combined Fleet had forestalled him, sailing out of Cadiz much earlier than we anticipated. By then it was too late so Peck remained and fought the enemy with us."

"And was killed honourably in battle, sir."

"*No!*" Harvey's cheeks were suffused with blood, his fists clenched until his knuckles showed white. "He died what he always was, a traitor. The fact that he was not able to bring about the downfall of his own country in no way changes anything. Had he lived, then he would have been executed here on board the *Téméraire* and his body buried anonymously and ignominiously at sea. Nothing changes that. A Spanish sharpshooter executed Peck and he will be buried at sea, the only marker inside his sailcloth coffin this treacherous missive which, thank God, failed to reach its intended destination."

"And for the record, sir?"

"No record, Toohig. There can be no trial to prove his guilt, just these sheets of paper. Peck will be listed as 'missing at sea'. The end result is the same except that we shall not have yet another traitor to tarnish this fine day and our history. Slide the corpse overboard after darkness has fallen and leave it at that. Tomorrow the British fleet will mourn the death of its finest admiral. Let nothing spoil that sombre day."

NELSON EXPECTS

Nigel Brown

Here is the second story set at Trafalgar. It is the first historical story by Nigel Brown (b. 1959), though he has had several science fiction, fantasy and ghost stories published. Brown tells me that he was born and raised in Portsmouth, within easy walking distance of the dockyard and the city's old naval fortifications, which he knows like his "own backyard". So much for our naval security!

"Do your duty, Berney!" said the young lieutenant, out of the darkness. Lieutenant Parks stood beyond the pale light of the frigate *Euryalus*'s deck lantern. "Get down into the dinghy. I'll teach you some guts."

William Berney turned away from Parks. Berney's years in the navy, since being pressed off the merchant ship *Mermaid* in 1802, had taught him that no able seaman answered a lieutenant back. He tugged at the rope hanging over the frigate's side, testing it. As he pulled, he could hear the small wooden dinghy bumping alongside the ship's hull as the *Euryalus* pulled it across the entrance to the Bay of Cadiz.

Parks stepped to the edge of the deck, then lifted his spyglass to watch the shore to leeward. William followed his gaze.

The lights of Cadiz burned at the southern end of the bay's entrance. Beyond them, invisible in the night, were the masts of Admiral Villeneuve's Combined Fleet of French and Spanish ships. The enemy. Parks turned the glass northwards, past Rota at the northern end of the bay.

Earlier, before nightfall, William had overheard Captain Blackwood instructing Parks to take the frigate's dinghy shoreward. Parks was to rendezvous at midnight with a Spanish fishing-boat bearing information about the enemy fleet at anchor in the Spanish port. Dangerous work, William knew, venturing so close to the enemy shore with so many lookouts and patrols swarming around the bay.

Now, standing alongside the brash lieutenant, he cursed his ill-luck that Parks had spotted him outside the captain's cabin before he could hide below decks. I'm no coward, William thought. I just want to see Jessie and my boys again. Jessie's face, her smile, her brown curls under her Sunday-best bonnet were as fresh in his mind as they were that last day in church together, before he left for London and the *Mermaid*.

"Time to go," said Parks, lowering his spyglass. His head dipped into the lantern's light; William noticed its peculiar narrow shape and jutting chin threw the grotesque image of a ship's prow across the pale decking.

They climbed down into the small boat, along with three other seamen, taking care to shield their pistols from the spray. Before long, William was too tired from rowing to worry about the closing enemy coastline. He pulled at his muffled oar, his arms and shoulders straining, his checkered shirt drenched in sweat despite the cool night breeze which blew in from the Atlantic. At fifty years old, he struggled to keep up with the younger seamen rowing beside him.

Parks drove the rowers relentlessly across the choppy water. At intervals he raised his spyglass, scanned the sea to coastward, but William noticed his agitation as they neared the Spanish mainland. It was past midnight. There was no sign of the fishing-boat.

Then a lantern flashed in the darkness to the north-east. Parks gazed at the spot, waiting for the expected second signal.

They rowed on, but the blackness to larboard remained absolute.

"One light," Parks muttered. Reluctantly, he asked the rowers, "I saw one light. Did anyone spot two, or was it just the one?"

William and the other seamen affirmed that they had only seen the one.

"Oars up," Parks ordered.

They sat quiet in the dinghy, bobbing up and down in the darkness, awaiting Park's directions.

William realized Parks was unsure if the light was their rendezvous or an enemy patrol. Thinking back, he remembered the *Mermaid*'s escape from pirates off Cuba, when they had allowed them to sail close enough for the *Mermaid*'s suddenly unveiled 12s to chase them away.

Like any merchant seaman he saw no reason to go looking for trouble, but when the navy dropped him in it . . .

"Return the signal, sir," William said. "They'll need to get close to us on the larboard side." He lifted up his pistol. "We'll see them first against the shore lights. We'll have the advantage if need be to pick them off easier, to slow them down so we can escape."

"We have a mission to complete, Berney," Parks replied. "Captain Blackwood expects his men to overcome adversity, not escape from it!"

Parks paused, considering the darkness, the distant lights of Cadiz, the silent crewmen watching him. Then he raised his lantern and replied to the signal. William noticed he had pulled his pistol from his belt.

Minutes passed, then: "Hoi!" A call in the darkness. "Engleesh?"

William straightened up at the voice, despite his aching back. He looked around, and spotted a sail's broad silhouette against the darker shadow of the Spanish mainland. The boat was even smaller than their dinghy, bearing a single occupant who crouched low in the stern.

"*Euryalus*," Parks called out. The word came out hoarse, a hissing sound over the crash of breaking surf on the nearby shore. William detected a tremor in Parks's voice. Did Parks fear this was an enemy trick, as he did? William had heard how quick the enemy were to shoot captured spies.

"There is leetle time!" said the voice. "Our friend was taken by the French this night. I must be back before it is the light."

Fast launches could be sweeping the water for them already. William looked up at Parks, hoping the lieutenant would realize this and order them back to the frigate. Parks's face turned away from him in the darkness.

"But is there any news?" Parks asked. "Any news when the fleet may sail? Any destination? Is it north to the Channel, or south to the Gut?"

"The Gut, as you call it," was the reply. "Gibraltar and then Napoli. But take this back with you – our friend charged me to tell you this: Vice-Admiral Rosily rides like the devil to Cadiz on Napoleon's orders to replace Villeneuve. Villeneuve has learned of this, and means to sail on the next tide to escape his fate. Good fortune!" The sail flapped in the wind, bearing the small boat away to shore.

The import of the man's words struck the English crew like a thunderbolt. They all knew that battle had come at last.

"Quick!" Parks cried. "Make haste there!"

William rowed as hard as the rest of them, but this time the effort failed to calm him. The long days of watching the enemy fleet were over. There was no avoiding battle for him now.

"Row harder, you lubbers!" Parks said. "I'll not stand a delay on account of slack work!" The bow surged through the waves with each heave of the oars. William twisted around, to see how far they had to go back to the *Euryalus*. Parks sat forward, leaning out across the rippling water. He looked as if he could will the dinghy faster through the water to carry his glory back to his captain. William knew Parks well enough. The lieutenant expected his name to be put before Nelson himself after such an important mission.

A faint glow of dawn lifted above the Spanish coastline. The men pulled harder at their oars. Their haven approached, with Captain Henry Blackwood on the deck of *Euryalus*. It was he who had found Villeneuve's fleet at Cadiz, then raced to England to carry the news to Nelson.

But Parks was too late with his news. Blackwood had already signalled his vice-admiral that Villeneuve was on the move. The *Sirius*, a fellow frigate in Blackwood's small squadron, further inshore, had signalled that the enemy's sails had hoisted. The ships were already leaving port.

William saw that Parks took the news badly. The man's gimlet eyes narrowed with anger. Their baleful gaze flicked towards William. William knew that Parks resented his sound advice over the signals; he also blamed him for slack rowing – this snatching of his moment of glory.

"Good work, Mr Parks," Blackwood said. His face showed a deliberate open expression.

Parks swallowed. "Yes sir! Are they coming out, Captain?"

"I hope so," Blackwood replied. He trained his telescope on the *Sirius*.

William heard no more, that busy Saturday morning. He kept out of the sullen lieutenant's way, but it was not difficult, even on the small frigate.

The *Sirius* signalled 370 to confirm that the enemy was leaving port. The alarm needed to be passed down the line of ships to where Nelson waited in the *Victory* 50 miles away, hidden over the horizon from the nervous Villeneuve. William spent his time up in the rigging, as the *Euryalus* sailed into the best position to observe the enemy fleet. Then Midshipman Bruce sent him to his gun, an eighteen-pounder, to help prepare it in case the enemy ships approached the watching frigate.

The first dog-watch, at four o'clock that afternoon, found him at the mainmast. The breeze had died at noon, and, 4 miles from the enemy, they could see that Villeneuve's main fleet was still in port.

Parks spotted him, then approached before William could disappear.

"I've been watching you since Portsmouth," Parks said. "You do less than anyone, and seem to think you get away with it. This is a King's ship you're on now."

"I do my duty, sir," William replied carefully. The other seamen around them had noticed Parks's raised voice. They paid close attention to their tasks, listening hard.

"Oh yes!" Parks exclaimed. "You do just enough, I think. That's not your duty! I've met your sort before. You merchant seamen are happy for our protection; you're paid more, you work less. You're not fit to sail the same seas as Nelson himself!"

"I have, sir," William muttered.

"What, man?" Parks had already turned away, satisfied with his work.

"I have sailed with Nelson, sir."

"So have many. Was it the *Agamemnon*? I can't believe he put up with you."

"We sailed thirty-three year ago, sir. Together on a West Indiaman," William replied. "I remember him well; a fellow Norfolk man. I were brought up near Burnham Thorpe. Knew his folks. Nelson was sick as a dog at sea, but I taught him his first seamanship. I were just two years older than him, but had served double that time before him."

Parks looked incredulous. He thrust his chin out, almost in William's impassive face.

"If it's true," he spat, "then your *fellow seaman* has put you to shame since. Get back to work."

William returned to his gun post. His attempt at turning the tables on Parks was not sweet, but bitter.

The next day found the frigate still near Cadiz, under thick clouds racing up from the south. William watched the sails of the enemy fleet move out of the bay. Today they looked determined to leave, despite the growing bad weather.

He fretted all morning. His words with Parks brought it home to him. Here he was, a lowly seaman among many, while his once-companion Horatio Nelson commanded the whole fleet. William had enjoyed following the lad's career from his own safer posting in the merchant fleet. He had drunk many a toast to Nelson after his successes at Cape St Vincent, the Nile and Copenhagen. He shook his head in wonder that the sickly lad had risen so far, so fast. Yet he had to admit, even then, that Horatio had shown an unusual regard for his honour. A reck-lessness of determination which was alien to William Berney.

By the afternoon, Blackwood took the frigate westward, closer to the waiting British fleet. He wished to signal Nelson directly that the enemy was not returning to port, despite the onset of bad weather. Heavy seas and rain squalls risked Villeneuve retreating back to Cadiz. In fact Blackwood saw that the French vice-admiral was directing his thirty ships westward, before attempting to turn south for Gibraltar and the refuge of the Mediterranean.

As another squall blew up, Parks approached William on his way up to the rigging to help reef the sails. The heavy rain stopped for a moment, and its curtain drew back to reveal the British fleet all around the small frigate.

"Look at this, man! England's finest!" He swept his hand in an arc, taking in the *Victory*, the *Britannia*, the *Ajax* and so many others filling the sea with their great wooden bulks, and filling the leaden sky with their masts, rigging and acres of canvas.

"Don't you feel it?" Parks asked, raising his voice against the crack of sails. He pointed at the *Victory*. "Nelson's aboard her. We'll not let him down."

Yet all William could think of was the clash of the fleets to come. Each of those gunports open, blasting pain and death on both sides. He was glad to be on the swift frigate. Better to be the messenger boy than the champion fighter in a battle.

It was late afternoon, the middle of the first dog-watch again, before Nelson signalled Blackwood to return to watching the enemy fleet. William felt a pang of relief as the masts of the ships dropped below the horizon to the west.

That Sunday night, the *Euryalus*, *Phoebe* and *Sirius* watched the enemy. After a fitful sleep, as the frigate rocked over the growing Atlantic swell, William was on first watch until mid-night, at his gun post.

Captain Blackwood instructed that two blue flares be sent up at hourly intervals, signalling "Enemy standing to the southward". Along the deck, William worked as the loader in his gun crew. He took the bulky cartridge from the boy Sims and slid it into the barrel. This was followed by the wad, then the shot. The eighteen-pounder was fired every hour, one of three in quick succession, signalling "Enemy standing to the westward".

"Looking forward to the action, tomorrow?" Parks's voice bellowed in his ear.

William had a band of cloth tied around his head to muffle the deafening sound of the gun. He pointed at it and stared uncomprehendingly at Parks. A look of disgust crossed the lieutenant's face. To William, the man's features looked inhuman by the blue light of the flare – like death itself come to visit him.

Dawn on Monday, 21 October found the *Euryalus* back among Nelson's fleet, off Cape Trafalgar. William was up in the rigging when he saw, through the mist over the calm sea, a forest of masts on the horizon. It was Villeneuve's fleet sailing south towards the Gut. He considered his chances of surviving the day. Nelson used the frigates as fast messengers between the large battleships. William was certain that Nelson would be determined to lead his ship into battle first. Hopefully the *Victory* would bear the brunt of the enemy, leaving the *Euryalus* to serve in the safer mopping-up operation afterwards. He smiled to himself, realizing that, in his calculations, there was no doubt in his mind that the British fleet, commanded by Nelson, would win.

Then the drum roll went out: "Beat to quarters!"

William climbed down the rigging, ready to take up his post at the gun. He was certain it was the safest place to be in the following hours. At times like this his usual bolt-holes around the ship would be false havens. Captain Blackwood would post marines around the *Euryalus* to prevent desertion from post.

"You! Where are you going?"

He halted, still swinging from the ropes in the growing swell.

"Clear for action, sir. To my post."

Parks shook his head. "No. I've advised your gun captain that you're to come with me. Sims will take over from you."

Parks directed William over to a group of seamen standing by the captain.

He saluted: "Crew assembled to take you over to *Victory*, sir!"

Blackwood nodded. "Thank you, Mr Parks."

The heavy, sultry weather added to the nightmarish atmosphere as William followed Parks, Blackwood and the rest of the men down the netting into the captain's gig. Dazed, he pulled at his oar, each stroke taking him closer to what he knew would be the thick of the fighting.

The side of the *Victory* drew nearer, like a city wall at sea. William saw hundreds of men swarming over her, preparing for the battle ahead: red-coated marines peering over the side at them, able seamen 100 feet above them scaling the shrouds and ratlines, the open gunports with the shadowy figures of the gun crews within.

They rowed around the stern of the *Victory*, the gig dipping up and down in the heavy swell coming in from the Atlantic. A blue-coated, white-haired figure was clearly seen through a framed window, watching the fleet. A murmur of excitement rippled through the boat crew. Parks caught William's eye in this moment of elation. William saw triumph there, and a challenge: I'll see if you sailed with Nelson . . .

Once they were onboard, they were told to wait on the gangway off the quarterdeck for further orders while Captain Blackwood went to consult with Lord Nelson.

This was the heart of British sea power. Despite his misgivings about being there, William was impressed by the co-ordinated movements of so many men on the flagship. Above him, seamen climbed rigging, hauled on ropes. He saw that Nelson had ordered full sails to make use of what little breeze there was; even the studdingsails were set to bear the *Victory* as quickly as possible towards the enemy. Below him, he could see into the ship's waist to the upper deck, where gun crews were preparing their twelve-pounders. He noticed, even here, that the flagship was short of crew for the guns. He shuddered at his vision of inferno to come, the blood-red painted walls, the screams of dying men.

Parks stood next to him, silent as they watched the *Victory*'s crew at work. Then William heard him stamp his feet to attention. Looking around, William stared straight into the deep-set eyes of Lord Nelson himself.

The face was one he remembered, peeling back the years in his mind's eye: the strong features, the wide mouth, the thick brows.

William drew in a breath, tried to greet his one-time apprentice, but found he was too shy to speak. He stood mute, surprised at himself.

"These are Blackwood's men," said a tall captain, standing beside the vice-admiral. William realized that this was Hardy, captain of the *Victory*.

"Take this message back to your fellows on *Euryalus*," Nelson said, in William's own Norfolk accent. "You've been my eyes for these last weeks. Now we're running the enemy down I promise you warm work, my noble lads!" Nelson paused, turned to look at William again, then was about to say something when a breathless midshipman came running up and handed a message to Captain Hardy.

Hardy scanned it, his heavy brows furrowed. "The enemy fleet is turning back north!" he exclaimed.

"They are trying to get back to Cadiz," Nelson replied. "We'll stop them!" The two men walked towards the poop, already lifting their telescopes up to view the distant masts.

Parks waited until they were out of earshot, then turned to the subdued seaman. "Did you hear Nelson?" Parks asked. " 'Warm work' his lordship's promised!"

"Yes, sir."

"Well? If he knew you, he hid it well. I noticed you didn't claim old fellowship, either!"

"No, sir."

Parks glanced around to check that the senior officers had gone, then he tapped William hard on the chest. A gesture of contempt, a deliberate push. William took a step backwards, tripped over a rope, and plunged off the gangway on to the deck below.

$\star$ $\qquad$ $\star$ $\qquad$ $\star$

William opened his eyes to near-darkness; a flickering lantern rocked above him, jerking with each muffled thud that shook the *Victory*'s hull. He was lying on a sea chest in the sick-bay, at the bottom of the ship.

Before he could gather his senses and stop himself from moving, his arms twitched, his legs shifted uncomfortably. At once, a rough voice said, "Get up, yer lubber! You're all right! We'll need that space soon enough for our work!"

A surgeon's mate brandishing an amputating saw grinned ferociously at him. He thrust a piece of paper in William's hand.

"Yer to report to Lieutenant Harvey on the aft lower deck."

William was stunned.

"But I'm with the *Euryalus*," he said.

"Get up there!" the man replied. "Harvey'll set yer straight."

The lower deck was one level above. William had a growing dread at what had happened to him. He hurried through the dim light, between the crowds of men and boys scrabbling about their duties. A marine sentry guarded the aft hatch to above.

"I'm to return to the *Euryalus*," William said, "with Captain Blackwood."

The sentry regarded William coldly. He was posted there to prevent crew from deserting their posts in battle.

"Only officers, midshipman or powder monkeys pass," he said. "Return to your post!"

A boy descended the hatch ladder, showed his empty gun-cartridge case to the sentry, and was allowed through to the magazines for replacement.

"I've orders to report to Lieutenant Harvey." He showed the sentry his paper. The man squinted at it in the dim light, hesitated, then stepped aside.

The lower gun deck housed the massive thirty-two-pounders. Cleared for action, William could see across the whole deck: the thirty guns, fifteen on each side of the *Victory*, 200 men ready to fire them. He spotted Harvey, the lieutenant in charge of the aft part of the deck.

"Able Seaman William Berney, sir, from *Euryalus*."

Harvey looked too busy to acknowledge him, but he lowered his speaking trumpet at once.

"Lieutenant Parks tells me you're a skilled loader, Berney. We're short on that gun there." He indicated a gun on the starboard side, near to the hatchway. "Take your post."

"But my place is on the *Euryalus*!" William exclaimed.

Harvey scowled. "You're with us now! Take your post!"

William hurried to join his new fellow gun crew. He guessed what had happened. Parks had sent him down to the sick-bay, they'd had to leave the *Victory*.

A prime target. The wedge of the fleet that was being driven directly at the enemy guns.

His position at the gun muzzle, to load cartridge, wads and shot, allowed him to look out of the gunport.

His suspicions were confirmed when he saw Captain Blackwood's gig below, the men rowing like mad for their frigate. It was the worst moment of his life, even more than when the press-gang had found him cowering in his hidey-hole at the bottom of the *Mermaid*. Lieutenant Parks spotted his face at the gunport, and threw him a mock salute.

A fountain of water erupted near to the gig. It tipped madly in the wake, but the men rowed on. Captain Blackwood sat calm, as if it were a pleasure trip on the Norfolk Broads.

That cannonball was one of the ranging shots of the nearest enemy ships. The thumps and splashes continued out of William's sight. A rumble and boom of gunfire told him that, elsewhere, battle had begun. Looking forwards out of the port, he could see the enemy battleships bristling with guns, all facing towards the oncoming *Victory*. He estimated they were about a mile away, closing slowly in the light wind that drove *Victory* on.

Ducking back, William decided there was little he could do now but get on with it; keep himself busy to forget the approach of hell. He checked that shot was to hand. He remembered to tie a strip of cloth around his head, to protect his hearing. The other seamen in the gun crew looked tense, yet expectant. The powder monkey stood nearby, a small boy clutching a bulky gun cartridge to his chest.

The enemy found their range. The *Victory* shuddered, slowed her progress as the first holes were shot through her sails.

There was a minute of dreadful silence, then a roar of dragons aft as the broadsides from four of the enemy fleet concentrated their firepower on Nelson's flagship. The *Victory* seemed to pause in the water from the onslaught. William saw smoke aft along the deck, heard screams as deadly splinters of shattered flying wood raked the seamen waiting at their posts.

Yet still there was no order to fire. William stood rigid, eyes down at the shuddering sand-strewn planks of the deck, his mind trying to call up prayers, but being swamped by the terrible cries of the dying men, the last shriek of a child.

Then a midshipman hurtled down the hatchway from above. William heard him call to Lieutenant Harvey, "There'll be a target soon! The *Bucentaure*. Their flagship!"

He glanced out of the gunport, unable to see anything through billows of smoke. The lieutenant cried though his speaking trumpet, "Larboard guns, run out!"

Not the guns on his side. Not yet.

The crews on the other side of the deck clustered around their guns for a moment, then hauled them by the gun-tackles, slammed their carriages hard up against the ship's side, jumped back before the gun captains triggered the guns with their lanyards. The sound of the thirty-two-pounders blasting at the enemy deafened William. Dazed, he saw the gun crews work their guns in a practised motion which belied the smoke, the jerking 3-ton monster, the seeming confusion of men.

The minutes passed. William stood waiting, coughing in the acrid smoke that consumed them all. He could tell from the gun crew's actions that they were doing terrible damage to the enemy. The smoke cleared for a moment. Through the opposite gunport he caught a glimpse of the *Bucentaure*, her stern shattered. His eyes, stung with smoke, took in a vision of splintered burning timbers, lurching men falling over, awash with blood. He wondered if Villeneuve was dead.

Then the men ceased their deadly fire on the larboard side. William could see an approaching ship through his own gunport; he recognized it – the seventy-four-gun *Redoutable*. He tensed, knowing what was to come. The Frenchman loomed closer, so close that he thought she was going to collide with *Victory*. He saw with amazement that most of the lower-deck gunports of the enemy were closed.

"Starboard guns, run out!" Lieutenant Harvey cried.

It was his turn now; his side of the ship.

The gunman opposite him nodded, pausing only to lift his sleeve, wiping grimy sweat off his face. They both grabbed at the heavy rope, a quick glance around to check that the rest of the crew were there, then they heaved the 32 together; it crashed up against the gunport, chafing William's hands as the rope suddenly twisted loose.

He leaped out of the way with the rest of the gun crew, the captain pulled the trigger-line, the gun fired – jerked back violently across the deck, only held from rolling across to the larboard side of the ship by its tackles.

William could not hear his own gun's roar above the general tumult. He could only see a few guns to the right, a few to the left through the thick, choking smoke. Yet all the men knew what to do: ramming a sponge down the muzzle of the spent gun, William – as loader – taking a fresh cartridge from the assistant loader, sliding it into the hot barrel, next the shot, then hauling the cannon back to the gunport, then stepping back to avoid the recoil when it fired.

He couldn't see what damage they were inflicting on the enemy ship. Then a loud crunch sounded outside the gunport. A grinding noise, the shuddering deck which almost threw him off his feet, and he knew that the *Victory* had collided with the *Redoutable*.

A midshipman ran up to them, ignoring the blood which streamed down his face. He carried a bucket of water.

"Throw this out after firing your gun!" he bellowed at the gun crew. "Must stop our Frenchie catching fire! It'll set us off!"

So the madness continued. They would fire their gun, throw out water, then fire again.

The man opposite him lifted his arm to wipe his face again, then stumbled forward with a cry. He looked down with horror at his leg, the spreading red patch, the ragged hole made by a deadly splinter. Before William could react, the rest of the crew stepped back from the cannon. William realized the danger, stepped around the carriage and wrenched the man backwards. The cannon roared. It jerked past William and the wounded gunman.

The man nodded his thanks, patted William on the shoulder, then stumbled away towards the hatch leading to below.

William paused, the impact of his act sinking in: mortification at the risk he'd taken; a strange feeling of pride when he recalled the man's grateful face.

He thought of Horatio Nelson, fighting somewhere above decks. It became intolerable to him that his old friend did not realize that he was there with him, the two of them shipmates again after all these years.

William turned towards the powder monkey for another bucket of water and saw a group of men climbing down from the hatch. A billow of smoke passed, and he realized that it was a marine sergeant and two seamen, carrying a fourth man. They paused to let the gun recoil cross their way, then continued downwards to the orlop deck. The hatch sentry stood back; William could see he was shocked by the identity of the injured man.

That pause, a shaking on the ladder from the concussion of the nearby cannon, and the wounded man's face turned towards William. It was Lord Nelson.

William stared through the smoke at the descending figures. He was nudged violently by his fellow, then handed the bucket of water. He threw the water out of the gunport, then put the bucket down.

Running to the hatch, he ignored the dazed sentry, reached down and tapped the marine sergeant's shoulder. The sergeant looked up, anguish on his face.

"You cannot do more for him than fight on!" the sergeant cried out.

William stared in horror as the men gently lowered Nelson downwards.

"Is he taken from us?" William asked.

The sergeant shook his head. "Not yet. Mr Beatty has removed many a cruel musket ball." They disappeared below.

William felt grief, but bitterness too. A rising self-disgust. Seeing Horatio there, the lad still ready to sacrifice himself for England despite his loss of limb and eye, William realized how much he had depended upon his friend's blazing career for his own pride – how much Horatio meant to him.

How much it would mean to lose him.

The sentry recovered his senses and barred William's way downwards.

William glared at the man, but could see there was no way off the deck.

Lieutenant Harvey emerged out of the smoke.

"You! Return to your gun!" he roared.

William spotted the marine sergeant climbing back up through the hatch. He was alone.

"Nelson . . ." William began to say, then stopped when he saw the frown on the man's dirt-streaked face.

The sergeant peered at him through the smoke. Turning to Harvey, he bellowed, "I need this man on the quarterdeck!"

Harvey looked back at the gun crew. They still continued apace, William's place taken by a seaman from the upper deck. Harvey agreed that William could be spared.

William followed the sergeant upwards, his anger now directed at the enemy. They passed others descending the ladders: some seamen down from the rigging to join depleted gun crews; others shiny with blood, moaning, gasping, being escorted down to meet the surgeons' saws.

Up top, the bright daylight dazzled William for a moment. His ears were nearly deafened by the roar of the cannon from the sea battle around the *Victory*; he heard the crack of musket fire which sent splinters pinging off the deck in front of him.

His eyes made no sense of the quarterdeck, a confusion of shattered wood, the remains of the *Victory*'s wheel, ropes, billows of smoke, bodies lying everywhere – some still, some with legs and arms spasming as their lifeblood seeped out on to the dust-covered deck.

The marine captain approached through the choking smoke. "Sergeant Secker!" he cried. "How's the admiral?"

"Lord Nelson's below in the cockpit, sir!" the sergeant said. "I brought this one up, Captain. He saw Nelson. I didn't want the news spread, sir."

The captain nodded. He handed William a musket. "Call up more from below, Secker! We'll board the enemy soon!"

Secker saluted, then returned below.

William peered up through the smoke and saw Frenchmen perched in the *Redoutable*'s rigging 30 feet above him, aiming their weapons down at the *Victory*'s decks. They were the source of the musket fire, the cause of so much carnage around him. William realized why Nelson had fallen so soon in the battle. He blinked back tears. His anger flared into rage.

A marine in front of him dropped forward on to the deck, clutching his side where a deeper crimson splashed out of his red jacket. A second shot pierced his back, then he lay still.

William lifted his musket and aimed upwards, at the *Redoutable*'s mizzen top. Three sharpshooters were perched there, firing down at the quarterdeck and the *Victory*'s poop.

A billow of smoke passed, clearing the view for a moment. William took careful aim, then shot one of the snipers. The man jerked backwards, tumbled off the beam, then plunged through the rigging on to the *Redoutable*'s deck.

His fellow swung his musket around, fired, but missed. A spray of splinters appeared at William's feet. They cut his legs, but he felt nothing.

Now the two remaining sharpshooters were both aiming their shots at the *Victory*'s poop. A seaman had survived the earlier grenades and musketry; he still returned their fire. William saw him shoot the second Frenchman off the beam.

William took ammunition off the dead marine, reloaded, then aimed his musket at the remaining sniper. He squeezed the trigger, but a blow knocked him sideways. His musket skittered across the deck. He stood there for a moment, amazed there was no pain. Then his legs failed him. He hit the deck and lay there, waiting for the sniper to finish him off. Above him, he saw the seaman on the poop shoot the remaining Frenchman off the rigging.

A loud crash roused him from his daze. The *Redoutable*'s mainyard came down. Eager Frenchmen were crowding up to their makeshift bridge to board the *Victory*.

A sharp pain grew in his side. It was enough to keep him awake as he was lifted up, then carried down the hatchway. A nightmare of smoke, shouting, searing pain; he was carried down the ladders to the cockpit.

One deck below the now silent thirty-two's, and the smoke was a little less, but the gloom, the bizarre shadows made by the jerking lanterns, made it seem like a deeper descent into the underworld. Hellfire was still above them, but the cries and groans of the wounded men, brought here to suffer the attentions of the surgeon and his mates, made it seem an even worse place. William's head knocked against a low beam in the confusion, sending him into a bliss of unconsciousness.

The cries of the man lying next to him roused William awake. He lay among the wounded and dying. He could move, if painfully. Someone had bandaged his side.

Gasping, he struggled to his feet. The sound of the battle above had died down; the *Victory*'s cockpit was crowded. William realized that hours could have passed – he could be too late.

There was no way of telling which of the bloody bundles was the vice-admiral. Then he spotted a group of men on the larboard side. They moved away. Lord Nelson lay on a mattress, his back propped against the side of the ship.

William stumbled towards the dying man, his heart thumping. He saw that Nelson's jacket and shirt were removed, replaced by a sheet. Several wounded men lay nearby among dropped cutlasses and broken pikes.

"My lord . . ." he began.

"What news?" Nelson asked, panting out the words between shallow breaths.

William hesitated, then explained: "I've come from the quarterdeck. Shot one of their men off the rigging. Maybe the rogue who shot you!"

Nelson managed a smile. This encouraged William to continue.

"My name is William Berney . . . Bill Berney. We sailed on Hibbert's West Indiaman together."

Nelson stiffened in surprise. "My time is done!" he gasped. "The ghosts of my past greet me now!"

"I'm no ghost!" William exclaimed. "We met earlier. I came over from *Euryalus*."

Nelson's eyes closed. He shifted his head, then stared at William with his good eye.

"I recall," Nelson answered, after a moment. "So, Bill, have I learned those first lessons of seamanship that you taught me?"

William nodded. His eyes were moist.

"Now you fight here, at my side. I am delighted you see this glorious day for England."

William bowed his head. "Yes."

Nelson gazed at his old friend in the gloom. "My back's shot through, Bill!"

William felt a hand on his shoulder. He looked up to see Captain Hardy, crouched over them in the gloom.

Hardy nodded to him, in acknowledgment that he had heard their words together, recognized who William was. "Thank you, Mr Berney," he said.

William withdrew to allow the captain of the *Victory* to confer with his vice-admiral. Another stood behind Hardy, who now came forward into the dim lantern light.

It was Lieutenant Parks, his face streaked with dirt, his eyes wide at the sight of the dying Nelson.

"Captain Blackwood has sent me over with messages for the

vice-admiral," Parks murmured. From the respect in his voice, William knew that he had heard Nelson's words as well.

But it no longer mattered to him. William turned his back on Parks, to pay his last respects to his friend Horatio.

THE KNIGHT ERRANT

Richard Butler

The following story provides some light relief. It is another in the adventures of Lieutenant Trubshaw whom we first met in "The Battle of Elephant Bay" in The Mammoth Book of Men O'War. *Once again it is based on a series of real events which happened soon after William Bligh – he of* Mutiny on the Bounty *fame – became Governor of New South Wales in 1805.*

Richard Butler was born and educated in England and emigrated to Australia in 1963. He spent several years as a teacher until the publication of his fourth novel, The Buffalo Hook *(1974) when he decided to risk not just one risky job, but two, becoming an author and an actor. He has published some twenty books including several historical novels.*

The East Indiaman *City of Lancaster*, ten weeks and four days out of Tilbury, rolled comfortably as she took the slate-grey Pacific swell on her starboard bow with a gentle thump and a spray of white foam. To the west lay the low coastline of the New South Wales colony, as grey and featureless as the ocean under the morning overcast. "Damned dispiriting prospect!" First mate Jethro McGinnis, young and freshfaced, snapped his glass shut. "Why Cook concerned hisself wi' it I can't think. Fit only for mother-naked Hodmedods, I reckon."

"And convicts." Captain Willis, stout and red of nose, cocked an eye at the leech of the mizzen course. Satisfied, he added, "Good place, this, for felons. Gawd knows what Milady'll make of it, and her of royal blood."

"Alice – er, that is to say, her maid, Miss Phillips, told me she thinks it to be like Tahiti. Nice place to join 'er 'usband, she thought." The mate sighed romantically. "A real beauty, Lady Sophia is. I'd say Colonel Bowen's a lucky man."

The captain grunted sceptically. "I'll wager she'll be off back to Lunnon once she sets eyes on Sydney town."

"An' caught a whiff of it." McGinnis chuckled.

"Below there!" A hail from the foremast lookout. "Sail, Cap'n! Two points to larboard!"

"What heading?"

"Easterly. Makin' for us, Cap'n."

"From the settlement, doubtless," Willis said. "The brig *Lady Nelson*, come to escort Lady Sophia into harbour." He cast a critical eye at the deck, holystoned as white as that of a King's ship. "Be prepared for visitors, Mr McGinnis." He opened his telescope and stared at the tiny rectangle, white as the wing of an ivory gull against the grey of the distant land. It vanished as the East Indiaman rolled. Soon it was the fore-topgallant of a brig, heeling to the warm south-westerly. "Aye, *Lady Nelson* it must be. We'll have the courses in, mister."

The hands went up the ratlines, agile as apes. The big merchant vessel rolled a little more as the way came off her. A girl appeared up the aft companionway, clinging to the hand-ropes – a pretty girl in a blue gown, her blonde hair blowing in the wind. The mate's face broke into a foolish grin. He touched his hat. "Good morning to ye, Miss Phillips."

"Good morning, Mr McGinnis. Captain." She gave a little bob. "Lady Sophia sends her compliments and wishes to inform you that the increased motion of the ship has caused her to spill her dish of tea."

"Convey my apologies," Willis said, "and inform her lady-ship that we are shortly to receive a visitor." He turned to point at the brig, which was closing rapidly. "From Port Jackson." He trained his telescope. He could see no flag. But, even as he watched, her gunports opened. He said, "She intends to salute your mistress, it seems. Prepare to dip the flag in reply, mister." At the same time, a jet of smoke puffed from a gun, to be blown away on the wind. The flat bang of the cannon reached them. A fountain of white foam sprang up a cable's length ahead of the *City of Lancaster*.

Willis gaped, thunderstruck. A shot across her bow!

A flag panelled in red, white and blue soared up to the brig's masthead. Willis said, "By God, a Frenchman! But in these waters?"

They heard a hoarse bellow. "Heave to or I'll sink yer!" The accent was American.

"Take in sail." Willis was no fighting captain.

As the hands swung aloft again, the brig launched a boat. It pulled across the sea to the ladder McGinnis had rigged. A moment later, four men appeared on deck.

"Jesus!" McGinnis said. The girl gave a squeak of horror.

For the first man was a creature of nightmare. Of middling stature, he had immensely broad shoulders from which his head, round as a cannonball, grew straight out without a neck. He seemed to have no hair beneath his greasy cap and his face, wrinkled and brown as tree bark, bore no eyebrows or beard. His bloodshot eyes bulged and were set strangely apart like those of a toad on either side of a flattened nose that bore a great black wart on the right side. And from the left sleeve of his jacket protruded brown feathers that ended in a three-pronged claw.

He strode aft, a pistol in his right hand. "Well, well!" He had a nasal Boston accent. "What have we 'ere?"

"Merchantman *City of Lancaster*, bound for Sydney, Mixed cargo. Provisions and clothing for the convicts, mostly. My name's Willis."

"That's just dandy, Willis," said the man with the claw. "And since we're bein' kinda sociable, I'm Cap'n Haggit. Hawkfist Haggit, on account o' this here." He waggled his claw.

"I knew ye were no Frenchman," McGinnis stared at him with contempt.

"Ah, but I am, matey." Haggit's strange frog-like eyes returned his stare. "Leastwise, I fought in Napoleon's navy aboard *Requin* there. Until me an' me shipmates thought we'd go a-privateering instead."

Deserted and murdered their officers after the carnage of Trafalgar, Willis thought, and took to piracy. Found Europe and the West Indies too hot for them, so came to prey on the Spice Islands and New South Wales.

Haggit leered at the girl. "And who might you be, my pretty?"

"I'm Alice Phillips," she said defiantly. "Maid to Lady Bowen, niece of King Frederick William of Prussia and daughter of the Earl of Bray—"

"A king?" Hawkfist showed brown teeth in a grin. "Well, who'd have thought it? We've got ourselves a royal bit o' muslin, by Christ! Where is she?"

"Downstairs," she said. "Dressing and not to be disturbed."

"Ho, is that so?" He spoke in rapid French to the huge black man and two white seamen who stood behind him. They laughed. "Well, we'll see about that when we gets her ashore. Where we'll also have little Alice to amuse us. *Nous nous amuserons bien avec la petite poule, eh, Jacques?*"

The big black nodded, grinning. Hawkfist shuffled over to the cringing girl and ruffled her fair hair with the pistol barrel.

McGinnis stiffened. "Leave her alone, you Yankee scum!" he snarled.

Hawkfist grinned. He stroked the pistol down her neck and jabbed it into her left breast. She whimpered with pain.

With a growl, McGinnis jumped at him, fists raised. He'd hardly moved when there was an explosion, a flash of flame, a jet of smoke. He staggered sideways and fell. Blood stained his breeches and spread on to the deck. The girl screamed and hid her face on the captain's chest. "Self-defence." Hawkfist shoved the weapon into his sash. "Ye all saw him attack me." He gestured to the two seamen. "*Aux poissons, mes amis.*"

The seamen seized McGinnis and threw him overboard in a

splash of bloody foam. A hand was raised. It vanished into the grey, rolling sea.

"My God!" Willis said, his red face mottled white. "He was still alive!"

"Stow it!" Hawkfist raised his claw until its needle tips were inches from Willis's face. "Ye'll think he was the lucky one before we're through with ye. Meanwhile, you'll follow *Requin* into my little hideaway. An' no tricks, *comprenez*?"

Lieutenant Percival Trubshaw had been given the highly responsible post of O/c RGH – Officer Commanding Refurbishment of Government House – in preparation for Lady Sophia Bowen's arrival. One of his duties was to superintend the wallpapering of the dining room with a flock paper patterned in a rather horrible purple floral motif. The work was being done by the elderly Able Seaman Nathaniel Scoggin who, fortunately for the project, took absolutely no notice of the orders the lieutenant gave him.

"Do not be wasteful with the paste, Scoggin," Trubshaw said, as the seaman's brush slopped to and fro. "A thin mixture of flour and water will suffice. We want no lumps". His eye fell on a large sack near the door. "What the devil are you doing with all that flour?"

"Wot flour, sir?" Scoggin peered about. "Ah! That flour." Scoggin could hardly explain that he was on a flash lay with the governor's cook and selling the flour to grub shops in the town – a flogging offence, at least. He gave the first answer that came to a mind made Machiavellian by fifty years in the navy. "It's for a steak an' kidney pie, sir."

"What?" Trubshaw's rather protuberant blue eyes protruded a little more. "Pie, did you say, Scoggin?"

"Yes, sir. 'Twas to be a surprise, sir, knowing as how you're partial to steak and kidney pie, sir. It's for your birfday, sir."

"But my birthday's eight months away!"

"Indeed, sir. But you're always a-telling us to be prepared, like, so—"

"And there's at least half a hundredweight here!"

"Better too much than too little, sir, as King Solomon said to 'is wives."

"King Solomon? Went in for wallpapering, did he? I'll be damned!" He paused. "Well, I must say, it's uncommon civil of you, Scoggin. None the less, it *is* government flour, so—"

To Scoggin's relief, the interrogation was cut short by a yell. "Trubshaaah! Report this instant!"

Trubshaw jumped with fright. The Devon accent and quarterdeck bellow of Governor William Bligh were vastly different from the calm voice of Captain Philip Gidley King, the previous governor. "Bounty" Bligh, outstanding navigator, first-rate seaman and faithful husband though he undoubtedly was, had a vile temper and did not suffer fools gladly. He had assigned Trubshaw to the fools category on sight and in consequence had frequently figured as the principal character in the lieutenant's nightmares, often swinging a hangman's noose in one hand and a cat o'nine tails in the other.

He sat behind his desk, portly and pale, his thinning black hair brushed flat, his aide, Lieutenant Philip Montague Codlington, at his side. Suave, elegant, good-looking, Codlington was also brainy, well connected and well organized – all the things Trubshaw was not.

"Trubshaw!" Bligh snarled. His bloodshot eyes put the lieutenant in mind of a mad bull. "What the devil are you about?"

"Me, sir?" Trubshaw, bent double in the act of bowing, peered sideways.

"Yes, you, sir, damn and blast you! How dare you present yourself in that condition! The mess on your coat, sir! Looks like vomit. And why are you crouching like a Bombay bumboatman with piles?"

His mind a-whirl, Trubshaw stood erect. He looked down at the spatters that Scoggin had sprayed as he worked. "Ah! it's paste, sir. My apologies, sir."

"Paste? Paste? Been eating the stuff, I suppose. Well, never mind the blasted paste, Trubshaw, it concerns Lady Sophia."

"The paste concerns her, sir?" Fright had caused Trubshaw's wits to addle even more than usual. "Well, she may rest assured there'll be no lumps—"

"What?" the governor shouted. "Lumps?" Codlington sniggered.

"None whatsoever, sir. The seaman mixing it seems to know all about the methods of King Solomon, an expert at wall-papering—"

"King Solomon? Are you insane?" The governor's face had turned a colour that matched Trubshaw's nasty wallpaper. He breathed heavily for a moment. "Now, attend, both of you. *City of York*, sister ship to that in which Lady Sophia is sailing, left Cape Town before *City of Lancaster* and arrived today. What does that signify, eh?"

Anxious to impress, Trubshaw said smartly, "Why, sir, that the taverns and bordellos will be kept uncommon busy to-night."

Codlington smiled a superior smile. "I think His Excellency intends us to apprehend that the arrival of *City of Lancaster* must be imminent."

"Precisely!" Bligh gave his aide a nod. "Therefore, as a courtesy to our ally, King Frederick William III of Prussia, I have resolved to send the government brig *Lady Nelson* to escort her in with an appropriate salute. How many guns for a King's niece, would you say, Trubshaw?"

"Two, sir?" Trubshaw said. When Bligh winced: "Fifty?"

Codlington rolled his eyes heavenward. In the navy, even-numbered salutes did not exist, even numbers being considered unlucky. He said, "For royalty, the customary twenty-one, sir?"

"Correct, Codlington, *Lady Nelson* will, of course, be under your command."

Was it Trubshaw's imagination or did a shadow of unease cross Codlington's classically handsome features?

"And you, Trubshaw," Bligh said, "will act as my aide during his absence."

"Aye, aye, sir." Trubshaw groaned inwardly. Not only would he have given his all for a cruise down the coast but to be closeted with the irascible Bligh every day . . . ! He could imagine no worse fate.

Codlington coughed. "Sir, while I am sensible of the honour you do me, perhaps I might remind Your Excellency that Trubshaw has more seagoing experience than—"

"No need for false modesty, Codlington! I need somebody who can manage a situation that requires a sense of style, courtesy and intelligence. You'll do very well, I know. Go and prepare. You leave in an hour."

In his quarters, Trubshaw tried to improve the appearance of his coat by rubbing it with a wet rag. That merely worked the paste into the cloth, stiffening it like board. The dreaded trumpet blare came again. "Trubshaah! Report instantly!"

He ran. "Poor Codlington has twisted his ankle badly," growled the governor. "So you'll take command of *Lady Nelson* with Scoggin as your cox'n. Someone else can do the refurbishing."

"Aye aye, sir," Trubshaw said delightedly. *Ha! Ha! Codlington is a landlubber who fears the sea!* "And thank you, sir. Rest assured that I will—"

"Be silent! Is that your best coat?"

Trubshaw stared at him dumbly.

"I asked you a question, sir!" Bligh beat the table in a rage. "Answer, you insolent wretch!"

Trubshaw spoke with his teeth together, sounding like an incompetent ventriloquist. "You commanded me to be silent, sir. It is in fact my only coat."

"You can't greet Lady Sophia looking like that. Borrow Codlington's best."

"Aye aye, sir!" He rushed to the dining room, collected Scoggin and was aboard *Lady Nelson* in half an hour in a coat that, although reaching down to his ankles, was almost new. "Cast off for'ard!" he shrieked happily. Even though her twelve guns were loaded only with powder, a 60-ton, Deptford-built brig was a distinct leg-up from the 29-ton schooner that had been his last (and only) command. "Cast off aft! Make sail, Mr Scoggin!"

"Who?" Scoggin looked around.

"Make sail, you confounded numskull!"

"Ah! Aye aye, sir!" That was the form of address Scoggin was used to. "Hands to braces!"

A 10-knot nor'-westerly took *Lady Nelson* on a broad reach down the vast harbour, through the Heads and into the blue Pacific. The mastheads swung against a cornflower sky studded with puffball clouds as she turned south in warm sunlight with the breeze on her starboard quarter, making a steady eight knots. Trubshaw stood in the shifting shadows cast by the sails, watching the coast trundle past and thinking that heaven could offer no greater happiness than this. And to top it all, he'd escaped the horror of being the governor's aide!

It was shortly after eight bells that the lookout bawled. "Deck, there! Column o' smoke! Point to starboard!"

"Blackfellers!" Scoggin grunted.

"Their village, think you?"

"Nah! They don't have no proper villages, sir. They moves about a lot."

"Natives that move about are called no muds," Trubshaw said.

"No muds, sir?"

Trubshaw said patiently, "They're called no muds because they have no mud huts, d'ye see? What's over there?"

Scoggin could neither read nor write but he could manage a chart. He struck a dirty finger on a large inlet. "That there's Tom Thumb's Lagoon. Discovered in '96 by Bass and Flinders an' named after their little boat."

"The smoke's a few miles south of it. We'll close the shore and take a look."

Oh, Christ! Scoggin thought. Here we go again! It wasn't the first time he'd tried to prevent Trubshaw from killing them both. "Sir, them blackfellers can turn proper nasty. They got spears an' little throwing clubs what go round in circles—"

"Be silent, Scoggin! It's possible that *City of Lancaster* might have come to harm and run ashore. Change course and take her in."

They crept in under jibs and fore staysail. Through his glass, Trubshaw could see sandhills. And, on the beach—"

A cackle of laughter from the lookout. "Deck, there! There's a cove on shore a-dancin' about wiv no togs on!"

A white cove, Trubshaw observed, waving frantically. "We'll anchor, Scoggin. I'll take a boat ashore."

"Sir, maybe it's a trap."

"Nonsense, Scoggin. Do as you're bid."

The sniggering sailors pulled for the beach. Scoggin, a pistol in his belt, said, "He'll be a Wild White Man, sir."

"What d'ye mean?"

"Convict what's absconded, sir, an' joined a tribe o' black-fellers. Wild White Men, they calls 'em. Sometimes the natives think they're dead chiefs what's come back to life. Easy time, they has. Free grub. Women. No work."

"Better life nor ourn, then," stroke oar muttered. "Wouldn't mind—"

"Be quiet!" The boat grounded. Trubshaw put a hand on the gunwale and vaulted gracefully into the shallows. "Damnation!" He sank up to the ankles into glutinous mud and lost both shoes. He bent down and groped. "Aagh!" He received a mouthful of the Pacific Ocean as a wave rolled in, soaking him completely. Shoes in hand, he struggled ashore.

The wild man was undersized and bandy-legged, his body, arms and legs covered in grey-white hair. A shaggy beard came down to his chest and his hair hung down to his shoulders. Being stark naked in front of the grinning sailors didn't seem to embarrass him in the least. "Never thought I'd . . . be glad to . . . see a King's ship." His voice sounded like a creaking door. The words came in bursts as he arranged his thoughts. "We needs 'elp."

"Explain yourself." Trubshaw tried to squeeze water out of Codlington's best coat. "Why are you improperly attired?"

"Not improper as far . . . as me tribe's concerned. Name's . . . Joshua Diggins, sir. Forgive me . . . manner o' speech. Ain't spoke King's English . . . in a while. Not since . . . Guv'nor Philip's time. Year . . . war began."

Fourteen years! Trubshaw marvelled. Fourteen years with savages! "Where do you live?"

He waved a hand. "Round 'ere. Wiv me . . . tribe. But those bastards . . . have snaffled our land . . . our sacred ground."

"What bastards?"

"Frogs."

"What! Here?" Trubshaw reacted pretty much as if he'd been told the plague had struck. "Where are the impudent Crappos?"

He pointed north. "Big inlet . . . league or so. They got a camp there. Frog brig. This morning they captured . . . ship wiv three masts—"

"My God! *City of Lancaster!*" He turned to Scoggin. "We'll have to go in and rescue Lady Sophia!"

"Yis! Yis! And 'elp us . . . get our land back!"

"Small difficulty there," Scoggin said. "We ain't got no ball for the guns."

"No matter!" Trubshaw said. "We'll try a dodge, like those Greek coves with their wooden horse."

"'Orse?" Scoggin was totally confused. "What 'orse?"

"Never mind. We'll go in firing, then let ourselves be captured."

"What?"

"Once we're in their camp, we turn on 'em, tie 'em up and sail off taking their ship with us!"

"No, sir!" It was precisely the kind of hare-brained scheme that Scoggin dreaded. "It's madness!"

"Nay, nay! Clever, that is, sir," Diggins said. His English was improving rapidly. "A prime fakement, that!" He turned and gave a call like a bird.

"Why, thankee, Diggins, – Oh Lord!" Above the line of sandhills appeared a line of black men, wearing nothing but paint and carrying spears and clubs. One strode forward, eyeing Trubshaw in a way he didn't care for at all.

Diggins rattled away in a language that sounded like dogs fighting. To Trubshaw: "This here's our chief. I said you're his friend wot's come in peace."

"I have indeed!" Trubshaw said. He bowed. "How d'ye do, my dear fellow? Capital weather for the time of year, wouldn't you say?"

Diggins spoke to the chief at length, then turned to Trubshaw. "Right, sir, 'ere's the lay. You goes in like wot you said. Gets took—"

"Not bleedin' likely!" Scoggin said.

"Be silent! Go on!"

"Tribe waits till nightfall, then attacks. You gets free—"

"How?" Scoggin demanded. "Tell me that, you bare-arsed baboon!"

Diggins whistled. A moment later an immensely fat woman, wearing only an apron and a broad grin, waddled over the crest of the sandhills. "This here's Mrs Diggins," Diggins said. "Real downy, she is, wiv herbs and such. Got a cure for anythin'." He spoke to her. She gave him a handful of dry leaves from a bag at her waist. "This 'ere's for when yer can't sleep. Crumble it to powder, sprinkle a bit in yer grub or drink and off yer go. Bagful o' this in the Frogs' dinner and they'll go out like bleedin' lights. Then you legs it while we croaks the Frogs."

"Capital!" Trubshaw said. "Do you wish to return to Sydney with us?"

He looked sly. "I'm an absconded felon, sir. They'd put me back in the road gangs. Besides, I got Mrs Diggins an' the little uns. Nah, I'll stay."

"We'll get under way, then." Trubshaw smirked at the chief. He smirked back and spoke to Diggins.

"Chief wants to exchange gifts." Diggins winked. "Got 'is eye on your coat, 'e 'as, sir."

"Why, to be sure." Cheerfully, Trubshaw handed over Codlington's soggy coat. The chief, still smirking, pulled something out of a bag hung round his neck and put it in Trubshaw's hand. It wriggled. He nearly dropped it.

It was a very large, very fat insect larva. He said to Diggins, "What the devil do I do with this?"

"Eat it."

"What? This grub?"

"To be sure. Great honour if the chief gives yer vittles."

"But . . . it's alive!"

"Well, o' course it's alive! 'E ain't a-going to give yer no nasty old dead grub, is he?" As Trubshaw hesitated: "Sir, 'tis a deadly insult if ye refuse."

"Just make believe it's a bit o' cold, fatty pork, sir," Scoggin said. "Different kind o' grub!" He chuckled at his ready wit.

Trubshaw looked at the writhing larva, then at the chief's needle-pointed spear. He shut his eyes. He put it into his mouth. Then swallowed very quickly before he could throw up.

The sky had clouded over, threatening rain, when they reached the entrance to Tom Thumb's Lagoon. As they went in they could see a brig at anchor, the French tricolor flapping languidly. An East Indiaman was between the brig and the shore, where boats were drawn up. Some crude wooden huts had been built on the strip of beach between the sea and the dense scrub. Men pointed, yelled and ran about when they saw *Lady Nelson*. Aboard the brig, two men – the anchor watch, presumably – gaped, then jumped over the side, clearly expecting the brig to be the target.

Trubshaw thought longingly of what he could do if only his guns were loaded with ball. But, since they weren't going to hit anything, they might as well fire off everything at once. "Open fire!" His stomach felt queasy. And no wonder, he thought.

Firing blanks made more noise and smoke than firing ball. As the twelve cannon went off the detonation was deafening. The shore vanished as the ship was shrouded in smoke that cleared slowly in the light wind. Coughing, Trubshaw saw the activity ashore stop, the French clearly baffled by the lack of damage.

Then, after some shouting, a boat full of men put out. "Here they come to cut our froats," Scoggin said gloomily.

"No resistance!" Trubshaw cried. "We're to be captured, not killed, remember."

The men in the boat were armed with pistols, cutlasses and

knives. "I 'opes as 'ow they knows that," Scoggin said. "Jesus, just look at their capting!"

Trubshaw stared with horror at the squat, hideous creature with the toad's face and the steel claw. Hawkfist shouted, "Strike, or I'll rip yer livers out!"

Without being told, Scoggin ran to haul down the ensign as the pirates scrambled aboard. "Well, thankee for the salute." Hawkfist grinned. "You goddam lime-juicers forgot yer ammunition, did yer?" To *Lady Nelson*'s crew: "Yer officers are to be hanged with any man who refuses to join me."

"We only got one officer. Him!" Scoggin pointed at Trubshaw. "And he's a bloody slave-driver! We all hates 'im! I'll join yer an' gladly. Name's Scoggin, ship's cook."

"You wretch, Scoggin!" Trubshaw said, playing his part. "You're a damned traitor! As for you, *mongsewer—*"

"Aw, stow it! Get in the boat!" Hawkfist snarled.

As had been previously arranged, *Lady Nelson*'s entire crew went over to the enemy. "A sorry lot," Willis said in the hut where he and his crew were confined with Trubshaw. "Only four of my men deserted. The rest of us are to die tonight at the feast they're going to have off my stores. Unless your black-fellows' potion works."

Lady Sophia, the captain had said, had locked herself in her cabin on the ship with her maid and, armed with a pair of pistols, had offered to shoot any who tried to enter. "So far nobody's been game," he'd said. "But when they've got some grog inside 'em . . ."

The light was going fast. Fires had been lit and, through a crack in the timber, Trubshaw could see a cauldron steaming over one of them. Scoggin was stirring it busily. Birds called in the bush as the sun set, painting the western sky a vivid orange and red. In groups, the pirates sat on the beach, passing bottles around. "*Dépêche-toi!*" Hawkfist yelled. "Hurry with the stew! I'm hungry!"

"Aye aye, sir!" Scoggin gave it another stir. "Ready now!"

Hawkfist went up with his dish. The others queued behind

him. Soon they were all sitting on the sand, eating, drinking and laughing. Trubshaw began chewing his fingernails. Would it work?

No! Hawkfist went back for another plateful, steady as a rock. When he'd eaten it, he emptied his bottle. Then, to Trubshaw's horror, he stood up and walked towards the prisoners' hut. "So much for your fancy scheme!" Willis said bitterly. "Bloody navy!"

Hawkfist fumbled with a key and undid the padlock, his men crowding behind him, grinning. "Now we're gonna have some sport." He cackled. "We're givin' ye a fair chance to escape." He drew his pistol. "Come out here, Willis. Get to the trees before I count ten an' you're safe. Give yer my word." His men roared with laughter. Stout, middle-aged Willis had no chance at all. "Go! One, two, three, four."

Desperately, Willis tried to run through the soft, clinging sand. When he'd floundered 10 yards Hawkfist raised his pistol. "Eight, nine, ten!" he said thickly. "Too bad, Willis." He fired. And missed. "What the hell!" He went down on his knees. Then slowly he toppled on to his face. One of the men behind him said, "*Merde!*" as his knees gave way. Then another. One tried to draw a knife, cursed and collapsed.

Trubshaw looked at the bodies spread around on the sand. He said to Willis, "You'd better go aboard before they wake up." The captain and his men hurried to the boats drawn up on the shore.

One of the bodies climbed to its feet. "Wouldn't have minded some of that there stew. Me belly thinks me froat's been cut."

"Never mind your blasted belly, Scoggin! You're commanding the crew that will take the Frog brig into Port Jackson! We'll be rich men on the prize-money!"

He saw Scoggin and his delighted band board the *Requin*. From the darkened shore came shrieks and howls as Diggins's tribe set about the pirates. What they were doing to them Trubshaw neither knew nor cared. He was rowed to the *City of Lancaster*'s ladder where Captain Willis received him. "My apologies, Lieutenant," he said, "for my slighting reference to the Royal Navy."

"I pray you not to speak of it, Captain. Where is Lady Sophia?"

"In her stateroom. Refuses to budge. I'll direct you."

He took Trubshaw below and pointed to a door. Then, to Trubshaw's surprise, he leaped up the companionway. Trubshaw tapped. Instantly, there was a loud bang, a shower of splinters and a large hole appeared in the woodwork to the right of his waist. He sprang back with a shriek. A calm, clear voice from within said, "I did warn you, you French monsters."

"If you please, ma'am," Trubshaw cried, "the Frogs are defeated. I am Lieutenant Percival Trubshaw, of His Majesty's Navy."

Silence. The door opened a crack and lamplight flooded out. The delicately worked barrel of a small pistol appeared, aimed at Trubshaw's head. Then an emerald-green eye. "If this is a trick—!"

"Nay, ma'am – your Majesty – that is to say, Your Royal Highness. We have retaken the ship. You are free once more."

The door opened further. In the golden light he could see that her jet-black hair was in disarray, her creamy complexion was flushed and her perfectly shaped mouth was set in grim determination but she was still one of the most beautiful women he had ever seen. He made his best leg. "Your servant, Your Royal Highness! I beg you will forgive my lack of a coat, Your Royal Highness!"

She smiled and he was totally enslaved. "I am Lady Sophia Bowen, so 'My Lady' will suffice, I think. You have truly defeated those barbarous wretches?"

"Indeed, Milady. With the aid of the blackfellows."

"I don't doubt that most of it was your doing, Lieutenant. I am in your debt."

He was sorely tempted to return to Port Jackson aboard the *City of Lancaster* but he had *Lady Nelson* to take home. The three vessels sailed up the harbour next morning.

He was halfway through Codlington's whining about the loss of his coat when the familiar summons reached him – but strangely muted! He saw why when he found Lady Sophia, her husband and Captain Willis with the governor. A beaming governor! One whose smile faded only slightly when he saw Trubshaw's paste-stiffened coat! Trubshaw could scarce believe it until he remembered that Bligh would receive a substantial share of the prize-money. "You've done well, Lieutenant," Bligh said. "I must say I misjudged you formerly but now Captain Willis has told me how you saved his life and that of his crew and rescued Lady Bowen and Miss Phillips from the vile French pirates."

"My knight errant!" Lady Sophia smiled deliciously at him. He all but swooned.

"I merely did my duty, sir."

"England expects no less, as my Lord Nelson said." Bligh nodded. "Well done, Lieutenant. That will be all."

Trubshaw bowed. Lady Sophia said, "One moment, Your Excellency! Surely Lieutenant Trubshaw deserves rather more than that? Surely, for such gallant service, a promotion would be fitting?"

Bligh smiled patronizingly. "Alas, my lady, the navy is not in the habit of handing out promotion for every trivial act that—"

"Your Excellency!" A hard note came into Lady Sophia's voice. "I must say, I find it surprising that you consider my release from danger to be a trivial act!" Clearly, she was not accustomed to being crossed, and by a mere governor at that.

"Ah!" Bligh's smile vanished. "That was not my meaning, my lady. But, you see, such a decision does not rest with me. No, I should have to refer it to my lords of the Admiralty—"

"Just as, if my recommendation is rejected, I should have to refer the matter to my uncle, King Frederick William III! He will, I know, consider that his family has been slighted by you and inform the Prime Minister of his—"

"Nay, nay, my lady!" Bligh had broken out in a light sweat. "I am sure we can avoid any misunderstanding of that nature. In the circumstances their lordships will undoubtedly endorse the promotion of Lieutenant Trubshaw to the rank of—" He spoke as if choking. "The rank of lieutenant commander."

"Sir!" He bowed low. "I am most truly grateful."

Lady Sophia smiled at him again. "Furthermore, I am sure that my uncle will wish to invest you with the Golden Eagle of Prussia in appreciation of your gallantry."

"My lady! I am deeply honoured." He bowed again. Promotion, a decoration and prize-money! His cup was filled to overflowing.

"And that's not all," Bligh said. "I have yet another reward for you. *City of Lancaster* has brought orders for Lieutenant Codlington to return to England forthwith. So I am appointing you as my permanent aide. What do you think of that, eh?"

"O my God!"

"What!"

"Merely an expression of my appreciation to the Almighty, sir," said Lieutenant Commander Trubshaw gloomily.

THE REVENGE OF THE GUNNER'S DAUGHTER

Peter Tremayne

This story takes place at the siege of Cophenhagen in September 1807. Copenhagen was bombarded for four days even though, at that time, Britain and Denmark were not at war! The attack was to get the Danish regent to surrender his fleet so that it was not taken by the French. Peter Tremayne uses this as the background for an intriguing murder mystery.

Peter Tremayne is the alias used by Celtic scholar Peter Berresford Ellis (b. 1943) for his mystery and weird fiction. The author of over sixty books, Tremayne is currently best known for his series of historical mystery novels featuring Sister Fidelma which began with Absolution by Murder *(1994). Tremayne counts among his ancestors Captain Rory Ellis, an Irish privateer regarded by the English as a pirate, who harried ships along the Irish coast in the first quarter of the seventeenth century.*

The last French shot had fallen a full quarter-mile aft of the *Deerhound* as she slipped into the sheltering fog which was rolling down through the Oresund from the Kattegat and across the Kjoge Bight, south of Copenhagen. That had been twenty minutes ago and since then there had followed an uneasy quiet, free of the noise of battle; the sea's quiet of creaking wooden spars, the fretful snap of canvas and the whispering waves against the sides of the twenty-two gun sloop as she became immersed in the thick white mist which now concealed her from her vengeful pursuer.

Captain Richard Roscarrock, captain of His Majesty's sloop *Deerhound* stood, head to one side, in a listening attitude on the quarterdeck, hands clasped tightly behind him, lips compressed. Finally he raised his head, his shoulders seemed to relax.

"Hands to shorten sail, Mr Hart." He turned to the midshipman next to him, a lad scarcely out of his teenage. "Quietly does it," he snapped hastily as the youngster raised his hand to his mouth to shout the order. "Quietly all! We don't want Johnny Frenchman to hear us. We'll take in the tops'ls and mains'l. Pass the word! And have the hands take a care for the damage on the mainmast; the maintop gallant mast seems to be badly splintered. And, for heaven's sake, get a couple of hands to secure the mainstay; it'll cause damage if it swings loose for much longer."

Midshipman Hart brought his hand to his forehead so that his original motion ended in a cursory salute. He went forward to gather the hands.

Gervaise, the first lieutenant, moved closer to his captain. His voice was quiet.

"I don't think the Frenchman has followed us, sir," he observed. "He's probably beating back into the Baltic now that he has discovered we are in these waters."

Roscarrock agreed mentally but gave a non-committal grunt by way of response. He had been long enough in command to realize that it was not politic to discuss his thoughts with his juniors.

Unstead, the second officer, joined them.

"Did you see the cut of her, sir? I'll bet ten guineas on that being the *Épervier* of Rambert's squadron."

"Will we try to rejoin Admiral Gambier, sir?" pressed Gervaise.

Roscarrock sniffed to indicate his irritation.

"In good time, Mr Gervaise. And I am well aware of what ship it was, Mr Unstead. We'll haul to and will use the cover of this fog to assess our situation. The French gunners were good and we have sustained some damage. Look at our mainmast."

The sloop had encountered the French seventy-four-gun man-o'-war by accident, sailing around the headland of Stevns Klint, and running abruptly under her guns before Roscarrock could wear the ship, turning the helm to windward. The Frenchman had opened fire almost immediately on the smaller vessel. The French guns had inflicted a lot of damage on the English sloop before her swifter sailing ability, good seamanship and the descending fog across the bight had allowed a means of escape.

Roscarrock knew that he must have sustained several casualties. He could see for himself that the maintopgallant mast had been splintered, the rigging and spars still hanging dangerously. The last shots the French had fired had been high and chain shot which had ripped into the rigging. Captain Roscarrock also knew there had been at least one, probably two shots landed on the gun deck. However, his first concern was whether the *Deerhound* had been holed below the waterline and his second concern was whether the damage to his masts was irreparable and would prevent him returning quickly to the main British fleet of Sir James Gambier to warn him of the presence of the French.

Lieutenant Gervaise had already read his mind and passed word for the master's mate, bosun, purser, cooper, chief gunnery officer and doctor: all the heads of the various departments that ran a ship-of-war.

The group of men came after in ones and twos and gathered before the captain on the quarterdeck. They were tired but wore that look of relief at finding themselves still alive. Faces were blackened by powder burns, clothes were torn and stained with blood.

"Has the word been passed for the gunnery officer?" Captain Roscarrock asked, looking round and not seeing the third lieutenant who fulfilled this role.

An elderly sailor, with petty officer insignia, touched his forehead briefly.

"Beg pardon, sir. Gunnery officer's dead. I'll make his report."

The first lieutenant blinked a moment. The second officer, Unstead, whistled tactlessly. Roscarrock broke in harshly as if he had not noticed their reactions.

"And where's the bosun?"

"Dead, sir," replied the master's mate dryly.

"Then his mate should be here."

"Dead as well, sir. I'll attend to the report," the man replied.

"Very well. Damage?"

"No shots below the waterline. Maintopgallant mast splintered and upper rigging tangled and dangerous. There is no way we can replace topmast shrouds nor the futtock shrouds. She should be able to take the mains'l and we can run without tops'ls though it will slow us down."

"What about the mizzentop mast?"

"We were lucky there. A chain shot went through the sheet but it can be patched. That was the shot that impacted against the mainmast."

Roscarrock nodded swiftly.

"Do your best. We'll attempt to rejoin the fleet as soon as this fog bank clears. Then we'll effect proper repairs. If our main fleet have already captured Copenhagen, we should have no problem." Roscarrock turned back to a grizzled petty officer. "What's the situation with the guns?"

The elderly man raised a finger to his forelock.

"Four guns and their crews out of action, Cap'n. Three guns totally destroyed."

Not as bad as Roscarrock expected; still eighteen guns remaining in action.

"Purser? What's our status?"

"Most of the stores are safe, sir. Only two water casks were smashed by shot but we can replace them. The biggest loss is one of the rum casks."

"The men will have to lose their rum ration until we can replenish the cask. Cooper, how about replacing the water casks?"

"I'll have new casks made by tomorrow if we have easy sailing."

Roscarrock was coming to the report that he disliked most of all.

"Mr Smithers, what's the total casualties?"

The sloop was lucky in that it carried a surgeon. Sloops of His Britannic Majesty's navy did not usually have the luxury of carrying a surgeon and had to rely on the cook-cum-barber to double in that capacity.

"Thirteen dead, twenty-four wounded, five seriously," intoned the florid-faced surgeon with an enthusiasm that seemed to indicate he relished his work.

Roscarrock's mouth thinned. "How seriously injured?"

"Three will be dead before nightfall, sir."

Roscarrock's jaw tightened for a moment. Then he asked, "What ranks among the dead?"

"Two midshipmen and . . . and Lieutenant Jardine; four petty officers, and the rest" – the surgeon shrugged – "the rest were other ranks. Of the wounded, all are seamen, sir."

Roscarrock glanced quickly at the surgeon. "Jardine was killed, you say?"

It was the petty officer gunner who answered.

"Beg pardon, sir. Lieutenant Jardine was on the gun deck, laying the guns, when he—"

Roscarrock interrupted with a frown. Lieutenant Jardine was the chief gunnery officer. There was no need for an explanation as to where his station had been during the action.

"We'll get the details later. And the midshipmen who were killed?"

"Little Jack Kenny and Tom Merritt," the surgeon replied.

"Very well," Roscarrock said after a moment's silence. "Very well, I want this ship cleared and ready for action again within the hour."

There was a chorus of "aye aye's" and the petty officers dispersed to their jobs. The surgeon went with them to take charge of the wounded.

Lieutenant Gervaise was shaking his head. "Jardine, eh?

There'll be a lot of ladies at Chatham who will shed a tear, no doubt." He did not sound grief-stricken.

Lieutenant Unstead was positively smug. "And there'll be a lot of husbands who will sleep more comfortably at night," he added sarcastically.

Jardine had been third officer on the sloop. He had been a youthful, handsome and vain man with a reputation for the ladies, especially for other men's wives. Roscarrock did not rebuke Unstead because he was aware that, before they had left the port of Chatham, Unstead had actually challenged Jardine to a duel: something to do with his wife Phoebe. The duel had been prevented by the Provost Marshal on shore and both officers were severely reprimanded.

Roscarrock did not bother to comment. He knew that most of the officers and men would not be sorry to hear of Jardine's sudden demise. His handsome looks disguised a cruel temperament. He had been too fond of inflicting discipline with a rope's end. Roscarrock had tried to keep Jardine in check but the man was possessed of a brutal nature which enjoyed imposing pain on those who could not retaliate. It was not good for discipline for a ship's company to see their officers in conflict and so Roscarrock was unable to show his disapproval of Jardine before the men. He had to support the punishments that his junior gave out and reprimand him only in private. No; there would be no false grieving in the *Deerhound* over Jardine.

"Mr Hart!"

The young midshipman came running forward, touching his hat to his captain.

"Lieutenant Jardine is dead. As senior midshipman, you are now acting third lieutenant. I want you to go round and make a list of all casualties. The surgeon will have his hands full tending the wounded."

"Aye aye, sir."

"Report back to me within the hour."

Roscarrock swung round, dismissing the youthful officer with a curt salute, and turned to his first officer.

"Make sure that the men know the urgency of our situation, Mr Gervaise. I shall be below in my cabin for a while."

In a sloop, a captain's quarters were small, dark and stuffy. A small curtain separated his sleeping quarters, a single bunk, a cupboard and space for a chest, from his day cabin in which there was space for a desk and a couple of chairs. Roscarrock went to the desk and pulled out a half-filled bottle of brandy. He uncorked it and poured out a glass. For a moment he held it up to the light that permeated through the cabin, seeing the amber liquid reflecting in the dull grey light. Then his features broke into a smile and he raised the glass, as if in silent toast, before swallowing in one mouthful.

He replaced the bottle, sat down and drew out the ship's log. Then he took out pen and ink.

"Kjoge Bight, 2 September 1807," he wrote at the top of his entry, and then sat back to consider how, in brief form, he should address the events of the brief but fierce engagement.

He had just finished the details and realized that Midshipman Hart had not returned with the list of names to enter in the log. But at that moment there was an urgent tap on the door.

Frowning, he uttered the word: "Come!"

Midshipman Hart stood flushed faced in the doorway. He seemed in a state of great excitement.

Roscarrock frowned irritably. "You're late! Do you have the casualty list?"

Midshipman Hart placed a piece of paper on the captain's desk but continued to stand in a state of some agitation. Roscarrock suppressed a sigh.

"What is it?"

"Beg to report, sir," he began, "concerning the death of Lieutenant Jardine . . ."

"What about the death of Jardine?" Roscarrock demanded sharply, causing the young man to pause awkwardly again as if trying to find the right phrases.

"There are some . . . some curiosities about the manner of his death, sir. I, I don't know quite how to put it."

Roscarrock sat back with a frown, placing his hands before him, fingertips together.

"Curiosities?" He savoured the word softly. "Perhaps you would explain what you mean by that word?"

"It would be better if you would come to the gun deck, sir. Begging your pardon, it would be easier to show you rather than to tell you."

The young man was clearly embarrassed. He added quickly, "I've asked the surgeon to join us there."

Roscarrock sat quietly for a moment or two. Then, with a sigh, he reached for his hat and stood up.

"This is highly unusual, Mr Hart, but I will come as you seem to set such store by my attendance."

"Thank you, sir, thank you." Midshipman Hart seemed greatly relieved.

As Roscarrock followed the young man up on to the deck and allowed him to lead the way towards the gun deck, his expression was bleak.

"I cannot see what is curious about a death in battle that needs a captain in attendance when a report is made of the fact, Mr Hart. I presume you have a good reason for dragging me to look at a corpse?"

Midshipman Hart jerked his head nervously. "I think you will understand when I show you, sir."

They descended on to the gun deck. The *Deerhound* mounted eleven cannon on either side. The first thing that struck one in that confined space, which had a clearing of only five feet between decks so that often the men crouched to perform their fighting duties, was the stench. The acrid gunpowder and smoke predominated but it mingled with the smell of burnt wood, recent fires that had been doused where French shot had ignited combustible materials. There, too, was that odour of charred flesh, that undescribable nauseous combination of the reek of the wounded and the stench of urine.

Captain Roscarrock drew out a square of lavender-soaked linen, which he always carried, and held it to his nose, glancing around him distastefully.

The deck was a shambles where the French shot had hit. Wood was splintered. Ropes and tackle lay in chaotic profusion. There was blood everywhere and canvas covered several bodies which had not yet been cleared away.

Roscarrock saw, at once, that the French shot had blown away part of the first four gunports on the starboard side, which had been the side of the ship he had presented to the enemy in his attempt to turn. Three guns were mangled heaps of metal almost unrecognizable. A fourth, as the gunner had reported, was damaged but not so badly as the first three.

Yet it was not to that scene of chaos that the young midshipman led him but to a gun that was listed in the gunnery chart as number six portside, the central gun position of the eleven gunport broadside. There was no damage here but an isolated body was lying just behind the gun, which was being lashed into its position by two sailors.

The florid-faced surgeon, Smithers, was standing by the body, over which a canvas tarpaulin had been placed.

Midshipman Hart came to a halt by it and turned to his captain. "Lieutenant Jardine, sir," he said, pointing almost dramatically at the body.

Roscarrock's eyes narrowed. "I think I presumed as much," he said without humour. "Now, Mr Hart, what exactly demands my presence here?"

Hart strained forward like an eager dog trying to please its owner.

"Well, sir, this position here, behind number six gun, was where the gunnery lieutenant was positioned to direct our broadsides."

Roscarrock tried not to sound irritated. "I am aware, Mr Hart, of the battle stations of my officers," he replied.

The boy actually winced and Roscarrock felt almost sorry for his sharpness. However, a ship-of-war in His Majesty's navy was not the place to deal in polite manners.

"Get on with it, Mr Hart."

Midshipman Hart swallowed nervously. "Well, sir, Lieutenant Jardine was not killed by French shot nor collateral damage from its fall."

The midshipman turned to the doctor. He was smiling as if amused by something.

"Lieutenant Jardine sustained his fatal injuries having been struck by that gun when in recoil." He indicated the cannon being lashed back to its bulkhead moorings.

Roscarrock stared at him for a moment.

"I see," he said slowly. "Are you telling me that when number six gun was fired, it recoiled into Jardine and killed him? That Jardine was standing too near the gun when it was fired?"

Smithers actually chuckled. "Precisely so, Captain. Precisely so."

Roscarrock knew there was no love lost between the surgeon and the late third lieutenant. He decided to ignore the man's humour.

"If he was so close behind the gun when it recoiled, then it would seem that this was an accident but that the fault lay with him. We will give his family the benefit of hearing he died in action and not by an accident that could have been avoided."

Midshipman Hart cleared his throat. "It was not exactly an accident, sir," he ventured.

Roscarrock turned quickly to him with a frown. "What's that you say?" he snapped.

Midshipman Hart blanched at his captain's disapproving tone but stood his ground.

"I do not think this was an accident, sir."

There was a moment's silence.

"Then, pray, sir, how else do you explain it?" Roscarrock allowed a little sarcasm to enter into his voice. "Jardine is standing behind the gun; when it is fired, the gun recoils and slams into him causing injuries from which he dies. Do I have the right of it, Surgeon Smithers?" he demanded of the florid-faced doctor, without turning to him.

"You do, sir; you do, indeed," echoed the stilling surgeon.

"Then we are agreed so far. Now, Mr Hart, if, as you claim, this was no accident, are you saying that Lieutenant Jardine deliberately stood in a position where he, as gunnery officer, knew the gun would recoil on him?"

"No, sir, I do not."

"Then what are you saying," Roscarrock demanded harshly, "for I am at a loss to understand your argument?"

"I am saying that murder may have been committed, sir."

There was an awkward silence.

The young midshipman stood defiantly under the close scrutiny of his captain.

When Roscarrock spoke, his voice was quiet. "Murder, Mr Hart? Murder? That is a most serious accusation."

Midshipman Hart raised his jaw defensively. "I have considered the implications of my accusation, sir."

"Then, perhaps, you would be good enough to take me through the facts which would lead me to follow your line of thinking."

Hart was eager now to demonstrate his arguments.

"I have accepted that Lieutenant Jardine was an experienced gunnery officer. His station in any battle was to stand amidships behind guns number six on both port and starboard, a position where he could command the broadsides on both sides of the ship. His usual position was centre ship where no gun could recoil back if properly secured."

Roscarrock said nothing. All this was common knowledge which was shared by even the young powder monkeys aboard. The boys who carried powder and shot to the cannon learned immediately they came aboard to avoid accidents such as getting caught in gun recoil.

Hart paused and when his captain made no further comment, he went on quickly.

"Each cannon is secured to its position by stay ropes which allowed for recoil but control the extent of the recoil. Therefore, a gun can only jump back a yard or so at most."

Roscarrock was still silent.

"In the case of number six gun" – Hart turned to where members of the crew had now finished lashing the gun back into its position – "the gun recoiled back across the deck and struck Lieutenant Jardine without being halted by the stay ropes."

Roscarrock's eyes narrowed slightly. "Are you telling me that the gun was not secured?"

"That is correct, sir. It was not secured. I believe that this was a deliberate act and no accident."

"Deliberate? It could have been caused by a frayed stay rope which had not been picked up during an inspection."

Midshipman Hart shook his head vehemently. "Two main ropes secure the gun. Both ropes would have had to be frayed and have snapped asunder at precisely the same moment. A frayed rope breaking on one side would not cause a straight recoil. The gun would have swung at an angle on its side as the stay rope on the other side would have pulled it to a halt there."

"What are you saying, then?"

Midshipman Hart turned to the gun and picked up a couple of rope's ends.

"These are the ropes that attached the gun to the bulkhead to limit its recoil." He held them out for Roscarrock's inspection. "If you will observe, sir, you will see that both ropes were cut almost through by a sharp implement, a knife, to the point where the force of pressure from the first recoil would have snapped the remaining strands."

Roscarrock examined the rope ends in silence before handing them back to the young midshipman.

"Very well, Mr Hart. Suppose we accept that someone did this in order to kill Lieutenant Jardine; we must then assume that whoever did it knew that in a battle Jardine would be standing behind that gun. His battle station was well known. But how would they been so sure as to the moment the gun was to be fired? They would have had to sever the ropes only when they were certain of an engagement, for tackle is inspected every three days on this ship."

Midshipman Hart inclined his head thoughtfully. "You are quite right, sir."

"Exactly so. You will agree that to achieve this purpose, the severing of the ropes had to be done just before we engaged the French. In those seconds during the very call to battle stations. There would surely have been witnesses to the deed."

"Lieutenant Jardine was not popular with the men, sir."

It was Surgeon Smithers who made the deadpan comment. There was no argument in that.

Roscarrock turned as if irritated to find Smithers still there, grinning broadly.

"Very well, Doctor. I am sure that you have other duties to fulfil. I would ask you not to comment to any other person about this matter until we have cleared it up."

Thus dismissed, the surgeon left to attend to those injured who needed his skills.

Roscarrock turned back to the young man. "Accepting the stay ropes on the cannon were tampered with in the way you suggest and for the purpose of causing the death of Lieutenant Jardine, and leaving aside the opportunity of that action, the surgeon is right – Lieutenant Jardine was not a popular officer on this ship. Any member of the crew could have done this. Even one of your fellow midshipmen."

Hart raised his eyebrows in protest.

"Yes," went on Roscarrock, before he could speak. "I know all about the punishments that Lieutenant Jardine handed out."

One of the spiteful punishments which Jardine liked to order was having the master-of-arms inflict floggings on midshipmen who fell foul of his temper. They were made to "kiss the gunner's daughter": that was, they were stretched over the barrel of a cannon and beaten with a birch stick. "The gunner's daughter" was naval slang for a cannon.

Roscarrock modulated his tone to speak in a friendly, reasonable fashion.

"Look, Hart, most of the ship's company will not shed a tear when Jardine" – he gestured to the body under the tarpaulin – "is tipped over the side. One-fifth of the ship's company are pressed men. Jardine was commander of the press-gang at Chatham. There's vengeance in their minds. And, as for the rest . . ." Roscarrock shrugged. "Better to forget the reason why; his family will rest more comfortably knowing that he died doing his duty."

Midshipman Hart stood his ground. A look of stubbornness seemed to fill the features of the young midshipman.

"Sir, my father is a parson and I was raised to believe in truth and justice. I cannot agree to such a subterfuge. If a man has been murdered then his killer must be found."

Roscarrock sighed wearily. "If you must pursue this matter, Mr Hart. I see no purpose in it when there are a dozen other dead and dying to be accounted for in this engagement and probably more of us will die before we reach our home port again."

"I would like to pursue my enquiry, sir," the young man insisted stubbornly.

"Who is the gun captain of number six, portside?" Roscarrock demanded ominously after a short pause. "Pass the word for him. Perhaps we can settle the matter now."

The gun captain was a muscular seaman in his late thirties. He stood nervously before them.

"How do you explain this, Evans?" demanded Roscarrock, a hand encompassing the gun and the body.

Evans shrugged slightly. "Ain't got no explanation, sir," he muttered. "The stay ropes jest snapped and the cannon went straight back into the lieutenant. Broke the rammer's foot as it jolted over it."

The rammer was the man who stood by ready to ram wad and shot into the barrel.

"Did anyone notice that the stay ropes were frayed before you put your match to the gun?"

Evans shook his head vehemently. "The Frenchie was upon us and firing, sir. We just loaded with shot and waited for the order to fire."

"Please, sir . . ." Midshipman Hart intervened, indicating that he wished to ask a question.

Roscarrock nodded his assent.

"Where were you when we beat to quarters, Evans?"

The gun captain shifted his weight from one foot to another.

"We were already on our way up from the lower deck. We'd heard the first cry that a Frenchie had been sighted and so we came running for the gun deck knowing a fight was in the offing. While we were running up, we heard the drum start beating to quarters."

"And when did Lieutenant Jardine arrive?"

"Why, he was already at his station and cursing us for our slowness, though 'twas unfair as we were one of the first guns ready and run out, begging your pardon, sir. However, I do swear he was on the gun deck before we sighted the Frenchie."

"You are sure about that? There was no time for anyone else to be on the gun deck at your gun between the sighting of the Frenchman and the arrival of Lieutenant Jardine?"

"The master's mate was with him, sir."

"Pass the word for the master's mate," called Roscarrock to a passing seaman. Then he turned back to the gun captain. "What happened then?"

"There came the command from yourself, sir." Evans glanced nervously at Roscarrock. "Lieutenant Jardine relayed your order to fire when our guns began to bear. The Frenchie got in a first shot that smashed number two gun and killed the crew 'fore they had time to fire. Then we fired and . . . well, you know what happened."

Roscarrock dismissed the man with a wave of his hand just as the master's mate arrived.

"Were you on the gun deck before we beat to quarters?"

The grizzled veteran frowned at his captain. "That I was. I accompanied Lieutenant Jardine who wanted to inspect the readiness of the gun deck. We were here a full ten minutes before we beat to quarters. Then I went directly to my station leaving the lieutenant here."

"That is all," dismissed Roscarrock, turning to the midshipman. "Well, Mr Hart, your theory seems to be flawed. If Lieutenant Jardine was already on the gun deck when we sighted the Frenchman, how could anyone have cut the stay ropes with the intent to kill him before the gun crews came into action?"

Midshipman Hart was evidently trying to fathom this out. His face brightened. "Unless the stay ropes were cut beforehand."

Roscarrock chuckled cynically. "Are you telling me that whoever cut them was foresighted? A fortune-teller? That he cut the ropes with the premonition that we would shortly be in action and Jardine would be standing in that position? Why, we might have gone this entire voyage without firing a shot in anger—"

"That's it! cried the young man excitedly. "Not in anger, not firing a shot in anger . . ."

Roscarrock regarded him with perplexity. "What are you talking about?"

"Don't you recall last night, sir? You called all officers to your cabin and said that there would be a gunnery drill some time this morning to check our efficiency. That explains why Lieutenant Jardine was already on the gun deck before we sighted the Frenchman. He was ensuring his guns were in readiness."

"I don't follow."

"All the officers knew that gunnery drill would take place. And every officer was told to ensure no crew member knew this so that it was to be a good measure of their efficiency. Even Surgeon Smithers was at the officers' call when you announced the drill."

"Are you now saying that one of my officers is responsible for Jardine's death? That knowing the gunnery drill was ordered and also knowing where Jardine's station was, they cut through the stay ropes and waited for the drill?"

"I am saying that one of the officers on this ship is responsible for his murder, sir. Only the officers knew of the impending gunnery drill and had time to tamper with the ropes."

Roscarrock pursed his lips. "I think that your argument is rather far-fetched. But" – he raised a hand to interrupt the midshipman's protest – "I'll not gainsay your wish to make further enquiries. Remember that you are making serious charges, Mr Hart. I will not record our conversations in the log until you come to me with evidence. Now, I am afraid that I have other pressing matters to attend to."

Returning to the quarterdeck Roscarrock found his first lieutenant, Gervaise, issuing orders to the ship's carpenter. He stiffened slightly as the captain approached and dismissed the craftsman.

"There's still some rigging tackle in a dangerous condition on the mainmast by the crow's nest. We won't be able to clear it until we get in port waters. The Frenchie was using some chain shot to try to dismast us. It's still lodged up there. We'll have to use the mizzen-top lookout position."

"Very well. What about the foremast?"

"The master's mate is overseeing the jury rig now. It'll mean a new sail there. We can be under way within half an hour."

Roscarrock glanced around at the enshrouding fog. "Unless it's my imagination, this fog is thinning. Let's hope the Frenchie hasn't stuck around to find out what has happened to us. We won't have the speed to outrun him without full sails."

Gervaise did not seem unduly worried. "Rambert's a cautious cove, sir. Remember how his squadron failed to support Admiral de Villeneuve off Cape Finisterre a few years back? It was Rambert then who ran for a fog bank to escape our squadron rather than engage us. I think he'll keep his ship back and not venture after us."

"Let's hope you are right, Mr Gervaise."

Gervaise hesitated awkwardly. "Sir, what's this Surgeon Smithers was chortling about Lieutenant Jardine's death?"

Roscarrock swung round in annoyance. Damn the loose-mouthed doctor to hell!

"What was Smithers saying?" he demanded.

"Oh, he seemed amused by the fact Jardine killed himself by accident and won't get the glory of dying in battle. Is it true?"

"Lieutenant Jardine was killed by a gun recoiling into him, that's all," Roscarrock said shortly.

Gervaise abruptly began to chuckle. "Bless me! It's really true? Not killed in action? No fame and glory in death for Jardine?"

Roscarrock's eyes narrowed. "I am fully aware that you didn't like Jardine, Mr Gervaise."

Gervaise stopped chuckling and his mouth suddenly hardened. "Didn't like him? That is an understatement. I hated him and if I had been a better man with sword or pistol, like young Unstead, I would have called out the bastard long ago.

Ask Smithers, as well. He once tried to foist his attentions on Smithers's daughter Prudence."

The words were spoken softly but there was vehemence in them.

Roscarrock turned away in embarrassment. He pretended to examine the drifting fog again.

"Hands on deck for the committal of the dead to the sea in half an hour. I want to be under way immediately afterwards if this clears." He made to turn down the companionway but then paused and added, "Make sure we can muster a fighting trim if Johnny Frenchman suddenly appears again."

Lieutenant Gervaise raised a hand to his hat.

In his cabin, Roscarrock sat for a while absently drumming his fingers on his desk top while listening to the faint sounds of shouted orders and answering cry of the hands as they performed their various tasks to return the ship to readiness.

Little time seemed to pass before there was a sharp tap on the door.

It was Midshipman Hart. His face wore a satisfied expression. He seemed bursting with news.

"Come in, Mr Hart," Roscarrock invited. "From your expression, I presume that you have solved your mystery?"

"I believe that I now know the means whereby it can be solved."

Roscarrock raised his eyebrows for a moment and then sat back, relaxing as far as his small wooden chair would allow.

"So what is your conclusion?"

"Exactly as I said, sir. Lieutenant Jardine's death was accomplished with malice aforethought. Knowing the gun drill was going to be held this morning, one of the officers of this ship cut the stay ropes some time during the night so that number six gun would recoil back and strike the lieutenant. However, before the gun drill was due to take place, a real engagement ensued when we sighted the Frenchman. The result was just the same. The gun killed the lieutenant."

"That much you have claimed before. You were going to

report to me when you could sustain your hypothesis. Can you do so?"

Hart smiled broadly. "As you gave me permission to pursue the task, sir, I took the liberty of searching Lieutenant Jardine's dunnage."

"You searched his personal possessions?"

"I did so, sir. I believe that given what I have found, I can demonstrate the reality of my theory and present a prima facie case against an officer."

Roscarrock leaned forward quickly. "How so?"

"It is well known that Lieutenant Jardine had innumerable affairs; that he was a lady's man, a seducer of women."

Roscarrock spread his hands, palm downwards on his desk. "Go on," he instructed.

"There were several letters in his locker all written to him by the same female hand and signature together with a small portrait. A portrait of a young lady. A rather attractive young lady."

"Well?"

"The letters were signed each time 'your own adoring P'. In one letter, dated on the very evening we left Chatham, this lady, "P", writes to Jardine that she fears for his life while on board the *Deerhound*. She suspects that her husband has discovered the affair and means to find an excuse to kill him. She begs him to find an excuse to absent himself from the ship at the earliest opportunity. There is some emotional material about them eloping to some foreign place together."

Roscarrock drew his finger along the side of his nose thoughtfully.

"The letters signed with the initial 'P' you say? I don't think that will get you far. By coincidence, I know the names of the wives of three officers begins with 'P'. Midshipman Hope is married to a young lady named Penelope. Lieutenant Gervaise's wife is named Peggy and Lieutenant Unstead's wife is Phoebe . . ." Roscarrock suddenly paused as if a thought had struck him.

Midshipman Hart was nodding excitedly. "Lieutenant Unstead already challenged Lieutenant Jardine to a duel in Chatham. It was stopped by the Provost Marshal. The cause of the duel was that Lieutenant Jardine had insulted Lieutenant Unstead's wife. Lieutenant Unstead's wife is named, as you say, Phoebe."

Roscarrock inclined his head as though unwilling to admit the possibility.

"It is still a theory. How can you prove it?"

"By the miniature portrait, sir."

"So far as I recall, no one on board, except Jardine, ever met Mrs Unstead, so we have no knowledge of her features."

"Then all we have to do is wait until we return to Chatham and then compare the portrait with the features of those of the officers' ladies whose names begin with 'P'. I will wager, however, that the features match those of Mrs Unstead. Then we will have our assassin."

Captain Roscarrock regarded the eager young midshipman with a serious expression.

"Mr Hart, I think you have done well. However, we cannot let a word of this slip out because if it was thought that you had this evidence, your own life would not be worth that of a weevil in a ship's biscuit. Do you have these letters and the portrait?"

Midshipman Hart reached into his uniform jacket and drew out a sheaf of papers and a small silver-framed oval object.

"I was going to give them to you, sir, so that you could lock them away until we return to Chatham."

He handed them across.

Roscarrock gave them a cursory glance.

"One thing, Mr Hart." He smiled softly. "Although you suspect Lieutenant Unstead, would it not be more appropriate to suspect all officers, for you might be doing him an injustice?"

"Indeed, sir. I am trying to keep an open mind in case I am wrong."

"Why, then, am I not among your suspects? I could well play the part of a jealous husband."

Midshipman Hart smiled and shook his head. "I did entertain the notion, sir, but then I dismissed it."

"Dismissed it? On what grounds, pray?" demanded Roscarrock in amusement.

"I found out from your steward, sir, that your wife's name begins with the letter 'M' and not 'P'."

Roscarrock's smile broadened. "You believe in attending to minutiae, Mr Hart. You are right. My wife's name is Mary. You will go far in the service. Very well. I shall keep these letters and the miniature portrait under lock and key until we are safely home in Chatham. Do not mention a word of such a find. Until we reach our home port, it might be wise to let it be known that your enquiries have been resolved and there is nothing suspicious about Jardine's death."

"Aye, sir."

Roscarrock turned and placed the letters in his locker with the miniature portrait.

There came the sound of a ship's bell.

"Nearly time for the burial service," sighed Roscarrock. "Ask Mr Gervaise to pass the word."

Captain Roscarrock had been wrong. The fog was patchy and did not thin immediately. It lay around the *Deerhound* for two hours more after the committal of the bodies to the sea. Roscarrock impatiently paced the quarterdeck for a while, awaiting its clearance but it hung with persistence. Now and then, Roscarrock heard officers exchanging a whisper and a chuckle. Crewmen passed to their duties, smirking. The reason was obvious. The news that Lieutenant Jardine had been killed in an accident was spreading round the ship. No glory for Lieutenant Jardine, just a casualty of bad fortune. It seemed that Midshipman Hart had spread the word that there was no more to the curious manner of the gunnery's lieutenant's death than ill fate.

Eventually, Roscarrock returned to his cabin and set himself to wait for the fog to clear. It was another hour before Midshipman Hart knocked on the door and touched his hat.

"Mr Gervaise's compliments, sir. The fog is clearing rapidly now. There is a nor'-north-westerly wind beginning to blow."

Roscarrock stood up.

"Excellent. Take a run up aloft and scan the horizon. I don't think the Frenchman has remained nearby but we don't want any surprises. I come on deck immediately."

Hart touched his hat again and turned out of the cabin.

Roscarrock reached for the brandy bottle and poured a generous glass from its amber contents.

Time seemed to pass interminably.

There was a sudden commotion on deck.

He raised his glass and swallowed quickly.

There was a cry: "Pass the word for the captain!"

Almost immediately one of the youngest midshipmen knocked at his door, a lad no more than fourteen years old.

"Mr Gervaise's compliments, sir," came his childish piping treble. "Would you come on deck immediately, sir?"

Roscarrock grabbed his hat and followed the boy on to the quarter deck.

He glanced around as he came out of the companionway.

"What is it, Gervaise? Is it the Frenchman?"

Gervaise's face was pale. "Young Hart, sir. He came on deck, sprang into the stays and went scrambling up the mainmast to the crow's nest. He was up there before I could warn him! Didn't I mention earlier that the chain shot had frayed the rigging and splintered the spars there? All above the mains'l was unstable. Young Hart just slipped, lost his footing and came crashing down to the main deck."

He indicated towards where a group of sailors were gathered around something that looked like a bundle of clothes.

Surgeon Smithers rose from his knees by it and glanced upwards towards the captain. He stood his head in a studied fashion.

"Neck clean broke, Cap'n," he called.

Roscarrock turned back to Gervaise.

"Was there no way the boy could have been warned before he went up the main rigging?" he demanded.

Gervaise shook his head. "What was the boy climbing up there for anyway?"

"I told him to go aloft," replied Roscarrock. "I wanted a

sweep around with the fog clearing to see if the Frenchman was anywhere in sight. I didn't realize that he would go for the mainmast. I thought everyone had been warned that it was unstable. I presumed that he would use the mizzenmast crow's nest, which would give a good clearance of the horizon, but . . ."

"Poor little sod," muttered Lieutenant Unstead roughly. He had been standing behind Lieutenant Gervaise. "One more body to go over the side, I suppose. I'll get the sail-maker to stitch up another canvas and shot."

An hour later the sloop was tacking across the wind, moving painfully slowly north-north-west across the bight towards the waiting British fleet.

Captain Richard Roscarrock sat at his desk and unlocked the cupboard, drawing forth the small miniature. He gazed down at the young, soft face, with the golden ringlets and pert red lips that smiled out from it. He stared in disapproval for a moment and then returned it, taking out the sheaf of letters which had been so emotionally addressed to Lieutenant Jardine and signed "your own adoring P".

They were outpourings of a desperate and naïve love. Hart had been right. The last letter had alerted Jardine to the young woman's suspicion that her husband had found out about their affair and was a threat to Jardine's life. It was clear that the husband, whose name was not indicated in the letter, was a fellow officer on board the *Deerhound*.

Roscarrock gave a low sigh, folded them up and returned them to the locker.

He drew some clean sheets of paper towards him and reached for the pen and ink.

He addressed his letter to "Mrs Mary Roscarrock, care of the Rat and Raven Inn, Chatham". Then he paused a few moments for thought before beginning: "My dearest wife, Polly . . ." He paused and smiled grimly to himself. It was a good thing young Hart's education had been lacking in that he had not realized Polly was used as a diminutive of Mary.

THE GAUNTLET

Jane Jackson

Although after Trafalgar it was generally regarded that Britain "ruled the waves", it didn't mean that she always got her own way. During this period Britain was not only at war with France but there were constant hostilities with the fledgling United States that would eventually erupt into the war of 1812. The following story is set in 1809, but shows just how strained relationships were at that time.

Jane Jackson is the author of around twenty books, mostly contemporary romances under the alias Dana James, plus several historical romances. Her most recent book is The Iron Road *(1999). Nick Penrose is the central character in a proposed series of novels featuring the packet ships during the Napoleonic Wars.*

Nick Penrose stood on the quarterdeck of the packet ship *Lady Sarah*, waiting as the men ran to their allotted places. For the next four hours, while one watch worked the ship, the other would practise gunnery. Behind him in the western sky a thick bank of cloud was building on the horizon. Two hours ago at sunrise the sky had blazed gold and red, warning of the change in the weather. Since then the swell had grown heavier, the sea had turned to pewter, and the wind had become erratic.

"Loose your guns!" he shouted, watchful as the teams cast off the tackles that held the two starboard guns hard against the ship's side. With handspikes and wedges the guns were levelled, the wooden plugs that kept the barrels dry were whipped away, and the side-tackles hauled on to run them out. The 6-foot long cannons were primed, pointed, fired, sponged and reloaded.

The echoes of the thunderous reports had barely died away, and the smell of gunpowder still hung hot and acrid in the air when Nick saw the doctor appear. He emerged from the larboard doorway leading into the captain's quarters below the quarterdeck and looked up, his plump red cheeks shiny, his jaw freshly shaved.

"The captain sends his compliments, Mr Penrose. Would you join him?"

Politely phrased, but an order none the less, Nick recognized. "Put up your guns!" he bellowed, and signalled to the bosun to take over.

Above the tang of turpentine and linseed oil rubbed into the rails to stop them turning black, the smell of coffee and frying bacon made his mouth water, and his stomach rumbled. The captain's steward, a small, skinny, evil-looking man, who fussed over him like a mother hen, would have breakfast ready for the captain and the doctor. As the only other officer, Nick had been invited to eat with them. But the atmosphere was not easy. Had it not been for the fact that mealtimes provided virtually the only opportunity to discuss ship's business with the captain, he would have preferred to eat with the carpenter and sail-maker.

He descended the steep companionway ladder to the main deck, automatically ducking his head as he went through the doorway and along the short passage. Tall, and strongly built, he seemed to spend his life with his head bent. The man he was following had come aboard with the captain, and styled himself Dr Downey. But to Nick's knowledge he had made no inspection of the ship, the food supplies, or the crew.

Nick passed his own tiny cabin, and the racks of muskets and swords.

"Have we another fine day in store, Mr Penrose?" Downey asked over his shoulder.

"There's a blow coming. So we'll certainly cover a fair distance."

"Oh dear. No doubt there'll be more injuries then."

Nick masked an ironic smile. The only person hurt during the last gale had been the doctor himself. He had fallen against the musket rack and gashed his head on leaving the captain's cabin after an evening of brandy and chess. Jenkins, the sail-maker, had stitched him up. The doctor hadn't known a thing about it until next morning.

A week into the voyage, concerned by the rarity of the captain's appearances on deck, Nick had asked the doctor if there was a medical reason.

Downey had bared his teeth in an ingratiating smile. "You can rest assured, Mr Penrose, that the captain has every confidence in you."

Nick shot the doctor a dry look. "Said that, did he?"

"Well." Downey's gaze shifted and he looked mildly uncomfortable. "Not precisely. If you want his *exact* words, they were: "Why keep a dog and bark yourself?"" He rushed on, "But you must not take offence. He is not a well man."

"What's wrong with him?" Nick had asked bluntly. Over the years he had sailed with several captains who, but for the new rules requiring them actually to sail with their ships or else forfeit their salary, had previously preferred to remain ashore, letting the mate take all the responsibility without additional pay.

Stiffening, visibly shocked, the doctor had spluttered, "You cannot expect me to tell you that! But I can assure you that though he endures many discomforts he is perfectly capable of carrying out his duties. Indeed he often declines my remedies in favour of a game of chess which, he says, enables him to put them from his mind, at least for a short while. His ability to exclude all but the game makes him a challenging opponent."

"The ship's loss is your gain," Nick had muttered. But the conversation had given him an idea. Though he didn't play he knew chess to be a game of strategy and tactics. Faced with a hostile crew, half of whom had no seafaring experience, being on the run from the law, the press-gang, or home, he had ordered every man to take a turn behind the wet velvet curtain, packing the narrow flannel cartridges, or filling the priming horns. Then he had divided each watch into teams that mixed old hands with new and made each team responsible for a particular gun or sail.

Rigged as a brigantine, the packet carried square sails on her foremast, and a huge gaff on her mainmast, plus a gaff topsail. When wind conditions permitted, Nick had pushed her to her limits: setting the foreroyal and skysail, and raising extra staysails and the flying jib. Then he had ordered them brought in again. He had repeated the manoeuvres until each man knew where he should be and what he must do. His next challenge had been the guns.

Nick entered the captain's day cabin. Light streamed in through the stern windows below which a padded leather bench seat ran the full width of the ship. Two polished mahogany tables, bolted to the cabin sole, stood at a wide angle to one another. One contained the ship's log, several charts, a chess board, an octant, a ruler, a small stand containing pens and a squat inkwell with a cork in it. The other was covered with a crisp white cloth laid with silver cutlery, folded napkins and fine china.

The captain entered from his sleeping quarters on the starboard side. Washed and shaved, he was smart in his undress uniform of dark-blue frock coat, black neckcloth and blue breeches with white stockings and buckled shoes. Nick sometimes wondered why he went to so much trouble when he so rarely left his cabin.

Short, stocky and tight-lipped, Captain Carne was also ex-navy. "Cleanliness and discipline, Mr Penrose," he'd barked across the table at their first meeting. "I expect high standards of both. See to it."

"Good morning, Mr Penrose."

"Captain."

"Mr Penrose," the captain began wearily. "The Postmasters General have, in their wisdom, ruled that packets must run rather than fight. And to enforce that decision they reduced the size and number of guns a packet may carry. You have now considerably reduced our stock of powder and shot. I should not need to remind you that the task of the Packet Service is to deliver His Majesty's mails, not to—"

"Captain, with respect, in order to fulfil that task we must reach our destination safely. And while we may not attack, by God, we have the right to defend ourselves. Smart firing could make all the difference between escape and capture. *Sir*."

"A fair point," the captain conceded graciously. "But one that has, I think, been adequately made. There will be no further *practising*, Mr Penrose. What remains must be conserved. Do I make myself clear?"

Nick clenched his teeth. "Sir." He didn't know the reason behind the captain's transfer from navy to Packet Service. The doctor – if indeed he knew – certainly wouldn't tell him. And as a relative stranger to the bosun, carpenter and sail-maker – a mate's usual source of information – there was no one else he could ask.

He recalled the difficulty he'd had persuading the captain to accept the need for regular firing practice.

"Sir, I'd like to suggest a competition."

Captain Carne's brows had climbed. Seated at the table in his day cabin, his journal open in front of him, ever-present chessboard with its game in progress pushed to one side, he had shaken his head, visibly doubtful. "Mr Penrose, I can't help wondering if you are wise to be fostering such division. Should we face a hostile encounter – God forbid – these men will be called upon to work together in warding off any attack. I can't help feeling—"

"With respect, sir, most of the new men came aboard not knowing one end of a gun or a sail from the other. Now they do. Sharpening their skills by pitting the teams against each other means that when a real fight comes we'll have a damn sight better chance of surviving it. Begging your pardon, sir."

Still the captain had frowned. "I don't know. The cost—"

"We have four barrels of white powder in the magazine, sir.

Being restored it might be of doubtful strength. We could use that. And we don't need to load shot every time." How in God's name was the packet supposed to defend herself if half the crew had never handled a cannonball, never mind reloaded a gun in a hurry? "But they ought to get used to the noise."

"Oh well, if you must." Sighing, Carne had waved him away, picked up his pen and resumed writing in his journal.

So, Nick had begun his self-appointed task. Each week the *Lady Sarah*'s guns had roared, and by the time she reached Barbados the surly rabble were beginning to resemble a strong, efficient crew. The doctor had tutted over the number of rope burns, powder burns, severe bruising and crushed toes requiring treatment. But as Nick pointed out, each time there were fewer, which showed lessons were being learned.

"Well, sit down, sit down." The captain now waved an impatient hand. He seated himself on the buttoned leather, and shook out his napkin. Nick and the doctor pulled out chairs from beneath the table.

"Captain—" Nick began.

"Later, Mr Penrose." Captain Carne turned to look expectantly at his steward who emerged from the tiny cubby-hole containing the stove on which he prepared their meals.

"Ah, Tremlett. Something smells good."

"Not till you've 'ad your fruit." The steward set down the dish of sliced mango with a thump and sniffed. "I'll fetch your coffee." He stumped out again.

"A singular fellow," the doctor remarked, and Nick looked down, masking an involuntary smile at this understatement.

"Indeed he is, Doctor," the captain agreed. "Where I go, Tremlett goes."

I bet that makes you welcome. Nick tried again "Captain—"

"Not while we're eating, Mr Penrose. Doctor, I was reading about Philidor last night. Have you ever attended any of his exhibitions at the chess club in St James's Street? Apparently he played three men simultaneously while wearing a blindfold."

"Indeed, Captain. I recall . . ."

Nick stopped listening. When they had finished the mango,

Tremlett brought in three platefuls of breaded pork strips fried crisp and golden. This, Nick conceded, was proper food. The steward might look like a dockside cut-throat but he could certainly cook.

Draining the last of his coffee, Nick wiped his mouth, refolded his napkin. "If you'll excuse me." He stood up, then looked at the captain, determined not to leave until he had made his request, and angry at being forced to beg for something anyone with a lick of sense would recognize as vital. Anyone but Captain Carne.

"Captain, about the gunnery practice—"

Carne's features were set, his eyes narrowed and hard. "The matter is closed, Mr Penrose. You may go."

Back on the quarterdeck Nick fought his rage. It was 21 December. And though they would not reach Falmouth for Christmas, or even New Year, at least they were on their way home. God willing, the repairs to *Kestrel* would be complete. But even if they weren't, he would not sail with Carne again, on that he was determined.

Taking a deep breath and shrugging off his anger, he listened to the sounds of the ship. The fitful gusty wind rattled blocks and snapped canvas as *Lady Sarah* drove her nose into the heavy swell then tossed her head and shouldered the dark water aside to leave a white foaming wake. He turned from the starboard rail, checked the binnacle, nodded to Johnson standing on the windward side of the wheel, and glanced up the foremast. He had trimmed the sails so that the topsail, topgallant and royal progressively angled away from the forecourse to catch and use every ounce of the variable wind.

"Deck ho! Sail on the larboard beam!"

He looked to the maintop where the elder of the ship's two boys was on lookout. "What is she?"

"British man-o'-war, Mr Penrose. She's running up a signal."

Snapping open his glass, Nick peered through the eyepiece. The packet was commanded to heave to for delivery of urgent despatches. Sails shortened, the *Lady Sarah* slowed. But in the fitful conditions Nick wanted to keep a certain amount of way on her, for without a degree of speed she would not answer her helm.

The warship's cutter had raced towards them across the dark swell. Nick had sent word down to the captain, but he had not appeared.

The young fourth lieutenant who clambered aboard carrying a flat leather despatch case brought welcome news.

"Another British victory. Two French frigates defending Guadeloupe, *La Loire* and *La Seine*, have been destroyed by Rear Admiral Sir Alexander Cochrane."

Behind him, Nick heard the soft rustle as the news was whispered through the crew.

"The admiral has already sent the squadron's sloop to try and intercept the Jamaica packet. But you will probably reach England first, and it's important the Admiralty and Foreign Office are informed as soon as possible." He looked around. "Where is your captain? I have something else for him."

"I'm afraid Captain Carne is—"

Shock widened the lieutenant's blue eyes, and his face paled. "Carne?" he whispered. "Not Captain Charles Carne?"

Nick nodded, frowning. "Why? Do you—"

Half turning, the lieutenant drew Nick aside, his voice low-pitched and urgent. "I have instructions to hand over a top-secret document from Admiral Cochrane addressed to Mr Pitt. It's of vital importance." He gnawed his lower lip.

"You know Captain Came?" Nick whispered, astonished.

The lieutenant gave a bitter nod. "To my sorrow." He wrestled with his conscience for a moment, but deep-seated rage overrode prudence. "He was commanding an eighteen-gun corvette and I was aboard a sixteen-gun brig convoying a merchant fleet when two French privateers attacked. Both our ships sustained damage, but we managed to cripple one of the Frenchmen. The convoy had scattered for safety, and my captain went after the other one. He signalled Carne to support him. But Carne backed off and went after the convoy ships instead."

"What happened to the privateer you were chasing?"

"After we'd holed him several times, he turned tail. But we'd lost a good part of our crew, killed or injured."

"Let me have the document," Nick said. "I'll make sure it's delivered."

The lieutenant was visibly torn.

"Listen, Carne has barely left his cabin the whole voyage. He may as well not be aboard. This morning he ordered me to stop gun drill."

Dismay shadowed the lieutenant's face.

"Trust me," Nick urged. "I'll get it safely to England. I give you my word."

Under cover of the despatch case, the lieutenant reached inside his jacket and withdrew a slim package sealed in oiled silk. Masking the transaction with his broad body, Nick took it and slipped it inside his shirt.

Handing him the despatch case, the lieutenant shook Nick's hand, his grip hard and firm. "God speed and good luck."

Moments later the little cutter was speeding back across the waves like a small white bird, the packet's crew cheering her.

After getting the *Lady Sarah* under way again, Nick went below and relayed the news of the admiral's victory to the captain.

"Thank you, Mr Penrose." Carne barely looked up from his journal. "I suppose we are to carry the news home? You may leave the despatch case on the table."

Nick walked out, aware of the oiled silk hidden against his skin.

The following morning Nick was once more on the quarter-deck. The men responsible for the square sails on her foremast had finished washing the fo'c'sle, while those who handled her mainmast sails had swabbed the after part and quarterdeck. The water falling away through the scuppers had run milky, clouded by the mixture of wood particles and caulking scrubbed loose by the holystones. Cleaning duties complete, the crew had slung the mess-tables and sat down to their breakfast of oatmeal and molasses.

Suddenly there was a shout from the lookout in the maintop. "Deck, ho! Sail on the larboard bow!"

Nick seized his glass from the holder by the binnacle. Raising the eyepiece he waited, holding his breath, as the packet surged up the face of the next swell.

"Deck ho! A schooner, two masts. She's a big 'un!"

Nick had her now. And just before the packet plunged into the trough, he glimpsed the pennant streaming from the top of the mainmast. An American privateer, probably coming from Bermuda. They prowled the ocean alone, unless they were chasing a merchant fleet. Then, like wolves, they hunted in a pack.

"All hands to stations!" Nick bellowed, snapping the glass shut. The deck swarmed with men, and for one dreadful instant the mêlée resembled the aimless panic of an ant-hill stirred with a stick. He gripped the rail, willing himself to wait. He began to count silently, and his heart kicked with relief as confusion separated into a semblance of order as those uncertain, or simply slow, were shoved roughly to their places.

"Stand by to wear ship!"

There was a rush to lift the halliard coils off the pins so they were clear for running when the order came.

Where was the captain? Surely he must have heard the noise? Seeing the bosun waiting, ready at the foremast, Nick made his decision. They would not be able to outrun the schooner. Their only hope was to head back to the protection of the squadron. But if the American had seen them, and there was still an outside chance she had not, would they be able to hold her off long enough? He glanced across at Johnson.

"Up your helm!"

The spokes blurred as the helmsman whipped the wheel round, and *Lady Sarah* swung away from her course into a tight turn that would take her back the way she had come.

"Raise tacks and sheets!" he roared. Then, "Haul away!" The huge gaff mainsail and the foresail yards swung across almost in unison, filling again with a crack. The air was noisy as the bosun's mates roared and bellowed, and men grunted and heaved, arms flying to haul in the slack. Yards trimmed and tacks boarded, Nick watched the swift coiling down. As soon as all the ropes were off the deck and on their pins out of the way, he gave the order to loose the guns. Tension increased.

The packet's four four-pounders and small stern-chaser were no match for a privateer. But if the American expected the *Lady Sarah* to be an easy catch, he was in for a surprise.

Where in hell was the captain? "Toby!" Beckoning the younger of the two boys, Nick sent him to find out. Then, rapping out orders, repeated by the bosun above the squeal and rumble of the gun trucks and the creak of the tackles, he watched the teams go through the sequence. Only this time it was no drill. This time the guns were being loaded with 3-inch balls of cast iron that would, once the powder was ignited, leave the barrels at 1,000 feet a second. This time they would be fighting for their lives.

Snapping open the glass, and bracing himself against the packet's increasing motion, he looked aft. The privateer had changed course. Lean and low, the American had raised a topgallant studdingsail on her foremast, and a jib topsail and, able to sail much closer to the wind than the brigantine, was slowly but surely closing on them. From the size of her, even at that distance, Nick guessed she carried eight or ten broadside guns plus a bow chaser. With a crew of up to seventy so that guns and sails could be worked simultaneously, she was a swift, efficient killing machine. Hearing the fast thud of feet on the companionway, Nick glanced round as Toby reappeared.

"Mr Penrose, the cap'n's packing away all 'is stuff into boxes full of sawdust. Tremlett and the doctor's 'elping un. I gived un your message and 'e said you was to carry on. 'E said," – the boy's thin spotty face puckered in his effort to relay the message accurately – "'e 'ad utmost confidence in you." He spread his dirty hands with a helpless shrug.

Nick couldn't believe it. The captain was giving priority to his china? "All right, Toby. Get back to the cartridge box. And keep the lid shut until it's wanted."

With a quick nod the boy raced away. Nick looked down on

the main deck at the team around each gun. The fireman had filled the buckets and scattered sand over the deck for purchase, the slow match burned in its little tub, the gun captains were ready with priming irons to pierce the cartridge already in the barrel, and two men held the side-tackles of each gun.

About to take the wheel and send the helmsman below to bring up the weighted leather bags containing the mails, Nick heard a dull *crump* echo across the heaving water. Jerking round, he saw the puff of white smoke clear against a grey sea and sky and felt his stomach contract.

The ball struck just below the maintop, shearing the saddle that held the mainsail gaff against the mast and blowing away the rest of the main and topmast. The lookout pitched overboard with a scream as the weight of the gaff ripped the sail free and crashed to the deck in a tangle of canvas and rope, pulverizing the quarterdeck rail and narrowly missing Nick and the helmsman.

A second explosion punched the air and, even as Johnson anticipated his order and hauled on the spokes, Nick knew it was too late. His shout was drowned by the deafening crash of splintering wood and glass as the ball struck the stern quarter and ploughed a path of devastation through the men on the deck. Tackles released as men were blown apart, the starboard guns rolled across the canting deck mowing down everyone their path. Ignited by Tremlett's stove, the captain's store of brandy exploded with a roar and tongues of flame leaped from the shattered stern windows. The ball knocked one of the larboard guns off its truck, smearing two men to bloody pulp and sending the sand-filled tub containing the slow match flying. It landed in powder spilled from a dropped priming horn. The powder flared, setting fire to the tarred cordage and torn canvas as the gun's weight and the heel of the ship sent gun and men crashing through the bulwarks and into the sea.

In seconds the packet's deck had become a scene from hell.

"Pengelly, get those fires out!" Nick yelled, and saw the bosun skidding through the carnage to rally what remained of the crew. Moments later a chain of bloodstained, smoke-blackened men were feverishly passing buckets, and desperately hurling water on to the flames. The doctor staggered out of the starboard doorway, and looked up at Nick, his ashen face streaked with crimson above gore-splattered coat and breeches. "Dear God!"

"The captain?"

The doctor shuddered violently and shook his head.

"Do what you can for the wounded."

"What of the dead?" The doctor's voice quavered.

"What about them?" Nick snapped impatiently.

"Surely . . ." The doctor gestured vaguely at the severed limbs, the bodies unrecognizable as men, then turned away looking as if he was about to vomit. It was then Nick realized this was the doctor's first experience of war at sea. And the *Lady Sarah* wasn't even a fighting ship.

"The sail-maker will provide shrouds." Looking aft Nick saw the privateer bearing down on them. Resistance would invite annihilation, and flight was impossible.

"Take in the foreroyal, t'gallant and flying jib." The staysails, which had been rove through blocks above and just below the maintop were already hanging in jumbled disarray. "Stand by to strike her colours!" His throat was dry, his nostrils full of the stench of blood and worse. But it was rage and frustration that made his stomach heave as he stumbled down the companionway.

The portmanteaux carrying the mails should have been stored on deck under a tarpaulin, but the captain had insisted they remain in his cabin.

"Where safer, Mr Penrose?" he had demanded, and turned away, the matter closed.

Nick gazed at the shattered panelling that had once partitioned the tiny cabins, cupboards and stores; at the shreds of crimson-soaked curtains, bedding and clothes; at the shards of china, and wood shavings that covered everything in fine golden curls. Half the cabin was scorched and blackened, the smell of burning and spirits still strong. He began a frantic search, his gorge rising as he glimpsed a glazed eye below white bone, and a hand lying palm-up, the fingers half curled revealing the captain's trimmed and polished nails. He swallowed hard, freezing at the sound of a speaking trumpet hailing the packet. The privateer would be alongside any minute.

He resumed his search, tearing at the debris, heedless of jagged wood and broken glass. Charred leather caught his eye and he grabbed the bag, hauling it free. The second bag had suffered less damage, and the despatch case, shielded underneath, was barely marked. Seizing all three he stumbled down the passage on to the deck, scrambled across the clutter of wood, rope and canvas to the larboard side and, hidden from the privateer, hurled the bags over the side. Weighted with shot, they sank immediately. As he wiped sweat and dust from his face with his forearm, a seaman muttered, "Boarding party, Mr Penrose." And Nick turned to see the privateer barely half a cable length away. The men lining her rails held muskets aimed at the *Lady Sarah*, and those in the rigging were armed with knives and cutlasses. A small boat was already crossing the distance between them.

The wounded unable to walk were carried below, and Nick sent Toby down to act as the doctor's loblolly boy. As the boat drew alongside, the remainder of the packet's crew left the gruesome task of placing what remained of their shipmates into canvas sacks, and gathered together behind Nick.

Two smartly dressed men climbed aboard. "Joseph Delaney, of the privateer *Charlotte*." Tall and fair-haired, the American bowed politely, his accent a soft drawl. "Thiz ma first mate, Henry Lovell. Whom do Ah have the pleasure of addressin'?"

"Nicholas Penrose, mate of the *Lady Sarah* packet," Nick was terse. "Captain Carne is dead."

The American shook his head sadly. "Ma condolences to ya." His manner altered subtly, and Nick glimpsed steel in the grey eyes. "Now, Mr Penrose, Ah'll tell you what we're gonna do. Any of your men who want to join me will be made welcome."

Behind him Nick heard grunts of disgust and someone spat.

Delaney ignored them. "You might tell 'em they could do worse. Ah'm a fair man. Bein' volunteers, ma crew all gets a share of the prize money. Truth is, Ah already have several o' your countrymen aboard, of their own free will Ah hasten to add. And they don't appear in no hurry to leave."

Conscious of the American's cool assessing gaze, Nick remained silent.

Delaney shrugged. "So be it. In that case you all will be put ashore—"

"What about the ship?"

Delaney smiled. "Why, Mr Penrose, she's our prize. We'll strip her, of course. Ah guess every man in your crew has a few barrels of rum stashed away to sell back home. Ah wonder what other trinkets and treasures we'll find."

It was no more than Nick had expected. "And then?"

"She'll burn, Mr Penrose."

There was a hiss of indrawn breath followed by a low rumble of anger. Nick heard Pengelly mutter a warning, and the men fell silent. Curling his fingers into his palms, Nick thought of the oiled-silk package next to his skin, of his promise to the young lieutenant. He had to get the *Lady Sarah* back to England.

Face and voice devoid of expression he announced, "I can't accept that."

Delaney's brows lifted a fraction. After a brief glance at his companion he turned back to Nick, his tone gently amused. "Mr Penrose, Ah don't see you have a choice in the matter."

Nick met the American's eyes. "Clearly this ship is no use to you. But nor is she a threat. Instead of burning her, sell her to me. I'll buy her off you, on behalf of her owners."

Delaney's eyes narrowed thoughtfully. "You're carrying bullion?"

"Yes, but you'll take that anyway. This is separate. A note of promise that the packet's owners will pay you her value. Only as a wreck, of course." He indicated the damage. "In this state she's worth little. But isn't that better than nothing? And nothing is what you'd get if you destroy her. I understand the banks have arrangements for such transactions."

Delaney studied him intently and Nick held both his breath

and the clear cool gaze. Then the American held out his hand. "You gotta deal, Mr Penrose."

The American captain left nothing to chance. While one party of his men plundered the packet, sweeping through her like a plague of locusts, stripping everything of value, another group herded the *Lady Sarah*'s crew together and held them at gunpoint. Only Toby, the doctor, and the most grievously wounded were excused.

The crew's fury and hatred of the marauders was almost tangible. Nick stood with them, demanding Delaney instruct his men to leave food, a hogshead of ale, and enough powder and shot for the packet to defend herself should she face another hostile encounter on the way.

"If we don't reach Cornwall, Captain," Nick pointed out, "you won't get your money."

The American sent his clerk to prepare two copies of a deed. Soon after they had both signed, the black schooner had all her kites flying and, finding wind where there seemed to be none, was creaming away across the oily swell.

Turning his back on the privateer, Nick put every able-bodied man to work. There were painfully few, but they turned to with a will. What could not be salvaged was heaved over the side. Rigging was replaced, and a makeshift saddle fashioned for the main gaff. He drove them hard, moving from group to group. The doctor emerged, bloodied to the elbows, from the fo'c'sle and slumped to the deck, his head hanging in exhaustion.

"How many more dead?" Nick demanded.

"Six."

"And the survivors?"

"One broken leg. The rest are just deep cuts and severe bruising."

"Can they work?"

The doctor raised dark-circled eyes, his lips quivering with indignation. "For pity's sake, Mr Penrose—"

"If a French frigate came upon us now, Doctor, do you think we could expect pity?" Nick snapped. "Can they work?"

The doctor nodded. "All but one, he's still unconscious."

"The boy can watch him. I need you up here." Nick turned. "Pengelly!" he yelled. "Get those men on deck." They had to find shelter soon in order to make repairs that would get them safely back to England. But there was one more necessary task to be completed first.

As the remains of their shipmates, wrapped in torn sailcloth and weighted with shot, were heaved over the side to a resting place far from their Cornish homes, Nick led his pathetically small crew in the Lord's prayer, then suggested that any man who wished might say a few words. Several muttered a phrase or two: their farewells no less poignant for being inarticulate. After a further moment's silence, Nick gave orders to get under way. His last glimpse of the chart had shown the packet due east of the Leeward Islands, and that was where he headed.

Eight hours later, the wind had strengthened. With the packet's foreyards braced hard round, her reefed mainsail straining the hasty repairs, Nick felt intense relief when the lookout in the bow yelled, "Land ho! Fine on the starboard bow!" And as dusk fell they limped into an anchorage on the south-western side of a small island with well-wooded slopes. After a makeshift meal, their wounds re-dressed, the crew finally succumbed to exhaustion. Only Nick remained awake, bone-weary, but too distracted to sleep.

Over the next two days they worked from dawn to dusk. Men sent to find water came back with news of a spring, plus fruit, sweet potatoes and the additional prize of a young wild pig. They had cut its throat and slung it between them on a sapling. The smell of roasting meat gave everyone new heart and work proceeded at a pace Nick had hardly dared hope for.

The gaping holes in the stern and bulwarks were re-planked. The water butts were filled, and more fresh fruit and vegetables stowed. Men who couldn't walk repaired torn sails, spliced ropes, and shook their heads over the carpenter's insistence that they painted black three 6-foot lengths of thick palm trunk with roughly bevelled ends. It was only when two of these trunks had been mounted on crude tripods and pushed out through the gunports that their purpose was realized.

Overhearing one man mutter, "Don't see the point of it," Nick wiped his face on his sleeve.

"Illusion, Mitchell. It would hardly be wise to let any ship we encounter believe we cannot defend ourselves."

"Well we can't."

"*They* dunno that," the bosun put in. "And anyway, tedn so. We still got two guns, and the stern-chaser."

"Much good they'll do us."

"You shut yer yap!" Pengelly lost his temper. "Dear life! Things is bad enough without you making 'em worse."

"I only said—"

"I knaw what you said, and I don't want to 'ear no more of it." He stomped off muttering, "Bleddy Jonah!"

The next morning the wind had backed and was blowing steadily from the south-west. Nick knew they must leave at once or risk being trapped here if the wind changed again. With the sun shining in a clear sky, Nick set as many sails as he dared and pointed the packet north-east. Picking up her skirts, the *Lady Sarah* knifed through the white-frilled water as if anxious to get home as soon as possible.

Day and night the wind remained steady, a strong breeze that kept the sails hard and full. With such a depleted crew, Nick took a regular turn at the wheel so that Johnson could snatch a few hours' sleep.

The days passed. And as their wounds healed, so the men's fears eased. With so few of them to work the ship, their days were long and exhausting, yet there was a new mood of comradeship aboard. Even the doctor had stopped complaining, and lent a hand when and where necessary. They had tasted hell and survived. And they were almost halfway home.

Though he had continued to post a lookout, sending Toby, the smallest and lightest, into the crudely repaired maintop, Nick was startled when the shout came: "Sail on the larboard bow!"

Seizing his glass, Nick raced to the bow. It was another

schooner, three masts this time. She had to be out of the Azores, the nearest land. He released the breath he'd been holding as he saw the Union flag fluttering at the top of her main topgallant mast. As he watched, the schooner changed course, heading towards the packet. Instead of lowering the glass and reassuring the crew, something made him wait. Moments later the red, white and blue flag was hauled down and replaced by the Stars and Stripes. Nick's throat dried, and his stomach tensed in a combination of rage and fear. *Not again*. Not when they had come so far and already survived so much.

Lowering the glass, he looked round, and saw the men watching him. He didn't need to tell them. They had already guessed. Someone muttered, "Bleddy 'ell."

"That's enough o' that!" Pengelly roared.

But something else had caught Nick's attention. A great black pall of cloud filled the entire horizon to windward. It crouched, low and threatening, as it crept towards them. Given the packet's sorry state, the promised squall could finish her off. But it might also offer her an escape route. Everything depended on timing.

Raising the glass again, Nick studied the schooner. Now she was closer he could see she was dirty and ill-kempt, and bore the scars of a recent battle. As he watched, her gunports opened, the long black barrels emerging, ready to spit death and destruction.

"Wear ship!" Nick yelled. Before leaving the island he had set up one real and one dummy gun on each side. Now he desperately needed a few extra minutes to move the other real one across. The crew worked like demons, the doctor hauling on sheets along with the rest, while the depleted gun teams strained and grunted to get the heavy cannon across to the larboard side.

A ranging shot from the schooner's bow chaser hit the water ahead of the packet. Nick glanced at the ominously darkening sky. The squall line seemed to be gathering speed as it rolled forward.

The *Lady Sarah* had come round in a full circle, and was heading directly for the schooner. Though she presented a narrow hull target, her masts and rigging were at risk from the privateer's bow chaser. Through the glass Nick could see men working frantically. Why hadn't they fired again?

"Clap on to those side-tackles! Level your guns! Out tompions. Run out! Prime!" His voice was harsh and cracking with strain. After another quick look through the glass, he rapped an order to the helmsman, and the packet started to bear away from the oncoming privateer. This would bring *Lady Sarah*'s guns to bear, but it was also the moment of greatest danger, as it exposed the greatest area of hull. "Point your guns, as they lie!" No time to elevate or change the angle, nor for another try. This was their one and only chance. "Fire!"

The powder hissed as the slowmatch was pressed down hard. There was a flash and the guns roared, bright flame lanced through the smoke. The trucks squealed and rumbled, and the tackles twanged as recoil hurled the guns backwards.

"Bosun, ready the stern-chaser! Bear away, Johnson, hard down!"

As the deckmen hauled on sheets, Pengelly and his mate desperately levered the smaller stern gun round.

The sky was ominously darkening as the privateer's bowsprit and jibboom disintegrated. Spars, rigging and canvas flew skyward, blown apart in a cat's-cradle of ropes, splintered wood and shredded canvas.

"Now, Pengelly! Fire as you bear!"

The stem-chaser's deafening report made his ears ring. As the purple-black cloud hurtled towards them, Nick knew he had literally seconds before the squall hit.

"Make fast your guns!" His throat was raw from shouting. "Stand by to shorten sail! Take in the fore royal and topsails." Canvas thrashed as the yards came down. "Two reefs in the mainsail!"

The cloud was a solid blanket, blocking out the sun to leave an eerie half-light. As the flying jib and staysails were dropped, a violent gust rocked the packet. The squall hit with a sudden blast of wind that lifted the *Lady Sarah* and flung her forward. Caught by a cross-sea, she slewed round, and lay her over on her side.

"Hold fast for your lives!" The words were torn from his lips by the roaring wind. Rain hissed and thundered: lashing down in blinding sheets, a solid wall of water that pounded the deck and cascaded down to the lee scuppers where it met the sea boiling in over the rail.

Clinging to the mainmast with one arm and the wheel with the other, Nick and Johnson fought the helm. The rudder was kicking like a wild horse, and Nick's muscles ached and burned with the strain as they struggled to turn her into the wind. If she broached to, turning broadside to the waves, it was all up with them, for she would simply roll over.

Nick could hardly breathe. His black hair was plastered to his scalp, his coat and breeches saturated and clinging like a second skin.

He couldn't see the schooner through the dense rain and spray: had no idea if his foolhardy act of defiance had worked. As the deluge eased, Nick ignored the howl and shriek of the wind in the rigging and the groaning of the ship, and altered the packet's course to the south-east in a desperate bid to put as much distance as possible between the *Lady Sarah* and the privateer.

"All hands, prepare to make sail!"

Blinking and gasping, the crew slid across the slippery planking to their stations, their curses lurid and heartfelt as they struggled with the heavy sodden canvas. As they loosed, hauled, braced and made fast, the packet leaped forward, heeling over, her sails hard and shivering. Nick dug his nails into his palms. Had he moved too soon?

The sails held. The screaming wind began to ease. The darkness slowly lightened, and the rain stopped as suddenly as it had started. Moments later the huge black cloud was rolling away to leeward and the sun emerged, shining from a cornflower sky on to sapphire water that danced and sparkled.

Dazed and exhausted by their frantic exertions, the men slumped against guns and bulwarks gasping for breath. Then Toby's voice rang out. "Look! She's going!"

All heads turned in unison. After a silence that lasted as long as it took to realize the boy was right, that their bluff with only two working guns had succeeded, the men roared their defiance and relief in a great rousing cheer.

The damaged privateer had taken also advantage of the squall, bearing off and returning to her original course.

Nick looked down at the soaked, filthy, red-eyed, grinning men, and smiled. "Right then. Home!" Patting his jacket he felt the oiled-silk package warm against his ribs. He would keep his promise.

HORNBLOWER AND HIS MAJESTY

C.S. Forester

We continue with the deteriorating relations between Britain and America in this rare short story featuring the famous character of Horatio Hornblower. C.S. Forester (1899–1966) did not write only the Hornblower series. He was the author of The African Queen *(1935), the basis for the famous film starring Humphrey Bogart and Katharine Hepburn. He wrote a biography,* Lord Nelson *(1929), a historical novel about Columbus,* To the Indies *(1940) and a novel set at the time of the war of 1812 featuring Captain Peabody –* The Captain from Connecticut *(1941). The first Hornblower novel to be published was* The Happy Return *(1937). He wrote two others,* Ship of the Line *(1938) and* Flying Colours *(1939), and pretty much called that an end to it apart from writing a few short stories such as the following. However the success of the books led him to continue the series starting with* Commodore Hornblower *(1945) and as he proceeded so he created new events that sometimes ran across the earlier stories. As a consequence he did not seek to have these stories reprinted and they have remained, pretty much forgotten, for the last sixty years!*

"Mind you, Sir Horatio," said Dr Manifold, "I think this treatment of His Majesty is unwise, very unwise."

"Indeed, Doctor?" said Hornblower politely.

"At the last consultation of His Majesty's physicians," said Dr Manifold, "those of my opinion were just outvoted, but I venture to say, Sir Horatio, that although mere numbers were against me – and it was only a trifling majority, you must remember – all that are most distinguished in the world of medical science were on my side."

"Naturally," said Captain Hornblower.

"In the matter of accumulated knowledge we were over-whelmingly superior. But the question of His Majesty's health was left to a mere counting of heads. Mark my words, Sir Horatio, this business of voting by numbers, without regard to position in the world, will be the curse of humanity for centuries to come, unless something is done about it."

"That seems only too likely," said Hornblower. One of his guiltiest secrets was the fact that he fancied himself a democrat and radical, but in the exalted circles in which he moved nowadays he had little difficulty in concealing it, because everyone he met took it for granted that he was the opposite.

"A sea voyage for His Majesty!" exclaimed Dr Manifold contemptuously. "Build up his strength! Distract him from his troubles! Fiddlesticks! A patient in His Majesty's unfortunate condition of mind should be kept low. It stands to reason. Bleeding, Sir Horatio – some ounces twice a week. A thorough course of purgatives with a low diet. Gentle confinement in the dark. That would give His Majesty's unhappy brain a chance to clear itself of its humours and to start again anew – with a *tabula rasa*, a clean sheet, sir."

"There is much in what you say, Doctor."

Hornblower was not lying when he said that; it seemed quite a logical treatment of insanity in the year 1812. But at the same time he was moved with pity at the thought of his poor mad King exposed to that sort of brutality. His instincts revolted against it, and his reason told him that as the treatment had been tried unsuccessfully for two years now, it might be as well to experiment with the reverse.

What he was more concerned with, if the truth must be told,

was the responsibility of his own position. This was his first command since his triumphant escape from captivity in France, and since he had received the accolade of the Bath at the hands of the prince regent. The command of the royal yacht during His Majesty's madness might have been a sinecure had not this decision been taken to give His Majesty a course of fresh air and change of scene. Sailing about the Channel with His Majesty on board while the sea swarmed with French and American privateers meant a grave responsibility for the captain – for him.

Hornblower looked round the decks of the *Augusta*, at the four stumpy six-pounders, and the two long nine-pounders fore and aft. He would not be able to make much of a defence against one of those heavily sparred, heavily gunned New England privateers. Dr Manifold seemed to be echoing his thoughts.

"Of course," he was saying, "there is no need for me to point out to you, Captain, the need for the utmost precautions against any shock to His Majesty. You have received orders, I fancy, against firing any salute?"

Hornblower nodded.

"And there must be no bustle and no excitement. Everything must be done more quietly than is usually the case on shipboard. And you must be careful not to run into any storms."

"I shall do my best, Doctor," said Hornblower.

A midshipman who had been perched up at the main-topmast crosstrees came sliding down the backstay, touched his hat to the captain and moved hastily forward. The crew assumed an attitude of expectancy.

"Here comes the King!" exclaimed Dr Manifold suddenly.

Hornblower merely nodded.

A little group of men on foot came slowly down the slope to the jetty against which lay the *Augusta*; it was not until they were no more than 50 yards away that Hornblower blew a single short note on his whistle and woke the ship to life. The side boys, in spotless white gloves and frocks, ran to their positions at the gilded gangplank. The pipes of the boatswain's mates twittered loudly. The six men and the sergeant of the marine detachment appeared miraculously upon the quarterdeck, pipe clay and buttons gleaming, the two drummers with their sticks poised beneath their noses. The crew fell in by divisions, the officers in their cocked hats and silk stockings, sword hilts and epaulettes shining in the sun, in front of them. The whole of the little ship was ready and welcoming at the moment when the party reached the shore end of the gangplank, not a moment too early, not a moment too late – it was a neat piece of work.

There was a brief delay at the gangplank. His Majesty was reluctant to come on board. Hornblower saw the hesitation; he saw the plump, white hands cling to the handrails, and saw them forced free again, unobtrusively, by two of the attendants. There was a burly lord-in-waiting, immediately behind His Majesty, wearing a fine plum-coloured coat with a laced waistcoat in a contrasting shade, crossed by the narrow ribbon of the Thistle – the bearer, presumably, of some historic name from beyond the border. He closed up behind His Majesty, closer and closer. The hands caught and clung again, and again were forced free, and the lord-in-waiting's ponderous stomach was planted firmly in His Majesty's back and propelled him almost unnoticeably but irresistibly along the gangplank, so that His Majesty arrived on the deck with just a shade of haste.

Every officer's hand came to the salute; the boatswain's mates set their pipes twittering loudly; the drums of the marines beat a long roll. Up to the main truck soared the royal standard, where its opulent folds flapped slowly open in the gentle wind. His Majesty had come aboard.

"Chickens and chimes. What? What?" said His Majesty. His clouded blue eyes caught sight of a seagull wheeling against the sky, and followed it in its flight. "What? What? Ducks and Dutchmen. What? What? What?"

The little group of courtiers and attendants pressing along the gangplank gradually edged him further on to the deck. Then his wandering glance caught sight of Hornblower standing at attention before him.

"Hillo!" said the King. A kindly smile illuminated his face. "Lessons going all right?"

"Yes, thank you, Your Majesty," said Hornblower.

The King reached up and took off Hornblower's cocked hat with its gold lace and buttons, and with his other hand he ruffled Hornblower's sparse hair.

"Don't let 'em beat you too hard," he said. "What? Don't let 'em. What? Good boys get guineas."

Dr Manifold had approached, and was standing behind Hornblower's shoulder. The King saw him, and cowered away suddenly in fear.

"Your Majesty!" said the doctor, bowing low, but his humble tone and demeanour did nothing to reassure the frightened being before him. The little court closed up round the King and herded him slowly away as before. Hornblower caught up his cocked hat from the deck where it had fallen from the King's trembling hand, and turned away to his duties.

"Fore- and maintops'ls, there!" he called. "Cast off those warps, Mr White!"

He felt he needed distraction after seeing the abject terror that had convulsed the face of his King at sight of the doctor who had tormented him. The air of the sea would feel cleaner than that he was breathing now.

With the royal standard at the main, and the white ensign at the peak, the *Augusta* nosed her way out of Newhaven harbour to where her escort, the twenty-gun corvette *Cormorant*, awaited her coming. Hornblower, looking through his glass at her, thought what a vivid comment it was on the strain to which the British navy was being subjected, that His Majesty, King George III, King of Great Britain and Ireland, could be escorted to sea only by a twenty-gun corvette at a time when 120 ships-of-the-line and 200 frigates flew his flag.

Times were changing. The royal standard at the main no longer sported the lilies of France – they had been quietly dropped a little while ago in favour of the harp of Ireland. And in the past six months the British navy had suffered a succession of minor reverses such as could not be paralleled in the history of the last fifty years. The reverses could hardly continue; now that England had learned the fighting power of the United States navy, she would certainly smother the infant sea power with a relentless blockade. But blockade could never prevent the escape of raiders and commerce destroyers – nineteen years of war with France had shown that. England would have to grin and bear her losses while the slow process of strangulation went on. What he was concerned about was that the *Augusta* should not be one of those losses.

"Signal midshipman!" he snapped. "*Augusta* to *Cormorant*. Take station one mile to windward."

The gay flags soared up and were acknowledged by the *Cormorant*. In her station a mile to windward she was interposed between the *Augusta* and any stray raider who might try to swoop down upon her.

The *Augusta* crept out from the shore, and turned down-channel on her cruise. Behind her stretched the cliffs of England, the Seven Sisters and the towering height of Beachy Head. Hornblower looked over at the King and his courtiers. He watched the pathetic, white-haired figure making its way here and there with uncertain steps while the short-sighted blue eyes examined everything, and he came to the conclusion that undoubtedly Manifold was wrong in his notion of the correct treatment. Surely this life, this clean air and these simple distractions were better for a diseased mind than the bleedings and purgatives and solitary confinement which Manifold desired to inflict.

The King's course had brought him close to Hornblower, and the vague blue eyes were studying Hornblower's face again.

"Little Sophia likes the sea," he said.

"Yes, Your Majesty."

Hornblower knew that Sophia was the King's favourite daughter, dead these twenty years and more; he had heard of the happy little holidays on the Dorset coast which the King had once enjoyed with his young family. The King's brow wrinkled as he struggled with his memory.

"Little Sophia!" he said. "Where is she now? She was with me a little while ago."

"Her Royal Highness is on a journey, sir," interposed the lord-in-waiting – there was a perceptible Scotch accent in his voice to match the ribbon of the Thistle which he wore.

"But why? She didn't tell me anything about it," said the King.

"She left the message with me, sir. Her humblest duty and respects, sir, but she did not have time to await Your Majesty's return to say goodby in person. Her Royal Highness will be back again on Tuesday, and meanwhile hopes that Your Majesty will remember to be as quiet and good as if she were here."

"Tuesday," said the King. "Tuesday. It is a long time to wait for little Sophia, but I suppose I must. I will."

Hornblower's eyes met the lord-in-waiting's, and Hornblower felt his heart warming suddenly to him. The kindly little deception, the dexterous hint of the need for quiet, showed that this Scottish lord had the sense and tact necessary for his position, and his smile showed that he cherished the same kindly feelings towards the mad King as Hornblower did. Hornblower suddenly ceased to remember how much higher the Order of the Thistle ranked above the Order of the Bath which ornamented his own breast.

"His Majesty," said the lord-in-waiting, "wishes to command your presence at dinner."

"That gives me great pleasure, sir," said Hornblower.

That was hardly a correct statement, Hornblower found. Not that the dinner was not quite excellent, despite the fact that the royal cooks were flustered and unhandy in their unwonted situation. The food was good, and the service, allowing for the cramped space of the great cabin, efficient. But it did Hornblower's appetite no good to see the King, his table cutlery limited to a spoon, seated with a watchful attendant at each side, and eating as clumsily as a child and daubing his cheeks with bread and milk. So it was almost a relief, despite the foreboding of trouble which it brought him, when a midshipman slipped into the Great Cabin and whispered in his ear:

"Mr White's respects, sir, and it's getting thick outside."

Hornblower laid aside his napkin, nodded apologetically to the lord-in-waiting, and hastened out; it was only when his foot was on the companion that he realized that he had completely forgotten about making his bow to the King.

Outside, as Mr White had reported, it was undoubtedly getting thick. Long, narrow bands of haze were drifting over the surface of the sea, the surest indication of an approaching dense fog. The *Cormorant* to windward was already nearly invisible. With night approaching, visibility would soon be negligible. Hornblower pulled at his chin and debated what he should do. Shoreham harbour lay to starboard, but the tide did not serve and the wind was falling; it would be risky to venture into shoal water in a fog. As with every captain in difficulties, his first instinct was to get out to sea away from the dangerous land. To seaward lay added dangers from raiders, but the chance of meeting a privateer was easily preferable to the certainty of shoal water. Hornblower gave his orders to the helmsman and called the signal midshipman.

"*Augusta* to *Cormorant*," he said. "Course south. Keep closer."

It was a distinct relief to see through the thickening haze the acknowledgement mount to the *Cormorant*'s masthead while the corvette turned obediently and shook out her mainsail to take up her new station; a quarter of an hour later it was too thick to see across the deck, and Hornblower thanked his stars he had decided to get out to sea instead of trying for Shoreham harbour.

"Get that bell ringing, Mr White," he ordered sharply.

"Aye aye, sir," said an invisible Mr White.

The loud rattle of the fog bell echoed dully in the heavy atmosphere, and the silence that ensued hung heavy as the *Augusta* crept slowly over the invisible water. It seemed a very long two minutes before it rang again. Seemingly close at hand the bell was answered by another on the port quarter.

"That's *Cormorant*, sir," said White at Hornblower's side – Hornblower did not condescend to reply to a remark futile in its obviousness. The next time the other bell sounded it seemed to be well to starboard.

"What the hell?" said White.

The direction of sound in a fog was always misleading – fog banks sometimes echoed back sound as effectively as a cliff face. The *Augusta*'s own bell rang long and harshly, and the *Cormorant*'s reply could only just be heard. Hornblower tried to remember all he knew about Melville of the *Cormorant*. Young, dashing, ambitious, he had been posted as captain after a bold cutting-out affair somewhere on the Biscay coast. But it was doubtful if his qualities were such as to enable him to perform the difficult task of keeping touch with a consort in a fog. Again the *Augusta*'s bell rang, and this time he could hear no reply at all.

Dr Manifold was on deck now, and approaching the sacred presence of the captain – the command of the royal yacht exposed him to these plagues, and Hornblower felt he would gladly exchange it for that of the crankiest ship-of-the-line in the Channel fleet.

"That noise disturbs my patient, sir," said Manifold.

"I am sorry, but it is a necessary noise," answered Hornblower.

"I insist on its stopping."

"There is only one man on board here," answered Hornblower, his exasperation boiling over, "who can insist on anything. And he insists that you go below, sir."

"I *beg* your pardon, sir."

"If I have to repeat myself, sir," said Hornblower, "I will call a couple of hands to carry out what I say."

"You are a boor, sir. I have the ear of a cabinet minister, and by George, sir, I'll—"

Dr Manifold cut his speech short as Hornblower turned to the midshipman at the quarterdeck with the evident intention of carrying out his threat. He bolted down the companion as nearly like a rabbit as his portly dignity permitted.

"Pass the word for my steward," said Hornblower as he had intended doing and, when the man came on deck, "Bring me a chair and a pea jacket."

Hornblower spent the night in the hammock chair, wrapped up in the thick coat – he was unwilling to leave the deck while this fog persisted. It was a weary vigil, and whenever he dozed off, he was awakened with a start by the clamour of the fog bell. At the end of the night, White was standing beside him.

"It must be dawn by now, sir," said White. "But I can't say it looks any different."

The fog was as thick as ever – the main yard was invisible from the deck.

"Listen!" said Hornblower, sitting up tensely. His ear had caught the faintest sounds somewhere astern – its acute analysis told him of the wash of water, the creaking of timber, the rattle of cordage, all blended and reduced in volume so as to tell him of the presence of a ship somewhere in the near distance. Then they both heard, plainly and distinctly, a voice in the fog say, "Call the watch."

"They're speaking English," said White. "That's *Cormorant*, then, thank God."

"Go and stop the fog bell, quick," snapped Hornblower, and White was impressed enough by the urgency of his tone to run to do his queer bidding without question, while Hornblower still listened.

"Keep the hands quiet!" said Hornblower on White's return. "I don't want a sound on board."

There had been something odd about the pronunciation of that word "watch". The vowel was broadened in a fashion no English officer would employ. Hornblower did not believe that it was the *Cormorant* that lay astern there.

"Send a hand to the chains with the lead," said the voice in the fog.

"Queer," whispered White; the explanation still had not dawned upon him – he was not as quick-witted as his captain.

Hornblower walked aft and stared through the mist over the taffrail. There was just the faintest thickening there, the merest, most inconsiderable nucleus in the fog – a ship was crossing their wake from starboard to port not 20 yards away, and unsuspecting. Hornblower watched until the nucleus had lost itself again in the fog over the port quarter.

"Mr White," he said, "I'm going to haul my wind. Port your helm quartermaster."

The *Augusta* swung round and headed on a course exactly opposite to that of the other ship. Hornblower could be confident that the distance between the two was widening steadily, though slowly; there was only the faintest of breaths of air to push the *Augusta* through the water.

Here came the King, up bright and early on this misty morning, attendants with him. Hornblower grudged the moments of distraction from his duty of staring into the fog. King George straddled on the slightly heaving deck like an old sailor – one way and another he must have spent a great deal of time at sea.

"Morning," said the King.

"Good morning sir," said Hornblower.

"Foggy day, what? Thick weather, what? What?"

There was a lucidity about his manner that had been totally wanting yesterday; perhaps his day at sea had really done him good. A gleam of light came through the fog, and suddenly there was sky to be seen overhead.

"There's *Cormorant*, sir," said White. "No, by gad, she's not."

A mile astern a ship was to be seen, headed on an opposite course; with every second her outline became clearer and sharper. As they watched she wove around in pursuit of them, revealing herself as heavily sparred and well-armed, with twelve gunports a side. She was hastily setting all sail – the white pyramids of canvas grew as if by magic in a fashion that would have been creditable in a King's ship.

"Set all sail, Mr White. Smartly now, men."

"Pretty, pretty," said the King, smiling in the sunshine; whether he was alluding to the ordered bustle of setting sail or to the appearance of the pursuing ship was not apparent.

The *Augusta* had all sail set as soon as the other ship, and Mr White was paying careful attention to their trim as she ate her way close-hauled to windward. It was some time before he could spare a moment to stare through his glass at the other vessel.

"A Yankee, by gad!" he exclaimed, as the red and white bars of the flag she hoisted danced into the field of his glass.

"Hoist our colours, Mr White. But not the royal standard."

There was no purpose in telling the American what a prize was being dangled under his nose. Hornblower peered through his glass at her. If she managed to work up within close range there was no hope for it – he would have to surrender, as the *Augusta*'s six-pounder pop-guns would stand no chance against the other's heavy metal. And then? Hornblower's imagination boggled at the thought of what would happen next. What would the Americans do with a captive King – the King against whom they had fought for so many weary years a generation ago? He tried to picture the effect of the news in New York or Boston.

He was so interested in the idea that he quite forgot that he, himself, and his career were in jeopardy. American boats would swarm out to the Narrows to meet them; there would be jubilation and excitement. And then – and then – there was a tradition of hospitality and kindliness across the ocean. Faults on both sides had brought about this war, faults that might easily be forgotten when America tried – as she surely would – to make the poor old King as comfortable as possible. The unnecessary war might end in a wholly desirable peace.

For one insane moment Hornblower was almost tempted to risk it, and he was positively shocked with himself when he realized the depths of the treason with which he was dallying. It was his duty to escape with the *Augusta* if he could; for that matter she would be a captive by now if his quick brain had not steered her towards safety the moment he had first heard that American voice through the fog. There was a bank of fog up there to windward; once let the *Augusta* bury herself therein and she stood a chance of safety. That fool Melville in the *Cormorant* was apparently quite lost.

A puff of smoke from the American's bows, and a fountain of water 100 yards on the starboard quarter.

"Take him below," said Hornblower curtly to the lord-in-waiting, with a gesture at the King.

"No!" said the King with a stamp of his foot, and Hornblower had no time for further argument.

"Clear away that nine-pounder," he said – the long nine on the quarterdeck might perhaps shoot away a spar and save them.

Another puff of smoke from the American, and this time there was a sudden howl overhead like devils in torment. She was firing with dismantling shot – lengths of chain joined to a common centre, rolled in a ball and fired from a gun. In the course of the projectile's trajectory the chains swung out and circled screaming in the air, spelling destruction to any rigging they might hit.

"Come on with that gun, there! Have you all got wooden legs?" Hornblower called.

The men threw their weight on the train tackles and ran it out. The gun captain crouched over the sights. As he did so, the American allowed her head to fall away from the wind; she showed her side, and when every gunport was in view, she suddenly enveloped herself in the smoke of a full broadside. It sounded like some devils' orchestra as the air filled with the din of the dismantling shot screaming all about them. Hornblower looked anxiously upward and was astonished to see how little damage had been done; then he remembered the same astonishment in other battles. The sea was so large, the target so small by comparison – a miss was so easy, a hit so difficult. A halliard had been cut – White had already started a hand up the rigging to splice it – and a long tear appeared in the maintopsail. And the American had lost 100 yards by yawing out of her course to deliver that broadside.

The bang of the stern-chaser beside him caught him off his guard and almost startled him out of his wits – he hoped no one noticed the nervous jump which nearly lifted him from the deck. No one could see where the shot fell – at least the American showed no sign of damage. The King was standing breathing in the smell of the powder smoke that eddied round him. He was clearly enjoying himself; mad or no, he was full of the traditional courage of his family. There was no sense in repeating the order to take him below in that case, for the flimsy sides of the royal yacht would be of small avail in keeping out twelve-pounder balls.

The American was yawing again. Hornblower watched, fascinated, as gun after gun of her broadside crept into view. Then came the gust of smoke and the howl of the projectiles, and an immense clatter aloft as everything seemed to go at once. The maintopsail yard lurched lopsided, its slings shot away. The foretopmast was gone altogether, and hanging overside. Ropes were parted everywhere, and the little *Augusta* lay crippled. She was hardly able to move through the water, and the American could overhaul her at her leisure now. There could be no question of making a hopeless fight of it, not with the King on board. All he could do was to try to prolong the chase by keeping the *Augusta* moving as long as possible.

"Clear that raffle away, Mr White," he said loudly and cheerfully for the benefit of the crew. "Fo'c'sle, there! Cut that wreckage clear! What are you thinking about?"

The men were leaping to their tasks, but the American was coming up, hand over hand, behind. She had lost ground to leeward through yawing, and now she was going about so as to get up to windward of the chase. Her other broadside would bear soon. Hornblower decided that when it did he would have to surrender. He found himself wondering again how the King would enjoy a visit to Boston or Philadelphia, and then shook off these idle thoughts to supervise again the work of clearing the wreckage.

And as he did so he caught a glimpse of a faint blot in the fog bank ahead. Something was looming out of it, growing sharper every second. He saw the headsails of a ship; so definite was the fog bank that the headsails were illumined by the sunshine before the after-sails were visible. He knew her – she was the *Cormorant* tardily retracing her course in search of her precious convoy. He cheered wildly and involuntarily, and the surprised

crew, looking in the direction in which he pointed, cheered with
him.

The *Cormorant* came flying down to them, with every sail set,
but as they watched they saw her upper yards thick with men as
she got in her royals ready for action. They gave her another
cheer as she went by; the American was clawing up to windward
trying to get the weather gauge in the approaching duel with
this formidable opponent. But the fog bank had reached the
Augusta by now. One or two little wreaths of mist drifted across
her deck, and then she plunged deep into it, and the battle they
were leaving behind was hidden from view. Hornblower heard
the two opening broadsides, each one sharp and distinct – sure
proof in either case of a well-disciplined crew. And then the
firing changed to a long, continuous roll of artillery.

Without the King on board, Hornblower would have turned
his ship about, crippled as she was, to join in the fight, but he
knew his duty. He was about to shout an order to Mr White,
when his attention was attracted by the approach of the King.

"A good boy," said His Majesty. "Good boys get guineas."

The smile on the foolish face was quite winning and charming; the King brought his hand out of the royal fob pocket and
put something into Hornblower's hand. It was not a guinea.
That desirable and elegant coin had disappeared from circula-
tion altogether now that England was in arms against all the
world. The coin epitomized the financial straits through which
England was struggling; it was a Spanish silver dollar, with,
struck into it, the profile of the King who had just presented it
to Hornblower – queer legal currency for the wealthiest nation
in the world.

"Thank you, sir," said Hornblower, doffing his hat and
bowing low as the spirit of the moment dictated.

They were through the fog bank now and the sun was shining
on them again, lighting up the face of the King. Far astern the
long roll of artillery came to a sudden end. Perhaps one ship or
the other had hauled down her colours. Perhaps at this moment
the boarders were fighting hand to hand on the littered decks.
Perhaps, after all, thought Hornblower, it might have been

better if the *Cormorant* had not arrived in time for the battle. Some lives would have been saved – many more, perhaps, if peace had resulted from an enforced visit of the King to the United States. He tried once more to picture the King landing at the Battery, but even his imagination boggled at that.

GUNFIRE OFF MAKAPUU

Jacland Marmur

It's time we saw the war of 1812 from the American perspective. The following story draws upon an actual battle off Hawaii in 1813. Too soon forgotten, Jacland Marmur (1901–70) earned a solid reputation in his day as an author of sea stories with such books as Wind Driven *(1932),* The Sea and the Shore *(1941) and* Sea Duty *(1944).*

In the robust northern latitudes where the ships of the Salem whalemen homed, dawn at this time of year would march boldly out of Massachusetts Bay, crystal cold and blustering with autumn's threat. There would be early frost on Winter Island and the bronze forecastle bells at Salem Quay would tongue with singular clarity, double-stroked sea music from a spar-branched forest of masts rooting along the foreshore because of the frigates of British blockade. But here in the islands of the Great South Sea where the warm, wet trade wind blew, the sun was a sudden shell-burst hurling spears of light against the rocky shield of Makapuu Head.

All night the red eye of a signal-fire from the land winked into velvet darkness. But its power, like the brilliant constellations high aloft, ended with the dawn. It, too, waned and seemed to expire before approaching day. The man who sat humped on the beach stirred his huge shoulders and stood up, his shadow immense behind him in the first dawn light. For some moments he remained very still, looking down at the young woman asleep beside the fire, wrapped in a blue sea-cape, her head pillowed in its hood, a small, lead-bound sea chest shielding her a little from the damp night air. An odd light was in his deep-pocketed eyes, something of reverence, something of awe. Cherokee Sam, his old brown face wrinkled as a Massachusetts winter apple, master harpooner of the Barton whaling fleet, did simple homage thus to the troubling mystery of womanhood he had never quite been able to solve in the way of his rough and often lewdly brutal life. For an instant it was almost tenderness that touched his weather-bitten face, a most singular thing for a powerful man with a lion's mane of grey hair bunching beneath a stocking cap, the marks of fifty sea years plain upon him. And it puzzled him with a vague annoyance he could not give a name. Like the wild exultation he had known some thirty years before when the Colonies went free by what wounds men like himself were stoically willing to take. That, too, had been a puzzling thing. And here was English war again and the Salem whaling fleet in threat. The old seaman frowned and turned away.

"Old man!" He put a grumbling complaint to himself. "Puzzling is a no-good thing. Only the whales you waif can fetch home any ile!"

He set chaff coffee to boil over a pocket of embers, his big red paws clumsily methodical about such unfamiliar work. From behind the volcanic boulder he had used as a back rest, he brought coconuts, a few plantain. In the distant brush two small, tethered burros grazed, making a rustling noise at forage. If the ships failed the rendezvous, he reflected, the animals would be needed to return to the village of Honolulu from this headland of the Island of Owheehee. Satisfied they were all right, he turned his weathered face to the sea, searching against blinding light. He saw the trade clouds piled in tumbling heights in the north, their upper peaks sombre yet with darkness, their lower ridges edged with flame. Southward, the coral reef sent long combers foaming with unhurried speed, lifting spray to the morning sky. In between the ocean stirred and vastly sighed till it reached the beach, where it sent questing little fingers of white water on exploration between the lava rocks. But there was no sail in sight.

Out of the corner of his eye he saw the girl stir in sleep. His ingenuous sense of propriety had apparently been on guard against this, for he seized his spyglass at once and, with his limping gait, he hurried out of sight around a jutting crag. When he came back, she was waiting for him, a slender, long-legged young woman in a tight-bodiced New England dress that moulded her bosom in youthful maturity; and the sunlight was golden on her yellow hair.

"Cherokee!" she admonished sternly. "The morning watch was mine."

"I felt no need for sleep, Miss Barton," he growled; and he telescoped his glass with exaggerated carelessness.

"Miss Barton!" she mimicked, putting her arms akimbo. Then she dropped gracefully to her heels by the fire, pouring steaming coffee into pannikins. With faint amusement in her clear grey eyes, she said: "It was always 'Naomi' in my father's ship."

"Aye." His big head nodded gravely. "But it is not fitten here."

"Oh-h." She pursed her small mouth, then let a short tinkling laugh escape her lips. She mocked, almost with gaiety: "You are fearful people will gossip?"

Cherokee Sam swallowed coffee, stirring his shoulders in embarrassment. "I have a place," was all the explanation he could make. Then he flatly announced: "We should not be here together at all."

"Why, that is Philadelphia nonsense! Davis says he hears of an English frigate sent to cruise the southern sea. Ike Davis is personal adviser to the great King Kamehameha and—"

"I take no stock in British men-o'-war 10,000 leagues from home. But if it should be true, the more reason for you to remain safely in Honolulu, and not be wanting to rejoin the whaler *Naomi Barton* and be running into gunfire. It would be your father's wish."

"You are too fearful, Cherokee. The fleet will rendezvous off Makapuu. We will have my brother's brig privateer for convoy, and the twenty-four-gun ship *Alert* besides. Between those two they can set the tune for any clumsy English frigate, very handily."

"Clumsy?" The old harpooner brought the crags of his brows together. "I have had to do with them before," he growled. "They have a guileless, simple look, these Englishmen. Here, a man would think, is an easy enemy. And then suddenly the iron sings! Napoleon himself is discovering—"

"The more reason, then, to burn a signal-fire here! There is searoom outside for a ship to choose her action space if there is need. Should they be caught at anchor in the harbour when a man-o'-war takes up blockade – If what we hear of what happened inside the Chesapeake is true, they are as handy as any Yankee crew at cutting out! No. We will keep our ships out of Kaiwi Channel with our warning if we can and sail from here together in convoy eastward round the Horn. And I will be in the barque my father named for me." She tossed her head. "She will be flying the full-ship pennant, too, when Luke Goodson brings her booming in from the whaling-grounds along the line!"

"Aye. No doubt. She is a lucky ship, that one, luckiest of all the Barton fleet your father built and sailed. He—"

Cherokee Sam's voice hesitated, then ceased altogether. For some moments there was silence while the creeping tide sucked and gurgled with a louder sound and the surf drummed distantly. Cherokee had seen this woman grow from awkward, gangling girlhood to young maturity on the decks of the Barton ships. She grew straight and tall, and that look of eager wonder came early to her eyes, the look the strong young have of expecting sure and splendid conquest beyond the pale horizon line. It gave her Northern loveliness a sense of smouldering fire and passion the old harpooner found it difficult to understand. It was the Salem heritage, no doubt, because it seemed to him her father had had that same sturdy look until the end. It made you remember the clean prospect of New England seaport towns in the walking winter mists; it made you remember the virile foreshore sounds; and it made you know these things were good. John Barton was gone now. It was four months since the barque sheeted home her topsails out of Honolulu Bay, leaving Cherokee Sam and Naomi ashore to care for the stern old man who needed no better protection against his age and fever than the familiar yellow muffler round his throat.

"Watch her good, Luke," he told his mate before he took his gaunt frame ashore; and, "Watch her good, Sam," he told his friend, the old harpooner, just before he closed his eyes. These had always been John Barton's deep concern – his ships and his girl. And these were strong recollections in the eyes of Cherokee Sam as he blinked against the sunfire of the Great South Sea. But when he spoke, it was of a different thing.

"It is not well," he grumbled in his chest, "to underestimate an enemy. They are a stubborn lot and proud as Lucifer, the men from the Narrow Sea. They keep a mad King safely hid and out of harm. No one speaks of it, because it is not fit. Lord Liverpool makes believe his Prince Regent never took the marriage vows with the papist Lady Fitzherbert while he makes sweet speech to the Princess Caroline. And no one speaks of that, either. So a foolish man might think the English folk are surely in the mire at last. Ho! The English folk survive their kings with ease. And when the need shapes up – the iron sings again! But I do not love them. No! I have some wounds to remember. Out of the Indian wars, and out of British boarding-pikes back in '81." The old harpooner's voice went flat, the tassel of his stocking cap rapping his cheek in emphasis. "I was twice impressed from Western Ocean ships," he snarled, "and I served brass guns that were not mine off Tripoli and off Cadiz! No!" he boomed. "I do not love the English! When I haul on breeching tackles, let it be beneath an ensign full of stars! The red St George's cross is not for—" He caught himself up. The savagery went out of his fierce blue eyes. "I am sorry, Naomi," he said with grave humility, "I had forgotten—"

"Well" – she smiled – "so it is Naomi again at last!"

"Aye. I had forgotten all about your Lieutenant Wainright." He grinned contritely. "He is man enough to be of Yankee breed, that one—"

"But he is not!" the girl interrupted quickly. "He is an English naval officer." She looked away, dismissing the thing. "The ships are overdue, Cherokee. They must not miss our signal when they make landfall here on Makapuu."

"You are fond of him," the old sailor persisted.

"Fond?" She continued to stare off against the empty ocean space, purple water ringed with cloud, the trade wind keen against her cheek. "Fond? How silly words can sound! We did not use such words, sailing a ship's yawl on Salem Bay and the weather in the east, or when we danced together in Jamaica and the King's band played before the war. It seems to me we used no words at all, because I can remember none of them. We laughed very much; that I do remember. We did not seem to be enemies. We laughed so much I cannot tell you if his eyes are blue or grey. But they can be fierce. They are North Country eyes. Like yours. I remember, too, that Father said he had an uncouth way of dancing, holding a girl too close. I think Father was right. The braid of his uniform could hurt." Her hand thoughtlessly touched her breast. "It hurts a little yet." Then she tossed her head to dismiss a thing she had never really intended to say. But when she turned to look at him, there was no shame on her at all. "You now, Cherokee! Did you never one day see a girl, and the two of you walk straightway towards each other as if you both knew all at once—" She laughed that sudden, tinkling laugh. "No. Of course not. Not tough old Cherokee Sam Slade!"

He looked at her for an odd moment of silence. Then: "No," he murmured gravely; and he stood up, picking his spyglass from the rock. "I will climb the crag a piece to see if whales still spout. Or perhaps a Yankee sail."

The old seaman climbed with precision, dragging his shorter leg a little and heaving his solid frame from one foothold to the other. She watched him reach a shelf of the promontory, where he drew himself erect to face the east. Here he rested his glass to study blinding outer emptiness with faithful care, the sunshine on the polished leather of his cheek. Then she walked to the water's edge where the trade wind tightly moulded the dress to her body, buffeting her skirts. And with the green jungle at her back the girl, too, peered outward towards the sea.

They kept that watch all day. The girl was fretful with eagerness, pacing the shale to and fro – for she was young and the young can waste no time awaiting an award. But Cherokee Sam had the long patience of those who know defeat and have learned at last how to stare it down boldly. The sunfire passed from the seaward face of Makapuu, dragging shadow slowly after it across the cliff. The eastward slopes of Owheehee lost their burning look as the sun went west. And it was late afternoon when the old harpooner steadied his glass on a point in the south and east. The girl sensed quick concentration in his posture. She came to stand below him, motionless and expectant, her small round face upraised.

"The Salem ships!"

He said nothing for some moments, his big red hand adjusting the focus screw. Then he growled out observation in terse, broken bits: "Three t'gallants . . . Broad-sparred. The *Alert* would have a cleaner cut. I can see no more. Now she lifts! No; she is not Salem-built. She comes up from the South. Starb'd tack. Wallowing her yards." He stopped. The girl remained unstirring. "Hull up," said Cherokee at last. Then all at once he snapped shut his telescope, climbing quickly down to stand before her on the beach and growl a single word: "English!"

The girl exclaimed: "Davis was right, then! Cherokee, if this frigate—"

"Frigate? She moves more like a barge-boat in the Thames."

"Well, then!" Quick excitement gleamed in Naomi Barton's sea-grey eyes, and her cheeks took fire. "A prize! A prize, Cherokee, for Leclerc's privateer *Alert* or for my brother Ira's brig the *Yankee Blade*, if only one of them will lift the land in time! Give me the glass, old bear." She plucked it from him, spun round, and swept the southern quarter where the sea ran blue and white. "Ah! She shows her courses." The girl's low contralto was rich, a little throaty. "Heavy tops, rope-railed. Gilt on her quarter galleries, and a beak bow square as a Dutch go-down."

"Indiaman!"

"No doubt of it."

The old harpooner frowned. "Why does an Honourable Company ship run westward round Cape Horn instead—"

"Because Isaac Hull and Davy Porter are hunting British ducks in the Yankee frigates off Cape Hope!" She swung her glass slowly in a northing arc, breathing eager excitement. "Leclerc, Leclerc!" she pleaded. "Here is prize-money enough for your fat Nantucket wife and all the seven babes, with no more worry for the winter pork if you only pry the horizon mist apart in time! Here—"

Her voice cut off, and the glass trembled a little in the balance of her small white hand. "The *Alert!* Cherokee! She swings three royals in the sky. She has the weather gauge and running free. Look there!" The glass came from her eye; she thrust it seaward like a lunging sword. "See her walking down the wind!"

Cherokee moved his head. In the north and east three pale grey banners swung, like little clouds in unison. His puckered sailor eyes could read the signs they spoke. The twenty-four-gun Yankee privateer *Alert* thrust her lower canvas upward like some wild and urgent growth reaching to heaven swiftly from the sea. Then her lean, dark hull ran free. The hot sun, dipping westward, hurled red bolts against her till, with heavy trade clouds solid-banked astern, her canvas glowed like three red pyramids of fire. White foam marched before her eyes as she came racing for the land, but Cherokee looked that way for only a moment.

"I do not like this thing," he growled, fastening his stare on the lumbering Indiaman. "She has—"

"He says he does not like it!" Naomi's voice rang quick and short with glee. "Cherokee, you are a most melancholy man! See now – Captain Leclerc has sighted prey! He hauls his wind to shut her off from searoom. I can see his gunports open and the muzzles glitter black. Presently we—"

"The Englishman means to run east. Foolish man! He tacks slowly. And yet—"

"All Englishmen tack slowly, Cherokee. A change of course is irreligious to a Britisher."

"She moves with a sluggish air," the old harpooner growled, "like a ship with her bottom foul. Yet she wears huge t'gan's'ls and the wind is fresh. And that white sheer line of her, broad from the mizzen channels to her bows. It is an odd strake for a ship of Honourable John to sport." He rumbled on, his instincts alert and fretful: "Two fo'c'sle guns at side, two at the quarter-deck. Probably carronades . . . *Ah!* She almost missed her stays! How odd that—"

"Stop mumbling, Cherokee! Honourable John has eight guns, ten at most; and those meant only for close defence against Malay pirate praus. The *Alert* is a twenty-four-gun privateer and fast as a hawk at wing. The Salem whalers must be close behind her, and no doubt my brother's brig. The ships will make the rendezvous in spite of all your grumbling. But first there is this ugly duck to pick. A pity Ira's *Yankee Blade* is not—" She broke off, her voice keening with excitement. "Leclerc's bow chaser talks!"

The action was in plain sight now to the watchers on the shore. The sun dipped to the burning peaks of Owheehee, setting shadows of the hills darkly marching out upon the sea. On the eastern board the tumbling trade clouds went afire with sunset light, aflame from the zenith to the ocean floor. But in between, where the last great pool of daylight still flooded the sea off Makapuu, the two ships stood etched in brilliant clarity. A small white cloud blossomed at the eyes of the running *Alert*; an instant later the single crash of gunfire came slamming to the land. The shot fell far short, sending a jet of spray aloft from where it dropped. The Indiaman held on, the gilt of her stern and quarter galleries aflame with sunfire. The *Alert* hauled further to the east to head her off from open sea, leaning now so her gunports bristled and her copper sheathing flashed. The

Yankee ensign whipped aloft to her mizzen peak as she rushed down with all sail set, eating up the sea space left between. Suddenly the Indiaman sent her canvas shuddering in stays again. She came through the wind's eye more quickly this time. On the starboard tack once more she plunged her beak bow deep, worrying closer to the land.

"Too late!" Naomi Barton's rich contralto sang, guessing the intention of the Englishman's manoeuvre. Her eyes burned brightly and her little fists were clenched. "You should have run for Kaiwi Channel from the start. Not now! Now you are—"

"She tacked with ease that time," growled Cherokee Sam Slade. "Now why—"

"You grumble like an old woman at her worrying. Watch how Leclerc will tuck her in his bag!"

The *Alert* stood up with her compensating change of course, the towers of her sun-drenched canvas dwarfing the narrow hull beneath. White smoke belched from her head once more, swallowing the crimson tongue of flame her bow gun spat. The explosion rocked against the cliffs and the solid shot geysered in the sea squarely across the wall-sided bows of the Indiaman.

"He takes notice this time!" Naomi Barton cried. "He slings t'gallants in the gear!"

The old harpooner made no response. His wrinkled face was set in an intense frown as he watched the Indiaman lay her mainsail to her mast in obedience to the signal to heave to, wallowing in the long deep swell. The *Alert* rushed down, standing closer inshore. Men were visible on her deck now, and far aft Jack Leclerc, tall beside the wheel. These things were plainly to be seen while the shadow of the land raggedly marched across the sea to touch the ships at war.

"She has showed no colours yet. She has not struck." Old Cherokee growled this out from deep in his chest, his eyes narrow against the last reflected light. "Leclerc! Leclerc!" he pleaded, remembering Cadiz and Tripoli and the waters off the Chesapeake. "Put yourself under his counter. Shorten down.

You are too reckless, standing in bow-on to be raked by slaughtering carronades. You—"

He said no more. A startled gasp escaped the girl. And then those two, side by side in half light on the beach, were silent with horror. What happened came swiftly, while shadow gathered deeper in the mist-hung, purple valleys of the land. All in an instant the white ensign of England with the red St George's cross slapped to the Indiaman's mizzen peak, the battle flags stiff in the wind from her lofty trucks. The broad white sheer lines running from her after chain plates to her bows fell as if by magic from her hull, broad, painted false strakes of wood, held in place by lashings. They dropped from both her sides to splash into the sea, drifting clear. Lifting gunports were revealed instead, then the maws of the guns themselves, thrusting out. What had appeared a lumbering, helpless Eastern Island merchantman showed for what she really was, a razeed forty-four-gun King's ship, HMS *Resolve*. And then the broadside thundered, almost at point-blank range.

The violent explosions rocked with a solid crash, one single mighty roar. This was no ragged broadside manned by merchant gunners, but the deadly work of well- and long-trained naval crews. The heavy carronades fore and aft followed almost instantly, orange fire licking through the heavy battle smoke, grape and canister pouring raking fire across the *Alert*'s rashly exposed deck, doing frightful execution. The deception had been perfect, the surprise overwhelming; the purpose of the Indiaman's seemingly foolish manoeuvre was apparent now. Three of the *Alert*'s forward pieces went off, singly, setting up new thunderous echoes to reverberate from the face of the seaward cliffs. Disastrously, she could bring no more to bear.

Grey-yellow powder-smoke engulfed the embattled ships like a sinister fog bank hanging low upon the wine-dark sea. Above it only upper spars were visible, musket-fire rattling from the Englishman's fighting tops. Now she put her canvas all aback, making sternway and yawing to let the *Alert*, with strong way still upon her, sharply overrun. It brought the razeed frigate's larboard broadside quickly into range, first the forward ordnance slamming out destruction, then each after heavy piece along the gun deck as it came to bear. Now the effect of that first overwhelming hail of solid shot was plain. High aloft, above the clouds of stinking powder-smoke, the fore-truck of the Yankee privateer was describing a little crazy arc. The royal canvas swayed with it, drunkenly careening in the sky. Then the whole mast rolled slowly down like a falling tree, torn cordage spilling with it. The mainmast followed, the snapping stays exploding like pistol shots, dragging the mizzen royal and topgallant with it in a tangled mass of wreckage.

With the smoke pall hanging, shielding her hull from sight, it seemed the *Alert* had disintegrated utterly. Till the trade wind, coming fresh with falling night, tattered that smoke to ribbons. And the horrified watchers on the shore could see her, what had such a little time before been a tall-sparred ship with life and power in her. She was a dismasted hulk now, black specks inert upon her deck. She wallowed, helpless, and defenceless, the wreckage dragging from her wounded hull – the English frigate, hardly scratched, wearing round in the north to bear down for the kill. Naomi Barton dropped her chin upon her chest and let a long hard sob come rackingly from her breast. She remained that way, hollow and empty of emotion. But the old harpooner, who had seen wars and devastations many times before, stood stiff and motionless, his face a stony mask of agony; and he could keep his hollow eyes on this disaster too.

He saw the final explosion rend apart what was left of the deck of the Yankee privateer *Alert*. It belched upwards in a mighty, roaring sheet of flame, wreckage spewing, charred timbers flying heavenwards.

The girl's head came up. "Cherokee," she sobbed, "Leclerc's Nantucket wife will have no—"

"He blew up the magazine." The seaman's voice was hoarse. "He sent overside what men were left and he blew her up to keep her powder and supply from the enemy. He did not strike." And Cherokee repeated, with a stubborn pride: "He did not strike!"

The charred corpse of the Salem privateer vanished quickly beneath the sea. There was nothing left now but survivors, clinging to some floating spars in failing light. That and the wall-sided frigate lumbering down, rigging boat whips to her yardarms to pick up her false sheer strakes and what men were still alive. Heat-lightning flashed silently across the eastern sky. The twilight deepened. The first phase of the Salem whale-fleet action off the Head of Makapuu was at its bitter end and those two who saw it knew the implications it could hold. Fascinated by the swiftness and horror of the catastrophe, they stood unstirring on the narrow beach of shale and sand, the tall New England girl with yellow hair and the old harpooner, his face square and set like a carving out of solid teak. The trade wind freshened, moaning against the cliff while the surf drummed distantly with a loud and lonely sound.

"Now my brother's brig is all that stands between this disguised man-o'-war and the helpless whaling ships." The girl's voice sounded dull and very far away. "A privateer eighteen against a frigate forty-four!"

"He is a rash and headstrong man, Captain Ira Barton of the *Yankee Blade*." Cherokee Sam Slade kept his wrinkled face against the wind, and he did not move his leonine old head. "He will make the rendezvous and he, too, will think he has an easy English merchant prize to pick. He will be destroyed! After that, this blasted razeed Indiaman will snap up the Salem ships at will. One by one. Like a bull sperm snapping squid." He raised his forearm; he opened and shut his huge fist in a gesture of sudden violence – once, and again. "Like that!"

"He must be warned." Naomi's voice had still that tone of dullness and of apathy. "Ira must be warned in time."

The old seaman's head snapped round. "Of course!" he barked. "And I stand here whining like—" He went round on his heel, striding robustly with his uneven gait towards the embers of the signal fire. "Quickly, Naomi! We will ride the burros. I will find a sloop, a cutter, anything that floats and sails! With luck I can intercept the *Yankee Blade* and give her warning of this in time to—"

"You would need more than luck." The girl whirled, sudden vitality in her voice once more. "The whaling fleet and Ira's brig cannot be far away under the horizon lip. The frigate already has the sea out there. You would have to beat around past Diamond Head – and do you suppose this Englishman would let a despatch boat go sailing past beneath his nose? You would need more than luck: you would need a miracle!"

"Then we will pray for one! The burros—"

He stopped short. The girl was hurling faggots on the live coals. For an instant he watched her in astonishment. Little purple flames took hold of the dry wood instantly, licking upwards in gathering gloom. Then he sprang forward, shoving her to one side, out of the light of the fire. "Are you made? You will bring a boatload of marines on us! You—"

"I will give them a beacon for their landing! Because they are already on their way."

He looked seaward. It was true. He was in time to see the English cutter lifting swiftly along the hump-backed crest of a running swell, darkly limned in sunset on a darker sea. The oars flashed all together, navy-style, catching some reflected fire as yet undrained from the ocean hills. In the east heat-lightning still tongued soundlessly, lighting the big Indiaman in brief instants of vivid relief where she wallowed with her mainsail laid against the mast, surging her headsails upward one moment, plunging her beak bow deep in the dark flood the next. The boat swept closer with seamanlike precision, the banked oars striking phosphorescent fire from the sea each time they dipped. He could see the muskets stiffly erect on the middle thwarts, the tarred hats, the pigtails of the seamen and marines.

"We must run for it! They would not follow the burros inland. Even if we have been seen we would be taken to be Kanakas. They cannot know who we are, and—"

"We will remain here, Cherokee, and tell them."

She said this with quick short emphasis, turning towards the sea at once. He eyed her narrowly, his mouth agape on a thing he left unsaid. Wild thoughts went plunging through his brain:

She was overwrought by what she had lately seen! So Cherokee gauged distances swiftly, his eyes darting towards the tethered burros, then out to the English cutter where the oar banks flashed. If that disguised frigate closed with Ira Barton's brig, the devilish ruse would work again! Who would take a clumsy-looking Indiaman to be a forty-four-gun King's ship at cruise in the southern sea? The *Yankee Blade* would be destroyed! And all the whaling fleet afterwards – unless warning came to her in time. For a single desperate instant Cherokee thought of making the dash himself. But he knew at once he could not leave her here alone.

"Naomi," he pleaded desperately, "run! I will cover you from their musket-fire. Run while—"

She did not stir. The next moment the cutter hailed the land. "Remain where you are, you two!" a thin, boyish voice cried through dusk. Cherokee Sam Slade groaned. It was too late! The boat grounded skilfully on the narrow beach between the jutting lava rocks. They were trapped. There was no escape now. They would have to bluff it. But time! This precious time was wasted, and there was little time to spare.

"Say nothing, Naomi!" he warned her in a deep, bass growl. "I am your father, a boat chandler of Owheehee, and we are simply fishing here. The action we saw means nothing to us. Remember, Naomi! Nothing at all."

She made no response. She remained stiffly erect against dancing firelight, a tautness on her and her cheeks aflame while the old seaman fished out a tobacco twist, carelessly shaving a pipeful with his knife into his horny palm. But from under his shaggy brows he saw the little midshipman leap spryly ashore, his hand proudly on the hilt of his dirk. He came briskly towards the fire, two musketed marines at his back. The remainder stood by the boat, ankle-deep in tidewash, passing a long narrow box drapped with the English ensign from the cutter to the shore. So that was it! Burial party for some officer fallen in the action who had requested it before he died. A ranking flag officer, at that! There was the chaplain with his prayer-book held high and dry as he waded ashore, the lieutenant in the sternsheets following, gold epaulettes, dress coat, and all. Cherokee frowned severely at that stern face under the naval hat, and odd thing tugging his memory. But darkness was settling down with the swiftness of the lower latitudes and the lanterns swinging there in seamen's hands just glittered on a narrow, troubled face with smouldering gunpowder eyes. And then the midshipman was snapping in his face to test his young authority.

"Well, by my ears!" he shrilled. "They're not brown men at all! Here, you! What the blasted hell you doin' here watching—"

"Mind your tongue, little English boy!" Old Cherokee raised his head with solemn dignity. "The mark of the beast's still on you."

The youngster flushed, reminded of the white patches on his uniform collar denoting his lowly rank. "Yankee, eh?" He recovered his dignity with effort. "I'll warrant you've felt a rope's end in a King's ship once or twice." He turned his head. "An old man, sir!" he called back to his officer. "Yankee, by his insolence. And a girl."

"A girl?"

"Aye aye, sir."

"Very good, Mr Vandershort. I am coming."

Naomi's head lifted at sound of that quiet voice. She stepped forward, a low gasp in her throat. And then she stopped short. The knife in Cherokee's hand ceased its deliberate movements. It remained poised in one fist, his tobacco twist motionless in the other. Across an open space those two faced each other in utter silence, the Salem girl with the hood of her sea-cape on her shoulders, firelight on her cheek – and the English naval lieutenant, leanly erect in the shadowy fringe where light and darkness merged. For that still moment the sound of the sea and the moan of the trade seemed inordinately loud. The murmur of gruff voices at the beached boat came dully, like a muttering from very far away. Cherokee Sam Slade looked quickly from one to the other. He saw the quick and bitter anguish in the eyes of both, and he left his big hands drop slowly to his sides. Then a cutlass scabbard rattled in the darkness where the lanterns swung. In that taut stillness it was a startling sound, like a brazen clash of cymbals in an empty place.

"Naomi!" the lieutenant said. She continued to look at him, making no sound. The light in her eyes went grim and cold, her fists mercilessly clenching down emotion, memory, the bright hope, the eager promise of the past.

He said her name again: then he came towards her slowly, waving the midshipman boy aside without taking his eyes from her face. Cherokee saw him walk to her that way, a man under a compulsion irresistible. Quite suddenly he remembered the girl's voice, still and deep with passion; and he remembered what she had said: "*Cherokee, did you never one day see a girl — and the two of you walk straightway towards each other as if you both knew all at once —*" He frowned, averting his grizzled head from such a troubling thing. Because her face was different now; it had a bitter, stony look. And her voice was icy and empty of all desire.

"Lieutenant Bruce Graham Wainright of the King's navy!" Her head was back; her eyes flashed; her red lips barely parted to let the thin iron of her words come curling through. "You ought to be so proud! Such a very clever trick with which to murder Salem men!"

"We are at war." He did not flinch. He stood facing her, gaunt and taller by a head than she. The fire flicked ruddy light and dark shadow on the sand between. It glittered on the buckles of his shoes, licked upwards now and then to flash glitters of reflected flame from the braid and epaulettes of his uniform. But the most of his face was in darkness, a narrow, solid English face with eyes that looked a little hollow in that uncertain light. "Your credit is misplaced. The ruse you saw in use was not a plan of mine. It belongs to Captain Sir Harry Neyland who—"

"Then you may tell your Captain Neyland that—"

"The captain was killed in the action," the lieutenant interrupted with a quiet weariness. "We are ashore to give him burial. It was his wish."

"I thought it strange to see a chaplain in an East India ship." The girl's voice went brittle with scorn. "Honourable John builds his merchantmen one single ton below the peacetime regulation register that would require a churchman be aboard on articles. It is too expensive to keep live men at peace instructed of their God. Only for the war dead, it would seem, can we afford a chaplain's hopeful words!"

"Naomi!" He raised one hand; then in irresolution let it fall again. Now he spoke rapidly, like a man with a thing which must be said: "I had no thought to find you here. Still, I am glad – because ashore you will be safe. You have been in my mind the whole long, bitter cruise – you in your father's whaleship and we bearing across the southern sea to—"

"To destroy us!"

"Yes, to destroy you. That is our commission. With Captain Neyland dead, the command of HMS *Resolve* is mine and—"

"And that thing you will do, Bruce Wainright. Yes; I know you will!" Her voice rose, taut with strain. "I know you well. Faithful eyes that laughed with me so many times. But always there was gunfire hidden deep beneath. I knew it then: I know it now. Tradition and duty are strong steels binding you. Men are faithful to such things."

"Men are faithful to other things as well." Some smiling memory seemed struggling desperately behind the flint and powder of his haggard eyes. Between them this tension lay like an iron bar. They beat their hands against it, reaching blindly to each other, to desire, to the long, bright hope that was so clear on Salem Bay and in Jamaica when the King's band played before the war. But they could not bridge that narrow space now. "Your father always said—"

"My father died in Honolulu. Cherokee and I brought him ashore from the *Naomi Barton* barque. We were here on the beach to rejoin her when—"

"Naomi!" Cherokee spun on his heel. "Be still!"

"And why should I be still?" she wildly cried. "You saw this cowardly trick his captain used against the privateer *Alert*. He had her already heavily outgunned but that, it seems, was not advantage enough for him. Well, do you think Lieutenant Wainright would not do the same again? Now tell us, sir!" She stepped directly in front of him, her burning face upraised. "You—"

The lieutenant said dully again, "We are at war. I should be missing in my duty otherwise. Yes; it would be done."

"Well, I have a duty too!" The girl's arms hung stiffly at her sides, her fists clenched tight. "I have a duty to the helpless Salem whaling ships and to my brother Ira Barton's privateer, the brig—"

"Naomi!" Cherokee sprang towards her, savagery in his eyes. He seized her arms to silence her. "You are giving information to any enemy who—"

"We already know." Lieutenant Wainright's voice was flat. "An armed brig. The *Yankee Blade* of eighteen guns to furnish convoy to the whaling fleet in consort with the ship *Alert*. She—"

Naomi shook off the harpooner's restraining arm. And suddenly she laughed, a wild keening laugh. "Her you will not murder! She shall be warned your sheer strakes are false and cover deadly guns. We shall see to it – Cherokee and I! Because we saw the *Alert*'s destruction, and we know. We sail at once in a Honolulu sloop to—"

She hurled this defiance at him before she stopped abruptly, choking off the rest with a fist that flew to her mouth too late. Cherokee groaned aloud. The lieutenant's shoulders sagged. A weariness crawled across his blue-grey eyes. "Naomi, you should not have told me that. Now I cannot let you go. If you had not spoken I —" He drew himself erect with effort. He looked away from what he saw behind her eyes. "I am sorry." The words were not spoken, rather they were torn from somewhere in his throat. "I must take you on board until after —" He spun on his heel. "Mr Vandershort! These two people are under your restraint."

He marched away at once, his sword chains making a tinkling

in the night. The girl's stare followed his swaying back, her small fist still tightly at her mouth. Her eyes seemed very bright and the steel no longer flashed, now she did not have to meet the challenge, the fierce, suppressed urgency of his desire. A slow sob gathered in her breast. "He did, Cherokee, what I knew he must and would. I knew. I knew."

"You said that thing to him, knowing he—"

"Yes!" The sob broke through at last. "Yes." Cherokee kept looking at her where the fireshine touched her pale, drawn cheek. "We could never find the *Yankee Blade* at sea. Never, Cherokee! Not with a little sloop. Not in time. She would be destroyed and—"

"Aye!" the old harpooner cut in with his bitter growl. "But *he* will find her! And the time he does, we will be on board this disguised frigate called *Resolve*! Helpless. We will see your brother's brig smashed. Smashed!" he repeated, gall and wormwood in his voice. "Aye! We will see Ira Barton's *Yankee Blade* deceived the way we saw poor Jack Leclerc's *Alert*! We will see her smashed and crippled, and her men die helpless at their guns. Before our very eyes!"

The little midshipman boy was striding towards them with elation. They saw his swinging lamp, a musketed marine on either side. But the girl remained unstirring. She stared blankly off across the ink-dark night where the stern lanterns of the English man-o'-war dipped and rose leisurely in the quiet murmur of the sea off Makapuu.

"Perhaps, Cherokee," she breathed, "perhaps we shall see a very different thing."

II

Mr Midshipman Percival Vandershort's pink cheeks glowed with wholesome British pride by the beached cutter of HMS *Resolve*, disguised third-rate frigate, forty-four. He could make nothing of the long-legged girl with the faraway look in her troubling eyes. She kept her face averted, intent on the stern lanterns of the man-o'-war swinging distantly off Makapuu in a

pool of phosphorescent seafire. But the wrinkle-faced harpooner with the stocking cap was understandable; he had the
seamark on him. The little midshipman, his naval hat at a rakish
tilt, was dreaming of promotion along the glory road, and that
dream was sweet. His spindly legs were wide-spaced on the
sand, his boy's thumbs tucked in his breeches belt where the
uniform coat flared away. If he wiggled his hands it set his dirk
chains jingling, giving him a feeling of good determination.

"We will teach you Yankees some manners yet!" he piped.
"So you would take a sloop a-sailing and warn your funny little
brig eighteen? Ho!" he chortled. "Well, we will keep you tucked
aboard to see you don't! And we'll swallow your brig like ginger
beer." He jingled his side-arm chains again. "After that we'll
sweep the southern sea of every Yankee whaler. By Nelson's
bones, we will!"

Cherokee Sam's head stirred in the lantern-light. "Be careful,
lad, should you sail prize-master of one of them," he sternly
growled, the acid of the *Alert*'s destruction and Naomi's rash
speech still gnawing. "Salem men are fond of the flesh of little
midshipmen boys. They bile them whole in the blubber pots.
Sperm ile is best, I understand. Then they lick their chops,
from the master down, in the dog-watch mess."

"Blasted Yankee insolence! You will—"

Whatever else Mr Vandershort meant to announce was
interrupted by the crash of musket-fire as the party of marines
did honourable salute over the fresh grave of flag Captain Sir
Harry Neyland, lately in command of HMS *Resolve*. The
muffled intonation of the chaplain was heard, the rattle of
grounding arms, an order issued in a low, stern voice. Then
the men returned. A grizzled sailor face revealed itself under a
stiff, tarred hat as yellow lamplight gushed across it. Then that
face withdrew and another took its place, pigtail gleaming over a
hairy neck. Lieutenant Wainright remained on the edge of
darkness, a silent figure with contemplative eyes awaiting the
cutter's launch.

When he came into the sternsheets the boat, urged forward,
lifted to the surf swell, then took the water fairly. The launchers

vaulted in; the long oars took up their rhythmic clicking in the thole-pins. Cherokee Sam, a grim bitterness on him, stared back at the signal-fire on the beach, till it winked a red eye and went out. Naomi had her gaze over a shoulder, watching the huge bulk of the frigate loom larger across a narrowing space of dark sea. Points of starshine sparkled on her canvas, her wall-sided hull rolling with a loud seawash. Lamplight showed at her entry gangway, and on a part of her false sheer strake being hauled up to be lashed in place once more. Then the cutter skilfully swung for the landing.

"Toss!"

The oars snapped up in two precise banks. The bosun's whistle shrilly piped the new commander's return, bare-footed side boys at salute. They looked goggle-eyed at the girl, coming aboard a King's ship, the harpooner limping after her. The second lieutenant, who had the deck, looked a little astonished too.

"They are out of one of the Salem ships," Wainright curtly explained, "waiting on the beach to rejoin her."

"Then they saw—"

"Precisely, Mr Columtree! You will see that she – they are given comfort and courtesy . . . Square the mainyard. The course is east."

"Aye aye, sir. Four of the *Alert* survivors have died of their wounds. Fourteen remain, sir. They are fit."

The girl came forward. She said coldly, "They are our people. Would it infringe on your duty to let us speak with them?"

Wainright nodded. "Mr Vandershort will escort you. You are to have my room, Naomi," he added quietly. "I will hold the deck."

"If you will allow" – she turned away, her voice flat – "I shall keep the deck myself."

He watched her grace of movement, her lithe young body giving thoughtless adjustment to the swinging deck before she passed out of wavering lantern-light. But he remained there, his weathered English face betraying no sign of emotion. Except his stern, unflinching eyes, clouded from ceaseless vigil on what things he had not said. Then he stirred, vaguely aware of his second lieutenant, mumbling – complimenting him upon command. He felt no elation, only the stern necessities of the business he had in hand. It was a rancour in him, this trickery against an enemy already inferiorly armed. But here was war, the long, interminable wars. And what had war to do with what a man imagined he could see in the sea-grey eyes of a Salem girl? There was rebellion in those eyes, and in the eyes of Cherokee, a proud rebellion Englishmen ought to understand. These people stemmed from England: they should not be England's enemies! Lieutenant Wainright coughed, moved stiffly aft to examine the traverse board, sweep a quick look aloft to the trim of his heavy spars: then he took to pacing steadily fore and aft along his quarterdeck.

So the long night passed. The ship lazed through the sea, only a main topgallant set above broad topsails in simulation of the cautious night habit of Honourable John's slow merchantmen. Seen that way from across an ocean distance in the first thinning of the night with her main battery gunports hidden from sight by a brightly painted wooden strake, no honest seaman would take her for a cruising frigate of Britain's battle-fleet. She had a look of ease and innocence, but there was deadly, disguised power in her as she swam eastwards towards the dawn, hunting the Salem ships for prey.

She emerged slowly out of darkness. First her courses touched watery shadow to her deck, ranging a little. The sea babbled; the steady trade made a pleasant singing in the lofty webwork of her gear. In that half light the vast ocean stirred like a grey giant restless towards the end of sleep. Pale shapes began to reveal themselves; the sailing-master by the heavy wheel at the quartermaster's shoulder; the angular frame of the commander still measuring the oak, his long shadow crossing and recrossing the gun carriage of the larboard carronade; the forecastle lookout, his striped shirt suddenly brilliant as he moved towards the belfry to strike the double notes. And in the waist the girl in her sea-cape beside Cherokee whose back was braced against the bulwark, his wrinkled face fretful even in his dozing. Because he remembered the *Alert*'s destruction, and he could not forget there was nothing left to oppose this deadly frigate now but a little privateer of eighteen guns. Even in a straightforward action the brig was hopelessly outarmed. Taken by surprise, she would not even be able to run, to refuse gunnery with this heavy-armed man-o'-war. The *Yankee Blade* was doomed. And after that the entire whaling fleet, to be picked off one by one.

Naomi Barton had that knowledge too. It was in her sleepless eyes, restlessly searching the sea. Westward only the peaks of Owheehee showed above horizon haze, a grey rumour of the land deepening to purple as the sunrise grew. Tension mounted in the girl with nearing dawn. The onus of this thing was on her; upon her alone. She stirred now, seeing the distant cloud masses flush with a sunfire not yet free of the rim of the sea. With a taut, quick motion, she brushed the hair from her face, looking to the fore crosstrees where the lookout hung, the long thin glass at his eye. Then suddenly the dawn exploded, flinging horizontal bars of fire across the ocean waste. And with it, as at a signal prearranged, came Mr Midshipman Vandershort's thin voice, urgently crying the deck.

"Sail ho!"

The girl spun her back to the bulwark, head upraised. Cherokee leaped instantly erect, feet planted wide, motionless and waiting. They heard the quarterdeck reply, the quick report from aloft, "Weatherbow, sir!" An instant of silence. "Two more sail. Three, sir! Bear a point in the north." Then, shrilly: "Four!"

Lieutenant Wainright sprang to the weather rigging, climbing swiftly, opening his telescope. Excitement flew through the ship, heads aloft, mouths a gape. "The *Yankee Blade*!" Cherokee Sam barked hoarsely. "With the Salem fleet rounding down for Makapuu to join the *Alert* with her ile casks full. The *Alert* is destroyed! And we—"

He broke off, helpless, his big paws clenched. The English

commander dropped smartly to his deck. Naomi moved her small head to watch him. In the stillness his low voice carried with extraordinary clarity. "Let the ship run as she goes for the present. They will catch the sunfire on our canvas soon enough." He put his head on his shoulder towards the wheel. "Steer large! Let her yaw like a clumsy merchantman." His voice was sharp with strain. "Get the tubs in tow astern, Mr Columtree, to check her way and make her awkward in manoeuvre. Overhaul the releasing gear on the false strakes. Charge the guns. Solid shot main battery, grape fore-and-aft carronades. We—"

"The deck!" the midshipman's hail came fluting from aloft. "The leading sail, sir. A brig. She hauls her wind aft and bears down!"

"Very good. Lay below, Mr Vandershort!"

"More luscious Yankee pie!" Mr Columtree's broad red face wreathed in a delighted grin. "A pity Captain Neyland is not here to see his clever trick in use again with—"

"Out fore and mizzen t'gallants!" Wainright cut in. "Get the royals on her. It must appear we mean to run. Keep the men out of sight. Shore coats over these uniforms!" He placed stiffly to the break of his quarterdeck. "Prisoners below!"

The girl stood below him, smiling coldly up, oblivious to the sudden rush of activity. For the first time his eyes wavered before what scorn he saw on her face. He wanted to speak, to tell her he had no relish for this deception a dead commander's cleverness had put to use and so put compulsion on him for its use again. But her voice came first, like a whiplash. "It is well to take no risks, having only a forty-four-gun frigate with which to engage a brig eighteen! I am surprised you send me below when—"

"Naomi, I beg you—"

"– when I could so well be used as a decoy!" she finished coldly.

"By my eyes, sir!" Mr Columtree's excitement exploded with violence. "She doesn't know it, but she's right! Let the Yankees have the deck. Who'd suspect us for a man-o'-war with a woman and that ragged crowd in view? We can have that brig in point-blank range! Point-blank, sir!"

"Mr Columtree, I am not scoundrel enough to put a woman in the way of gunfire."

"There is not the slightest danger, sir. You know it! We can have them all below to the cable tier in easy time. Before the first broadside goes." He stared hard at his superior who had so lately assumed command. "I submit, we are at war!"

Lieutenant Wainright's shoulders sagged. Yes; they were at war. Every advantage must be used and if that burden were refused there was treason, or at least disgrace, to face. He heard Naomi's ironic laugh. If only she had held her peace! His lips pressed tight. Against his will, he forced the barely discernible inclination of his head. It made Mr Columtree chortle with glee before he spun away. But Naomi remained at the foot of the ladderway, that odd, strained pain behind her eyes.

"Cherokee," she breathed to the astonished harpooner at her side, "go for'ard. Mix with the *Alert* prisoners when they come on deck to—"

He cut in hoarsely, "I will never understand why—"

"Joe Blanding will tell you." She started up for the quarter-deck. "Cherokee, do as I say!"

The brig lifted rapidly against the sunrise, leaving her un-armed consorts still hull down. It was plain she too considered HMS *Resolve* a lumbering merchantman to be picked up for an easy prize. There was reason for it. The man-o'-war, towing invisible drags astern, moved slowly despite her press of canvas. On the foredeck the clustered *Alert* prisoners could be seen, and the figure of a girl far aft. A privateer had little to fear from such a ship. So the brig rushed down into the deadly trap, lofty and heavy-sparred, fast as a cloud, flinging her bow wave wide. Suddenly she yawed to bring her bow gun on, the Yankee ensign snapping to the peak. A puff of white bloomed at her eyes; then the faint report was heard. The solid shot sent a spout aloft far short of HMS *Resolve*.

Mr Columtree laughed. "Insolent beggar! Presently we—"

"In royals. Hang t'gallants in the gear. Ready about! Starboard broadside to her." Lieutenant Wainright's orders barked angrily. "Pass the word to the gunners. Mr Columtree" – his voice was savage now at what he had to do – "you will personally see the girl and the men are underdecks before the false strakes drop or—"

He let the rest hang. The brig was still beyond long range when the *Resolve* put down her helm. She came clumsily through stays, slapping and surging. During this time Naomi had watched the skilful deception with burning eyes. Sure of easy victory, the men aft paid no attention to her. Now she moved carelessly towards the pinrail. Forward, the men of the destroyed *Alert* did likewise, milling protectively around Cherokee. The girl threw a sharp glance across the sea to where the unsuspecting brig piled canvas to the morning sky, her lean hull dark beneath. Then she raised her arm, a quick fierce signal. Instantly, she seized a heavy pin from its seat, racing to the starboard bulwark. Forward, Cherokee had done the same. And the rest happened with a startling suddenness.

Almost together they brought their heavy irons slamming down against the tripping gear that held the false white strakes in place against the frigate's hull. Somewhere a hoarse voice bellowed warning. Mr Columtree spun on his heel, crying rage. But he was too late. The restraining ropes, released, skirled through the fairleads. Squarely in the vision of the onrushing brig the broad disguising wood dropped with a banging clatter from her side, revealing at once her solid row of closed gunports, showing her unmistakably for what she was, a razeed man-o'-war, deadly and heavy armed.

Mr Columtree rushed to the break of the quarterdeck, drawing his pistol, roaring for a ship's corporal. The men of the *Alert* seemed undisturbed, Cherokee in their midst grinning sheer delight. And Naomi stood with her arms stiffly at her sides, her small fists clenched, her stare intent across the ocean space towards her brother's privateer. She heard Lieutenant Wainright cry down his second-in-command's murderous rage, but she paid no heed. Not until she saw the sudden flutter of those distant headsails; watched the brig stumble in her headlong rush into disaster; saw the big yards swing as Ira Barton, seizing the situation and its meaning instantly, wore his command sharp round upon her heel. Only then did she move her head.

"I must thank you for permitting me to warn the brig. You remember I told you I would."

He stared at her. "Do you mean you deliberately goaded me—"

"Do you suppose I would blurt out to you at Makapuu we meant to sail a sloop to the brig if I really intended to? I am not such a child as that. How would we find her in a small boat? No! We could never have reached the *Yankee Blade* that way – not in time. But I could make you *take* me to her. That," the girl cried, a wildness on her, "that I did!"

There was an instant of silence between them. Then: "I am almost glad." The lieutenant said this softly. "Now the action will be straightforward, the way action in a King's ship ought—"

"Action indeed!" Mr Columtree snarled a large disdain. "There is no disgrace in a brig eighteen refusing action with a frigate of forty-four! She runs like a stag! We will have to chase—"

"I think differently, Mr Columtree." Wainright could almost smile, now the weight of distasteful, and what he considered dishonourable, trickery against an inferiorly armed enemy was lifted from his shoulders. "The brig will know she stands alone between us and the annihilation of every Yankee whaleship in the southern sea. She—"

The girl cut in, her voice taut with strain: "Yes! He will return! He is a rash and headstrong man. He will sacrifice his brig. He will destroy himself!" The tension in her snapped. She hid her face in her hands, the long sobs racking her. "That is my brother over there. And you, Bruce, you are—"

She said no more. She turned away, rocking a little as she went. And the man in command of HMS *Resolve* was grateful he no longer had to look upon what her anguished eyes revealed. Speech, desire, trembled in him. He had no way of knowing how much longer he could clench it down. This lay between them, this dark and narrow gulf they must not bridge. Not now

– not facing the dreadful business presently in hand. He blinked; and when he spoke his voice was the naval voice, the grim, hard, autocratic voice of the quarterdeck.

"Mr Vandershort! You will see the prisoners safe in the cable tier." He spun sharply on his heel, discarding the distasteful coat to reveal plainly the naval uniform and all the naval lace. "Beat to quarters, Mr Columtree! Cut the towing tubs adrift! Release that larboard strake. Gunports wide! Sheet home the t'gallants. Put the royals on her. Topmen aloft!" His eyes snapped to his upper spars, then hard at his sailing-master. "Steer her small, Mr Gaines! He will want the weather gauge. I doubt we can beat him to it. We shall see!"

THE rattle of the drums took charge, crackling through the ship. The white St George's ensign and all the battle flags snapped smartly to the peak and trucks. Naomi heard that sinister drum chatter, felt the throat-catching impact of it, the tempo of quick excitement running like a flame along the deck. She found Cherokee moving along beside her down the gangway, his eyes burning, his nostrils aflare like an old war-horse hearing the battle bugles blow. And the survivors of the *Alert*, growling elation because they had saved the brig from surprise. But Naomi felt no elation. She knew her brother Ira, who commanded the *Yankee Blade*; she knew the will and passion that lived like steel and powder in that man. And she knew Bruce Wainright and what the gunfire meant behind his smouldering eyes.

Along the battery deck the powder boys stood ready at the gangways. The gunners were stripped to the waist, hauling the breeching tackles of the heavy guns; the shot racks full; matches dripping into the swabbing tubs. She remembered these quick visions with a violence of clarity, and the last sight she had of the *Yankee Blade* clouded under canvas in the brilliant sun, rushing away to the east with her signal halyards full to warn disperse-ment to the helpless whaling ships. But in the dank and gloomy cable tier there was nothing to see but the glittering eyes of her compatriots. Silence was down here and hard breathing. Silence and the noise of the rushing sea against the heavy plank. Silence and timbers groaning as the ship went tautly on the wind. Cherokee put an arm awkwardly about her heaving shoulders. But he kept his wrinkled stare upon an oaken knee as if he thought, looking there in fascinated concentration, he might hear familiar sounds to reveal and interpret how the dreadful battle went.

But on the quarterdeck of HMS *Resolve* the action took a clear and precise shape. The frigate stumbled no longer in manoeuvre. Deception and trickery were at an end. With that need no longer on him, the weary look of irresolution dropped from Wainright's weathered face. His ship showed colours, guns, battle flags, all the trappings of her trade in honest view. Against courageous men, anything less than this touched dishonour; it could hold no glory for a Yorkshire man. Now he could stand erect, doing full honour to the cloth he wore, keenly judge the battle space, test the strength and temper of the weather, gauge the method of his antagonist. Deep within him there was still another pride. The girl with the yellow hair had caught at opportunity; carried it through with daring skill. He was almost grateful. Perhaps an English girl might have done as much; she could have done no better. At any other time Lieutenant Wainright would have smiled. But now there was this business to attend.

The HMS *Resolve* reached west of north, lifting the sunburnished head of Makapuu again as she hunted the weather gauge well clear of the southern reef. Distantly the brig's signal buntings dropped, snapped aloft, shot down once more. The whaling fleet scattered; the last royal dropped below the rim of the sea. Then, like a cock quail perched on a farmer's fence rail who will not move until his brood is across the open dust and safely in the brush, the headsails of the little privateer flushed red with sunfire as she came about. Taking the starboard tack on a narrowly converging course she, too, rushed to the west of north.

Watching how her bow wave grew, Mr Columtree could

grunt: "We have a hawk to sail against! By God, sir, you are right! She means to accept the action!"

Lieutenant Wainright said nothing, quietly gauging the sea-room left him between the lee shore of Owheehee and the tumbling reef.

The facts, the necessities of the situation walked with calm clarity through his alert brain now. He had his enemy heavily outgunned; she had him as heavily outsailed. She had the weather gauge, could hold it, retaining choice of battle space. He could not force the action, must accept it as she chose. Against a heavier, or even an equal, opponent there would be worry in that land under his lee with the reef to the south and a hawk to keep him penned. His grey, gunpowder eyes were level, but wildfire raced across his brain. If he were that swallow there against the eagle's claws, his instinct told him, he would board. With speed. With brilliant daring. At once! There would lay the only hope of victory.

"Ready about!" – He would test that thing! – "Lay her east!"

The heavy ship came smartly through her stays. Wainright kept his eyes glued on his antagonist, a small brig with twin pyramids of canvas dwarfing a dark hull. Instantly she hauled her wind aft, holding her distance but running astern instead of meeting the opposite tack to lose the precious gauge. His eyes began to glow. There, then, was a seaman who knew his trade! Why not? It was Captain Ira Barton who was a Salem man, and Wainright had some knowledge of the Salem breed.

"Ready about!" he snapped again. "Steer small!"

The privateer hauled up as before and at once. She cruised the bottle's neck. And knew it! The hard dry glitter set in the lieutenant's eyes. Now he knew the temper, the capacity of his enemy. "Trice up the nettings, Mr Columtree! Prepare to repel boarders, Mr Vandershort. Pike and cutlass. Stand to!" The commander knew the vital, deadly effect of the first heavy broadside correctly used. "Hold fire till the word is passed!"

The shrill whistles piped. Bare feet raced the sanded decks to stations. The topmen braced themselves aloft. Hands sweated on the musket holds. Eyes flamed with the suppression of excitement, the hot unbearable tension of courage and down-clenched fright, of unspoken hope, of still resolve, of some dear human memory crystal-clear in that instant before action and death and glory burst its flaming torrent overhead and the gods of battle did their will with those the gods alone would choose in grim, ironic jest. Till that feeble little brig took aft her wind, choosing her moment now. She stood down with her eyes aboil, her hawspipes dripping brine like gore. And that way the fevered tension lay, stillness mounting like a living thing across the sea and in the ships at war.

"Ease helm, Mr Gaines." How loud, how commonplace the commander's words could sound! Like a fateful, hollow echo in a hollow, empty ship. "In royals. T'ga'ns'ls in the gear. Steady . . . *Steady!*"

So she waited for explosion and gunfire off the head of Makapuu, ponderously rolling, the seawash strong. Sure. Undisturbed. She had the weight and pride of Empire to sustain her at her back. She had Drake, Hawkins, Nelson; fabulous sea fighting giants with the seadogs' eye to stand in shadowy assistance on that uneasy quarterdeck. But the little brig came down against tradition's heavy weight, against deadly armament. She flew down boiling, gallant, foolhardy, the young Yankee ensign taut. What did *she* have, so willingly to spring against death's obliterating jaw? Little enough. A dangerous dream, a new nation's hope, a vision of human freedom pulsing in that hidden place where some men know for sure the spirit lives. As little as this there was to give her sustenance in moments before men knew they were about to die.

She closed the range with appalling speed. The blocks knocked out along the battery of HMS *Resolve*, and the depression screws worked lower, preparing for destructive, point-blank fire before the enemy closed to board; the gunners lay their gleaming eyes along the dispart sights. On the quarterdeck Mr Columtree cried out, "She yaws!" And scornfully: "At range a quarter-mile?"

A bloom of gushing smoke blotted her bow; an instant later the solid crash of a single gun smashed the expectant stillness to ribbons. The shot fell short – a ranging gun. Still Lieutenant Wainright frowned. That geyser in the sea was most astonishingly close! Her bow swung on again, but did not hold. She moved part of her port battery to bear. A trickle of doubt about her started upward along the commander's spine, that trickle in him growing as he watched, gushing upward to his brain, exploding there. The brig did not intend to board, but only make it appear she would! The dark shape of a man hung halfway up her after shrouds, growing in stature till his arm flung down. A single gun of her larboard battery lashed flame and smoke, testing the range again.

In a man forward the tension snapped. "Blasted Yankee pointers!" he shrilled. "Do they think—"

The explosion rocked across the brilliant sea. A humming sounded in the air. The man's voice ended in a scream of agony and was still. The heated shot crashed splinters from the bulwark opposite. They were outranged! In that bitter moment Wainright knew for certain the brig's strategy for the first blow had outwitted him.

"Starboard gunners, Mr Columtree!" Wainright's voice was harsh. "Lay her—"

The brig's broadside, bearing full, smashed with a single mighty roar. The smoke belched upward over her in enormous clouds. The shot sang insanely, then tore at solid oak. The British battery answered. But the range and point was new, unexpected. The fire came ragged. She luffed, ponderously – and as she did, the quarterdeck could see the brig's yards swing above the yellow smoke as she hauled sharp round to check her overrun and bring her starboard battery to rock new echoes from the cliffs of Owheehee. Then she took her wind abaft the beam and, leaning deeply, shot away beyond the range of Mr Columtree's beloved guns.

THIS was the pattern of her audacious battle plan. Taking full advantage of her speed and her most expert gunnery, she stood off to swab and reload in safety, dancing on the sunlit sea as momentarily the battle smoke went clear.

The surprise of that first hammer blow could never be repeated, but it had served its purpose well and she had delivered it almost unscathed. The first dead dotted the deck of HMS *Resolve*, the first wounded were being carried to the cockpit below. And the mizzen mast, swaying, sent the topmen wildly sliding to the deck before it rolled down with a rending crash, carrying main tophamper with it.

"Cut away that blasted raffle!" roared red-faced Mr Columtree. Then he swung around, flinging his arm to windward. "He fights his ship flying all his highest kites, that ragamuffin there!"

He referred to Ira Barton, still hanging hooked in the brig's main shrouds. He had a pipe between his teeth; he wore a flaming flannel shirt and a battered, shapeless, grey felt hat; and he looked as if he had just caught casual sight of the spout of a pod of whales instead of the drooling guns of a British man-o'-war.

Now distantly he took his brig through the eye of the wind once more, bearing her east by south to keep the frigate penned between the peak of Makapuu and the southern reef while he himself ran free. Lieutenant Wainright's eyes were burning. The fever of battle touched him. But there was admiration there, a twinge of regret behind relentless blue-grey eyes that men like these were enemies.

"Hold the larboard fire!" He wondered if these calm and quiet words were really his. "Mr Gaines! Lay me close aboard."

It was a master's mate who answered; Mr Gaines was not in sight. And the little brig flew down, all her lofty, sunshot canvas reaching to the sky. Once more her lean hull sheathed itself in flame and smoke, winging death across an empty space. The frigate took dreadful punishment to close effective range. Then her overpowering broadside spoke, rocking in one convulsive roar. This time her heavy guns bit deep. The drifting smoke poured over her. Rifting here and there, it revealed the brig's scuppers trickling red. Hulled in half a dozen places, tatters of torn gear streaming aloft, her lower canvas gap gaping, she stumbled away, leaving what destruction she could behind. But still she kept on coming down. Again and again she limped off, her functional loveliness maimed and broken, only to work through stays and bear doggedly down once more: the swallow against the hawk – the terrier against the wounding, crippling lion's claws.

Lieutenant Wainright clenched his fists. Through the stinking smoke of battle he could still see Captain Ira Barton leaning above his narrow quarterdeck with one arm idly hooked around a shroud. Strange compulsion came upon him, to scream out to that gaunt and tattered shape comfort and some reassurance. As a man would to another he found he could admire . . . Strike! Strike, you gallant fool! You cannot tear a King's frigate forty-four apart, with bare hands. Not with that look shining behind your stony eyes! You want guns for that. Guns! And we've the guns. I have no stomach for the murdering of honest men. Strike! You can do no more. You have already done enough! . . . This urge welled chokingly in Wainright's chest; he could barely fight it down.

But all the time he knew that brig would never strike that tattered, starry ensign from its place – he knew it by the careless look which that young seaman in a shapeless hat could hold while his ship splintered apart beneath his very feet.

"By my eyes!" Wainright heard his second-in-command bellow this echo to his thought, sudden admiration torn from Mr Columtree against his will. "He could have sailed with Nelson, that ragged whaler there!"

So went that famous action off the head of Makapuu, in view of whitely marching trade clouds while the sun climbed steadily and the ocean heaved with a vast, indifferent disdain. Down below, in the cable tier of HMS *Resolve* the shuddering impacts came like a mad convulsion of the sea. Down there one man kept growling incoherent rage; and when the still spaces came he sobbed and was abruptly still – till the thunder roared once more and the ship heeled down to the cannonade. Then he took his meaningless shouting up at once, knowing the brig must be, miraculously, still afloat. They heard the smashing roar of wreckage overhead, the rumbling gun carriages, the dull crying, the muffled screams.

Cherokee Sam Slade just stared, his eyes wild and wide on emptiness.

"Her mizzen – by the board." The old harpooner growled hoarse and broken words. To himself and no one else. "That would be Ira's master gunner. Caleb Brown has a keen, grey pointer's eye."

But Naomi Barton kept her fine head bowed, her chin upon her chest, only her shoulders moving now and then "A brig, Cherokee." She kept repeating this over and over in a dull tone. "Ira's feeble brig eighteen against a heavy frigate forty-four. It's Ira and Bruce. Ira and Bruce!"

When the final stillness came, it was a thing to be given no credence or trust. They looked at each other – quick, questing glances out of shining eyeballs. In a moment more the guns would surely roar. But this time the silence held. Like a stillness ultimate and absolute. The hurricane lamp splashed yellow light and weird shadows over the hawser fakes. Then a heavy tread sounded; the gangway opened; a gruff voice spoke words of doom in a booming, hollow cave: "You may come on deck."

No one stirred. They remained where they were, like people entranced. They took no belief in the substance of that voice, till it repeated itself, an echo that came too late: "You may come on deck!"

Cherokee Sam's leonine head gave way at last. His voice grated brokenly.

He said, "She is gone."

And Naomi Barton sobbed: "She is destroyed!"

They followed the powder-grimed marine in silence where the battle lanterns smoked, hearing sounds from the cockpit it is better for men soon to forget. Till they reached the sight of heaven and the shambled deck of HMS *Resolve*. Here they stopped suddenly at what met their eyes. The frigate's deck was a welter of confusion and rubble, gun-carriages askew, her woodwork splintered, her mizzen mast a jagged stump, her mainmast severed at the top, foregear streaming ragged in the wind as the heavy ship rolled down. Grotesque shapes spotted the sanded oak, oddly blotched. There was nothing left of Mr Vandershort except a cocked midshipman's hat tipped against a dismounted carronade as if someone had idly tossed it there. He would never wiggle his boy's fingers any more in his breeches belt to hear his dirk chains clink. And far aft Mr Columtree still stood amidst the wreckage of the quarterdeck, Lieutenant Wainright towering beside him. He was crying out across a narrow space of sea.

Crying? Odd! And to whom?

Cherokee moved his head. "The brig! She floats!"

Now they saw her plainly. She was such a sight upon the heaving swell as men could not forget. A broken cheer started welling from a dozen throats; froze suddenly and died away.

For the brig was completely dismasted. Two jagged stumps stood above her broken deck, littered with rubble and inert dots. Her wheel was splintered. Her hull looked black against the violence of sunlit blue. The sea took hold of her, lifted her a little, then dropped her in a pool of foam, making a loud, clear, gushing noise. She was down by the head, her shattered bowsprit heel afloat. No wonder the Yankee men no longer had the heart to cheer. But they could move aft, compelled that way by what they saw and heard.

Two men stood aft in that maimed and dying ship, chaos all around them, the brazen sky aloft, a tattered ensign bearing fifteen stars and fifteen stripes nailed to a whipstaff lashed to the mainmast stump. One of them stolidly chewed on a cud of Salem twist, holding a boarding-cutlass in his hand. The other was lean and tall and narrow-shaped. His face was angular and bony, as if built up of little teakwood blocks catching highlights where the sun had weathered its crags a deeper hue. He wore a flannel shirt, and on his head a battered old felt hat. He had a Massachusetts squirrel gun loosely by the barrel in his big brown fist, the carved butt at his feet.

The men and Naomi moved aft; they moved in silence,

urgently drawn closer to that man: He had such strength in him, and that look imperious. And then they heard a sharp New England drawl sounding on the north-east trade, the voice of home, giving purpose and meaning to death and gunfire off the head of Makapuu.

"This ship" – he said it with a clearness that was firm and absolute – "this ship will strike to no craft afloat!"

"Who asks your ship to strike?" they heard Lieutenant Wainright roar in a strange and sudden thrust of pride. "You have saved your convoy and the whole Pacific whaling fleet! We could not chase or take a shallop now, the shape your brig has put me in. The best we can do is work down Kaiwi Channel under jury rig to refit or interne in Honolulu Bay. Who in blazes asks your colours down? You have fought your ship to glory and—"

"I do not fight for glory, sir, but for what things men must!"

Ira Barton stirred at something that caught the corner of his eye. On the forecastle head of HMS *Resolve* a stunned seaman staggered to the broken rail, the cannonade still ringing in his half-deaf ears. Seeing still the colours of his enemy, his arm thrust out instinctively, the pistol cocked. On the sinking hulk the man in the shabby hat moved with a quick, unhurried ease, the squirrel gun discharged at his hip. The seaman's pistol exploded upward harmlessly, leaving him to stand with a look of puzzled bewilderment at his suddenly bloodied arm.

"Cease firing!" bellowed Mr Columtree, his red face smeared with powder-smoke. "Blast you all! Cease firing for'ard or—"

"*Bruce!*"

Naomi cried out the commander's name in a wild alarm, her fist at her mouth. Cherokee looked sharply at her, then across the sea space between the ships of war. He saw a wounded Yankee gunner on the poop of the broken brig drag himself painfully to one knee. Roused by the renewed sound of firing, that man saw the British quarterdeck through blurring eyes, and all the British naval lace. Towards it his cocked musket pointed, the muzzle trembling with the intensity of his final will.

"Bruce!"

Cherokee sprang instantly in front of her, thrusting her away, a low growl in his throat. He took the narrow ladder in a single leap. He hurled himself in front of Wainright, having time for nothing else. That musket flashed; the shot crashed out; then the Yankee gunner collapsed, his arms sprawled wide, his weapon clattering.

The impact of the ball staggered the old harpooner. But he held his feet, stumbling to the rail. Here he dragged himself upright, hanging on. And that way he stood when Naomi reached him, a wild pride in his wrinkle-pocketed eyes commanding her to silence. Because he understood this thing at last, and all the puzzlement was gone. Here was the meaning of the cutlass wounds of '81, the long anguish, the throat-catching glory he had felt but never quite made out. Now it lay revealed, with a blinding clarity as sharp as pain. It was in the look of that ragged master, erect on the shattered deck of a foundering little brig with an old felt hat on his head and a smoking gun held idly in his fist.

"He has a navy," Cherokee could growl, "a navy and a nation in his eyes!"

He hung on, severely frowning, hearing Lieutenant Wainright's voice.

"The brig sinks beneath your feet! Damn it, man! Bring your wounded clear."

"There is no boat."

"Longboat away!" Mr Columtree roared it out to cover what unwilling admiration stirred in him. "Blast you! Have we no sailors left? Longboat! Longboat away!"

So they came over, the wounded, the man who calmly chewed on a cud of Salem twist, and Captain Ira Barton. Those two stood in the sternsheets with their weapons in their hands, a stained cutlass and a Massachusetts squirrel gun, symbolizing no surrender, symbolizing no defeat, their ensign still left lashed to a whipstaff fished to the mainmast stump of a fighting brig called *Yankee Blade*. The boat bumped the ponderous side of HMS *Resolve*. Ira started up the ladder for the entry port.

And when he did the prisoners of the destroyed *Alert* moved together toward, the rail. They moved out of instinct. They gave it no conscious thought. Some inner urge alone impelled them. They could think of nothing else except to stand there in a silent, ragged, respectful cluster when a shipmaster out of Salem stepped the deck.

Mr Columtree saw them. His face flushed a deeper red. He blinked his eyes, and then he set his naval hat aright. "Dress ship!" his gruff voice rasped. "Where's a blasted drummer boy? Have we no bosun left? Or at least a bosun's mate to pipe the whistle when a naval captain comes on board!"

So the English whistles shrilled and an English boy with a bloody face gave the long dry ruffle on the drum to honour Ira Barton when he reached the planks of oak. He stopped there an instant, looking quietly around.

"Hello, Joel," he drawled to one of the tattered side boys. "Good to see you, Ned," he told another. "I left your woman and the babe both well." Then he touched his hand to an eye in salute to the quarterdeck. "Your disguising, false sheer strakes, sir," he drawled dryly to the commander of HMS *Resolve*. "Very neat! But you released them a little too soon. Otherwise we—"

"It was your sister, Captain Barton. She cleverly goaded me into bringing her aboard a King's ship so she could give you warning as she did."

Ira came towards Naomi, dragging his gun butt along the deck. Cherokee still clung to the rail, pain taut along his wrinkled cheek. He was watching the look in Lieutenant Wainright's eyes, seeing that man too come walking towards the girl. He sagged a little, as if his legs were leaden now.

"Cherokee," he heard her say in her throaty voice, "Cherokee, why—"

It came clearer. The gathering mists no longer troubled him. "There was a high-breasted girl with chestnut hair," he growled, something like a smile behind his stubborn eyes. "I remember now! How we once walked straightway towards each other, as if we both knew all at once—"

He stopped on that, moving his head with a slow and grave deliberation. He sighed. How lovely this ocean, how warm and sweet the pleasant north-east trade. Now the stillness after gunfire seemed intense, the burbling sea and the wind's low moan inordinately loud as the crippled frigate surged off the sunshot head of Makapuu. That way the silence held while they watched a battered, mastless little brig quickly settling, beginning her last long slide with all the light of heaven on her. Cherokee thought he heard voices: The British commander's English tone, and Ira Barton's drawl. They really sounded much the same, he thought.

"You, sir" – that was the tall lieutenant, no mistake – "you have a familiar North Sea look. Like kin of my own at home. You have the look of a Yorkshire man."

"It can hang on. Our grandfather came from the wolds of York. But we" – the Yankee captain said this hard and firm – "we are Salem men!"

"There ought to be room in a place like that for one more Salem man."

Some brittle thing quickly slipped past Ira Barton's lips. "There is no more room in Salem for an Englishman than there was in Boston Harbor for excised English tea!"

Cherokee frowned. That was the steel and powder that lived and burned in Ira Barton's heart. It wasn't right, he thought. Men from the wolds of York should not be enemies. He ought to tell them! But he found he couldn't, for the lieutenant's voice reached to him like a sound from very far away. "But I am speaking of Americans, Captain. Surely there would be room in Salem town and in a Salem ship for another one. And for his wife. After the wars are done."

Presently Cherokee would smile at that. But not yet. The old harpooner's apple-wrinkled face took on a look of concentrated effort. There was a thing he had to see before the darkness closed. He watched for it with utmost care. Now there! That ragged ensign flying still, taut and close above the lipping foam.

He reached out, in silence pointing to it. He saw it pluck under, but it didn't matter; he was certain it would lift again another time and in another place.

"The whaling fleet, sir!" he said, going slowly down. He meant much more than that. He meant shabby Continentals, freezing at Valley Forge. He meant bearded men from the Chesapeake, dying with Hull and Porter and John Paul Jones. He meant the look of Salem Quay and Massachusetts Bay. He meant the flame kept bright in darkness, signalling men some promise and a little hope. But words were difficult for Cherokee to find and form. No matter. Words were unimportant while men like Ira Barton lived. The time was short. This would have to do: "The Yankee whaling fleet," he said with firm and stubborn emphasis, "the Yankee whaling fleet is safe."

THE GUNS OF THE *GHOST*

Charles Partington

We first encountered Jack Gallant in "Gallant's Gamble" in my earlier anthology The Mammoth Book of Sword and Honour. *The following story takes place about a year before the events described there. Charles Partington (b. 1940) is a printer by profession who has been writing short stories for over thirty years.*

The north-westerly finally blew itself out after raging unabated for close on thirty-six hours. When the sea subsided and while Old Eashal slept, Jack Gallant made what repairs he could to their hurriedly lashed-together raft.

Their ship, the post office packet *Bonny Mary*, bound for Gibraltar and a rendezvous with units of the Mediterranean Fleet, had suddenly foundered in the teeth of the shrieking storm. Gallant and Old Eashal, both pressed deckhands, had managed to survive. The rest of the crew and its officers had all perished. Now they were alone and adrift in the Atlantic without food or water.

Gallant was used to being alone, accustomed to fending for himself. He was as inured to hardship as any eighteen-year-old could be. A big-framed youth, he was already taller and stronger than most full-grown men. A desperately hard upbringing had toughened his sinews and put raw strength in his muscles. His stone-grey eyes watched life dispassionately, though when anger flared in them, few would attempt to stare him down. He had high cheekbones, a strong jaw and an easy smile that revealed a set of fine white teeth. A head full of glistening, slightly curled, black locks grew down to the wide collar of his frayed linen shirt, which was soaked through by spray and fastened by a plaited leather thong. Gallant had learned from bitter experience never to despair, never to anticipate. He was content just to endure. And if possible, survive.

Gallant was still working with the lashings when Eashal suddenly dragged himself to a sitting position on the raft, groaning with cramp. It lacked an hour till dawn and the sky was almost as black as the sea, but the old man's eyes became fixed on the indeterminate horizon.

"Jack!" he gasped, pointing. "Look over there! Are me old eyes a'playin' tricks, or is that a ship I see?"

Gallant lifted his head, staring hard in the direction Eashal was pointing. He saw nothing at first. Then at the extreme edge of visibility, where sea and sky merged into infinity, he saw a trembling mote. "There's nothing wrong with your eyesight, Eashal. That's a ship all right!"

Hope flared in Eashal's eyes. "Right, son, pick up that oar, and start paddling," he demanded. "If we lose her, we may not get another chance . . ."

As the distance between them shortened, it became apparent that the ship was carrying no sail and was heaved to, probably running a sheet anchor.

"Looks like she's been involved in action recently," Eashal remarked. "Most of her spars and rigging's been shot away." His craggy face wrinkled as he thought through the possibilities. "But why haven't the crew run up a temporary rig?"

"Maybe there's no one on board," Gallant suggested. "Could be a derelict. Maybe she's a plague ship and everyone's dead."

Eashal growled uncomfortably. Like most blue-water men, the old man had a superstitious dread of the unknown or the inexplicable.

Details of the wallowing hull steadily became clearer. "What

kind of ship is it?" Gallant strained his eyes, fervently hoping
she was a merchant vessel. "Maybe she's an East Indiaman."

"She's no trader," Eashal observed, rubbing at his whiskers.
"I'd say she's a ship-of-the-line. A two-decker for sure and
either a seventy-four or an eighty-gun third-rater."

"A naval ship?" Gallant knew they were facing the prospect
of almost certain conscription again. Still, he reflected, *any*
seaworthy vessel was preferable to their slowly sinking raft.

"You'd just better hope she's one of ours," Eashal noted.
"Till we know for sure, it might be best to approach her real
cautious like. Don't go a-whoopin' an' a-hollerin' when we get
within callin' distance. If she *is* a French-crewed ship, any
marines on board her are as likely to use us as target practice as
help save our skins."

Gallant nodded silently. Ex-soldiers hanging round the Cin-
que Ports all rumoured that the land war was going well in
Europe, that the allied forces were preparing to march on Paris.
Yet at sea, France's navy remained a running sore despite the
English fleet's growing superiority.

Anxious not to make even the slightest noise in the dim light,
they paddled ever closer to the silently drifting hull, praying
they wouldn't be noticed by anyone standing up on deck or
staring out of the stern gallery windows.

"Look!" Eashal pointed at the elaborately carved prow, his
superstitious nature momentarily reasserting itself.

Gallant could see the figurehead clearly now. It took the form
of a wraith-like woman, her long hair streaming back from her
elegantly spectral face, her hands reaching towards the horizon.
Emblazoned below was the ship's name, the *Ghost*. As if to
accentuate Eashal's accumulating terrors, a faint, discontinuous
moaning and wailing could be heard from low down inside the
ship's hull, a distressing noise like the clamouring of tormented
souls.

Gallant could see the fear and apprehension on Old Eashel's
face. "It'll be the crew," he said, reassuringly. "What else could
it be?"

The port side of the hull showed minimal damage from

cannon-fire, though shrouds and ratliness and other bits of rigging trailed down below the waterline. Clearly, gaining entrance to the *Ghost* was not going to be difficult.

But as they prepared to scramble off the raft, Eashal let out a curse and began hauling on one of the sunken lines. With a swirl of bubbles, something came bobbing up to the surface. Entangled in the line was a body. The English naval uniform identified the dead man as a ship's officer. The mouth had dropped open in a spasm of agony and the eyes were blank and staring. Eashal pulled the bloated corpse alongside the raft, inspecting it closely, turning it over in the water. Gallant watched the grisly operation with dismal curiosity.

"This man was executed!" Eashal raged, unable to keep his voice below a whisper. "His hands are still bound and he was shot in the head at close range. Look, you can see powder burns around the entry wound. Blew the back of his skull clean out." He peered below the water. "Jack! There's another body snagged in the lines. What the hell's been happening here? Mutiny? Have *all* the officers been slaughtered?"

Gallant cautioned Eashel to lower his voice, unless he wanted to end up like these unfortunate souls. "Take it quietly and carefully," he whispered.

Stepping off the raft, Eashel began clambering up the entangled rigging towards the lower rungs of the entry port ladder. Gallant took a deep breath and followed, trusting the old man's judgment that they were doing the right thing. Just below the open gunports, they paused for a moment, listening intently. Yet no one came to stare down at them.

"Right, wait there a minute!" Gallant whispered, setting off up the ladder again.

"Where you going, boy?"

"See if I can find out what's happening."

"Well, watch what you're doing," Eashal grumbled. "You'll like as not get us both killed."

Reaching the top of the ladder, Gallant carefully raised his head high enough to peer between the deck rail supports. Eashal's guess had been right. Considerable damage had been inflicted amidships, mainly to her starboard side. The masts, sails and rigging had all been carried away by cannon-fire. Lamps were glimmering on the quarterdeck and a group of figures were drinking and conversing in the light spilling through the open door of the master cabin. He knew a few words of French, enough to recognize the language when he heard it spoken. Eashal's insistence on caution looked like timely advice now. Ducking his head below the rail, he set off back down the ladder.

He only got as far as the main gun deck, when a hand reached out from the nearest open port and grabbed hold of his jerkin. Eashal's gaunt face popped into view. "In here!" the old man urged in a whisper. Gallant nodded. Swinging across on the tangled ratlines, he crawled in beside him.

There he stopped, rooted to the spot, staring in amazement. Shafts of blood-red light from the rising sun were streaming through the open ports of the gun deck, illuminating the gleaming barrels of a row of massive thirty-two-pounder cannon. He gazed dumbstruck at the gaping muzzles, trying hard to imagine what the ear-shattering noise and fury would be like when these huge, heavy-calibre weapons fired in anger.

Immediately behind the guns, running along the middle of the deck from the bows to the stern, was a flimsy screen made of bits of wood and scraps of canvas. Forced to eat and sleep in the cramped spaces between the guns, the port crews stored their rolled-up hammocks and personal possessions in drawbags hanging from nails hammered into the screen supports on one side, while the starboard crews did the same on other side.

"You goin' to stand there gawping all mornin', boy?" Eashal hissed. "Or might you consider telling me what you saw up there?"

Gallant shivered, banishing the image from his mind. "I saw Frenchies up on deck, Eashal, just like you figured I would. Looks like they've got control of the ship."

Eashal nodded. "Must be a prize crew. Probably executed all the *Ghost*'s officers, then banged her crew up in the hold. Well, we've got to get our boys out of there, Jack. Then we'll give those murderin' French scum a taste of their own medicine. But how're we going to do it? The Frenchies must have posted guards around the hatchway. There's only two of us and we ain't got even so much as a pistol or cutlass between us."

The young man thought for a while, remembering tales he'd heard from sailors. "What do sailors fear most when they're at sea?"

Eashal's face drained of its colour. Gallant could tell from his expression he was thinking of the nameless demons of the deep, but all Eashal could bring himself to say was, "Drowning . . . I guess."

Gallant shook his head. "No, not drowning, Eashal. Or denizens of the depths. Not by a long shot . . ."

Eashal's eyes narrowed as he wondered at Gallant's plan, but followed him as he crept quietly along the gun deck, halting at the central hatchway. Carefully, both men peered into the echoing space of the orlop deck. There were no ports or windows down there. Lanterns, swinging from the ceiling struts, added to the faint light filtering down the ladderway. A group of four French sailors were seated on low benches, playing cards on an upturned barrel. Their conversation was a mixture of cursing declamations and slurred banter. Clearly, all had been drinking heavily. As the ship tilted in the light swell, empty rum bottles rolled and rattled across the deck. Nearby, three more men, snoring soundly, were sprawled in an untidy heap across a stack of spare sails. Every man on the orlop deck carried a pistol at his belt. Muskets fitted with long bayonets lay within easy reach.

Jack Gallant watched, grim-faced. When the cries of the English crew imprisoned in the hold grew too loud for their captors' ears, a pistol barrel was thrust through the hatch grating and a shot fired off indiscriminately. All the Frenchmen laughed. Gallant had seen enough. He drew his head back, his grey eyes glittering with anger. "Is this the only way on to the orlop deck, Eashal?" he whispered.

"'Course not. There's another stairway towards the bows

and one at the stern. An' in between there's a couple of ancillary hatches without stairways just for the loading of supplies."

Both men froze for a moment as the sound of several pairs of booted feet, clattering along the deck above their heads, re-verberated through the ceiling planking. Gradually, the foot-steps grew fainter and voices, raised in discordant caterwauling, faded with them.

Gallant went over to the nearest gun. Pushing aside the jury-rigged table, he began rummaging around in the crew's draw-bags, dragging out and discarding spare woollen shirts and socks, canvas jerkins, linen coats, even lengths of twine and small tools. Everything was discarded with grunts of disap-pointment.

Eashal scratched his head, then grabbed Gallant by the arm. "What the hell are you looking for, Jack?"

Gallant turned on him impatiently. "For anything that will give off a lot of smoke without bursting into flame."

"You're goin' to try and smoke 'em out?"

Gallant nodded. "If they're half as drunk as they seem to be, I'm guessing they'll panic and think the ship's on fire. Their first thought will be to get the hell out of there. In the confu-sion, we may be able to get the hatch open and get our men out."

Eashal scratched at one of his ears. "What about using a pitch-bucket?" he suggested. "That stuff belches smoke like the fires o' hell once it's alight. I guarantee, Jack, you won't be able to see a hand in front of your face down there after a minute or two."

"Perfect!" Gallant exclaimed. "Where can we get some?"

"Carpenter's stores up in the bows," Eashal replied and, with no more ado, led the way.

After forcing the door to the carpenter's storeroom, they chose two old metal buckets containing just a few inches of pitch, then tied lengths of rope to their handles. Carrying lighted tapers with which to ignite the pitch, both men returned to the gun deck. Jack Gallant took up his position near the aft ladderway, waiting for a moment to give Eashal time to reach the stern ladderway. Then he dropped the glowing taper into the bucket. Almost immediately the pitch caught fire, hissing and spitting and beginning to exude a plume of dense, acrid smoke. As the fire intensified and the smoke thickened, Gallant lowered the bucket down the ladderway.

When the rope went slack, indicating that the bucket of burning pitch was now resting on the deck, Gallant dropped the rope. To help him breathe, he pulled his handkerchief over the lower half of his face. Inevitably, some of the choking smoke was already beginning to rise up the ladderway but he could see that it was also having the desired effect down on the orlop deck.

Dense smoke was now billowing towards the French sailors from both ends of the ship. It took only a matter of seconds before the first questioning, uncertain cries came from the surprised Frenchmen. Followed moments later by screams of, "*Mon Dieu, feu! Flamme!*" Then the sounds of a great clattering and stampeding in the smoke-filled darkness as, coughing and gasping, they struggled drunkenly to their feet and began clambering to safety up the rungs of the midship's ladderway.

Jack Gallant had been waiting for just this opportunity. Taking a deep breath, he slithered down the rungs on to the orlop deck. There, he could hardly see a thing. Even filtered through his handkerchief, the fumes from the burning pitch irritated his lungs and his eyes streamed with tears. Even more smoke was being generated than Gallant had anticipated, yet so violent had been the blaze that the pitch had already almost exhausted itself. The lower half of the iron bucket was radiating a dull red glow, but apart from a little charring, the section of wooden decking below it showed no indication of bursting into flame.

Disoriented, but grimly resolute in his purpose, Jack Gallant began walking along the lower deck with outstretched hands until he saw something gleaming faintly through the smoke fog. It was one of the storm lanterns the Frenchmen had used to illuminate their card-game. His heart lifted. The hatch grating must be somewhere nearby. Lifting the lantern off its peg, he swung it across the floor, searching in every direction.

"Men of the *Ghost*!" he yelled raggedly, aware that the imprisoned crew should be able to hear him now. "Where are you? I'm English. I'm trying to get you out!"

This brought a sudden outcry of bawling and yelling from somewhere to his left. Following the direction of the sound, he reached the hatch cover. The faces of a dozen anxious men were pressed against the iron grating, with more crowded behind them.

The flickering lamplight revealed something of the terrible conditions. More than 150 miserable souls were crammed together in the confined space. Many were huddled on the tops of provision boxes and wooden casks in an effort to keep out of the stinking bilge water slopping about between the bulkheads. Some of the men were clearly in a bad way. Filthy bloodstained bandages had been wrapped around appalling wounds. Little else had been done to alleviate their suffering.

A thin-faced man, his bruised right eye wrapped in filthy strips of cloth, challenged him. "Who the 'ell are *you*, mister? What you doin' on the *Ghost*? Got a sniff of the treasure lyin' behind that bulkhead, 'ave you?"

"Shut up, Joe!" a voice hissed behind him.

"Treasure?" Gallant shook his head. "No, me and my shipmate, Eashal, we were shipwrecked in the storm and reached the *Ghost* on a raft. We—"

Someone growled urgently, "Never mind all that, friend. Just you hurry up and get us out of here before we burn to death!"

Gallant had been easing back the rusting lock-bolts. "You're not going to burn," he assured them, snapping the bolts free and swinging the grating clear of the hatch. "There's no fire." He reached down, grasping hands and arms, helping the first men climb out. "The smoke's just a decoy to get rid of the guards. But it won't fool them long. They'll be coming back soon as they realize it's a false alarm."

From somewhere in the smoke-filled darkness there came a metallic clanging and clattering, followed by a yell of pain and an instantly familiar voice complaining, "God damn it! Who put those there?"

"Eashal?" Gallant called out. "We're over here!"

"I *know* where you are, Jack!" the old man answered testily. "I'll be with you in a moment." There were more bangs and scufflings. Then a few seconds later, Eashal's familiar wrinkled face was revealed by the lamplight.

"Look what I tripped over, Jack!" the old man grunted. He was staggering under the weight of half a dozen muskets and a similar number of cartridge pouches, all abandoned by the guards during their pell-mell flight to the higher decks. "Thought we could make better use of them than the Frenchies." He dumped them on the deck. Those of the *Ghost*'s crew who had already climbed out of the hold eagerly started arming themselves.

A gun captain, a broad-backed heavily tattooed man with massive forearms, a shaven head and a neck like a bull, displayed a mouthful of metal-capped teeth as he grinned at Eashal. "Hey, pass me one of those firearms, old-timer. And make sure Tucker here gets one, too. He's the best shot on the boat." The gun captain ran a finger along the needle-like blade of the bayonet, his eyes glittering icily. "We'll find a use for these stickpins those bastards never anticipated Why, we'll—"

His sentence was never completed. At that moment a French seaman, clutching a lantern in one hand, came clattering down the midships ladderway to investigate the supposed spread of the flames. Instead, through the dissipating smoke, he saw the freed crewmen. He let out a yell of horrified alarm and tried to climb back to the gun deck, but the man named Tucker raised the barrel of his flintlock musket and squeezed the trigger. Tucker could hardly have missed. The Frenchman was killed instantly as the heavy ball smashed through his skull.

The English crew cheered appreciatively as the lifeless body of one of their tormentors slithered down the ladderway. But their joy was short-lived. The muzzles of several pistols appeared over the lip of the gun-deck hatch and a short barrage of hastily aimed shots was fired.

Down below, someone extinguished the storm lantern, plunging the orlop deck into uncertain gloom. The Englishmen scattered, seeking what cover they could behind the deck pillars or the mast heels, diving into the cable coils or crouching behind the massive anchor capstan. Fusillades of shots were now being exchanged. Powder flashes dazed the eyes and the explosive detonation of gunshots deafened the ears in that confined space. Lead shot whistled through the air, slamming into the deck planks or gouging deep holes in the inner hull cladding, sending splinters flying, ripping into unprotected flesh and producing howls of pain and anger.

The fight was of short duration. The French prize crew, comprising fewer than twenty men in total, were no match for the *Ghost*'s complement of over 150 furiously angry, maltreated sailors. A brief token resistance was offered, but it soon collapsed in a total rout. Unable to defend the approaches to the three ladderways and both loading hatches, the disordered Frenchmen frantically withdrew to the upper deck where half their number tried to delay the Englishmen long enough in a futile final stand, while the rest struggled to launch the only serviceable longboat. But when three of their number fell, killed outright by well-aimed musket balls, and four more collapsed with disabling wounds, the rest threw up their hands in surrender.

It wasn't difficult for the crew of the *Ghost* to decide what they were going to do with their French prisoners. After three of the more sadistic members of the prize crew had been given severe beatings, they were all marched below decks and locked in the hold, where they would be kept until they could be handed over to the appropriate authorities in England. The action was not without its irony.

Half starved after having been denied any proper rations for almost three days and restricted to drinking only rank-smelling water during their incarceration, the crew's first thought turned to satisfying their stomachs. Several barrels of biscuits, salt-pork and smoked fish were brought up from the purser's storeroom, which were washed down with copious amounts of rum and beer. Gallant and Eashal were equally hungry. So when the gun captain came up to where they were sitting on the scuttle combing and handed them each a wooden platter piled high with food and a large jug of beer, they fell to with relish.

"Looks like we're indebted to you two gentlemen for our freedom, temporary though it may well be," the gun captain said. He extended a huge hand.

Gallant grasped the hand warmly. "I'm Jack Gallant. And my shipmate here is Eashal Tillet."

"Jim Sayce," the big man responded. "Pleased to make your 'quaintance."

"Don't need no thanks, Mr Sayce," Eashal said, sniffing. He abhorred all displays of sentiment. "We only did what any Englishman would 'ave in the situation."

The gun captain nodded. He took a swig of his own beer, then wiped his lips. "Me and my mates, well, we've been wonderin' how you two got on board the *Ghost*."

"From a raft," Gallant explained. "Our ship sank during the storm. We were adrift for two nights and a day. If the wind and currents had taken us in another direction . . . Well, I guess we were just lucky."

"Lucky?" Jim Sayce glanced towards the horizon. "Maybe, gents. Maybe not."

"That don't sound too cheerin', Mr Sayce," said Eashal, spraying biscuits as he spoke.

"Ever heard of the *Princesse*?" he asked.

Jack and Eashal's expressions remained blank.

"Top o' the line French ship, around 140 guns. You may be makin' her acquaintance real soon."

"How so?" Eashal pressed.

"On account o' what we got stashed below decks."

Gallant studied Sayce carefully, recollecting a reference one of the crew had made earlier concerning treasure. For an instant he glanced at Eashal, who shook his head warningly. "Maybe you'd better start at the beginning?" Gallant suggested.

Sayce scratched his shaven, tattooed head, his glance wandering towards the horizon again. "Looks like we got time, gents." He held up a massive arm, waving his empty beer jug.

"Longman!" he yelled in a voice like a foghorn. "More beer, mate. And another bottle o' that rum."

Sayce shaded his eyes from the sun for a moment. "Three months ago, gentlemen, the *Ghost* was signed on under Admiralty letter for a voyage to South America. She was the junior member of a small flotilla that included two first-rate vessels, the *Lilac*, of 96 guns and the *Herald*, carrying 112 guns. Fine ships they were, good seasoned crews, though us lads on the *Ghost* were no embarrassment to the commodore, Sir Cecil James Rawden. All three ships had been placed under his command. His orders – as we found out later – were to proceed to the Gulf of Venezuela where we were to cruise the waters as far south as Cayenne for as long as the flotilla's provisions held out. We were supposed to engage any French squadrons we encountered and – wherever possible – relieve all commercial transports of any valuable cargoes."

Sayce gathered his thoughts for a moment, remembering. "In the very first week of our arrival, less than 2 miles outside the mouth of a great river – 'eard mention it was the Orinoco – we surprised a twenty-gun sloop flying the French colours." Sayce smiled. "She tried to run, o' course, but her crew were poor sailors and lackin' in spit. One broadside from the *Lilac* and that was enough; she pulled to and hauled down her colours. Well, Commodore Rawden sent a boat across and his officers discovered that she was carrying a fortune in gold and silver bullion. What none of us knew, or could have known, was that the sloop's master had arranged to rendezvous with the *Princesse*. A formidable vessel, the *Princesse*, large enough to outgun even the *Herald*. Seems her captain – the Count de Vaugelas or some-such – is a part-time corsair. Earned himself a reputation as a disreputable, vicious bastard by those who should know. A great captain, by all accounts, but a real bad lot.

"Anyway, before arrangements could be made to transfer the ingots into the *Herald*'s safe-keeping," Sayce said, shaking his head, "what should 'appen but the *Princesse* came sailing into view around the headland. Well her captain could see right away that he'd got the 'up' on us. Sitting ducks we was, with all sails furled and the bowers down. And you can be sure that Count de Vaugelas lost no time in engagin' us."

Sayce took a long swig from the rum bottle, then offered it round. "In all the confusion, the crew of the sloop overpowered the *Herald*'s small boarding party, cut loose and headed for cover towards the coastal fog banks. Commodore Rawden must 'ave been mad as 'ell to see his prize slipping from his grasp. Signalled us he did, orderin' the *Ghost* to give chase. Every man jack of us wanted to stay put and 'elp slug it out with the *Princesse*. But orders is orders, an' I suppose it made sense. We carried only eighty guns, with half o' them bein' Culverins, and we took the least draught. So I guess that the old man was right that the *Ghost* was more suited to follow the sloop into the uncharted shallows.

"Made for hazardous sailing though, I can tell you. But Cap'n Cragg obeyed his orders to the letter and gave chase. We stood off from the fog much as we could. Taking continual soundings. An' used the endless squawkin' of the parrots an' the hootin' and screamin' of the monkeys in the treetops to judge how far away the shore was. When the breeze dropped to a whisper, headway could be maintained only by 'aving the ship towed by both longboats. Eventually the noise of battle faded far behind us and the midday sun burned off the mist, yet we didn't see 'ide nor 'air of our quarry. But by late afternoon, as the breeze picked up again, Cragg's persistence paid off. We overhauled the sloop. She was stuck fast on a mud flat and every effort to refloat her 'ad failed. No doubt fearing reprisals, the crew abandoned her as the *Ghost* 'ove to. They fled into the jungle without firing a single shot."

Sayce laughed at the thought of how easy it had all been. He took another swig of rum and continued.

"So all we had to do was transfer the gold and silver ingots into the *Ghost*'s hold. Now this may surprise you, gen'lmen, but so heavy was the treasure that a fair part of our iron ballast and shingle had to be jettisoned just so the ship's trim could be maintained. Our purser reck'ned the value of the bullion at over £950,000."

He paused, savouring the amount and letting the reality of it settle.

"'Course, it presented Cap'n Cragg with a real dilemma," he continued suddenly. "Common knowledge it was that we could do one of two things. We could return to the mouth of the Orinoco to see how the battle had gone and see if our assistance was needed; or we could immediately set sail for home, to make sure that the bullion reached the coffers of the English treasury without further mishap. Must 'ave been an 'ard decision to make. Knowing that Commodore Rawden would support his decision, Cap'n Cragg ordered that we embark for England.

"We were barely a week into the voyage, when every soul on board was appalled to see the sails of the *Princesse* looming up behind us. She had either escaped from both our first rates or, more worryingly, had triumphed over them. A long chase ensued and a good run for the money we gave those French bastards. Twice we nearly got away. But in the end, the *Princesse* over'auled us and nearly blew us out of the water. Lost two of our masts in the first broadside. Nothin' could be done. We were forced to surrender. Count de Vaugelas sent a prize crew aboard us and we was banged up in the hold while Cap'n Cragg was took over to the *Princesse* on the pretext of making terms. Terms!" Jim Sayce spat venomously. "Can't make terms with scum like that!"

For a moment the gun captain's eyes were full of despair. "The seas were runnin' too high for the bullion to be transferred by longboat, so the French attempted to establish a tow line between the *Ghost* and the *Princesse*. The light was failing and the weather suddenly worsened, blowing up real savage. So fierce was the storm that both ships quickly found themselves in difficulty. The *Princesse*'s rudder snapped and both ships were driven apart in the growing darkness. Realizing that all they could do was sit tight and ride out the bad weather, the French prize crew deployed the *Ghost*'s sheet anchor and waited for the storm to blow itself out and the *Princesse* to return . . ." Jim Sayce sniffed, then gave Jack Gallant and Eashal a grim smile. "And that's one thing you can be sure of, shipmates. The

Princesse is coming back. Mark my words, she's a-hunting for us right now. There's no way her captain would contemplate turning his back on £950,000. 'Specially not after havin' chased us clear across the Atlantic."

Now Jack Gallant understood why the crew of the *Ghost* seemed so tense, why they cast frequent, anxious glances towards the horizon and why they continually fell into arguing among themselves over what should be done next. Around forty or so of the men wanted to rig up a jury mast and sails and make for England as quickly as possible, while the majority of the crew were clearly unhappy about abandoning Captain Cragg to the French without putting up a fight. Yet lacking any kind of even halfway feasible plan to rescue him, they were clearly at a disadvantage. More and more of the crew were siding with those who wanted to cut and run. Widespread dissatisfaction on both sides resulted in the outbreak of minor scuffles. Fuelled by the steady intake of liquor, these sporadic outbursts of unrest were growing more and more heated.

"Can't you do anything, Jim?" Gallant asked, turning to the gun captain. "The men seem to respect you; maybe you can get them to listen to reason."

"Ain't that easy, Jack," Sayce replied. "They're good men, all of 'em, but they're lost without authority being imposed on them from above. They need to be led. It's what they're used to. But they know me too well. They won't wear it coming from one of their own."

Gallant nodded. Taking a deep breath, he dragged the pistol out of Jim Sayce's belt. Then, before anyone could stop him, he leaped on to the fo'c'sle and fired a shot into the air. The loud report had the desired effect. Every one of the crew turned in surprise to look at the young stranger. For a moment an uncertain silence held sway.

"Listen, men," Gallant told them firmly. "All this arguing and fighting won't solve a thing. You've got to work together, agree to a plan that accommodates everyone's concerns. Then stick to it."

"Oh yeah?" a red-bearded man called out from where he was

leaning half slumped against the weather rail. "An' you got such a plan, mister?"

Gallant nodded. "Though it's not without risks."

"Not without risks?" The red-bearded man laughed cynically. "I get the idea that you're gonna suggest that we stick around until the *Princesse* shows up and take her on. If you think that a half-wrecked third rate can stand against one of the largest ships the French ever built, then you're crazy, mister!"

"Hear me out!" Gallant demanded, fixing his man with an icy stare.

Another member of the crew piped up. "Why should we? Reckon you look a bit fresh to be a-lecturin' us, sonny!"

"Hold on there, Peters!" Jim Sayce roared, standing up and shouldering men aside as he pushed his way through to the fo'c'sle ladder. "Jack here wasn't too fresh to spring us from the hold, was he?" the gun captain pointed out. "But for this lad's courage and presence of mind we'd all still be cooped up below. I say he's earned the right to be heard out!"

There were murmurs of assent.

Jack Gallant's plan relied on surprise and preparation. He deliberately kept his voice low while explaining what he had in mind, forcing the crew to pay attention to what he was saying. Some of the hands, he told them, would be required to start jury rigging a shortened foremast and bowsprit which would carry a forecourse and inner jib. These sails, once the sheet anchor had been raised, would allow a manoeuvre to be performed which was critical to the success of the exercise: the *Ghost* could be brought about very quickly. The Count de Vaugelas, naturally assuming that the English ship was still safely in the hands of his prize crew, would approach her with no suspicion of danger in his mind. Apart from a handful of men on watch, his gun crews and marines would be resting, most of them probably relaxing in their hammocks. The *Ghost* would look a sorry sight, at least the view he had of her. During the pursuit across the Atlantic, the third rate's starboard side had taken several heavy broadsides from the *Princesse*, incurring heavy damage. Spare sails, rigging and spars would be brought up from storage and scattered across the upper decks, adding further to the impression of destruction and impotence. But on the *Ghost*'s port side, the gun crews would be standing by with their thirty-two- and eighteen-pounders loaded, ready to be fired repeatedly at close quarters, the instant the ship was turned to come alongside her unsuspecting adversary.

"An' if we *do* go along with this crazy plan of yours, Mr Gallant," the red-haired man said, "an' I'm not saying yet that we will – least, not all of us – how long do we wait for the *Princesse* to appear? You given that any thought?"

Gallant glanced at the sky. It was still early morning and a long day stretched ahead. "What if we maintain position here until nightfall? If by then the *Princesse* hasn't returned, we up anchor and head home."

A short, overweight deckhand with thinning hair matted across his forehead had a question. "Even ignoring the difference in weight of shot, young fella, the *Princesse* is a big ship. She'll be quartering nearly 400 crew and marines in all. There's only 150 or so of us. What makes you think we've got a chance?"

"Because," Gallant told him, "after the *Ghost* was ordered away to pursue the sloop, I'm sure the *Herald* and *Lilac* wouldn't have surrendered their colours without giving a good account of themselves. You think that's right, mister?"

The deckhand nodded.

"Well it seems to me," Gallant suggested, "that no French ship – however big she is, can have come out of a fire-fight with two English first rates without suffering casualties. Lots of them. Because of that, I don't think there's anything like 400 fit men aboard the *Princesse*."

"Aye, that's right enough," the overheight deckhand agreed. "There'll be a good many o' them Frenchies nursing wounds or down in Davy Jones' Locker after all the English shot that was poured into her."

"What I don't understand, matey," another crewman shouted belligerently, "is why you're concerned about all this? What's in it for you? You an' your mate hopin' to get a share of the treasure?"

Jack Gallant, his eyes full of fury, reached out and grasped the man by the collar of his jerkin. "Just before we boarded the *Ghost*," he said, "we saw something floating in the water caught up in the riggings."

The sailor tried to knock his hand away. "Yeah, an' what was that, mister?"

"Two of your officers," Gallant said quietly. "Their hands had been tied behind their backs. They'd been shot through the head and their bodies dumped overboard. Seems almost certain that all of the *Ghost*'s officers were murdered. Let's just say it's a matter of conscience with me. I'd just like to get even with the Count de Vaugelas and his men, if possible."

The startled expressions and shocked silence with which the crew of the *Ghost* greeted this revelation suggested that attitudes might be about to change – permanently.

The dreadful retribution meted out to the French prize crew for the murder of the *Ghost*'s officers was as lacking in mercy as the original crime. They were brought up from the hold, screaming and wailing in terror, but not a man was spared and the method of execution was identical. Jack Gallant could not bring himself to watch the spectacle but he harked to Eashal's advice not to get involved. Instead, accompanied by Jim Sayce, he went below decks, breaking into the bosun's locked storeroom where the light arms were kept. There they found ample stocks of muskets, pistols and ammunition, which were distributed among the crew. All the remaining weapons, over 200 pieces, were loaded and placed in advantageous positions behind the deck rails ready for instant use.

After emptying the quartermaster's store of anything that could be used in the coming struggle, Sayce pulled a long wooden box off the shelves with a grunt of satisfaction. Knocking off both locks with the butt of his pistol, he opened the lid. Inside the velvet-lined compartment was a small bronze Lady cannon about 2 feet long. Fastened alongside it was an elaborately decorated swivel mount and deck stand. Clipped inside the lid was an iron rammerhead fitted with a sponge and ram.

Several boxes of small shot took up the rest of the available space. Sayce lifted the Lady cannon out, staring at it admiringly.

Eashal burst out laughing. "That's too small a toy to put any fear in the Frenchies, Jim."

Sayce just shrugged. After attaching one end of a broad leather strap around the trunnions and clipping the other to the cascable, he slipped it over his right shoulder, assessing the miniature cannon's balance and weight, pointing it straight ahead from waist height.

"Jim, you're not serious!" Eashal cried. "It'll break your back if you try to fire it like that!"

"We'll see, old fella," was all that Sayce conceded.

The crewmen working up top had finished lashing the replacement bowsprit and the inner jib into place on the foremast. Both sails were lowered and the sheet anchor wound in. Then, in the light wind, with Eashal at the wheel, coming sharp to port was rehearsed with increasing efficiency. The *Ghost* responded well, though once she broached to, wallowing helplessly in the wave troughs for several minutes until control could be regained. Watching these manoeuvres from amidships, the more experienced hands muttered uncertainly, casting doubts on the whole exercise, but Jack Gallant was convinced it gave them the advantage they would so desperately need.

As one of the acting gun captains, Jim Sayce personally saw to it that half the six-pounders mounted on the quarterdeck and fo'c'sle were loaded with musket balls to discourage prospective boarders, while the rest were stuffed with mixtures of chain and hammer to bring down the *Princesse*'s spars and rigging.

On both gun decks the crews made sure that the port cannon were cleaned, checked and loaded, ensuring that each piece was ready to be rolled out ready for firing the moment the order was given. Extra charges were prepared in the powder room and each gun had an ample supply of shot at hand. As a final act of deception, a tricolor was hoisted to the top of the shortened foremast, despite everyone's unease about sailing under the French flag.

There was little left to do now but wait. The sun was an hour past its zenith, already making its slow descent towards the evening horizon. The crew lolled about, smoking and drinking weak beer, wondering who might be the first to glimpse the *Princesse*'s approaching sails. As the hours dragged by, those on board the *Ghost* cursed with imagination were torn in opposing directions by their fears and aspirations.

A deckhand dozing with his legs straddling the cathead was the first to sight large sails about 8 leagues off to the south-east. He rubbed his sleepy eyes, staring intently. In the trembling blue haze it was difficult to tell what kind of ship she was. His excited cries alerted everyone and within seconds every soul on board the *Ghost* had gathered near the fo'c'sle bulkhead, watching curiously. It was only when the distant ship came hull up that the high decks and triple rows of gunports revealed her to be a large warship. A low excited muttering travelled through the crew. The tricolor was flying above her main royal. It had to be the *Princesse!*

The French warship was fairly flying along in the light breeze. Her studding sails were boomed out and she was closing on the *Ghost* at 7 to 8 knots. With every minute that passed the distance between them grew visibly shorter. Already Gallant could clearly see the damage inflicted on the great ship by the *Herald* and *Lilac* during the encounter in the mouth of the Orinoco had become visible. Then, when separated by perhaps 2 nautical miles, the *Princesse* started gathering in her canvas prior to a slow approach and fired off a signal cannon.

Jack Gallant nodded to Eashal who fired one of the six-pounders in response. Tension mounted as the long seconds slipped past.

Yard by yard, the two ships closed on each other and inertia alone was carrying the ever slowing *Princesse* forward now. Gallant waited until the gap had been reduced to a distance of three ship lengths. Then, anxiously, he turned to Eashal and demanded, "Now?"

Eashal shook his head. "Not quite, Jack." His weather-beaten hands were gripping the wheel tightly, his eyes fixed on the ever narrowing gap. "Maybe another . . . chain's length." His face was creased in concentration. "Just . . . there!"

Judging the direction of the wind and the position and motion of both ships exactly, Eashal spun the wheel hard over. Timbers groaned under the strain and the sails fluffed, flapping idly. Wherever they were, down on the gun decks or hiding in the quarterdeck cabins, everyone on board the *Ghost*, alert to what was happening, held their breath, their hearts pounding and pulses racing. One sudden, errant gust or unexpected lull in the wind now and all would be for nought. But round the *Ghost* came, dipping and rolling as the forecourse and inner jib filled again, presenting her port side to the *Princesse* which had all but drifted to a stop. Eashal's seamanship had been exemplary. A stretch of less than two yards of churning water separated both vessels. The moment had arrived. A great rousing cheer went up as Jack Gallant, after running down the French flag struck the English third rate's colours.

As Jack Gallant arrived breathless and stumbling on to the lower gun deck, all the flames of hell were unleashed from the metal snouts of the *Ghost*'s cannon. For a moment his senses were stunned by the ear-rending noise and the ferocity of each discharge, and he stood unmoving beside the ladderway, gazing in disbelief at the frightful scene. Then steeling himself, he ran forward, offering what assistance he could wherever the under-manned crews needed help. Gallant found himself being called from one gun position to the next, lending the strength of his arms to help heave on the breech-ropes, rolling the 9-foot-long, 55-hundredweight guns forward into the firing position. Once their muzzles were pointing through the ports, each gun captain took control, aiming the huge weapon and bellowing, "Stand clear!" before igniting the charge.

As the black powder detonated, the air was racked by a deafening explosion, followed by the howl of the departing ball and the jarring recoil as the heavy gun was sent running inboard on its wheeled carriage until brought to a halt by the groaning breeching-tackle. Then with smoke pouring from the muzzle, the barrel was sponged out, a new cartridge of black powder inserted and rammed home and the heavy iron ball loaded. Even lacking manpower, the *Ghost*'s well-trained, sweating crews were firing off a round every two minutes and the damage these guns were inflicting on the *Princesse* at such close quarters was appalling. Jack Gallant grabbed a moment to peer out through one of the gunports. Already, the French warship's four-inch-thick planking had received a frightful hammering. The bombardment of 32- and 18-pound cannonballs was smashing through her hull as easily as if it had been weakened by dry rot. From inside the ship, terrible screams could be heard coming from the wounded and the dying and it was obvious that utter confusion reigned on board the great warship.

Maintained speed of fire was essential now. The vital objective, which had to be achieved quickly if the *Ghost* was to have any chance of victory over the much larger French warship, was to try to dismount as many of the *Princesse*'s heavy guns as possible by shattering their carriages with direct hits. To this end, rapid and accurate fire was essential, otherwise the more heavily armed warship would soon begin to press home her advantage of superiority in weight of shot once her officers and crew, after recovering from their surprise, began returning fire.

The *Ghost*'s port side armament consisted of her main battery of twelve thirty-two-pounder demi-cannon on the main gun deck and sixteen eighteen-pounder Culverins on the upper gun deck; while ranged along the quarterdeck and fo'c'sle her twelve six-pounders had been brought into action, firing mixtures of chain and hammer shot intended to rip down the *Princesse*'s spars and rigging and to keep her crew pinned well down. That made a total of forty cannon, each discharging a shot every two minutes or less. A withering rate of fire. And so far without response.

Neither ship could break away from the engagement now. Snapped through by a clean hit, and trailing lengths of standing rigging and shrouds, the *Princesse*'s main foremast came slowly crashing down on to the deck of the *Ghost*, forming a bridge between both ships. Grabbing the opportunity and ignoring the hail of musket fire directed at him, Eashal leaped like a madman towards the now horizontal mast and began winding several loops of the snapped forestay around it, tying the line off securely to one of the timber heads. Both ships were now locked together. It was to be a fight to the finish.

Tremors continually shook the *Ghost* from stem to stern as her guns vomited destruction, shattering the curved hull of the great French ship to matchwood. Risking another glance out of one of the gunports – far more dangerous now that a hail of musketry fire was being exchanged by the *Ghost*'s deckhands and the *Princesse*'s marines positioned on her higher decks – Gallant could see that gaping holes had been ripped into the French ship's hull. The English gunners had been successful. Many of the French weapons had been silenced even before they could fire a shot, their carriages shattered or the decks below them ripped away, tilting the heavy guns over and rendering them useless. Despite the tremendous damage inflicted on the *Princesse*, the one-sided barrage could not continue much longer without reply. A number of the French cannon remained operational, and their crews were highly trained. Now the fire was returned, balls blasting great holes in the hull, shattering sections of timber framing and sending jagged splinters flying across both decks. The screams of the injured and the dying were coming from both ships now, but discipline held fast and the rate of fire from the English ship never faltered.

But the French had one weapon left that might yet turn the tide of battle in their favour. And the danger was instantly recognized when the brass monster fired her first shot. The *Ghost* staggered under the impact as if hit by a giant hammer. A large hole was blasted in the gun deck and two of the demi-cannon carriages were blown apart. Eight men were killed by that one shot.

"Cannon-of-7!" Jim Sayce cried out, warning his men with all the breath in his lungs.

Jack Gallant, his face streaked with sweat, caught the gun captain's eye. "What is it?" he asked, standing aside as the loader hurriedly rammed another charge home.

"One of the biggest cannon ever made, Jack," Sayce answered, pouring priming powder into his gun's touch-hole. "Fires a 42-pound ball! It'll rip us apart at this range, unless we can—"

Again the great brass monster spoke. Another huge hole appeared in the *Ghost*'s hull. The giant ball smashed into one of the mid-deck braces, demolishing it instantly. The carriage wheels of one of the upper deck eighteen-pounders dropped into sight as the planking gave way with an agonized groan of cracking wood. Crewmen below it tried to get out of the way as the 17-hundredweight gun fell on to the main deck, wreaking terrible destruction and knocking out two more of the *Ghost*'s main weapons. Jim Sayce had seen nothing of this. He had been knocked sprawling when a section of shattered deck beam caught him full in the face. He was either dead or unconscious.

Jack Gallant knew what he had to do now. The thirty-four-pounder was loaded and ready to fire. "Leave him!" he roared, grim-faced, as the gun crew tried to drag their captain to safety. "Grab that breeching tackle. Let's get this gun rolled out or we're all dead!"

Sweating and straining, the eight-man crew heaved on the ropes. The heavy cannon jerked forward, trundling across the deck on its wheeled carriage until the muzzle poked through the open port. Jack Gallant squinted along the sightline, tapping in another quoin to raise the elevation slightly, waiting – as he'd seen Jim Sayce do – for the swell of the waves to flatten out. Beyond the gunport, a dense fog of cannon smoke hung low over the water between both ships. Then through a gap in the heavy vapour, he saw, less than 30 feet away, that the elaborately decorated bronze barrel of the Cannon-of-7 was being dragged into position on the *Princesse*. Its gaping muzzle was pointed straight at him, and Jack Gallant felt as if he were staring down the throat of hell.

Ignoring the yells and cries of the French gun captain urging his crew to work faster aboard his own vessel, Gallant stood with the spluttering slow match in hand, and waited; waited for the exact moment when the swirling sea subsided and his sightline drew a bead on his monstrous target. Across the narrow strip of water that separated the ships, Jack Gallant could see the face of the Frenchman crouched behind his own weapon, also waiting. These were desperate moments. The *Ghost*'s wrecked gun deck was filled with the stench of black powder, the confusing concussions of those guns still firing and the tortured cries of the wounded. Then the moment came and Gallant ignited the thirty-two-pounder's priming powder. With a booming roar the charge exploded, sending its heavy iron shot screaming across the gap, straight down the throat of the Cannon-of-7.

The impact, as the French gun's charge exploded, ripping apart its brass barrel, was catastrophic. The force of the explosion ripped out the *Princesse*'s hull timbers right down to the waterline, utterly wrecking all her gun decks and spewing the maimed bodies of her dead and dying into the sea.

A great cheer went up from every man on board the *Ghost*. Jim Sayce struggled to his feet, and wiped away a trickle of blood oozing from a gash above his left eye. Staring out of the gun port at the wrecked French ship, he clapped Jack Gallant on the shoulder. "Well done, lad!" He grinned. Then swinging the strap of the Lady cannon across his shoulder, he ran towards the ladderway, crying, "Right! Come on, boys! Let's 'ave the bastards!"

Yelling murderously, pistols and cutlasses glinting in their hands, the surviving crew of the *Ghost* ran up on to the quarter-deck and over the bulwarks. Running along the fallen mainmast, they scrambled through a hail of musket fire towards the deck of the French warship.

For several minutes the surviving French marines, many of them wounded, formed a determined phalanx, struggling desperately with their small arms and razor-edged lances to repel the *Ghost*'s boarding party. The unequal stand-off could not be maintained indefinitely. And the Englishmen broke through, pouring on to the deck of the French warship, hot blood singing in their ears, vengeance beating in their hearts.

Hand-to-hand fighting ensued on all decks and the stench of new-spilt blood mingled with the sharp taste of burnt powder and drifting cannon smoke. The air was rent with the clangour and clashing of cutlass and hanger against bayonet and double-edge sword. Screams of agony and the triumphant yells of the victorious deafened the ears. In the vicious mêlée Jack Gallant was forced to hone his fighting skills quickly, narrowly avoiding death and serious injury on a number of occasions as a panicking French sailor lunged at him with a blood-smeared hanger, or a cornered marine loosed off a round that missed its target by a hair's breadth. His cool head, even more than his strength, agility and cat-like reflexes, served to keep the young man alive where others perished.

Hacking and stabbing about him, Gallant was fighting his way towards the officers' cabins, intending to try and help Old Eashal, where a final stand was being mounted outside the closed and locked door of the captain's stateroom. But while climbing the stairs to the quarterdeck, he was suddenly felled by a powerful blow from a musket-butt. Pain flared behind his eyes and for a moment the world jarred. As his assailant closed for the kill, Gallant swung his cutlass round in an ascending arc, slicing open the man's bowels.

Gallant, his head still reeling, watched horrified from the floor of the quarterdeck. As the stateroom door was thrown open, a determined group of marines wearing iron helmets and breastplates brought loaded muskets to bear on Eashal and the Englishmen fighting alongside him. Armed only with cutlasses and hangers, they froze, helpless in the face of the expected volley.

Now Jim Sayce appeared at Gallant's side, the straps supporting the Lady cannon crossing his left shoulder. "Eashal!" he yelled. "All of you! Out of the way!" And he levelled the barrel of the miniature cannon, aiming and triggering the flintlock in one fluid movement as the Englishmen scattered.

The powerful blast sent the gun captain staggering backward as a plume of dense black smoke and flaring powder erupted from the muzzle. Its heavy load of deadly chain and hammer shot shrieked across the deck, ripping into the French marines, smashing through their armour as if it had been made of butter. Not a single man escaped and the wounds they suffered were horrendous. Even the heavy doors behind them were shattered to matchwood by the ferocity of the Lady cannon's discharge. But now the way was clear. Scrambling over the ruined bodies of the dying, all the Englishmen poured through the stateroom into the Count de Vaugelas's living quarters.

The sumptuously furnished living quarters were empty. Heavy chairs had been upturned, a carafe of red wine had been spilled, staining maps and personal letters on the richly covered table. Small boxes containing jewels and gold coin littered the carpeted floor. Everything gave clear indications of hurried, recent evacuation. The carved doors leading out on to the stern gallery hung wide open. And tied to the rail, a rope ladder trailed down in the breeze.

The Englishmen rushed to the rail and stared at the sea. Below them, bobbing about on the light swell, was a small skiff. Four oarsmen were powering the little craft away from the *Princesses*; her single sail fluffed and began to fill in the breeze and the boat began to surge forward. Aft of the rowers crouched a woman, a long cape pulled close about her, shielding her from the spray. But in the prow of the skiff sat a resplendently dressed and coiffured man, his white uniform encrusted with gold braid and medallions, a regimental sword hanging at his belt. Not once did he look back.

"God damn it!" Eashal cursed. "We've lost the bastard!"

"Where's Tucker?" Gallant cried, weighing up the scene in an instant and grabbing hold of Jim Sayce. "You said he was that best shot on the *Ghost*? Did you mean it?"

Sayce nodded. "Yea, but . . . That would be some shot even for Tucker."

"Get him, quick!" Jack Gallant insisted.

Tucker was hurriedly brought to rail and a loaded musket thrust in his hands. Staring at the skiff, his face fell. "Hell, that boat must be almost 500 yards away," he muttered. "I'll only get one shot before it's right out of range." Resting the barrel on the rail he took a deep breath, and stopped slightly to peer along the sight. Then, cocking the hammer, he carefully took aim.

"What are you are aiming at?" Gallant demanded, grabbing hold of the barrel.

Tucker glared up at him, exasperated. "The Count de Vaugelas, up in the prow. Can't miss him in his white uniform."

"Aim at the woman!" Jack Gallant ordered.

"You sick bastard!" Tucker cursed, spinning towards him.

"Jack?" Eashal gasped out loud.

"Listen, that's not a woman," Gallant said through clenched teeth. "That's de Vaugelas."

Tucker glanced hesitantly at Jim Sayce. The gun captain shrugged unhappily. "I don't know, Tucker. It *may* be de Vaugelas . . ."

Gallant grabbed Tucker by the collar. "Do it!" he demanded. "I'll take full responsibility!"

Tucker jerked a thumb at the heavens. "Up there too?"

"If necessary," Gallant agreed.

Sweating visibly, Tucker lined up the sights again and his finger curled around the trigger. "The good Lord have mercy on us both if you're wrong!" he muttered. Then his finger tightened and the hammer came down.

The priming powder flared, and the charge detonated, kicking out the heavy iron ball with a roar and a flash of flame. For a long moment nothing else happened then the figure seated at the rear of the skiff went suddenly rigid and slumped sideways. Before the rowers' reaching hands could grasp and support it, the figure fell overboard. Entangled in one of the rowlocks, the voluminous cape was pulled away from the lifeless body, revealing a man dressed in the full regalia of a French naval uniform. While around it, darkening the white-crested waves, was a spreading stain of blood.

A ragged, breathless cheer went up from the crew of the *Ghost*. And many hands slapped both Gallant and Tucker on their backs.

"Never doubted you," Tucker revealed impishly, blowing down the smoking barrel of the musket.

Gallant turned to Jim Sayce. "What about you?" he asked.
The gun captain stared at him critically. "Lucky bastard!"

Old Eashal nodded wisely. "I'd say that's just about the measure of the lad, Jim. A *real* lucky bastard . . ."

THE LAST ENGAGEMENT

John Frizell

The following story is set after the exile of Napoleon on Elba. After so many years of conflict between Britain and France it took the navy a while to accustom itself to the fact that there was, in theory at least, peace. Officers returned to Britain from their various postings, though not all of them looking forward to the outcome.

John Frizell is a Canadian by birth though now lives in England. A biochemist by profession, he works for the environmental group Greenpeace where he has had considerable experience of the sea pursuing whaling ships.

It was the sort of day that made a sailor glad to be alive. The water was slipping aside in white foam from his ship's bows. A pair of dolphins were riding the bow wave, sometimes rolling on their sides to watch the ship with a bright, knowing eye; under the clear blue sky her wake was as straight as if it had been drawn with a ruler over the gentle swells of the sea, but for the long morning since they had sailed, James Wheeler had been unable to take any pleasure in the day. The impending loss of everything bulked too large in his mind.

In 1794, when the war had been raging hot, the navy had wasted no time in returning a crippled lieutenant to duty at sea in a posting where he could free an able-bodied one for combat. Now with the war over and Napoleon reduced from emperor of

Europe to king of a Mediterranean island smaller than the Isle of Wight, the nation rejoiced and, within a fortnight of the capture of Paris, French wine and brandy were openly shipped across the Channel and French fashions could again be worn in public. Gone for ever was even the faint chance of a successful engagement with a French ship of superior force – the only way James might have gained promotion and the security of being a post captain, a captain by right, not by courtesy. And the navy had decided that an ageing one-armed lieutenant could be put ashore on half pay to give a well-connected young lieutenant the experience of independent command.

When his ship docked in England, James would be superseded. The injustice of it ate at him, corroding the joy out of life. But for now he had all the minutiae that plague a captain to keep him busy.

"I am sure you can see the legal force of my position, Captain Wheeler," Lord Swanborough was saying. "My men must have more space." A few days ago Swanborough had been John Hunter, a younger son in charge of the family plantation and enjoying all the pleasures that Jamaica had to offer. Now he was a passenger on the *Princess Caroline*, a passenger with the first written contract of passage that James had ever seen, a contract guaranteeing his men 24 inches for their hammocks and 36 inches for himself. Although James was old enough to be his father, the young lord had run rings around him in business matters. James hid his irritation and gave in gracefully.

Lord Swanborough left the cabin. This made enough room for William White, the master's mate who was the closest thing to a first lieutenant the tiny ship possessed, to enter.

"Will the men wear it?" asked James, once he had explained the new berthing arrangements.

"There is an odd mood to them," said William. "Strangest I have felt in years. But I reckon there'll be no trouble. Passengers are popular now."

As captain, James received a token payment for each passenger. For the past three years he had spent most of it on doubling the men's rum ration on days he thought it safe to do so and on distributing free tobacco, thus making carrying passengers popular with the crew who had always regarded them as a curse in the past.

"It was a right strange leave-taking, though," said James, pouring a mixture of coconut milk, fresh lime juice and Jamaican rum from a small jug on the table and offering it to his subordinate. The jug, a bowl of mangoes, papayas and oranges, and the two glasses took up the whole surface of the table.

"The men know the navy can't hold them now that Boney's finished and there's peace," said William. "With the cross-Channel trade opening up, any man that wants a job can find one. It makes them skittish."

It had certainly made Stroud even more skittish than normal. James had tracked him through low bars and brothels until just before dawn. It was not the first time James had done this: Stroud often made half-hearted attempts to desert. But William had been out half the night rounding up men who had never before attempted to jump ship.

"All that want to go can leave legally when we get back to England," said James. "Which ones do you think will go and which will stay?"

Working together, they drew up a list for James to give to his successor. It was his duty to hand over the *Princess Caroline* in the best possible condition. When his wound had forced him into the little world of packet vessels he had quickly learned that speed counted for everything since there was no other criterion by which they could be judged. He had thrown himself into seamanship, becoming well respected for his ability to find ways to squeeze out an extra fraction of a knot but he had always found that experienced crew who knew the quirks of their ship were the key to effective operations.

"Call the captain," came a voice from over their heads, heard clearly through the skylight. "There's something wrong with that ship."

James was out of the cabin door before the message could be properly delivered. There had been only one ship in sight when he had gone below: some sort of merchant vessel, probably carrying cargo between the islands, crossing his course well to windward.

"What do you see?" he asked the lookout. He did not need to raise his voice. The *Princess Caroline*'s mainmast was only 50 feet high.

"She's turned to run down on us. She was right in the eye of the wind, then she turned."

Working to windward and then closing was the definitive move of a predator. The strange ship was certainly a pirate. Her sails shivered and she heaved to as if deciding whether the little ship under her lee was as helpless as she looked. James gave the orders to heave the *Princess Caroline* to as well. They pitched slightly as they watched the watcher.

"This will be like that privateer off the Azores," said James in a clear carrying voice the crew could hear.

"I'm sure it will be, sir," replied William in a public voice, but for a moment their eyes met and James could see that his friend knew as well as he did that the happy outcome of that long-ago day was not going to be repeated here.

James glanced around at the eleven men who formed the *Princess Caroline*'s crew. They were mostly old experienced seamen and they all looked apprehensive. The *Princess Caroline* was built for carrying mail, not for fighting, and she was armed with the smallest guns the navy issued. She was a very fast vessel but not fast enough to escape the enemy waiting for him to windward.

"What are you going to do?" said Lord Swanborough, walking uninvited on to the little quarterdeck. James suspected that the man resented him because he had brought the letter telling him of his father's and brother's deaths, even though it was also news of his ennoblement. He ignored the peer's transgression of naval custom, his trembling hands, his obvious fear.

"I shall close with him, my lord."

He gave orders to bring the ship back to the wind, sailing towards the enemy. The men looked sulky but although their world was changing about them they were still in the iron grip of discipline; they would do their duty.

The peer pointed at the two three-pounder guns which comprised the *Princess Caroline*'s broadside. "That ship is twice our size. More. She must have heavier guns. More men. Is this wise?"

"I have no choice, my lord."

This was true. There were no banks of fog where he could hide. No tricky shoals where the experience of a lifetime at sea might give him an advantage. Privateers and pirates tended to mount heavy guns on their bows; if he ran, the faster enemy would subject him to a raking fire as it caught up with him. Broadside to broadside was better, even if he could hold his pitiful broadside in his one hand. And it would be over quickly.

"You could be of great service, my lord. Were you to lead the passengers in musketry against the enemy, I am sure they would respond nobly. I believe you have some fine weapons?"

His lordship was much given to hunting and James had seen muskets, rifles and fowling pieces being carried on board as his crew had laboured to prepare for the voyage. He would have preferred a bundle of red uniforms. His fifteen passengers dressed as marines and drawn up in rigid lines might have been enough to convince a pirate to look elsewhere.

The pirate was hull up from the deck now. He examined it through his glass. Five gunports a side. Too many men to count.

"Brown. Sawyer. His lordship's guns are in the fore hold. Get them out for him. Issue a horn of powder to each passenger and ship's muskets to any who are unarmed after his lordship has distributed weapons. My lord, I am grateful for your assistance and will certainly mention it in my despatch."

Lord Swanborough followed the two seamen. The light swell let him walk easily as if he were a seaman himself. He looked calmer for having been given something to do and perhaps reassured by the idea that the *Princess Caroline*'s captain would be alive and writing despatches when the engagement was over.

William had cleared away the three-pounders; they were crewed, loaded and run out.

"She's under way, sir," said the lookout from his post aloft.

The pirate had come back to the wind and was running down towards him. It was the action of a confident commander. Anyone with an ounce of doubt that the *Princess Caroline* might be a threat would have waited for her to work to windward, watching her as she came. The pirate was growing visibly in size – ships close quickly on reciprocal courses.

"Edge away, Stroud."

Stroud, the most skilled steersman on board, was steering awkwardly, standing as close to the stern as he could and reaching forward to hold the end of the tiller; the *Princess Caroline* was so small she steered with a tiller, not a wheel. He was trying to stay as far from James as possible. Everyone knew that the ball that had taken James's arm had also killed his captain. Shipboard superstition dictated that no one would stand near the *Princess Caroline*'s captain in battle.

"Mr White, try the range when they bear. Aim low."

If he aimed high, a 3-pound ball had almost as good a chance of cutting a critical piece of rigging with a lucky shot as a larger ball, but he had so few guns that a lucky shot was very unlikely. Better to fire low and hope that balls coming on board the enemy might unsettle him.

The guns went off together. The wind instantly blew their modest clouds of smoke away. The 3-pound shot raised impressive columns of water but they were at least a cable short.

Smoke jetted from the pirate's bows. A waterspout burst from the sea to the *Princess Caroline*'s larboard. The ball went skipping away down the wake; the trade wind brought a patter of drops from the splash on board. A six-pounder or a nine, and either a very lucky crew or a very good one. A 9-pound ball hitting the *Princess Caroline*'s mainmast would cut right through it.

James focused his glass on the pirate's bow and watched the gun crew as they wormed, sponged and loaded. They were almost as fast as a navy crew. A man behind the gun crew stepped forward with a glass and for a moment the two captains regarded each other, then James turned his attention back to the gun crew. They were priming.

"Stroud. On my word, make a jig to leeward."

The *Princess Caroline* gave a little lurch to leeward. James took a step towards the bow so Stroud would come forward and get a better grip on the tiller.

"Wait for it, Stroud. Wait for it."

The pirate gun was run out. A tiny figure swung an arm towards the touch-hole.

"Now, Stroud."

The *Princess Caroline* fell off course and then came back to the wind, her new course parallel to the old. There was an enormous humming overhead and a hole appeared in the maincourse. His manoeuvre had taken him directly into the line of fire. The enemy captain had anticipated his move.

"Another broadside, Mr White. A double rum ration tonight for the first crew to hit her."

The *Princess Caroline* yawed. The guns fired, one, two.

"Both hit amidships, sir."

It was good shooting. But the gun crews were much more likely to be prisoners or dead by nightfall than to be enjoying their extra rum unless he could think of some way to even the odds. No inspiration came. No tactics, no surprise, no hope of help under the clear blue sky of that perfect day.

The gun on the pirate's bow was running out again. It looked much larger than before.

"Stroud. Let her waver to leeward then hold her steady and wait for my order to jig."

The *Princess Caroline* gave a small lurch and steadied. James could feel the tiller man's tension as silent seconds went by.

The pirate fired. The ball raced by head-high and 50 feet to their starboard, right where they would have been if James had given the order.

Lord Swanborough came on deck with the armed passengers just in time to see the ball skipping away. He stared at the pirate which had doubled in size and James could see the passengers twist and fidget as his nervousness spread to them.

He should have appointed William to lead them but it was too late now.

"This will be great sport," said James. "Had these fellows known how many Englishmen we have on board, they'd never have dared to attack. May come to their senses yet and run. So aim carefully, make each shot count and show them how Englishmen fight."

The pirate's bow gun was running out again. What would the enemy expect him to do? Straight again or jig? An even chance of disaster.

"Stroud. A jig to leeward when I say but only half as far as last time. Now."

The *Princess Caroline* dodged. The ball hummed by 10 feet to windward. The passengers stared.

The *Princess Caroline* yawed and fired. For a moment the tang of powder-smoke enveloped them all and the passengers cheered when water leaped up near the enemy.

James wondered why the pirate did not turn and fire a broadside. The most likely reason was that she was armed with carronades – guns that were lighter, cheaper, easier to use and above all of heavier calibre than the long guns that could be carried by a ship of that size. A single broadside from five heavy carronades at close range would tear the *Princess Caroline* to pieces.

But for the first time before a close engagement he was without fear. Perhaps this pirate was come to deliver him from the empty life of half pay and the tedium of being for ever bound to the land. He signalled William to con the ship.

"Steady as she goes, Mr White."

William's face was remote, resigned. All the correct tactical decisions had been made but he must know as well as James that there was little chance of surviving this engagement.

James left William with Stroud and spread the armed civilians out, making sure that each had a clear field of fire so they would not shoot one another or the *Princess Caroline*'s crew. At the same time he watched the enemy. The pirate would have time for one more shot from that deadly bow chaser. But there was little activity around the bow, much more on the deck. The pirate wheeled to present her broadside.

"Hard over, Stroud," yelled William.

Better to be hit broadside than to be raked. Smoke fountained from the pirate's gunports. But not from all of them. Even as shot howled around him and hulled the *Princess Caroline*, James registered that the number four port had not fired. And the amount and shape of the smoke blooming from each port was different. One was a carronade but a light one, probably a six-pounder – a boat gun. Two were long guns not much bigger than his. And one was just a swivel gun being fired through a gunport. Hope flared.

"Hands about ship."

Seamen ran from the guns to the rigging. The *Princess Caroline* carried just enough crew to sail her; she could not work both her sails and her guns at the same time.

He must get as close as possible and fight it out, broadside to broadside. But not too close. The civilians would be of no use against boarders and the pirate had five times his crew. James brought his ship around in a smooth curve and backed sails to stop her 50 feet from the pirate. He nodded to William, who rushed the men back to the guns, his face beaming. James could hear him ordering double shot.

The enemy were still reloading their guns. They were not nearly as quick as they had been with the bow chaser. Perhaps the men on the bow were the only real gun crew the pirates had and they were now scattered among the broadside guns, each trying to control a raw team. The pirate's crew might not be hardened corsairs at all, just a scratch crew of out-of-work seamen, fishermen, even ferrymen, picked up at ports from Tobago to Jamaica. But there were well over a hundred of them.

The *Princess Caroline*'s guns fired with a sharp crack. Four balls slammed into the enemy, raising splinters from her side and making ripples in the crowd on her deck. The pirate's carronade went off a moment after they hit but James saw no sign of the ball.

The passengers opened a vigorous and surprisingly accurate

fire, knocking down a marksman who had climbed into the pirate's rigging as if he were a bird sitting in a tree. Lord Swanborough picked off a man standing in an improvised crow's nest and then put down his empty gun and accepted a loaded one. He had his four servants seated in a circle, loading guns for him. Blood was dripping down the side of the pirate ship and into the sea. Two more pirate guns fired. One ball hit low on the *Princess Caroline*'s hull, the second punched a neat round hole in the Bermuda cedar of her side and passed between James and Stroud. Stroud edged back towards the stern.

The whipcrack of the *Princess Caroline*'s overcharged guns sounded again and once again all the balls went home. Dust and splinters burst from the enemy hull. After a moment James realized why he was seeing the impact so clearly: the enemy was drifting down on him. A large man wearing a red bandana climbed on to the taffrail and began whirling a rope with an iron hook on it. James took a pistol, fired and missed. Pistols were not very accurate but they were the only gun a one-armed man could use. He took another from the bucketful at his feet and fired and missed again.

Lord Swanborough turned. For a moment his musket pointed directly at James then it traversed an inch, steadied and fired. James heard the ball go by. The man in the bandana went over backwards. Lord Swanborough, the light of battle shining on his face, dropped the musket, snatched a fresh one and shot a second man as he leaned over the rail to recover the rope.

On a proper warship, James would be calling for canister but there was no canister on board. He turned to see William standing over the bow gun with a soup ladle in his hand, ladling musket balls from a little keg into its muzzle.

The pirate hulled the *Princess Caroline* again, the ball piercing both sides. Musket balls were peppering her decks but she was thinly manned and so far her luck held. The gap between the ships was dwindling fast. Pirates were pouring into the rigging and lining the sides. James fired pistols to some effect. Lord Swanborough and the passengers were more effective than James would have believed possible. Swanborough was actually directing their fire, managing them as if they were a workforce with deliveries to make, but although they inflicted many casualties they could no more stop the attackers than a man can hold back a wave with his hands.

James was aiming another pistol when the *Princess Caroline*'s guns went off. The man he was aiming at and those on either side of him turned to tumbling cloth puppets and disappeared. The air was full of red mist.

"Hands about ship."

As he gave orders to get the *Princess Caroline* under way, the hulls of the two ships came together with a grinding crunch. It was the moment the pirates had died for. James grabbed another pistol from the bucket and cocked it, waiting for the rush that would overwhelm them. The wind filled the *Princess Caroline*'s sails. There were strange sounds of rigging breaking and fittings torn from the wood as the *Princess Caroline* ground down the pirate's side. Every man on board, except Stroud at the tiller, faced the enemy with a weapon in his hand but the seconds dragged on and no boarders came. There was a final rending sound as the hulls pulled apart. James brought the *Princess Caroline* to the wind, turned to cross the enemy's bows and settled on a tack to windward.

"What are you doing, James?" said William as the opportunity to rake the enemy began to slip by. He shook his head and collected himself. "She is ours, sir. If we back sails we can rake her until she surrenders. We can take her, sir."

"We'd get nothing for her as a prize."

He pointed at the pirate's hull and the raw red of recent, inexpertly done repairs, no doubt concealing rot within. The sails had patches on top of patches.

"Do you think she is any danger to us now?"

The pirate's deck was covered with dead and wounded. The sound of men screaming and crying came clearly across the water.

The ferocity faded from William's face. The man James knew as a friend returned.

There was neither money nor honour to be had from this

engagement. The navy would not change its decision just because he had beaten five-to-one odds: warships are expected to defeat pirates.

Lord Swanborough approached, his face glowing. He spoke of the need to eradicate all pirates, of mass hangings and commanded James to go back.

"It is your duty, Captain Wheeler."

James knew it was his duty. He could be hanged for not doing it if the navy decided he had "run cowardly" from the fight. But just as the men were in a state of flux, so was he, passing from a world of duty to another world he could only dimly comprehend. The pirates knew what they faced; they would not surrender. Should he hazard the men on the *Princess Caroline* to destroy utterly these pirates, most of whom would never sign on a buccaneer again? His decision crystallized, became irrevocable. His duty was finished. He did not need to kill these men on behalf of a navy that had forsaken him. And he was damned if he would end anyone else's time at sea.

"I cannot go back, my lord. We are carrying post. It is a capital offence to delay the mail."

He watched Swanborough closely, wondering if he would accept the explanation.

"I see," said Lord Swanborough. "Still, it was a well-done thing." he shook hands with James. "Damn well done. We are all in your debt, Captain Wheeler."

They beat steadily to windward, plugging holes and repairing damage. James left William to it while he reflected. Did the loss of the navy have to mean the loss of the sea? Would his skills in getting the best from a ship be of value in peacetime? Swanborough's family owned ships and with peace bringing an expansion of trade they were likely to acquire more; might the debt of gratitude Swanborough had publicly acknowledged be repaid by employing him? The unfamiliar sensation of hope for the future illuminated him like the sun from the cloudless sky and, as the *Princess Caroline* cut steadily through the water, the strange notion of a life without the navy, without duty, began to take on shape and form.

GOODBYE TO HIS MASTER

Arthur Conan Doyle

We close this anthology with a story set in the very final days of Napoleon when in exile on St Helena. Sir Arthur Conan Doyle (1859–1930) is best remembered for his stories of Sherlock Holmes, but he preferred his historical fiction, especially The White Company *(1891),* Sir Nigel *(1906) and* Uncle Bernac *(1897). Among these works were a series of stories featuring the French soldier, Etienne Gerard. Running in* The Strand Magazine, *where the Holmes stories had first appeared, they were collected as* The Exploits of Brigadier Gerard *(1896) and* The Adventures of Brigadier Gerard *(1903). The following is the last story of the series.*

I will tell you no more stories, my dear friends. It is said that man is like the hare, which runs in a circle and comes back to die at the point from which it started. Gascony has been calling to me of late. I see the blue Garonne winding among the vineyards and the bluer ocean towards which its waters sweep. I see the old town also, and the bristle of masts from the side of the long stone quay. My heart hungers for the breath of my native air and the warm glow of my native sun. Here in Paris are my friends, my occupations, my pleasures. There all who have known me are in their grave. And yet the southwest wind as it rattles on my windows seems always to be the strong voice of the motherland calling her child back to that bosom into which I am ready to sink. I have played my part in my time. The time has passed. I must pass also. Nay, dear friends, do not look sad, for what can be happier than a life completed in honour and made beautiful with friendship and love? And yet it is solemn also when a man approaches the end of the long road and sees the turning which leads him into the unknown. But the Emperor and all his marshals have ridden round that dark turning and passed into the beyond. My Hussars, too – there are not fifty men who are not waiting yonder. I must go. But on this the last night I will tell you that which is more than a tale – it is a great historical secret. My lips have been sealed, but I see no reason why I should not leave behind me some account of this remarkable adventure, which must otherwise be entirely lost, since I, and only I of all living men, have a knowledge of the facts.

I will ask you to go back with me to the year 1821. In that year our great Emperor had been absent from us for six years, and only now and then from over the seas we heard some whisper which showed that he was still alive. You cannot think what a weight it was upon our hearts for us who loved him to think of him in captivity eating his giant soul out upon that lonely island. From the moment we rose until we closed our eyes in sleep the thought was always with us, and we felt dishonoured that he, our chief and master, should be so humiliated without our being able to move a hand to help him. There were many who would most willingly have laid down the remainder of their lives to bring him a little ease, and yet all that we could do was to sit and grumble in our *cafés* and stare at the map, counting up the leagues of water which lay between us. It seemed that he might have been in the moon for all that we could do to help him. But that was only because we were all soldiers and knew nothing of the sea.

Of course, we had our own little troubles to make us bitter, as well as the wrongs of our Emperor. There were many of us who had held high rank and would hold it again if he came back to his own. We had not found it possible to take service under the white flag of the Bourbons, or to take an oath which might turn our sabres against the man whom we loved. So we found ourselves with neither work nor money. What could we do save gather together and gossip and grumble, while those who had a little paid the score and those who had nothing shared the bottle? Now and then, if we were lucky, we managed to pick a quarrel with one of the Garde du Corps, and if we left him on his back in the Bois we felt that we had struck a blow for Napoleon once again. They came to know our haunts in time, and they avoided them as if they had been hornets' nests.

There was one of these – the Sign of the Great Man – in the Rue Varennes, which was frequented by several of the more distinguished and younger Napoleonic officers. Nearly all of us had been colonels or aides-de-camp, and when any man of less distinction came among us we generally made him feel that he had taken a liberty. There were Captain Lepine, who had won the medal of honour at Leipzig; Colonel Bonnet, aide-de-camp to Macdonald; Colonel Jourdan, whose fame in the army was hardly second to my own; Sabbatier of my own Hussars, Meunier of the Red Lancers, Le Breton of the Guards, and a dozen others. Every night we met and talked, played dominoes, drank a glass or two, and wondered how long it would be before the Emperor would be back and we at the head of our regiments once more. The Bourbons had already lost any hold they ever had upon the country, as was shown a few years afterwards, when Paris rose against them and they were hunted for the third time out of France. Napoleon had but to show himself on the coast, and he would have marched without firing a musket to the capital, exactly as he had done when he came back from Elba.

Well, when affairs were in this state there arrived one night in February, in our *café*, a most singular little man. He was short but exceedingly broad, with huge shoulders, and a head which was a deformity, so large was it. His heavy brown face was scarred with white streaks in a most extra ordinary manner, and he had grizzled whiskers such as seamen wear. Two gold earrings in his ears, and plentiful tattooing upon his hands and arms, told us also that he was of the sea before he intro-

duced himself to us as Captain Fourneau, of the Emperor's
navy. He had letters of introduction to two of our number, and
there could be no doubt that he was devoted to the cause. He
won our respect, too, for he had seen as much fighting as any of
us, and the burns upon his face were caused by his standing to
his post upon the *Orient*, at the Battle of the Nile, until the
vessel blew up underneath him. Yet he would say little about
himself, but he sat in the corner of the *café* watching us all with a
wonderfully sharp pair of eyes and listening intently to our talk.

One night I was leaving the *café* when Captain Fourneau
followed me, and touching me on the arm he led me without
saying a word for some distance until we reached his lodgings.
"I wish to have a chat with you," said he, and so conducted me
up the stair to his room. There he lit a lamp and handed me a
sheet of paper which he took from an envelope in his bureau. It
was dated a few months before from the Palace of Schönbrunn
at Vienna. "Captain Fourneau is acting in the highest interests
of the Emperor Napoleon. Those who love the Emperor should
obey him without question. – Marie Louise." That is what I
read. I was familiar with the signature of the Empress, and I
could not doubt that this was genuine.

"Well," said he, "are you satisfied as to my credentials?"

"Entirely."

"Are you prepared to take your orders from me?"

"This document leaves me no choice."

"Good! In the first place, I understand from something you
said in the *café* that you can speak English?"

"Yes, I can."

"Let me hear you do so."

I said in English, "Whenever the Emperor needs the help of
Etienne Gerard, I am ready night and day to give my life in his
service." Captain Fourneau smiled.

"It is funny English," said he, "but still it is better than no
English. For my own part I speak English like an Englishman.
It is all that I have to show for six years spent in an English
prison. Now I will tell you why I have come to Paris. I have
come in order to choose an agent who will help me in a matter

which affects the interests of the Emperor. I was told that it was at the *café* of the Great Man that I would find the pick of his old officers, and that I could rely upon every man there being devoted to his interests. I studied you all, therefore, and I have come to the conclusion that you are the one who is most suited for my purpose."

I acknowledged the compliment. "What is it that you wish me to do?" I asked.

"Merely to keep me company for a few months," said he. "You must know that after my release in England I settled down there, married an English wife, and rose to command a small English merchant ship, in which I have made several voyages from Southampton to the Guinea coast. They look on me there as an Englishman. You can understand, however, that with my feelings about the Emperor I am lonely sometimes, and that it would be an advantage to me to have a companion who would sympathize with my thoughts. One gets very bored on these long voyages, and I would make it worth your while to share my cabin."

He looked hard at me with his shrewd grey eyes all the time that he was uttering this rigmarole, and I gave him a glance in return which showed him that he was not dealing with a fool. He took out a canvas bag full of money.

"There are a hundred pounds in gold in this bag," said he. "You will be able to buy some comforts for your voyage. I should recommend you to get them in Southampton, whence we will start in ten days. The name of the vessel is the *Black Swan*. I return to Southampton tomorrow, and I shall hope to see you in the course of the next week."

"Come now," said I. "Tell me frankly what is the destination of our voyage?"

"Oh, didn't I tell you?" he answered. "We are bound for the Guinea coast of Africa."

"Then how can that be in the highest interests of the Emperor?" I asked.

"It is in his highest interests that you ask no indiscreet questions and I give no indiscreet replies," he answered, sharply. So he brought the interview to an end, and I found myself back in my lodgings with nothing save this bag of gold to show that this singular interview had indeed taken place.

There was every reason why I should see the adventure to a conclusion, and so within a week I was on my way to England. I passed from St Malo to Southampton, and on enquiry at the docks I had no difficulty in finding the *Black Swan*, a neat little vessel of a shape which is called, as I learned afterwards, a brig. There was Captain Fourneau himself upon the deck, and seven or eight rough fellows hard at work grooming her and making her ready for sea. He greeted me and led me down to his cabin.

"You are plain Mr Gerard now," said he, "and a Channel Islander. I would be obliged to you if you would kindly forget your military ways and drop your cavalry swagger when you walk up and down my deck. A beard, too, would seem more sailorlike than those moustaches."

I was horrified by his words, but, after all, there are no ladies on the high seas, and what did it matter? He rang for the steward.

"Gustav," said he, "you will pay every attention to my friend, Monsieur Etienne Gerard, who makes this voyage with us. This is Gustav Kerouan, my Breton steward," he explained, "and you are very safe in his hands."

This steward, with his harsh face and stern eyes, looked a very warlike person for so peaceful an employment. I said nothing, however, though you may guess that I kept my eyes open. A berth had been prepared for me next the cabin, which would have seemed comfortable enough had it not contrasted with the extraordinary splendour of Fourneau's quarters. He was certainly a most luxurious person, for his room was new-fitted with velvet and silver in a way which would have suited the yacht of a noble better than a little West African trader. So thought the mate, Mr Burns, who could not hide his amusement and contempt whenever he looked at it. This fellow, a big, solid, red-headed Englishman, had the other berth connected with the cabin. There was a second mate named Turner, who lodged in the middle of the ship, and there were nine men and one boy in the crew, three of whom, as I was informed by Mr Burns, were Channel Islanders like myself. This Burns, the first mate, was much interested to know why I was coming with them.

"I come for pleasure," said I.

He stared at me.

"Ever been to the West Coast?" he asked.

I said that I had not.

"I thought not," said he. "You'll never come again for that reason, anyhow."

Some three days after my arrival we untied the ropes by which the ship was tethered and we set off upon our journey. I was never a good sailor, and I may confess that we were far out of sight of any land before I was able to venture upon deck. At last, however, upon the fifth day I drank the soup which the good Kerouan brought me, and I was able to crawl from my bunk and up the stair. The fresh air revived me, and from that time onwards I accommodated myself to the motion of the vessel. My beard had begun to grow also, and I have no doubt that I should have made as fine a sailor as I have a soldier had I chanced to be born to that branch of the service. I learned to pull the ropes which hoisted the sails, and also to haul round the long sticks to which they are attached. For the most part, however, my duties were to play écarté with Captain Fourneau, and to act as his companion. It was not strange that he should need one, for neither of his mates could read or write, though each of them was an excellent seaman. If our captain had died suddenly I cannot imagine how we should have found our way in that waste of waters, for it was only he who had the knowledge which enabled him to mark our place upon the chart. He had this fixed upon the cabin wall, and every day he put our course upon it so that we could see at a glance how far we were from our destination. It was wonderful how well he could calculate it, for one morning he said that we should see the Cape Verd light that very night, and there it was, sure enough, upon our left front the moment that darkness came. Next day, however, the land was out of sight, and Burns, the mate, explained to me that we should see no more until we came to our port in the Gulf of Biafra. Every day we flew south with a favouring wind, and always at noon the pin upon the chart was moved nearer and nearer to the African coast. I may explain that palm oil was the cargo which we were in search of, and that our own lading consisted of coloured cloths, old muskets, and such other trifles as the English sell to the savages.

At last the wind which had followed us so long died away, and for several days we drifted about on a calm and oily sea under a sun which brought the pitch bubbling out between the planks upon the deck. We turned and turned our sails to catch every wandering puff, until at last we came out of this belt of calm and ran south again with a brisk breeze, the sea all round us being alive with flying fishes. For some days Burns appeared to be uneasy, and I observed him continually shading his eyes with his hand and staring at the horizon as if he were looking for land. Twice I caught him with his red head against the chart in the cabin, gazing at that pin, which was always approaching and yet never reaching the African coast. At last one evening, as Captain Fourneau and I were playing écarté in the cabin, the mate entered with an angry look upon his sunburned face.

"I beg your pardon, Captain Fourneau," said he. "But do you know what course the man at the wheel is steering?"

"Due south," the captain answered, with his eyes fixed upon his cards.

"And he should be steering due east."

"How do you make that out?"

The mate gave an angry growl.

"I may not have much education," said he, "but let me tell you this, Captain Fourneau, I've sailed these waters since I was a little nipper of ten, and I know the line when I'm on it, and I know the doldrums, and I know how to find my way to the oil rivers. We are south of the line now, and we should be steering due east instead of due south if your port is the port that the owners sent you to."

"Excuse me, Mr Gerard. Just remember that it is my lead," said the captain, laying down his cards. "Come to the map here, Mr Burns, and I will give you a lesson in practical navigation.

Here is the trade wind from the south-west and here is the line, and here is the port that we want to make, and here is a man who will have his own way aboard his own ship." As he spoke he seized the unfortunate mate by the throat and squeezed him until he was nearly senseless. Kerouan, the steward, had rushed in with a rope, and between them they gagged and trussed the man, so that he was utterly helpless.

"There is one of our Frenchmen at the wheel. We had best put the mate overboard," said the steward.

"That is safest," said Captain Fourneau.

But that was more than I could stand. Nothing would persuade me to agree to the death of a helpless man. With a bad grace Captain Fourneau consented to spare him, and we carried him to the after-hold, which lay under the cabin. There he was laid among the bales of Manchester cloth.

"It is not worth while to put down the hatch," said Captain Fourneau. "Gustav, go to Mr Turner and tell him that I would like to have a word with him."

The unsuspecting second mate entered the cabin, and was instantly gagged and secured as Burns had been. He was carried down and laid beside his comrade. The hatch was then re-placed.

"Our hands have been forced by that red-headed dolt," said the captain, "and I have had to explode my mine before I wished. However, there is no great harm done, and it will not seriously disarrange my plans. Kerouan, you will take a keg of rum forward to the crew and tell them that the captain gives it to them to drink his health on the occasion of crossing the line. They will know no better. As to our own fellows, bring them down to your pantry so that we may be sure that they are ready for business. Now, Colonel Gerard, with your permission we will resume our game of écarté."

It is one of those occasions which one does not forget. This captain, who was a man of iron, shuffled and cut, dealt and played, as if he were in his *café*. From below we heard the inarticulate murmurings of the two mates, half smothered by the handkerchiefs which gagged them. Outside the timbers creaked and the sails hummed under the brisk breeze which was sweeping us upon our way. Amid the splash of the waves and the whistle of the wind we heard the wild cheers and shoutings of the English sailors as they broached the keg of rum. We played half a dozen games and then the captain rose. "I think they are ready for us now," said he. He took a brace of pistols from a locker, and he handed one of them to me.

But we had no need to fear resistance, for there was no one to resist. The Englishman of those days, whether soldier or sailor, was an incorrigible drunkard. Without drink he was a brave and good man. But if drink were laid before him it was a perfect madness – nothing could induce him to take it with moderation. In the dim light of the den which they inhabited, five senseless figures and two shouting, swearing, singing madmen represented the crew of the *Black Swan*. Coils of rope were brought forward by the steward, and with the help of two French seamen (the third was at the wheel) we secured the drunkards and tied them up, so that it was impossible for them to speak or move. They were placed under the fore-hatch as their officers had been under the after one, and Kerouan was directed twice a day to give them food and drink. So at last we found that the *Black Swan* was entirely our own.

Had there been bad weather I do not know what we should have done, but we still went gaily upon our way with a wind which was strong enough to drive us swiftly south, but not strong enough to cause us alarm. On the evening of the third day I found Captain Fourneau gazing eagerly out from the platform in the front of the vessel. "Look, Gerard, look!" he cried, and pointed over the pole which stuck out in front.

A light blue sky rose from a dark blue sea, and far away, at the point where they met, was a shadowy something like a cloud, but more definite in shape.

"What is it?" I cried.

"It is land."

"And what land?"

I strained my ears for the answer, and yet I knew already what the answer would be.

"It is St Helena."

Here, then, was the island of my dreams! Here was the cage where our great Eagle of France was confined! All those thousands of leagues of water had not sufficed to keep Gerard from the master whom he loved. There he was, there on that cloud-bank yonder over the dark blue sea. How my eyes devoured it! How my soul flew in front of the vessel – flew on and on to tell him that he was not forgotten, that after many days one faithful servant was coming to his side! Every instant the dark blur upon the water grew harder and clearer. Soon I could see plainly enough that it was indeed a mountainous island. The night fell, but still I knelt upon the deck, with my eyes fixed upon the darkness which covered the spot where I knew that the great Emperor was. An hour passed and another one, and then suddenly a little golden twinkling light shone out exactly ahead of us. It was the light of the window of some house – perhaps of his house. It could not be more than a mile or two away. Oh, how I held out my hands to it! – they were the hands of Etienne Gerard, but it was for all France that they were held out.

Every light had been extinguished aboard our ship, and presently, at the direction of Captain Fourneau, we all pulled upon one of the ropes, which had the effect of swinging round one of the sticks above us, and so stopping the vessel. Then he asked me to step down to the cabin.

"You understand everything now, Colonel Gerard," said he, "and you will forgive me if I did not take you into my complete confidence before. In a matter of such importance I make no man my confidant. I have long planned the rescue of the Emperor, and my remaining in England and joining their merchant service was entirely with that design. All has worked out exactly as I expected. I have made several successful voyages to the West Coast of Africa, so that there was no difficulty in my obtaining the command of this one. One by one I got these old French man of war's-men among the hands. As to you, I was anxious to have one tried fighting man in case of resistance, and I also desired to have a fitting companion for the Emperor during his long homeward voyage. My cabin is already fitted up for his use. I trust that before tomorrow morning he will be inside it, and we out of sight of this accursed island."

You can think of my emotion, my friends, as I listened to these words. I embraced the brave Fourneau, and implored him to tell me how I could assist him.

"I must leave it all in your hands," said he. "Would that I could have been the first to pay him homage, but it would not be wise for me to go. The glass is falling, there is a storm brewing, and we have the land under our lee. Besides, there are three English cruisers near the island which may be upon us at any moment. It is for me, therefore, to guard the ship and for you to bring off the Emperor."

I thrilled at the words.

"Give me your instructions!" I cried.

"I can only spare you one man, for already I can hardly pull round the yards," said he. "One of the boats has been lowered, and this man will row you ashore and await your return. The light which you see is indeed the light of Longwood. All who are in the house are your friends, and all may be depended upon to aid the Emperor's escape. There is a cordon of English sentries, but they are not very near to the house. Once you have got as far as that you will convey our plans to the Emperor, guide him down to the boat, and bring him on board."

The Emperor himself could not have given his instructions more shortly and clearly. There was not a moment to be lost. The boat with the seaman was waiting alongside. I stepped into it, and an instant afterwards we had pushed off. Our little boat danced over the dark waters, but always shining before my eyes was the light of Longwood, the light of the Emperor, the star of hope. Presently the bottom of the boat grated upon the pebbles of the beach. It was a deserted cove, and no challenge from a sentry came to disturb us. I left the seaman by the boat and began to climb the hillside.

There was a goat-track winding in and out among the rocks, so I had no difficulty in finding my way. It stands to reason that all paths in St Helena would lead to the Emperor. I came to a gate. No sentry – and I passed through. Another gate – still no sentry! I wondered what had become of this cordon of which Fourneau had spoken. I had come now to the top of my climb, for there was the light burning steadily right in front of me. I concealed myself and took a good look round, but still I could see no sign of the enemy. As I approached I saw the house, a long, low building with a veranda. A man was walking up and down upon the path in front. I crept nearer and had a look at him. Perhaps it was this cursed Hudson Lowe. What a triumph if I could not only rescue the Emperor, but also avenge him! But it was more likely that this man was an English sentry. I crept nearer still, and the man stopped in front of the lighted window, so that I could see him. No; it was no soldier, but a priest. I wondered what such a man could be doing there at two in the morning. Was he French or English? If he were one of the household I might take him into my confidence. If he were English he might ruin all my plans. I crept a little nearer still, and at that moment he entered the house, a flood of light pouring out through the open door. All was clear for me now, and I understood that not an instant was to be lost. Bending myself double I ran swiftly forward to the lighted window. Raising my head I peeped through, and there was the Emperor lying dead before me!

My friends, I fell down upon the gravel walk as senseless as if a bullet had passed through my brain. So great was the shock that I wonder that I survived it. And yet in half an hour I had staggered to my feet again, shivering in every limb, my teeth chattering, and there I stood staring with the eyes of a maniac into that room of death.

He lay upon a bier in the centre of the chamber, calm, composed, majestic, his face full of that reserve power which lightened our hearts upon the day of battle. A half-smile was fixed upon his pale lips, and his eyes, half-opened, seemed to be turned on mine. He was stouter than when I had seen him at Waterloo, and there was a gentleness of expression which I had never seen in life. On either side of him burned rows of candles, and this was the beacon which had welcomed us at sea, which had guided me over the water, and which I had hailed as my star of hope. Dimly I became conscious that many people were kneeling in the room; the little Court, men and women, who had shared his fortunes, Bertrand, his wife, the priest, Montholon – all were there. I would have prayed too, but my heart was too heavy and bitter for prayer. And yet I must leave, and I could not leave him without a sign. Regardless of whether I was seen or not, I drew myself erect before my dead leader, brought my heels together, and raised my hand in a last salute. Then I turned and hurried off through the darkness, with the picture of the wan, smiling lips and the steady grey eyes dancing always before me.

It had seemed to me but a little time that I had been away, and yet the boatman told me that it was hours. Only when he spoke of it did I observe that the wind was blowing half a gale from the sea and that the waves were roaring in upon the beach. Twice we tried to push out our little boat, and twice it was thrown back by the sea. The third time a great wave filled it and stove the bottom. Helplessly we waited beside it until the dawn broke, to show a raging sea and a flying scud above it. There was no sign of the *Black Swan*. Climbing the hill we looked down, but on all the great torn expanse of the ocean there was no gleam of a sail. She was gone. Whether she had sunk, or whether she was recaptured by her English crew, or what strange fate may have been in store for her, I do not know. Never again in this life did I see Captain Fourneau to tell him the result of my mission. For my own part I gave myself up to the English, my boatman and I pretending that we were the only survivors of a lost vessel – though, indeed, there was no pretence in the matter. At the hands of their officers I received that generous hospitality which I have always encountered, but it was many a long month before I could get a passage back to the dear land outside of which there can be no happiness for so true a Frenchman as myself.

And so I tell you in one evening how I bade goodbye to my master, and I take my leave also of you, my kind friends, who have listened so patiently to the long-winded stories of an old broken soldier. Russia, Italy, Germany, Spain, Portugal, and England, you have gone with me to all these countries, and you have seen through my dim eyes something of the sparkle and splendour of those great days, and I have brought back to you some shadow of those men whose tread shook the earth. Treasure it in your minds and pass it on to your children, for the memory of a great age is the most precious treasure that a nation can possess. As the tree is nurtured by its own cast leaves, so it is these dead men and vanished days which may bring out another blossoming of heroes, of rulers, and of sages. I go to Gascony, but my words stay here in your memory, and long after Etienne Gerard is forgotten a heart may be warmed or a spirit braced by some faint echo of the words that he has spoken. Gentlemen, an old soldier salutes you and bids you farewell.